Sultry Nights

ABBY GREEN

ANNIE WEST

CATHY WILLIAMS

MILLS & BOON

First published in Great Britain 2012
by Mills & Boon, an imprint of Harlequin (UK) Limited,
Eton House, 18-24 Paradise Road, Richmond, Surrey TW9 1SR

SULTRY NIGHTS © by Harlequin Enterprises II B.V./S.à.r.l 2012

Mistress to the Merciless Millionaire, *The Savakis Mistress* and *Ruthless Tycoon, Inexperienced Mistress* were published in Great Britain by Harlequin (UK) Limited.

Mistress to the Merciless Millionaire © Abby Green 2009
The Savakis Mistress © Annie West 2009
Ruthless Tycoon, Inexperienced Mistress © Cathy Williams 2009

ISBN: 978 0 263 89706 7
ebook ISBN: 978 1 408 97074 4

05-1112

Printed and bound in Spain
by Blackprint CPI, Barcelona

Claiming his mistress! Sinful seduction!

Sultry Nights

Three exciting, passionate novels from
favourite authors Abby Green, Annie West
and Cathy Williams

MISTRESS TO
THE MERCILESS
MILLIONAIRE

BY
ABBY GREEN

Abby Green got hooked on Mills & Boon® romances while still in her teens, when she stumbled across one belonging to her grandmother in the west of Ireland. After many years of reading them voraciously, she sat down one day and gave it a go herself. Happily, after a few failed attempts, Mills & Boon bought her first manuscript.

Abby works freelance in the film and TV industry, but thankfully the four am starts and the stresses of dealing with recalcitrant actors are becoming more and more infrequent, leaving more time to write!

She loves to hear from readers, and you can contact her through her website at www.abby-green.com. She lives and works in Dublin.

This is for Lorna Mugan and Anne Warter, whose
friendship I value so much.

PROLOGUE

KATE LANCASTER stood at the very ornate stone font where her two-month-old goddaughter was being christened. The holy water was being poured onto her forehead as the priest said a blessing in French. The ceremony was achingly beautiful, in a tiny ancient chapel in the grounds of her best friend Sorcha's new home, a stunning château just outside Paris. Kate had been at her wedding in this same chapel just nine months previously, as maid of honour.

And yet this moment in which Kate wanted nothing more than to focus fully on the christening was being upstaged effortlessly by the tall man who stood to her right. *Tiarnan Quinn.*

He'd also been at the wedding, as best man; he was Sorcha's older brother.

Kate tried to stem the pain, hating that it could rise here and taint this beautiful occasion, but she couldn't stop it. He was the man who had crushed her innocent ideals, hopes and dreams. The man who had shown her a moment of explosive sensuality and in the process ruined her for all other men. And yet she knew she had no one to blame but herself. If she hadn't been so determined to— She ruthlessly crushed that line of thinking. It was so long ago she couldn't believe it still affected her. That it still felt so fresh.

Despite her best efforts to block him out she could feel the heat from his large body envelop her, his scent wind around her, threatening to burst open a veritable Pandora's Box of memories. The familiar weight of desire she felt whenever she was near him lay heavy within her, a pooling of heat in her belly, between her legs. Usually she was so careful to avoid him, but she couldn't here—now. Not at this intimate ceremony where they were being made godparents in this traditional ritual.

She'd survived the wedding; she'd survive this. And then walk away and hope that one day he wouldn't affect her so much. But how long had she been hoping for that now? A sense of futility washed through her—especially as she recognised that if anything her awareness of him was growing exponentially stronger.

Her jaw was tight from holding it so rigid, her back as straight as a dancer's. She tried to focus on Sorcha and Romain. They were oblivious to all except themselves and their baby. Romain took Molly tenderly from the priest, cradling her easily with big hands. He and Sorcha looked at one another over their daughter's head, and that look nearly undid Kate completely. It was so private; so full of love and hope and earthy sensuality, that it felt voyeuristic to be witnessing it. And yet Kate couldn't look away or stop her heart clenching with a bittersweet pain, momentarily and shamingly jealous of what they shared.

This was what Kate wanted. This was all she'd ever wanted. A fulfilment that was so simple and yet so rare. Tiarnan shifted beside her, his arm brushing against hers, making her tense even more rigidly. Against her will she looked up at him; she couldn't *not*. He'd always drawn her eyes to him, like a helpless moth to the certain death of a burning flame.

He was looking down at her and her heart stopped, breath faltered. He frowned slightly, an assessing look in his gaze as he seemed to search deep within her soul for her secrets. He'd looked at her like that at the wedding, and it had taken all her strength to appear cool. He was looking at her as if trying to figure something out. Figure *her* out. Kate was so raw in that moment—too raw after witnessing Romain and Sorcha's sheer happiness and love. It was worse than the wedding. She had no defence here with a tiny baby involved—a tiny baby she'd held in her arms only a few moments ago. Holding that baby had called to the deepest, most primitive part of her.

Normally she coped so well, but with Tiarnan looking at her so intently her protective wall of icy defence was deserting her spectacularly, leaving in its place nothing but heat. And she couldn't do anything to stop it. Her eyes dropped betrayingly to his mouth. She quite literally yearned to have him kiss her, hold her. *Love her.* Look at her the way Romain had just looked at Sorcha. She'd never wanted that from any other man, and the realisation was stark now, cutting through her.

Against her volition her eyes rose to meet his again. *He was still looking at her.* Despite everything, she knew the futility of her secret desires; the feelings within her were rising like a tidal wave and she was helpless to disguise them, caught by the look in his eyes. She also knew, without being able to stop it, that he was reading every raw and naked emotion on her face, in her eyes. And as she watched his blue eyes darkened to a glittering shade of deep sapphire with something so carnal and hot that she instinctively put out a hand to search for something to cling onto, seriously fearful that her legs wouldn't support her.

He'd never looked at her with such explicit intensity…it had to be her imagination. It was all too much—and here she was, pathetically projecting her own desires onto him…

It was only after a few seconds that she realised Tiarnan had clasped her arm with a big hand. He was holding her upright, supporting her… And right then Kate knew that all her flimsy attempts to defend herself against him for years were for naught. He'd just seen through it all in an instant. Seen through *her.* Her humiliation was now complete.

CHAPTER ONE

One month later. Four Seasons Hotel, downtown San Francisco

KATE felt even more like a piece of meat than usual, yet she clamped down on her churlish thoughts and pasted on her best professional smile as the bidding continued. The smack of the gavel beside her made her flinch minutely. The fact that the gavel was being wielded by a well-known A-list Hollywood actor was not making the experience any easier. Despite her years of experience as a top model, she was still acutely uncomfortable under scrutiny, but she had learnt to disguise it well.

'Twenty-five thousand. Twenty-five thousand dollars to the gentleman here in the front. Am I bid any higher?'

Kate held her breath. The man under the spotlight with the unctuous grin was a well-known Greek shipping magnate. He was old, short, fat and bald, and his beady obsidian eyes were devouring Kate as he practically licked his lips. For a second she felt intensely vulnerable and alone, standing here under the lights. A shudder went through her. If someone else didn't—

'Ah! We've a bidder in the back—thirty thousand dollars from the new arrival.'

A rush of relief flooded Kate and she tried to strain to see past the glaring spotlights to identify who the new bidder was. It appeared as if the ballroom lighting technicians were trying to find him too, with the spotlight lurching from coiffed person to coiffed person, all of whom laughed and waved it away. The bidder seemed determined to remain anonymous. Well, Kate comforted herself, whoever it was couldn't be any worse a prospect to kiss in front of all these people than Stavros Stephanides.

'And now Mr Stephanides here in the front is bidding *forty* thousand dollars…things are getting interesting! Come on, folks, let's see how deep your pockets are. How can you turn down a chance to kiss this lovely lady *and* donate generously to charity?'

Kate's stomach fell again at Stephanides' obvious determination—but then the actor spied movement in the shadows at the back. '*Fifty* thousand dollars to the mysterious new bidder. Sir, won't you come forward and reveal yourself?'

No one came forward, though, and inexplicably the hairs rose on the back of Kate's neck. Then she saw the look of almost comic indignation on Stephanides' face as he swivelled around to see who his competitor was. The Greek's expression visibly darkened when someone leant low to speak in his ear. He'd obviously just been informed as to the identity of the mysterious fellow bidder. With an audible splutter Stephanides upped the ante by raising the bidding in a leap to one hundred thousand dollars. Kate held in her gasp at the extortionate amount, but her smile was faltering.

She became aware of the ripple of hushed whispers and a distinct frisson of excitement coming from the back; whoever this person was, he was creating quite a buzz. And then whoever it was also calmly raised their bid—to a cool two hundred thousand dollars. It didn't look as if her ordeal was going to end anytime soon.

Tiarnan Quinn wasn't used to grand, showy gestures. His very name was the epitome of discretion. Discretion in everything: his wealth; his work; his life, and most definitely in his affairs. He had a ten-year-old daughter. He didn't live like a monk, but neither did he parade his carefully selected lovers through the tabloids in the manner so beloved of other men in his position: a divorced heterosexual multi-billionaire male in the prime of his life.

None of his lovers had ever kissed and told. He made sure that any ex-partner was so well compensated she would never feel the need to break his trust. He always got out before any messy confrontations, and he always kept his private life very private. None of his lovers ever met his daughter because he had no intention of marrying ever again, and to introduce them to Rosalie would be to invite a level of intimacy that was reserved solely for his family: his daughter, sister and mother.

His lovers provided him with relief. Nothing more, nothing less.

And yet here he was now, bidding publicly, albeit discreetly for the moment, in the name of charity, for a kiss with Kate Lancaster—one of the most photographed women in the world. Because something in his mind and body was chafing, and for the first time in a long time he was thinking discretion be damned. He wanted this woman with a hunger he'd denied for too long. A hunger he'd only recently given himself permission fully to acknowledge and to believe it could be sated.

And it had been a long time building—*years*. He could see now that it had been building with a stealthy insidiousness into a subconscious need that was now very conscious—a burning necessity. His mouth twisted; those years hadn't exactly been uneventful or allowed much time for contemplation. A short-lived marriage and an acrimonious divorce, not to mention becoming a single parent, had taken up a large part of that time. If he'd had the luxury of time on his hands he might have realised a lot sooner— He halted his thoughts. No matter. He was here now.

His attention came back to Kate, focused on Kate, and he had the uncanny sensation of being in the right place at the right time. It was a sensation he usually associated with business, not something more emotional. He corrected himself; this wasn't about emotion. It was desire. Unfulfilled desire.

Perhaps it was because he'd finally allowed himself to think of it again—that moment ten years ago—but it was as if the floodgates had opened on a dam. It had been little more than a kiss, and yet it was engraved more hotly onto his memory than anything he'd experienced before or after. It had taken all of his will-power and restraint to pull away from her that night. Since then Kate had been strictly off-limits to him for myriad reasons: because that incendiary moment had shaken him up a lot more than he cared to admit; because she'd been so young *and* his little sister's best friend.

He remembered the way her startlingly blue eyes had stared directly into his, as if she'd been able to see all the way into his soul. As if she'd wanted him to see all the way into hers. *She'd looked at him like that again only a few weeks ago.* And it had taken huge restraint for him to allow Kate to retreat back into her shell, to ignore his intense desire. Until *now,* when he knew he could get her on her own, could explore for himself if what he'd seen meant what he thought it did.

His sister's wedding had sparked off this burgeoning need, this awareness. He hadn't been thrown into such close proximity to Kate for years. But all through the ceremony and subsequent reception she'd held him back with that cool, frosty distance of hers. It was like being subjected to a chilly wind whistling over a deserted moor. He'd always been aware of it—yet that day, for the first time in years, it had rankled. His interest had been piqued. *Why* was she always so cool, distant?

Admittedly they had a history that up until now he'd been quite happy not to unearth. He knew on some level that that night ten years ago had marked a turning point for him, and perhaps it was one of the reasons he'd found it so easy to relegate Kate to a place he had no desire to re-explore. Her studied indifference over the years had served to keep a lid on those disturbing memories.

And yet he knew he couldn't deny the fact that he'd always been aware of her—aware of how she'd blossomed from a slightly gauche teenager into a stunningly assured and beautiful woman.

He'd thought he had that awareness and desire under control, but one night some years ago a girl had bumped into him in the street: blonde, caked in make-up, and wearing an outfit that was only a hair's breadth away from a stripper's. The feel of her body slamming into him, her huge blue eyes looking straight up into his, had scrambled his brain and fired his libido so badly that he'd sent his date home that night with some pathetic excuse and hadn't been able to look at another woman for weeks—turned on by a girl in a tarty French maid's outfit because she'd borne some resemblance to—

Tiarnan halted his wayward thoughts right there. He chafed at the resurgence of something so minor he'd thought long forgotten—and at the implication that Kate had occupied a bigger place in his mind than he'd admitted to himself. He reassured himself that he'd had his own concerns keeping him more than occupied—and lovers who'd been only too warm and willing, making it easy to shut out the frosty indifference of one woman. Seeing Kate just once or twice a year had hardly been conducive to stoking the embers of a latent desire.

But just a few weeks ago…at the baptism…she'd turned and looked at him and that cool façade had dropped for the first time. She'd looked at him with such naked blatant need in those fathomless blue depths that he'd felt as if a truck had just slammed into him. For the first time Tiarnan had seen the heat of her passion under that all too cool surface. It was a heat he hadn't seen since that night, when it had combusted all around them. It could have ended so differently if he hadn't found a thread of control to cling onto.

In one instant, with one look, Tiarnan had been flung back

in time, and all attempts to keep her off limits had been made redundant. It was almost as if he'd been put to sleep after that night, and now, with a roaring, urgent sucking-in of oxygen, he was brought back to painful, aching life.

She'd clammed up again after a few moments, but it had been enough of a crack in her armour...

Blood heated and flowed thick through his veins as he took her in now. She was dressed in a dark pink silk cocktail dress, strapless, showing off the delicate line of her shoulders and collarbone, her graceful neck. Her long, luxuriant blonde hair—her trademark—hung in loose waves over her shoulders, a simple side parting framing her face. And even though he was right at the back of the room those huge blue eyes stood out. Her soft rose-pink lips were full, the firm line of her jaw and straight nose transforming banal prettiness into something much more formidable. True beauty. There was fragility in the lines of her body, and yet a sexy lushness that would have an effect on every man in that room—something Tiarnan was very aware of. Uncomfortably so.

He felt a proprietorial urge to go and sweep her off that stage and out of everyone's sight. It only firmed his resolve, strengthened his sense of right.

His eyes drifted down with leisurely and very male appreciation, taking in slender shapely legs, it was clear why she'd become one of the most sought-after models in the world. She was, quite simply, perfect. She'd become a darling of the catwalks despite their predilection for a more emaciated figure; she was the face of a well-known lingerie company among countless other campaigns. Her cool, under-the-surface sensuality meant that people sometimes described her as cold. But the problem was he knew she wasn't.

He had the personal experience to know that she was very, *very* hot.

Why had he waited so long for this?

Tiarnan clamped down on looking again at what had made him suppress his desire for so long—apart from the obvious reasons. He dismissed the rogue notion that rose unbidden and unwelcome that she'd once touched something deep within him. It must have been an illusion, borne up by the fact that they'd shared a moment in time, imbuing the experience with an enigmatic quality.

She'd displayed a self-possession at the age of eighteen that had stunned him slightly. He had to remind himself that he'd overestimated her naivety. She'd known exactly what she'd been doing then, and she was a grown woman now. Tiarnan's body tightened in anticipation. She was a woman of the world—the kind of woman he could seduce. She was no longer an innocent... A sharp pain lanced him briefly. It felt awfully like *regret,* and Tiarnan crushed it back down. He didn't do regret. He would not let her exert this sensual hold over him. He would not let her bring him back in time and reduce him to a mass of seething, frustrated desire with one look because of a *kiss!* He would seduce her and sate this lust that had been burning for too long under the surface. It was time to bring it out into the open.

All he could think about was how urgently he wanted to taste her again, touch her. She had once tried to seduce him. Now it was his turn. And this time they wouldn't stop at a kiss.

His attention came back to the proceedings. He saw Stephanides bid again. He had no intention of letting that man anywhere near Kate's lush mouth. But the Greek was stubborn and out to prove a point—especially now that he'd been informed who it was bidding against him. He and Stephanides were old adversaries. Tiarnan casually made another bid, oblivious to the gasps and looks directed at him, oblivious to the whispers that came from nearby as people speculated if it was really *him.*

People's idle speculation and chatter was of little interest to him. What was of interest was Kate Lancaster, as she stood there now, with her huge doe eyes staring straight at him but not seeing him. She would—soon enough.

Stavros Stephanides finally admitted defeat with a terse shake of his head. A sense of triumph filled Tiarnan and it was heady. He hadn't felt the sensation in a long time because triumph invariably came all too easily. With no idea as to how much he'd finally bid for a kiss with Kate, and not in the slightest bit fazed, he stepped out of the shadows and strode forward to collect his prize. Not just the kiss he was now due, but so much more. And he *would* collect—until he was sated and Kate Lancaster no longer exerted this mysterious pull over his every sense.

Kate simply didn't believe her eyes at first. *It couldn't be.* It just could not be Tiarnan Quinn striding powerfully through the seated awed crowd towards her, looking as dark and gorgeous as she'd ever seen him in a tuxedo. Her face flamed guiltily; he'd been inhabiting her dreams for weeks—and a lot longer— jeered a taunting voice, which she ignored. Only the previous night she'd woken shaken and very hot after a dream so erotic that she was sure it must be her rampant imagination conjuring him up now.

Fervently hoping that it *was* just her imagination, she took him in: the formidable build—broad shoulders, narrow hips and long legs—the loose-limbed athletic grace that hinted at his love for sports, his abhorrence of the gym. His hair was inky black, cut short, and with a slight silvering at the temples that gave him an air of sober maturity and distinction. As if he even needed it. Kate knew his darkly olive skin came from his Spanish mother. She felt weak inside, and hot.

His face was uncompromising and hard. A strong jaw and proud profile saved it from being too prettily handsome. He was intensely male—more intensely male than any man she'd ever met. Years and maturity had added to his strength, filled out his form, and it was all hard-packed muscle. But his most arresting feature was his eyes—the strongest physical hint of Celtic lineage courtesy of his Irish father. Icy blue and utterly direct. Every time he looked at her she felt as though he saw all the way through her, saw through the paltry defences she put up against him. She tried so hard to project a professional front around him, maintain her distance, knowing that if he ever came near her he'd see in an instant how tenuous her control was.

And he had. The memory sickened her. Just a month ago, at Molly's christening, he'd caught her in that unguarded moment when her naked desire for him had been painfully evident. It had been just a look, but it had been enough. He'd seen it, and ever since then she'd been having those dreams. Because she thought she'd seen a mirror of reaction in his eyes. And yet she had to be wrong. She wasn't his type—she might have been for a brief moment, a long time ago, but it had been an aberration.

A dart of familiar pain gripped her momentarily. She knew she wasn't his type because she'd seen one of his incredibly soignée girlfriends at close quarters, the memory of which made her burn with embarrassment even now. She'd been out with a group of girlfriends, visiting her in New York from Dublin, celebrating a hen night. Kate, very reluctantly, had been dressed in a French maid's outfit, complete with obligatory fishnet tights and sparkly feather duster, when she'd walked slap-bang into Tiarnan as he'd been emerging from an exclusive Madison Avenue restaurant, an arm protectively around a petite dark-haired beauty.

Kate had felt about sixteen and fled, praying that he hadn't recognised her. And then, to add insult to injury, one of her friends had chosen that moment to relieve the contents of her stomach in a gutter nearby… She'd never forget the look on Tiarnan's face, or his date's, just before they'd disappeared into the darkened interior of a waiting chauffeur-driven car.

Bitter frustration at her weak and pathetic response to him burned her inside. Would his hold over her never diminish? And now she was imagining him *here,* walking towards her, up the steps. Coming closer. Desperation made her feel panicky. When would the world right itself and the real person be revealed? Someone else. Someone who wasn't Tiarnan Quinn.

She was barely aware of the Hollywood actor speaking in awed tones beside her, but when he said the name *Tiarnan Quinn* everything seemed to zoom into focus and Kate's heart stopped altogether. Reaction set in. It *was* him—and he was now on the stage, coming closer and closer, his eyes narrowed and intent on her.

Kate's instinct where this man was concerned was always to run, as far and as fast as possible. And yet here and now she couldn't. She was caught off guard, like a deer in the headlights. And alongside the very perverse wish that she could be facing anyone else—even sleazy Stephanides—was the familiar yearning, burning feeling she got whenever this man came near.

'Kate.' His voice was deep, achingly familiar, and it impacted on her somewhere vulnerable inside, where she felt her pulse jump and her heart start again. 'Fancy meeting you here.'

Somehow she found her voice—a voice. 'Tiarnan...that was you?'

He nodded, his eyes never leaving hers. Kate had the strongest sensation that she'd been running from this man for a long time and now it was over. But in actual fact he'd caught her a long time ago. A wicked coil of something hot snaked through her belly even as she clamped down desperately on every emotion and any outward sign of his effect on her.

With a smooth move she didn't see coming, Tiarnan came close and put his hands around her waist, thumbs disturbingly close to the undersides of her breasts. His touch was so shocking after years of avoiding any contact beyond the most perfunctory that she automatically put her hands out to steady herself, and found herself clasping his upper arms. Powerful muscles were evident underneath the expensive cloth of his suit. Her belly melted and she looked up helplessly, still stunned to be facing him like this. Shock was rendering her usual defences around him useless.

He was so tall; he'd always been one of the few men that she had to look up to, even in the highest of heels. He towered over her now, making her feel small, delicate. She was aware of every slow second passing, aware of their breaths, but she knew rationally that things were happening in real time, and that no one was aware of the undercurrents flowing between them. At least she hoped they weren't.

'I believe you owe me a kiss?'

This was said lightly, but Tiarnan's grip on her waist was warm and firm, warning her not to try and run or shirk her duty. She nodded, feeling utterly bewildered; what else could she do in front of the wealthiest, most powerful people in San Francisco? How much had he paid in the end? She'd forgotten already. But it had been a shockingly high amount. Half a million dollars? She had the very strong feeling that he was claiming far more than a kiss, and that coil of heat burned fiercer within her.

He pulled her closer, until their bodies were almost touching, and all Kate could feel was that heat—within her and around her. It climbed up her chest and into her face as Tiarnan's head lowered. Overwhelmed at being ambushed like this, and feeling very bewildered, Kate fluttered her eyes closed as the man she'd failed so abysmally to erase from her memory banks pressed his firm, sensual mouth against hers. It had been ten years since they'd kissed like this, and suddenly Kate was eighteen again, pressing her lips ardently against his…

Kate put a shaky finger to her mouth, which still felt sensitive. As kisses went it had been chaste enough, fleeting enough, but the effect had been pure devastation. She'd been hurtled back in time and Pandora's Box was now wide open. A flare of guilt assailed her; she'd fled the thronged ballroom as soon as she'd had the chance.

They'd been grabbed for photos with the press pack behind the stage straight after Tiarnan had claimed his kiss. Dizzy with the after-effects, she'd stood there smiling inanely. His hand had been warm on her elbow, his presence overwhelming. It was still a complete mystery to her as to why he was here at all, but she hadn't even had the wherewithal to stick around and make small talk. She'd run. Exactly like that night in New York on the street.

Bitter recrimination burned her. She was falling apart every time she saw him now, and if she'd not already made an ass of herself in France, mooning at him like a lovesick groupie, then tonight would certainly have him wondering what on earth was wrong with her. How was it possible that instead of growing immune to him she was growing ever more aware of him? Where was the law of physics in that?

She'd fled, not really thinking about where she was going, and now she realised that she was in the hotel bar, with its floor-to-ceiling windows showcasing a glittering view of downtown San Francisco in all its night-time vibrancy. The sound of a siren wailing somewhere nearby failed to root her in reality. The bar was blissfully dark and quiet. A pianist played soothing jazz in the corner. Kate took a seat at a table by the window. After a few minutes someone approached her. She looked up, thinking it would be the waiter, but it was a stranger—a man. He was wearing a suit and looked a little the worse for wear.

'Excuse me, but me and my buddies—' he gestured behind him to two other men in crumpled suits at the bar, who waved cheerfully '—we're all agreed that you're the prettiest woman we've ever seen. Can we buy you a drink?'

Kate smiled tightly, her nerve ends jangling. 'Thanks, really…but if you don't mind I'm happy to get my own drink.'

He swayed unsteadily, with a look of affront on his face, before lurching back to his friends. Then she saw one of the other men make a move towards her, as if taking up the baton. She cursed her impulse to come here, and turned her face resolutely to the window, hoping that would deter him.

She heard a movement, a deep voice, and then a looming dark shape materialised in the glass. She looked up and saw the face of her dreams reflected above her own. Disembodied. Throat dry, she looked round and up. Tiarnan stood there, looking straight at her, eyes like blue shards of ice against his dark skin. Her heart leapt; her palms dampened.

A waitress appeared next to him, and when she asked if they'd like a drink Tiarnan just looked at Kate and said, 'Two Irish whiskeys?'

Kate nodded helplessly, and watched as Tiarnan took the seat opposite her, undoing his bow tie as he did so and opening the top button on his shirt with easy insouciance. His voice, that distinctive accent with its unmistakable Irish roots, affected her somewhere deep inside. It was a connection they shared—both being half Irish and brought up in Ireland.

He jerked his head back towards the men sitting at the bar. 'You could have sent me packing too. They must be devastated.'

A dart of irritation and anger sparked through Kate at Tiarnan, for being here and upsetting her equilibrium. Her voice came out tight. 'I know you. I don't know them.'

His brow quirked. A hint of a smile played around his mouth. Kate felt very exposed in her strapless dress. Her breasts felt full against the bodice. She strove for calm, to be polite, urbane. This was her best friend's brother, that was all. They'd bumped into each other. That was all. On the surface of things. She wouldn't think about what was happening under the surface, the minefield of history that lay buried there. She smiled, but it felt brittle.

'What brings you to San Francisco, Tiarnan?'

Tiarnan's eyes narrowed. He could see very well that Kate was retreating into that cool shell he knew so well. The shell that for years had deflected his attention, made him believe she didn't desire him. But he knew better now, and he saw the pulse under the pale skin of her neck beat hectically even as she projected a front so glacial he could swear the temperature had dropped a few degrees.

He fought the urge to say, *You,* and instead drawled, 'Business. Sorcha mentioned you were here for the annual Buchanen Cancer benefit.' He shrugged easily deciding not to divulge the fact that he'd specifically booked into the same hotel as her. 'I'm staying here too, so I thought I'd come look for you. It would appear that I found you just in time.'

A vision of being kissed and groped by Stavros Stephanides came back into Kate's head. She lowered her head slightly. Some hair slipped forward over her shoulder. She longed for something to cover herself up, and berated herself for not going straight to her room. What had compelled her to come here? She forced herself to look up. She couldn't go anywhere now.

'Yes. I never thanked you for that.' And then curiosity got the better of her. 'How much did you pay in the end?'

'You don't remember?'

Kate burned as she shook her head, knowing very well why she didn't remember.

He seemed to savour his words. 'Seven hundred and fifty thousand dollars. And worth every cent.'

It would be. Tiarnan watched her reaction, the shock on her beautiful face, those amazing blue eyes framed with the longest black lashes. Saw the way the candlelight flickered over her satin smooth skin, the slope of her shoulders, the swell of her breasts above the dress. His body hardened and Tiarnan shifted, uncomfortably aware that he wasn't used to women having such an immediate effect on him. He enjoyed always being in control, and yet he could already feel that control becoming a

little shaky, elusive… Sitting here with Kate now, the thrill of
anticipation was headier than anything he'd felt in a long time.

He'd paid over half a million dollars, just like that. The amount
staggered Kate, and yet she knew to Tiarnan it was like small
change. That was a fraction of what he gave to charity every
year.

'At least it's for a good cause,' she said a little shakily.

The waitress arrived then, with two glasses. She placed
napkins down, and then the drinks, and left.

Tiarnan reached out a strong, long-fingered hand and raised
his glass towards her, an enigmatic gleam in his eyes. 'A very
good cause.'

Kate raised her glass too and clinked it off his. She had the
very disturbing impression that they weren't talking about the
same thing. Just then his fingers touched hers, and a memory
flashed into her head: her arms wrapped tight around his neck,
tongues touching and tasting. Tiarnan's hands moving to her
buttocks, pulling her in tight so she could feel the thrillingly hard
ridge of his arousal. She could almost hear their heartbeats, slow
and heavy, then picking up pace, drowning out their breathing—

Kate jerked her hand back so quickly that some of her drink
slopped out of the glass. Her skin felt stretched tight, hot. She
couldn't believe this was happening. It was like her worst nightmare and her most fervent dream.

She took a quick sip, all the while watching Tiarnan as he
watched her, hoping that he couldn't read the turmoil in her
head, in her chest. The whiskey trickled like liquid velvet down
her throat. She wasn't used to this, that was all. Tiarnan didn't
seek her out. She only ever saw him with Sorcha, or when lots
of people were around. When Sorcha had lived with her in New
York and Tiarnan had called round or invited them out to dinner
Kate had always made an excuse, always made sure she wasn't
there as much as possible.

But facing him now…that kiss earlier… She was helpless to escape the images threatening to burst through the walls she'd placed around them. Tiarnan leant back, stretching out his long legs, cradling his glass as if this were completely normal, as if they met like this all the time. The latent strength in his body was like a tangible thing.

Kate had to close her eyes for a second as she battled against a vision of him pulling back from kissing her, breathing harshly—

'So, Kate, how have you been?'

Her eyes snapped open. What was *wrong* with her? Normally she managed to keep all this under control, but it was almost as if some silent communication was going on that she knew nothing about—something subversive that she was not in control of, messing with her head. She'd never been so tense. But she told herself she could do this—do the small-talk thing. And after this drink she'd make her excuses and get up and walk away—not see Tiarnan for another few months, or even a year if she was lucky.

So she nodded her head and smiled her most professional smile, injecting breeziness into her voice. 'Fine. Great! Wasn't Molly's christening just gorgeous? I can't believe how big she is already. Sorcha and Romain are so happy. Have you seen them since? I've been *crazy* busy. I had to go to South America straight after the baptism. I got back a few days ago and I flew in tonight for the benefit—'

She took a deep, audibly shaky breath, intending to keep going with her monologue, thinking *Just talk fast and get out of here even faster,* when Tiarnan leant forward and said with quiet emphasis, 'Kate—stop.'

CHAPTER TWO

KATE'S mouth opened and closed. With just those two words she knew that he was seeing right through her—*again.* Silly tears pricked the backs of her eyes. He was playing with her, mocking her for her weakness, as if he'd known all along. So she asked the question, even though she knew it would give her away completely,

'Tiarnan, what are you *really* doing here?'

His face was shuttered, eyes unreadable. The dim lights cast him half in shadow, making him look dark and dangerous. Like a Spanish pirate. His shoulders looked huge. Kate's insides ached as only the way a body recognising its mate ached. Its other half.

Her soft mouth compressed. She'd tried to tell herself that what had happened between them hadn't been unique, hadn't been as earth-shattering as she remembered, but…it had. Since that night, no one had ever kissed her the way he had—with such devastating skill that she'd never been able to get over him. He'd imprinted himself so deeply into her cells. Just one kiss, a mere moment, that was all it had been, but it had been enough.

She repeated the question now, a throb of desperation mixed with anger in her voice, even leaned forward, put her glass down. She wanted to shout at him to just leave her alone, let her get on with her life so she could realise her dream: find someone to love. Have a family. *Finally get over him.*

'What are you doing here, Tiarnan? We both know—'

'We both know why I'm here.' His voice was harsh. The piano player was between numbers, and the words hung almost accusingly in the soft silence. Time seemed to hang suspended, and then the piano player started again and so did Kate's heart, and she desperately tried to claw back some self control and pretend that he *wasn't* referring to that night.

'I don't know what you're talking about.'

Tiarnan took a swift drink and leaned forward to put his empty glass down on the table. The sound made Kate flinch inside.

'You know perfectly well what I'm talking about. That explicit look you gave me in France, and what *didn't* happen that night.'

Oh, God. Kate felt the colour drain from her face. She was officially in her worst nightmare. She *knew* he'd seen her weakness in France—but she just hadn't been able to hide it. And if Tiarnan Quinn was known for anything, it was for sensing weakness and exploiting it ruthlessly.

She forced herself to meet his gaze, even though it was hard, and her voice came out low and husky. 'That night was a long time ago—and you're right. Nothing happened—' She stopped ineffectually. What could she say? *If you're thinking if I still want you, even after a humiliating rejection, then you're right.* Bitterness rose within her.

He was still sitting forward—predatory, dangerous. He said softly, in that deep voice, 'I'd call that kiss something happening, and that look told me that you've been just as aware of this build-up of sexual tension as I have.'

Kate shook her head fiercely, as if that could negate this whole experience. Shame coursed through her again at her youthful naivety, and yet her body tingled even now, when humiliation hung over her like the Sword of Damocles.

Why was he bringing this up *now?* Was he bored? Did he think he'd seen an invitation in her eyes that day at the christening? She burned inside at the thought and rushed to try and fill the silence, the gap, to regain some dignity.

'Tiarnan, like I said, it was a long time ago. I barely remember it, and I've no intention of ever talking about it or repeating the experience. I was very young.'

And a virgin. That unwanted spiking of regret shocked Tiarnan again, and suddenly the thought of other men looking at her, touching her, made him feel almost violent...

He said nothing for a long moment. He couldn't actually speak as he looked into clear blue eyes not dissimilar to his own. They were like drops of ice but they couldn't cool him down. Tiarnan fought the urge to reach across the table and pull her up, crush her mouth under his, taste her again. Instead he finally said, 'You're a liar, and that's a pity.'

Kate felt winded, breathless. The way he was looking at her was so *hot*—but she didn't think for a second that it meant anything. She didn't know why he was bringing this up now. She just wanted to stay in one piece until she could get away.

'I'm not a liar,' she asserted, and then frowned when she registered what he'd said. 'And what do you mean, it's a pity?'

Tiarnan sat back again, and perversely that made Kate more nervous than when he'd been closer.

'You're a liar because I believe you *do* remember every second of that kiss, as well as I do, and it's a pity you don't intend repeating it because I'd very much like to.'

Kate sat straight and tall. Somewhere dimly she could hear her mother's strident voice in her head: *Kate Lancaster, sit up straight. I won't have you let me down with sloppy manners. Show your breeding. You're a young lady and you will not embarrass me in front of these people!*

Her focus returned to the room. She wasn't ten years old. She was twenty-eight. She was an internationally renowned model: successful, independent. She struggled to cling onto what was real: the pianist was playing a familiar tune, the dark, muted tones of the bar, the lights glittering and twinkling outside. The waitress appeared again, and Kate could see Tiarnan gesture for another drink. His eyes hadn't left hers, and she thought that she might have misheard him. He might have said something entirely different. But then she remembered the way his hands had felt around her waist earlier, how close his thumbs had brushed to her breasts. The way he'd looked at her. The way he was looking at her now.

Ten years on from one moment with this man and she was a quivering wreck. Despite a full and busy life, despite relationships… If he had decided, for whatever reason, that he wanted her, and if she acquiesced, it would be like opening the door, flinging her arm wide with a smile on her face and inviting catastrophe to move in for ever. If she was this bad after a kiss, what would she be like after succumbing to the sensual invitation that was in his eyes right now? Because that look said that a kiss would be the very least of the experience. And awfully, treacherously, any insecurity she'd harboured since that night about her own sexual appeal died a death in a flame of heat. But it was small comfort. He had rejected her clumsy, innocent advances and she had to remember that—no matter how he might be making her feel right now.

The fact that this moment was a direct manifestation of her most secret fantasies was making her reel. The waitress came and deposited more drinks, taking away the empty glasses. Kate shook her head, feeling her hair move across too sensitive skin. She knew all about Tiarnan Quinn—she'd always known all about him. One of the perks of being best friends with his sister. So Kate knew well how he compartmentalised women, how he inevitably left them behind. She'd witnessed his ruthless control first-hand. She wouldn't, *couldn't* allow that to happen again. Not even when his softly spoken words had set up a chain reaction in her body that she'd been ignoring for the past few earth-shattering seconds.

She shook her head harder, even smiled faintly, as if sharing in a joke, as if this whole evening wasn't costing her everything.

'I don't think you mean that for a second.' She took a drink from her glass, put it down again and looked at Tiarnan. 'And even if you did, like I said, I've no desire to re-enact that kiss for your amusement. If all you're looking for is a convenient woman, there are plenty available. You don't need me. I don't think I need to remind you that you made your rejection of my advances quite plain that night.'

Tiarnan chafed at her sudden assuredness—and at her reminder of his clumsy rejection. That feeling of regret spiked uncomfortably again. Her smile was almost mocking—as if she pitied him! He'd never been an object of pity, and he wasn't about to start being one now.

He smiled tightly and saw Kate's eyes widen, the pulse trip in her throat.

'I rejected you because you were inexperienced, too young, and my little sister's best friend.' His jaw clenched. '*Not* because I didn't desire you, as you may well remember. I'm looking for a lot more than a re-enactment of that kiss, and believe me, I don't expect it to be amusing. I'm not looking for a convenient lay, Kate. I'm looking for *you.*'

All of Kate's precious composure crumbled at his raw words.

'You can't possibly mean that…that you—'

'Want you?' He almost grimaced, as if in pain. 'I want you, Kate. As much as you want me.'

'I don't.' she breathed.

He arched a brow. 'No? Then what was that look about at the christening, when you all but devoured me with your hungry blue eyes? And the way you trembled earlier under my hands?'

Kate flushed brick-red. 'Stop it. I wasn't. I didn't.' This was too cruel. Her humiliation knew no bounds. The sword had fallen spectacularly.

Tiarnan grimaced again. 'Don't worry. It's mutual.' His blue eyes speared hers. 'You've never forgotten that night, Kate, have you? It's why you always freeze me out every time we meet.'

She shook her head, his intuition sending shockwaves through her whole body. 'Don't be ridiculous. It was so long ago…of course I've…' She hitched up her chin defiantly. 'I've more than kissed men since then, Tiarnan. What did you think? That I've hugged my pillow to sleep every night, dreaming of you?'

The awful thing was, she could remember the mortification that had led her to rid herself of her virginity as soon as was humanly possible after that night—and what an excruciating disappointment it had been.

His mouth had become a thin line of displeasure. 'I wouldn't imagine for a second that you haven't had lovers, Kate.'

He reached out and took her hand, gripped it so that she couldn't pull away, and Kate was caught, trapped by her own weak responses: lust, and the building of guilty exhilaration. Her heart beat frantically against her breastbone.

'But did any of them make you feel the way I did after just a kiss? Did any of them make you want them so badly that it was all you could think about? Dream about?'

Tiarnan felt momentarily shocked by his words and the emotion behind them; until recently, until he'd set on this course to seduce Kate, he'd never really allowed himself to acknowledge what her effect on him had been. Touching her now, confronting this for the first time, was bringing it all back in vivid detail. Her hand felt small, soft and yet strong. He could feel her pulse beating under the skin.

Kate saw a red mist descend. The exhilaration dissipated. His words were so close to the bone—*too* close to the bone. She pulled her hand from his grasp and curled it tight against her chest.

'How dare you? How dare you come back into my life like this, making assumptions? Judgements? Asking me about things you've no right to know?'

Tiarnan looked at her and felt more sure than ever.

'I have a right, Kate, because one kiss clearly wasn't enough. This has been building between us all these years…this *desire* to know what it might have been like.'

Anger rushed through her, gathering force, and she used it before she could dissolve again. She stood up on shaky legs and looked down as imperiously as she could. But then Tiarnan stood too, altering the dynamic, taking some of the fire out of her anger, making her remember just how tall he was, how broad and strong.

She hitched her chin. 'I think *dormant* is a more appropriate word, and dormant is how it'll stay, Tiarnan. What's brought on this revelation? The fact that you thought you saw something in France? You saw nothing except what you wanted to see. I've no intention of becoming a notch on your bedpost just to satisfy some belated curiosity on your part.'

She walked around the table, as if to leave, but Tiarnan moved too and blocked her way. Kate saw a couple of people looking at them in her peripheral vision. She stalled and looked up, tried to shut out the way looking into Tiarnan's eyes had always made her feel as if she was drowning. She gritted her teeth.

'Could you please move? You're blocking my exit.'

'Need I remind you,' he said silkily, 'that *you* were the one so determined to score that notch in the first place? We both know that if I hadn't stopped when I still could I would have taken your innocence on the rug in front of that fire…'

Those softly spoken words smashed through the last vestiges of Kate's dignity and defence. She looked up at him and beseeched with everything in her. 'Please. Get out of my way, Tiarnan.'

He shook his head. 'I'm walking you to your room.'

'I'm perfectly capable of walking myself, and have been for some time now.'

His voice had steel running through it. 'Nevertheless, I'll walk you to your room—or do you want me to make a spectacle of both of us and carry you out of here?'

One jet-black brow was arched. Kate didn't doubt him for a second. Tiarnan had never been one to give a damn about what people thought.

She felt unbelievably prim as she bit out, 'That won't be necessary. You can escort me to my room if you insist.'

He finally moved aside to let her pass, and Kate stalked towards the entrance of the bar feeling stiff all over, her shoulders so straight and tense that she felt as if she'd crack if someone even touched her. She pressed the button for the lift and looked resolutely up at the display above the door as she waited. Tiarnan stood beside her, a huge, impossibly immovable force. Heat and electricity crackled between them. There was such tension in the air that Kate wanted to scream.

No one reduced her to this. *No one.* She was dignified, calm, collected. She knew she had a reputation for being cool and it hurt her—she was the least cold of people. She could turn it on when it suited her, but it wasn't really her. Cold histrionics and dramatics had been the territory of her mother. Kate had learnt at an early age to be a pretty, placid foil for her mother's effervescent beauty.

The lift arrived and the bell pinged, making Kate jump and then curse silently. She hadn't thought about her mother like that for a long time; Tiarnan's disturbing presence and even more disturbing assertions were effortlessly hurtling her back in time.

He stepped into the lift with her, and the space contracted around them when the doors closed. Kate pressed the button for her floor and looked at Tiarnan irritably when he didn't make a move to do the same. 'Which floor?'

Tiarnan looked at her glaring up at him. She was so beautiful. All fire and brimstone underneath that icy façade. Her eyes were flashing, her cheeks were pink and her breasts rose and fell enticingly under the bodice of her dress. She was rattled, seriously rattled, and he had to admit he was surprised at what was so close to the surface.

In truth he'd imagined this happening much more easily. He'd imagined a sophisticated woman embarking on a well-worn groove, both of them knowing and acting out their parts. But right now he was rattled too. She was resisting him. He couldn't think. All he wanted was to stop the lift, drag her into his arms and plunder her soft mouth. It had been too long since he'd tasted that inner sweetness, and the brief all too chaste kiss earlier had only proved to make his desire even more pronounced. But he knew he couldn't. He had to tread carefully or he might lose Kate for ever—and he didn't like the panicky feeling that generated. He didn't *do* panic.

Kate turned and folded her arms crossly, inadvertently giving Tiarnan an even more enticing view of her cleavage. She was sending out desperate silent vibes: *Get away from me! Leave me alone!* And as the lift climbed the floors with excruciating slowness that was exactly what he did. He actually moved further away. Back towards the wall. And when Kate sent him a suspicious glance she saw that he was leaning back, hands in his pockets, looking at the ceiling. He was even whistling softly.

The lift finally came to a smooth halt and Kate all but ran out through the doors, taking her door key from her purse as she did so. She expected him to be right behind her. She'd seen a new side to him tonight: implacable, ruthless. Determined. It intimidated her. *It excited her.* She got to her door and slid the key into the slot, her hands barely steady after that revelation.

But if he thought for a second that she was going to meekly turn around now and invite him in— Kate turned and pasted on a bright smile, words trembling on her lips…only to find the corridor empty. For a split second she had the bizarre and terrifying notion that she'd imagined the whole thing. Dreamt it all up.

But then she saw him. Leaning against the open lift door nonchalantly, one foot stopping it from closing, his huge shoulders blocking the light inside. That was why she hadn't seen him straight away. He inclined his head,

'Goodnight, Kate, it was good to see you again. Sweet dreams.'

And with that he stepped back in and the doors closed with a swish. Kate's mouth dropped open. All she could see in her mind's eye was that nonchalance and the bright dangerous glitter of blue eyes under dark brows. All her pent-up fury dissolved and she literally sagged like a spent balloon. She stepped inside her door and closed it, stood with her back against it in the dark for a long moment. Her heart beat fast, her skin tingled and her lips still felt sensitive. And yet more than all this was the ache of desire. She felt raw, as if a wound had been reopened.

Damn Tiarnan Quinn. He was playing her—playing with her. She didn't believe for a second that he was going to meekly walk away. No more than she would have meekly let him into her room. He was undoubtedly the most Alpha male she'd ever known. He always had been. He'd been born Alpha. And she'd set him a challenge with her refusal to acknowledge what had happened between them. There was no sense of excitement in knowing this, no sense of anticipation. She'd been too badly hurt in the past. She'd spent too long disguising her feelings, pretending to herself that she didn't want him. Hiding it from others, even from Sorcha.

She couldn't help but feel—knowing his reputation, which was legendary albeit discreet—that she was posing a challenge to him in large part because he'd let her get away. Was this the banal satisfaction of some long-forgotten curiosity? Kate knew well that there would be a very small number on Tiarnan Quinn's list of women who had resisted his charms, for whatever reason. She had the uncanny prescience that hers might be the only name. And yet that night it had been *he* who had stopped proceedings, not her. He was absolutely right; if she'd had any say that night ten years ago they would have made love on that rug in front of the fire.

For whatever reason, he'd obviously decided that he wanted to carry on from where they'd left off. And Kate knew with every bone in her body that if she didn't resist him she would be the biggest fool on this earth. The one shred of dignity she'd clung onto all these years was the very fact that they hadn't slept together.

Tiarnan stood at the window of the sitting room in his luxurious suite. The best in the hotel. He felt hot and frustrated, hands deep in the pockets of his trousers as he looked out at the view, not seeing a bit of it.

All he could see was his own reflection in the window and the slightly tortured look on his face—tortured because Kate Lancaster was lying in bed some floors below him in the very same hotel, and right now Tiarnan would have gladly given over half his fortune to be in that bed with her. She'd emerged from the mists of memory to assume a place that no other woman had ever assumed.

He could smell Kate's light floral scent even now. And yet she'd walked away, resisted him. Tiarnan couldn't remember a time when any woman he'd wanted had resisted him. From the moment the divorced wife of one of his father's friends had seduced him as a teenager he'd seen the manipulative side to women and had been initiated into their ways.

His mother had dealt him his first lesson. Cold and martyred. He'd seen how she'd made life hell for his father. Not happy to have been brought to inclement Ireland from her native Spain, she'd subjected his father and him to the frost of her discontent, eventually driving his father into the arms of another woman who'd been only too happy to accommodate him. Tiarnan could remember his father's secretary, how she would cajole and plead with him to marry *her*. He'd witnessed those scenes as he'd played outside his father's office, listening to the crying and hysterics. And then she'd taken the drastic step of becoming pregnant in a bid to secure her own happiness, and Tiarnan had been forced to collude in a devastating lie.

He forced his mind away from dark memories. He'd witnessed too much as a child. He knew well enough that his father had been no innocent party, but the machinations of the first female role models in his life had inured him to their ways and moods as he'd grown up. He'd vowed long ago not to be at the mercy of any woman, and yet despite everything, all his lessons learnt, he'd been caught too. Rage still simmered down low in acknowledgement of that.

A ripple of cynicism went through him. Even in Kate's innocence ten years ago she'd been manipulative too, just like the rest. Her innocence had been hidden beneath a veneer of sophistication that had fooled him completely until the moment he'd felt that hesitation. A telling gaucheness, an untutored response. It had cut through the haze of lust that had clouded his judgment that night.

Tiarnan could remember the spiking of betrayal and desperation he'd felt. He'd believed her to be experienced. For a second he'd been seduced into believing them to be on equal ground, both knowing what was happening.

Certainly there'd been no indication when she'd found him alone in the library. He'd offered her a drink and she'd taken it… Her hair had gleamed like spun gold in the firelight. A storm had howled outside. There had been a Christmas party going on in the house. Tiarnan had been making a rare home visit…

She had been wearing a dark red silk dress. Ruched and short, it had clung to her breasts and the curve of her hips. Her long legs had been bare, she'd worn high heels. She had taken the glass of whiskey and smiled at him, and for the first time Tiarnan had allowed himself to really notice her. In truth he'd noticed her as soon as he'd arrived that evening, and he hadn't been able to take his eyes off her. Some defence of his must have been down.

He'd noticed her before—of course he had—he'd have to have been dead not to. But strictly as his sister's friend. They'd both been tall and gangly, giggling blushing girls, but that night for the first time Tiarnan had seen that Kate had become a woman.

It was a quality that his own almost eighteen-year-old sister still hadn't quite achieved. But he'd had to concede that Kate had always possessed a quiet air of mature dignity, of inherent sophistication. A quiet foil to Sorcha's rowdiness and effervescence. Sorcha, his sister, had just come through a traumatic time after the relatively recent death of their father, and Tiarnan had taken the opportunity to thank Kate for being there for her.

Kate had blushed and looked down into her glass before looking back up, something fierce in her eyes. 'I love Sorcha. She's the closest thing I have to a sister and I'd do anything for her.'

Tiarnan could remember smiling at her, seeing her eyes widen in response, and then the flare of his arousal had hit so strong and immediate that it had nearly knocked him sideways. The air around them had changed in an instant, crackling with sexual tension. Even though Tiarnan had tried to deny it, to regain some sanity.

Standing there with her skin glowing in the firelight, her lush body firing his senses… He could remember how choked his voice had felt with the need to push her away when all he'd wanted to do was kiss her into oblivion.

'You know I've always considered *you* like a sister too, Kate.'

For an infinitesimal moment Kate had just looked at him, and then she'd carefully put down the drink and come closer to him, her blue eyes glittering, pupils huge. And she'd said huskily, 'I don't see you as a brother, Tiarnan. And I don't want you to see me as a sister.'

His arousal had sky-rocketed. On some level Tiarnan hadn't been able to believe he was being so wound up by an *eighteen-year-old girl*. But in fairness she wasn't like other eighteen-year-olds. She'd already been a model for a couple of years, was already living independently in London. And he couldn't believe she was standing there and seducing him. Or how out of his depth he felt in that moment. At the age of twenty-eight he was no novice around women, but he'd felt like one then.

She'd stepped right up to him and placed her hands around his face. Then, stretching up, she'd pressed her mouth to his. He'd put his hands on her waist, to try and set her back—but he'd felt her curves, and then she'd leaned closer into him, her soft breasts pressed against his chest…and he'd been lost. From that moment Tiarnan had been overtaken for the first time in his life by pure, unadulterated lust. It had felt like the most necessary thing in the world to pull her even closer, to deepen the kiss, taste her with his tongue.

Things had become heated and urgent in seconds, and only that telling movement she'd made, which had brought him back to sanity, had stopped the night ending a lot differently.

Tiarnan's focus came back from the heat of that memory. The vividness of it shocked him. He knew if he was asked he wouldn't be able to recall his last sexual liaison with such clarity. He stepped away from the window with a jerky movement and did the only thing he could do to ensure he'd have a modicum of sleep that night. He took a cold shower and vowed to himself as he did so that very soon he'd have Kate Lancaster in his bed—once that had happened these provocative memories would return to where they belonged: in the past.

Madrid, one week later

'Signorina Lancaster, you have a call.'

The phone felt slippery in Kate's hand. She knew who it was, and her body was already responding as if he was right there in the room with her.

'*Gracias.*'

She heard a click on the line and then a voice, deep, authoritative. 'Kate.'

His voice reached right down inside her and caused a quiver. She pressed her legs together and gripped the phone even tighter.

'Tiarnan. What a surprise.'

'Hardly,' he responded drily. 'I live about ten minutes from your hotel, and Sorcha told me you'd got the messages I've left. Apparently you've been too busy to get back to me.'

'I did speak to her earlier—and, yes, I've been extremely busy.'

'But now you're finished working?'

'Yes.' Relief rushed through her. Escape was in sight. She was still getting over the shock of having been sent on this last-minute assignment to Madrid—right into Tiarnan's territory, and so soon after their last meeting. Which she had no intention of repeating.

'I'm going home tomorrow—'

'Evening,' Tiarnan finished smoothly for her. 'So you have plenty of time to let us take you for lunch tomorrow.'

'I'm afraid I—' Kate stopped. He'd said *us*.

'Rosie is here. She'd like to see you.'

The words of a lame excuse died in Kate's throat. As much as she hated him for doing this to her, she knew that he would never in a million years use Rosie in any kind of manipulative way. He would know that she'd spent time with Rosie, but probably had very little idea just how much. Kate liked Rosie. She'd used to help Sorcha look after her whenever Tiarnan was in New York on business—which had been frequently enough, as he had offices there. He had sometimes left Rosie with Sorcha for a night or two a couple of times a year when she'd been younger. It had always turned into a joint effort, as Sorcha had been living with Kate in New York until just before she'd met her husband.

Sorcha, up until her pregnancy and the birth of her own daughter, hadn't possessed a maternal bone in her body, so Kate had always been the one to make sure Rosie was wrapped up warm, had eaten well and was tucked in at night. Sorcha used to joke that Kate had been born with a double helping of maternal instinct to make up for the lack of her mother's. The three of them would go to Central Park on adventures, or to the movies and for ice cream afterwards. Kate had always felt a kinship with the small, serious dark-haired child, whose mother had all but abandoned her after her divorce from Tiarnan.

'I'd like to see Rosie too. It's been a while.' Kate's voice felt husky, and already in her head she was rationalising giving in. She *was* leaving tomorrow evening, and with Rosie at lunch too Tiarnan was hardly going to ravish her, was he? And then once she got back to New York she'd be safe again…it would be fine.

'Good. We'll pick you up at midday from the lobby. See you then, Kate.'

And with those softly spoken last words, almost like a caress, the phone line went dead and Kate had the horrible feeling that everything was *not* going to be fine.

CHAPTER THREE

THE following day at midday Kate sat in the lobby of the impossibly chic hotel where she'd been staying. She'd already said goodbye to the crew who'd been with her for the shoot. They were all leaving on an earlier flight, heading to London and their next assignment. Her nerves were coiled tight, making her belly constrict. The thought of the lunch ahead was daunting, to say the least.

And then, as if pulled by an invisible thread, Kate's head came up and she saw Tiarnan silhouetted in the doorway. A huge, imposing figure. Not even giving her time to collect herself, prepare herself. Kate's nerves intensified to a crescendo as she stood up jerkily. Tiarnan strode authoritatively towards her—a man clearly on his own turf. Confident, powerful.

He was dressed in black trousers and a white shirt, open at the neck, his dark skin visible and the strong bronzed column of his throat. Kate hadn't been sure what to wear, and her wardrobe was limited, so she'd gone for a plain black shirt dress and accessorised it with a bright red scarf around her throat. She'd pulled her hair back in a ponytail, trying to project an image that said *friend* and not *lover*. Except right now she felt as if her scarf was strangling her as Tiarnan came to a halt right in front of her. *Too close.* Especially when he took her hands and leant forward to kiss her on both cheeks.

His scent wound through her, and she felt that quiver between her legs again. He had his own very uniquely male scent. She'd always been aware of it. He was one of the few men she knew who didn't douse himself in cologne. Kate had developed an acute sensitivity to smell after years of having to promote various perfumes, almost to the point that strong scents made her feel ill. But Tiarnan's scent was simply soap and water and *him*. Headier than any manufactured scent.

He let her hands go and they tingled. He looked around her. 'Where are your things?'

Kate fought to sound calm, aloof. 'The concierge has my bag. I've arranged for a car to pick me up from here to go to the airport later.'

Tiarnan shook his head and took her by the elbow to lead her over to the desk. 'That won't be necessary.'

In shock, Kate heard him instruct the concierge to cancel the cab and get her bag. The man jumped straight away, clearly recognising Tiarnan. She rounded on him, incensed that he was already dictating. 'What do you think you're doing?'

He looked down at her, leaning nonchalantly against the concierge desk. 'I have to go to the airport later too. You might as well come with me. It'll give us more time together.'

Kate realised something then. Suspicion sparked from her eyes and she crossed her arms. 'Where's Rosie?'

Tiarnan straightened as Kate's small case was delivered by the concierge, who all but bowed to Tiarnan.

He took Kate's arm again, giving her no choice but to trot after him unless she wanted to create a scene. She felt slightly bewildered. She wasn't used to seeing this side of Tiarnan. They emerged, and Kate saw a Range Rover and realised that he still hadn't answered her question. He opened the passenger door and turned to her, the intense blue of his eyes rendering her speechless.

'Rosie's at home. I thought we'd have lunch there.'

She chafed at his easy dominance, at the feeling of being backed into a corner. Tiarnan still had a hand on her elbow and he helped her into the passenger seat. Then, after putting her case in the back, he came around and got into the front, pulling away from the hotel with smooth ease.

The journey to Tiarnan's home didn't take long. It was in the Salamanca area of Madrid, one of the oldest *barrios* and home to some of the most exclusive houses, shops and hotels. It was just off Calle de Serrano, near a charming park, where he turned into a set of huge wrought-iron gates which opened slowly.

Kate looked around her, seriously impressed. Madrid was one of her favourite cities—it always had been. She loved its vibrancy, its history, the café culture, and could spend days wandering around, taking in the museums and galleries. Even now, though it was well into autumn, people were strolling in the lingering warm sunshine. Tiarnan waited to let a woman pass with a baby in a pushchair, and Kate had a sudden vision of what it might be like to live here, have this life. *Be that woman with the pushchair.*

She glanced at Tiarnan's profile as he drove forward when the gates were fully open. He looked distant, and not a little harsh. A shiver went through her even as she felt hot inside. He'd never be part of a dream like that. He'd made it clear a long time ago that as far as he was concerned he'd done the family thing. Sorcha had often told Kate how strongly Tiarnan felt about never marrying again. How Rosie had fulfilled any need he might have had for children.

'Here we are.'

Kate's turbulent thoughts came to an abrupt halt when she realised that they'd stopped outside a huge baroque townhouse. The colour of warm sandstone, it had a crumbling grandeur, with wooden shutters held back from gleaming windows. Bright flowers burst from ornate wrought-iron window box railings and from pots set around the steps and door. Trees surrounded the house, so that it seemed to nestle into the foliage. It was beautiful.

Tiarnan came around to join her. He carried her case in one hand. Kate asked suspiciously, 'Why are you taking it out of the car?'

Tiarnan's blue gaze mocked her for her suspicion. 'Because my driver Juan will be taking us to the airport.'

'But how do you know what time I have to be there?' Kate was struggling not to give in to Tiarnan's effortless domination.

His mouth quirked and her belly flipped.

'Because I know everything, Kate. Stop worrying. I'm not going to jump on you like some callow youth. You're quite safe.'

Just then the massive front door opened, and Kate saw a small dark-haired figure appear. Genuine emotion rushed through her. Tiarnan was forgotten for a moment.

'Rosie!'

Kate started forward instinctively, but then faltered. Rosie wasn't running to greet her as Kate remembered she'd used to do. She was standing there looking very serious. In an instant Kate curbed her instinct to go and hug Rosie, sensing that the child had changed since she'd seen her last. And it *had* been a while. Rosie hadn't come to Molly's christening. Instead, when Kate reached her she just smiled and bent to kiss her formally. She pulled back and looked into dark, wary eyes, wondering what had made her so cautious.

'Rosie, you're all grown up since I last saw you. You're becoming quite the young lady.'

Kate couldn't help tucking a strand of long dark hair behind her ear. Rosie's cheeks flushed pink as she seemed to fight something, and then she mumbled an incoherent reply before turning and running back inside—presumably to her room.

Kate sensed Tiarnan behind her, sensed his impatience. 'I'm sorry about that. Rosie is going through a difficult patch. She spent time with her mother recently, which never ends well.'

Kate's heart went out to the child. She could remember her own trials and tribulations, how *her* mother hadn't wanted anything to do with the fact that her daughter was growing and developing into a young woman. She could remember the turmoil she'd felt. Maybe Rosie was going through the same thing? From what Kate could remember, Stella Rios, Rosie's mother, had never been warm.

She looked at Tiarnan. 'It's fine. You don't have to apologise.'

A buxom housekeeper bustled into the hall, and Kate tried to keep track of the rapid Spanish as Tiarnan introduced them. The woman's name was Esmerelda, and Kate greeted her warmly in Spanish. She could sense Tiarnan looking at her and turned.

'I forgot that you speak Spanish.'

Kate shrugged and coloured slightly. 'Enough to get by.'

She had spent a lot of time working in Spain some years previously, and had kept up Spanish classes when she'd returned to the US.

He regarded her for another long moment, and then gestured with an arm for her to precede him. 'We have some time before lunch is served—let me show you around.'

Kate duly followed Tiarnan through the house, her awe mounting as he revealed a sumptuously formal reception area that led into a dining room which could seat up to twenty people. But just when she was starting to feel too intimidated he drew them away, towards the other side of the house and a much more relaxed area: a comfortable sitting room, complete with overstuffed couches and shelves heaving with books, a widescreen TV, videos and DVDs on the shelves alongside it.

Something in Kate's chest clenched. This was truly a home. Warm and inviting, with colourful rugs on the exposed stone floor.

At the back of the house Tiarnan revealed an idyllic garden with sunlight glinting off an aquamarine pool set among the bushes. A slice of paradise right in the middle of one of the most cosmopolitan cities in the world.

'You have a beautiful home, Tiarnan.'

Kate said the words but they felt ineffectual, stilted. How many women had stood here and told him that?

Tiarnan was looking around them. 'Yes,' he said, almost absently.

Kate shot him a look but he was already moving, walking back towards the house. With a last lingering look at the stunning peaceful garden, Kate followed.

Tiarnan heard Kate's soft footfall behind him. Something forceful and inarticulate was rising in his chest. He'd stood outside and showed her his idyllic paradise, and yet for the first time since he'd bought it he was aware of something inherently empty about it. The image of Rosie appearing at the front door came into his mind's eye. There had been something so lonely about that image too…

He didn't know what it was that was suddenly making him so introspective. He had Kate here. He had no grand plan where she was concerned, apart from getting her into his bed. When it came to women he found it easy to detach. But right now he was feeling anything but detached. He assured himself that it was just because he knew Kate already—they had a connection. And that was why she was here. He was going to use whatever means necessary to show her that he wanted her, to get her to admit to her own desire…

Lunch was in a smaller, less formal dining room just off the huge kitchen. Esmerelda was bustling back and forth with delicious food and warm smiles, but that didn't help dissipate the slight tension in the atmosphere. Despite the fact that Tiarnan was being utterly charming and mesmeric in a way that made Kate feel extremely flustered.

Being the focus of his attention, albeit with Rosie there too, was nothing short of overwhelming. The coiled energy in his taut muscular body connected with hers and she felt jumpy. It was a monumental struggle just to try and keep up with the easy enough conversation.

Rosie was largely silent and monosyllabic when Kate tried to talk to her. Kate had realised that the faint underlying tension was between father and daughter, and she guessed it went deeper than Tiarnan had let on. Rosie was picking at her food, and when she asked in a small, ever so polite voice if she could leave the table, Tiarnan said tightly, 'You've barely said two words to Kate.'

Kate directed a quick smile at Rosie and said, 'I don't mind. She can go if she wants. I remember how boring it can be, listening to adults.'

Rosie immediately jumped up and ran out, her chair scraping on the ground as she did so, making Kate flinch slightly. Tiarnan made as if to go after her, but Kate caught his arm, jerking her hand away again when she felt the muscles bunch under the thin material of his shirt. 'Really, it's fine, Tiarnan. I don't mind.'

He sat down again and sighed heavily. 'When we moved here from the outskirts of Madrid I changed her school. It's not been the easiest of transitions, and I'm currently public enemy number one.'

Kate thought of Stella again—Tiarnan's ex-wife. She'd never really known why the marriage had ended, and Sorcha had never talked about it either, but then Tiarnan's marriage break-up and subsequent fatherhood had coincided with a hard time in Sorcha's life... Kate's attention had naturally been taken up with her friend. In all honesty she'd used every and any excuse to avoid talking or thinking about Tiarnan. And the fact that she was thinking about his marriage now irritated her intensely.

Just as that thought was highlighting the juxtaposition between how she'd always so carefully protected herself around this man and how much he'd already reeled her in, the door opened and a woman came in—someone Kate hadn't yet met. She was middle-aged, and her face was white and tense. She looked as if she'd been crying.

Tiarnan stood up. 'Paloma, this is Kate—an old friend.'

Kate stood and extended her hand. As the woman came in it was extremely obvious that she'd been crying. She shook Kate's hand and managed a distracted watery smile.

Tiarnan was looking from her to Kate. 'This is Paloma—Rosie's nanny.' Belatedly noticing Paloma's distress, he said, 'What is it? Something with Rosie?'

Kate could feel the tension spike, and guessed in an instant that Rosie had probably been giving Paloma a hard time too.

The woman shook her head and fresh tears welled,

'No, it's not Rosie, it's my son. He's been involved in an accident and he's been taken to hospital. I'm sorry, Mr Quinn, but I have to go there immediately.'

Kate put her arm around the woman's shoulders instinctively as Tiarnan quickly reassured her. 'I'll have Juan take you. Don't worry, Paloma, you'll be taken care of.'

'Thank you, Mr Quinn. I'm so sorry.'

He waved aside her apology, and with a look to Kate strode out of the room to make arrangements. Kate did her best to help out. They went to Paloma's room and Kate helped her pack.

A short while later, as they stood on the steps and watched Tiarnan's chauffeur-driven Mercedes pull away with Paloma in the back, he turned and ran a hand through his hair. 'I'm sorry, Kate. I invited you for a quiet lunch and it's been nothing but drama. I didn't intend for it to be like this.'

Kate looked up into those glittering blue eyes and felt out of her depth. Tiarnan had taken control of the situation and despatched Paloma with an assurance that she must have as much time off as she needed. She'd heard him make a call to the hospital where Paloma's son was to make sure that he was getting the best of treatment, arranging for him to be moved to a private room.

Kate knew that he would personally oversee any payment. His innate goodness and generosity made her feel vulnerable.

She shrugged a slim shoulder. 'That's OK. It couldn't be helped.'

A shadow passed over Tiarnan's face and he swore softly under his breath. He looked out past her to where the car had disappeared.

'What is it?'

He looked back to her. 'I'm due in Dublin this evening, for the AGM of the board of Sorcha's outreach programme. I promised Sorcha and Romain I'd do it for them while the baby is so small.'

'Oh…' Kate would instinctively have asked what she could do to help, but she was due on her flight back to New York herself. She knew how important Sorcha's outreach youth centre was to her. And while she'd no doubt Romain would jump on a plane to Dublin for an important meeting like this for his wife, she knew Tiarnan wouldn't want to let them down.

'Can't Esmerelda help out?'

Tiarnan shook his head. 'She's a lot older than she looks, and while she does live here, in an apartment out the back, her husband is old too and needs taking care of… I couldn't ask her to take on Rosie.'

'Your mother?' Kate knew that Mrs Quinn had moved back to her native Madrid as soon as Sorcha had left home.

'She's down in the south, staying with her sister until the spring.'

'Oh…'

'The other problem is that I'm due to fly straight to New York from Dublin tomorrow. I'm taking part in talks with a senator, the mayor and one of the major banks. It's something I couldn't get out of even if I wanted to…'

Kate's conscience pricked her. She had to say something, because she knew when she got back to New York she didn't have any work lined up. She'd told her formidable agent, Maud Harriday, that she wanted to start scaling back her work commitments, and Maud with typical brusqueness had declared that all she needed was a holiday. So now, for the first time in a long time, Kate had a few clear weeks of…nothing.

'Look, I don't have any work lined up for the next…' she stopped herself revealing too much '…the next while. I could stay here and watch Rosie if you want. I mean, if that's OK with you?'

Kate couldn't decipher the expression on Tiarnan's face. She knew he was fiercely protective of his daughter. Perhaps he didn't trust her? That thought lanced her.

'I'd enjoy having an excuse to stay in Madrid—and a chance to see Rosie properly again…'

Tiarnan looked down at Kate, taking in her clear blue gaze. She was surprising him again. Offering to take on responsibility for Rosie like this. A few lovers after his divorce had hinted at wanting to get to know Rosie, to try and become more intimate. He instinctively wanted to say no to Kate's suggestion, but found himself stopping. The immediate feeling that he could trust her with Rosie surprised him.

Kate saw him deliberate, and felt compelled to insist on helping him. She refused to investigate *that* impulse.

'Tiarnan, you're stuck. If you want to go to Dublin in two hours and New York tomorrow, who can you get to mind Rosie at such short notice? And you know if you say you can't go then Romain will have to leave Sorcha on her own with the baby.'

She was right. Tiarnan knew if Kate wasn't here, offering this solution, he would have to take Rosie with him on his trip—and that was never ideal. Especially when her routine was of paramount importance right now. And Kate wasn't some random stranger. Tiarnan knew that she'd spent time with Rosie whenever Sorcha had looked after her for him before, and his discreet security team would make sure that Rosie and she were well protected. Rosie was an independent, mature girl for her age, so she really just needed to have company. Esmerelda would be on hand too. But…

He seemed to be considering something—and then he took Kate by surprise, moving closer. She froze.

He cocked his head slightly. 'You wouldn't be doing this just to avoid me, would you, Kate? Now that you know I'm going to New York? Or even because you're hoping that this will foster some kind of longer-lasting position in my life?'

Kate clenched her fists, surprised by the strength of the hurt that rushed through her at this evidence of his cynicism, and felt anger at his arrogant assumption that her capitulation was a foregone conclusion. His mention of New York hadn't even registered—*or had it?* The evidence that she might have been faced with his relentless determination again within days sent a flare of awareness through her. She damped it down, hating that he might see something.

'No, Tiarnan. Believe it or not, I'm just trying to help.'

She saw a suspicious light flash in his eyes, as if he didn't trust her assertion. He came even closer and lifted a hand, trailing a finger over the curve of her cheekbone and down to the place where her jaw met her neck. Since when had that small area become so sensitive that she wanted to turn her face into his hand and purr like a cat?

'Good,' he said softly. 'Because I had been planning on asking you out for dinner in New York. We can discuss it when I get back.'

Suspicion slammed into Kate, clearing her lust-hazed mind as she remembered the frenetic call from Maud about this assignment, the apparent urgency. She reached up and took down Tiarnan's hand. It felt warm and strong and vital, but she forced herself to let it go and glared up at him. 'Did you have anything to do with my being sent here for this impromptu shoot?'

Tiarnan crossed his arms and looked down at Kate, completely at ease. Smug. He shrugged minutely. 'Not…exactly…'

Kate crossed her arms too, as suspicion turned into cold certainty and not a little fear at how Tiarnan was determined to manipulate her. 'What's that supposed to mean?'

His eyes turned steely. 'It means that I *might* have encouraged the CEO of the luxury brand Baudé, who is a personal friend of mine, to hire you. I was aware he was looking for a suitable model…'

Shock spread through Kate—his influence had meant that within a week of seeing him in San Francisco he had managed to get her all the way across the world to Madrid, practically giftwrapped on his doorstep. The realisation stunned her. Evidence of his determination made her feel funny inside—confused.

'How dare you use me like that? I'm not some pawn you can just move around—'

Tiarnan took her hand, and her words halted and died.

'Kate. You know I want you. I will do whatever it takes to convince you of that and get you to admit that you want me too.'

'But…but…' Kate spluttered. The effect of him just holding her hand was sending her pulse into overdrive. 'That's positively Machiavellian.'

He came closer and lifted her hand to his mouth, pressed a kiss to the underside of her wrist. 'No. It's called desire—and it's a desire I've denied for a long, long time…'

Ten years. It hung there between them like an accusation.

'Tiarnan,' Kate said weakly. 'It was so long ago…it was just a kiss…we're not the same…'

'So why does it feel like it was only yesterday, and that it was more than just a kiss?'

And right then, with Tiarnan holding her hand and standing so close, it slammed back into Kate with all the intensity as if it had been yesterday. It was exactly the same for her. The only problem was it had never diminished for her, while he'd been busy getting married, having a baby. Forgetting her. Until now. Because he was bored, or intrigued to know what he'd refused?

Kate tried to pull her hand away, but he was remorseless, wouldn't let go. She glared up at him, feeling panic rise, feeling inarticulate.

Tiarnan's voice was eminently reasonable. 'I may have suggested you to someone for a campaign. That's all I did. I wanted to meet you here, show you that I meant what I said in San Francisco…and then in New York I was hoping that you'd agree to go out with me. Give us a chance.' He grimaced. 'What happened with Paloma today was out of even *my* control.'

Kate flushed and looked down for a moment. The panic was still there, but she fought it down. 'Of course it is. You couldn't have known that would happen.'

She looked up then, and finally managed to pull her hand from his. She stepped back to give herself space. But she knew it was useless. Tiarnan Quinn was fast filling every space within her and around her—as only he could.

'Look, I'm offering to stay and watch Rosie till you get back. Apart from that…' She shook her head. 'I—'

Tiarnan put a finger to Kate's mouth. 'Just…think about it, OK?'

Kate looked into his eyes for a long moment, and what she saw there alternately scared the life out of her and made her want to wrap her arms around his neck and have him kiss her— exactly as she'd been wanting him to since the christening in France. Eventually, feeling weak, she nodded. It was only a small movement, but it seemed that Tiarnan was happy enough with that. She was afraid he'd seen some capitulation in her eyes that she wasn't even aware of.

'Good. And thank you for offering to stay.' He stepped back too, and gestured for her to precede him back into the house. 'I'd better see if Rosie's OK with this, and fill you in on all the details of her routine.'

Kate walked back into the house and felt as if she was stepping over a line in the sand. She just hoped and prayed that someone would come along and divert Tiarnan's attention in New York. And yet as soon as she had that thought the acid bile of jealousy rose. Kate was very afraid that when Tiarnan returned she wouldn't have the strength to resist him…

Kate's eyes were tired. She put down what she was working on and sat back in the couch for a moment, closing her eyes, pinching the bridge of her nose. She was waiting up for Tiarnan. He was due home at any time now. He'd been gone for three days.

Kate was all geared up to be clear and firm. She fully intended flying back to New York first thing in the morning. The thought of Rosie, though, made her heart clench. It had taken some time—a couple of days of Kate walking her to and from her new school nearby, chatting easily about this and that—for a sense of the familiar old accord to come back. And while it wasn't exactly the way it had been, things were definitely thawing. Rosie clearly had a lot going on in her serious little head.

Earlier that evening, after Kate had bent down to kiss her goodnight, she'd been surprised and touched when a pair of skinny arms had crept around her neck and held on tight for a second. Rosie had said nothing, and Kate hadn't pushed it, just crept out of the room, her heart swelling with emotion. Emotion she shouldn't be allowing herself to feel for the little girl. *Or* her father.

Kate was surprised to admit to herself that in the past few days she'd felt an increasing sense of relaxation stealing over her. It had been so long since she'd slowed her pace. Stopping at the local café on her way home from seeing Rosie off to school each day, taking time to just read the paper had reminded her of how long it had been since she'd devoted any time to herself.

Sorcha had phoned earlier, and Kate hadn't missed the open curiosity in her voice. Kate hated misleading her friend, keeping the real nature of what was going on with Tiarnan from her, but Sorcha was just too close, so she'd passed off the chain of events that had led her to Madrid as just coincidence. But it was no coincidence that she was sitting curled up on Tiarnan's couch, waiting for him to come home, and no coincidence that was causing this churning mixture of excitement and turmoil in her belly…

Tiarnan stood at the door of the living room. The house was silent, warm. A sense of peace washed over him—the same peace he always felt when he got home and checked that Rosie was safe, tucked up in bed asleep. And yet tonight, after checking on her, that quality of peace was deeper, more profound.

One dim lamp was lit and on the couch was the curled-up figure of a woman. Kate. Here in his house. *His.* Satisfaction coursed through him. He walked in, the rug muffling his steps. She was asleep, hair tumbled over one shoulder in a bright coil of white-gold. His eyes travelled over her lissom form—what he could see of it in faded jeans and plaid button-down shirt. Her feet were bare, delicately arched, toenails painted with clear gloss. Desire was instant and burning within him.

He shrugged off his jacket and threw it onto the edge of the couch, sitting down beside Kate. She moved slightly in her sleep, sliding towards him, towards the depression he'd made. Tiarnan put an arm across the back of the couch and leant towards her face, which was turned towards him.

'Kate,' he whispered softly. She didn't stir.

He'd never been turned on by sleeping women, usually preferring them awake and willing, but there was something so perfect about Kate in sleep, her cheeks flushed a slight pink, her mouth in a little *moue,* that he couldn't resist the temptation to bend even closer and press his mouth to hers.

Kate knew she was dreaming, but it was too delicious a dream to wake herself from just yet. A man's mouth was moving over hers enticingly, softly, as if coaxing a response.

And, as if watching herself from outside her own body, she gave full rein to her imagination and let it be Tiarnan; let it be *his* hard, sensual mouth. It felt so good, so right, and on a sigh that seemed to draw in pure lust she opened her mouth against his.

She felt his deep moan of approval. It rumbled through her whole body, sensitising every point, making her breasts tighten, the tips harden into points. When his tongue sought entry to explore and tease, she smiled against his lips, her own tongue making a bold foray, tasting his, sucking it deep. She arched her body, wanting to feel more…

On some level, even while Kate knew she was dreaming, she was also very aware of the fact that she was in Madrid, in Tiarnan's house, waiting up for him to come home from the US… As if she'd climbed too high in consciousness to stay where she'd been, the shocking realisation came that she was no longer dreaming…what was happening was very real. *Tiarnan!*

Kate's eyes flew open, and at the same time she became aware of her heart racing and her breath coming hard and fast. She also became aware of slumberous blue eyes looking directly into hers. As if he'd sensed her wakefulness before she did, Tiarnan had moved back slightly. Her hands were on his shoulders, *clutching them to her,* not in the act of pushing him away. Her mouth felt bruised, sensitive. She remembered the hunger of that kiss just now. And yet amongst the shock and dismay that splintered her brain was pure joy at seeing him again.

It was all too much for her to process for a minute, seeing him here like this. She reacted against that feeling of joy and tried to push him away with all her might.

'What do you think you're *doing?*'

She gave another huge push, but Tiarnan was like a rock and still far too close. His mouth quirked sexily and everything seemed to slam into Kate at once: the dimness of the room, his scent, his body so close to hers. *Her wanton reaction.*

'Waking you with a kiss.'

She reacted violently to his voice, feeling acutely vulnerable—he'd taken deliberate advantage of her, and the more he did it, the less she could argue to him or herself that she was immune to him. If he knew how close this was to the fantasy she'd had for a long time…

She pushed again, feeling heat rise in her face. 'Finding me asleep did *not* give you the right to molest me.'

Tiarnan finally rolled back and away, releasing her, but a mocking look on his face cut right through her flimsy attack.

'Kate, believe me, I wasn't— *What the—?*' He suddenly jumped up like a scalded cat, holding something in his hand.

Kate immediately saw what it was.

'What the hell is that?' Genuine pain throbbed in his voice, and Kate allowed herself a small dart of pleasure; that would teach him.

She stood up and took the offending article from him. 'It's a knitting needle.' She indicated the couch and the pile of knitting that had rolled off her lap when she'd fallen asleep. 'I'm knitting a jumper for Molly, for Christmas.'

His mouth opened and closed. Kate saw a genuine lack of comprehension in his eyes, and then she looked down to where his hand still held his side, just above his trousers. A dark shape was flowering outwards through a small rip in his shirt, under his hand.

Shock slammed into Kate, turning her cold in a second. 'Tiarnan—you're *bleeding.*'

His mouth was a tight line. 'It went right into me.'

Acting on pure instinct, and feeling a shard of fear rush through her, Kate reached out and ripped open the bottom of his shirt. The wound was a small puncture, but it was pumping blood, and when she looked up at Tiarnan he'd gone white. Too panicked to feel bemused at his obvious distaste for blood, Kate held his shirt to the wound and led him out to the kitchen, where she found the first aid kit under the sink.

She made him rest back on the huge wooden table as she opened his shirt all the way to tend to him. She felt shaky. 'I'm so sorry, Tiarnan. I'd no idea you were leaning on the needle...'

He just grunted, and Kate busied herself stanching the blood. She applied pressure to a piece of cotton wool over the wound for a long moment, and looked at him warily. Colour had come back into his cheeks and his eyes were now glittering into hers.

He arched an incredulous brow. 'Knitting?'

She smiled weakly. 'It's a hobby. Something I took up to pass the time backstage at the shows.'

'Reading would have been too boring, I take it?' His tone was as dry as toast.

She smiled again. 'And smash the stereotype that all models are thick?'

A glint of humour passed between them, and suddenly Kate became very aware of the fact that Tiarnan was lounging back, lean hips resting on the table, shirt open, impressive chest bare. In a surge of awareness, now that the panic was gone, she unthinkingly applied more pressure, making Tiarnan wince.

'Sorry,' she muttered, lifting the cotton wool to check if the bleeding had stopped. To her relief it had, and it didn't look as if the needle had gone too deep. But now all she could think about was the fact that she was right between his splayed legs. The material of his trousers was pulled taut over firmly muscled thighs. His belt buckle glinted and a line of dark silken hair led upwards over a hard flat belly, like an enticement to his chest, which was covered with more dark hair. She had a sudden burning desire to know what it would be like to have her bare breasts pressed against his chest...

She grew hot again as she busied herself cleaning the wound and getting a plaster to hold it in place. Her hands didn't feel steady, and she prayed that Tiarnan wasn't noticing her meltdown.

What Tiarnan *was* noticing was the tantalising display of her breasts, just visible as she moved, in the vee of her shirt. From what he could see she wore a plain white bra, and her breasts looked soft and voluptuous. Perfectly shaped. He could remember how they'd felt, crushed against his chest. Her soft, evocative scent wafted up from her body as she moved. Her legs looked impossibly long in the faded jeans. He shifted on the table as she bent down and unwittingly came closer to where he was starting to ache unmercifully. The pain of where the needle had lanced him faded in comparison. The incongruity of finding that she'd been knitting in the first place—not a hobby that he associated with a woman like her—had faded too, in the heat of his arousal.

If she looked down… He gritted his teeth, trying to control his body, a muscle throbbing in his jaw as her soft small hands worked. Her hair slid over her shoulder then, and whispered against his belly. Everything in him tightened, and he couldn't help a groan. Immediately Kate looked up with wide, innocent eyes, inflaming him even more.

'Did I hurt you?' He shook his head. She was finished putting on the plaster. He could hear the tremor in her voice when she said, 'There—all done.'

He reached out and held her elbows, dragging her imperceptibly closer, and closed his legs around hers slightly. He could see her widening eyes, pupils enlarging, and it had a direct effect on his arousal levels. She was tantalisingly close to where his erection strained against his trousers. But not close enough.

His voice felt as if it was being dragged over gravel. 'Not all done yet… I think you should kiss it better.'

Kate's insides seemed to be melting and combusting all at once. She was unable to look away from Tiarnan's gaze. It held her like a magnet. Time stood still around them. She was so close now. One little tiny step and she'd be right there, captive between his legs, and she would be able to feel… She had to stop this madness. She had to remember that he'd deliberately set out to get her to Madrid to seduce her—had to remember her vow to be strong, resolute. She *couldn't* let this happen. She struggled to swallow.

'Tiarnan, you're not four years old...' Her voice sounded pathetically weak and feeble.

'You stabbed me with your knitting needle,' he growled. 'The least you can do is kiss me better.'

What they were saying should have had a thread of easy humour. But humour was long gone. This was deadly serious.

Kate's heart was pumping so fast now she felt sure he would be able to hear it. His hands on her elbows were strong, rigid. He wasn't going to let her go, and she didn't even know if she would have the strength to step away without falling down. This was the most erotically charged moment she could ever remember experiencing. Her throat was as dry as sandpaper.

'One kiss and then you'll let me go?'

Without taking his eyes from hers, he nodded.

Kate pulled away slightly and Tiarnan let go—cautiously. He leant back a little farther and rested his hands behind him on the table. It made him appear vulnerable and even more sexy, his torso long and lean, shoulders broad. Kate looked down at where the wound was. She put her hands behind her back, as if she couldn't trust herself not to run her fingers over the ridges of muscles that rippled over his belly. She felt weak inside— hot and achy.

She bent down over his chest, and down further, her mouth hovering over where the plaster was. His skin was dark olive, taut and gleaming, begging to be touched, kissed. She imagined it to be hot to the touch, and pressed her mouth just above the plaster. Without having consciously intended it, her mouth was slightly open. She could feel and hear his indrawn breath. Acting on pure instinct, Kate darted her tongue-tip out for the tiniest moment. His skin was warm, and slightly salty on her tongue. Lust coiled through her like a live flame. She could smell the musk of arousal and didn't know if it was hers or his.

She wanted with a desperate urgency to explore further, to press herself close and feel if he was aroused…

With every atom of strength Kate possessed, she managed to straighten up and look Tiarnan in the eye. Her hands were still clenched tight behind her back. She felt feverish. His eyes burned into hers, and suddenly Tiarnan's hands gripped her upper arms and he pulled her right into him. Caught off balance, she fell forward. He caught her full weight, and her hands came out automatically to splay across his chest. Desire flooded her belly and between her legs with traitorous urgency.

'Your wound…' she gasped.

'Will be fine.'

She was desperate now. As desperate for him to keep holding her as she was to get away—and that killed her. 'You said one kiss.'

He looked at her for a long moment. Kate felt her breasts crushed to his chest and, worse, felt his arousal hard against the apex of her legs. She was right in the cradle of his lap, unable to save herself from falling headlong into the fire. Her whole body was crying out to mould into his, to allow it to go up in flames.

She repeated herself, as if that might change the direction things had been taking since he'd walked up to her on that stage in San Francisco.

'You said one kiss.'

Tiarnan snaked one arm around her back, pulling her in even tighter. The other went to the back of her head. She was his captive, and she couldn't move even if she wanted to.

'I lied.'

CHAPTER FOUR

TIARNAN'S mouth came down onto Kate's with all the devastation of a match being put to a dry piece of tinder. Ten years of build-up exploded inside her. Her hands curled into his chest and he pulled her so close to his body that all she could feel was rock-hard muscle and his arousal. Kate could feel moisture gather between her legs and she moved unconsciously, as if she could assuage the need building there.

With a move she wasn't even aware of Tiarnan shifted them, so that Kate was now sitting on the table and he was leaning over her. Eyes closed, Kate could only feel and experience, and give herself up to the onslaught on her senses. Tiarnan's hands were in her hair, around her face. His mouth was relentless, not breaking contact, his tongue stabbing deep—and she was as insatiable as he.

Her arms wound up around his neck, clinging, hands tangling in his short silky hair. She finally broke her mouth away for a brief moment, sucking in harsh breaths. Her heart hammered as she felt Tiarnan's hands move down, moulding over her waist, cupping under her buttocks, pulling her into him even more.

She opened her eyes, but they felt heavy, Tiarnan's face was close, his breath feathering across her face, his mouth hovering. Feeling bereft, Kate reached up again and pressed her mouth feverishly to his, her whole body arching into Tiarnan's, revelling in his hard strength. No other man had ever made her feel so hot, so sensual.

Tiarnan's hands went to her shirt and she could feel him open the buttons, fingers grazing her skin, the curve of her breasts. She didn't protest—she couldn't. Impatient to touch him too, she pushed his shirt off completely, so his chest was bare, and ran her hands over the smooth skin of his shoulders. She felt the muscles move under his skin as his hands pushed aside her shirt. His mouth left hers and blazed a trail of kisses down over her jaw and neck. Kate's head fell back. All she was aware of was here and now and how badly she craved this touch. *His* touch.

Tiarnan's arm supported her as he tipped her off balance slightly so she leant further back. His mouth was on the upper slope of her breast and all her nerve-endings seemed to have gathered at the tip, so tight it hurt.

When she felt him pull down her bra strap and then her bra to expose her breast, her breath stopped. Tiarnan cupped the voluptuous mound with one hand, his thumb passing back and forth over the hard aching tip. Kate bit her lip and looked down. She was breathing fast, one hand behind her, trying to balance, clenched into the table as if that could stop her tipping over the edge of this sensation. Between her legs she burned, and she could feel herself fighting the urge to push into Tiarnan's body.

'So beautiful…' he breathed, looking down at her cupped breast with its pouting dusky peak.

Before Kate could gather her fractured thoughts and steady her breathing he lowered his head and his mouth closed over her nipple. She let out a long moan somewhere between torture and heaven as he drew it into the hot cavern of his mouth and suckled.

This felt so right—as if they had been transported back in time and this was a natural progression of that kiss. And yet…it shouldn't be. Not after ten years. How could ten years of other experiences be obliterated so easily? Wiped out as if they hadn't even existed?

It was that tiny sliver of rationality seeping into her head that woke Kate from her sensual trance. She became aware of the fact that she was practically supine on the kitchen table, and when she felt Tiarnan's hand search for and find the button on her jeans, about to flick it open, she struggled upwards, battling a fierce desire to just give in.

'No…*no*, Tiarnan. *Stop*.' Her hands were on his arms, pushing him back.

After a long moment he stood up, chest heaving, cheeks flushed, eyes glittering. Kate knew she wasn't much more composed. She dropped her hands. Her voice felt raw.

'We can't do this. Rosie might wake and find us…or Esmerelda.'

He looked at her for a long moment and finally took a step back, raking a hand through his short hair. He emanated veritable waves of danger, his face stark with a raw masculine beauty that nearly made Kate throw herself back into his arms. But she didn't.

She stood from the table on shaky legs and pulled her bra up, her shirt together, turning her back to him for a moment. She felt dizzy.

His voice cut through her dizziness. 'A few moments more and here would have done fine… But you're right. This isn't the time or the place.'

She rejected the almost violent need that beat through her body. She knew he was right; a few more moments and here *would* have been fine. Anywhere would have been fine. *The rug in front of the fire.* Any feeling of exhilaration that their desire had been mutual was lost in the humiliation that burned her again. Her voice was fierce.

'There won't *be* a time or place, Tiarnan.'

Kate felt a hard hand on her arm and she was pulled around to face him. His face was glowering down at her, taut with a frustrated need that had to be reflected on hers too.

'How can you deny what just happened here?'

Tiarnan saw Kate's eyes widen and he let her go. The force of need running through him was so strong he was actually afraid he couldn't contain it. She'd felt like nothing he could describe or articulate in his arms. Soft and fragrant and pliant…and so passionate. But he was shocked to come to his senses and acknowledge that if she hadn't stopped him he would be taking her right now on the kitchen table, overhead lights blazing down, like some overgrown teenager who couldn't wait.

Where was his sophistication? His cool logical approach to such matters? *She'd* had to remind *him* about Rosie. She stood, holding her shirt together, hair tousled over her shoulders, her cheeks flushed, lips red and engorged with blood. His hormones were already raging back to life. He had to get a grip.

Kate struggled to close her shirt. She felt as though she'd just been through some kind of seismic earth shift. She watched as Tiarnan's face closed down. He bent to pick up his shirt, muscles rippling across his back, and when he put it on her eye was drawn to the rip and the dark stain of blood. Her belly clenched. She couldn't answer his words. Couldn't deny what had happened.

She looked down, struggling with her bottom button, feeling tears threaten. *God.* How could she have been so un-utterably weak?

'Kate.'

She composed herself and finally closed the button before looking up. She hoped her face was blank, her eyes giving nothing away. She couldn't count on her years of training around Tiarnan any more. Her control was shot to pieces.

His shirt was back on, haphazardly done up, making Kate's heart turn over and making her want to do it up properly for him. She clenched her hands by her sides, fought the urge to tidy her hair, which was all over the place.

His eyes snared hers. She couldn't look away. Her mind blanked.

'I never meant to leap on you the minute I walked in the door…but you can see what happens between us…'

'I—'

His face tightened. '*Don't* deny it, Kate. At least don't do that.'

Kate shut her mouth. She hadn't been sure what she was going to say, but he was right. She'd been about to try and make some excuse for what had happened.

Tiarnan turned away and paced for a moment, before coming back to stand right in front of her. He looked grim. 'I was going to ask you tomorrow, but it seems as if now is as good a time as any.'

'Ask me what…?' Kate said nervously.

'Rosie's school is giving them some holidays from the day after tomorrow while they do some unavoidable renovation work. We're going to our house in Martinique. I'd like you to come with us.'

Kate could feel herself pale. She took a step back and started shaking her head, her heart beating fast.

Tiarnan watched her. 'You know why I'm asking you, Kate. You know what will happen if you say yes. But know this—if you say no, if you insist on returning to New York tomorrow, it won't change anything… I'm not letting you go. Not when we have unfinished business between us. Not when we have *this*.'

He reached out a hand and cupped her cheek. Immediate heat suffused her whole body and electricity made the air between them crackle. He was determined. Nevertheless, she had to hang onto some control. She pulled down his hand and stepped back.

'I need to leave here by eleven to catch my flight. I'd appreciate it if you could call a cab for me in the morning.'

Kate saw Tiarnan's jaw clench, but he just said, 'You won't need a cab. I'll take you if you want to go. *If* you want to go.'

'I will—'

Tiarnan cut her off, changed tack, and surprised himself when he said, 'When I went in to check on Rosie earlier she looked more peaceful than she's done in weeks.'

Kate shook her head, her heart constricting. 'Tiarnan, don't do this.'

Surprise at that admission, and at the way Kate was reacting, made him sound harsh. 'Look, you did me a huge favour minding Rosie. You've got time off, and you probably haven't had a holiday in months…'

Years, she said in her head, and right now it felt as if she'd been running from something for years. That sense of peace that had been stealing over her these last couple of days was elusively seductive, but there was no way she would relax around this man.

'I *would* like you to come on holiday with us. I spoke to Rosie on the phone about it earlier, and she said she'd love to have you come. I asked her not to say anything until I'd spoken to you… Just sleep on it, OK? And let me know in the morning.'

His tone brooked no argument. Pure arrogance. Kate felt tense.

'Fine. Tell yourself what you want. I know what I'll be doing tomorrow.'

Escaping from you again.

Kate backed away while she could and turned away. And felt as if she were being hounded by jeering voices all the way to her room.

Tiarnan watched the space Kate had left for a long moment. She'd rapidly taken up a place in his life he wasn't used to women occupying. He'd already drawn her into an intimate space that no other woman had occupied just by inviting her here, by letting her take care of Rosie. Apart from family, his wife was the only other woman who'd been that close; familiar darkness filled his chest. *She* didn't count.

And even his wife had never taken such control of his every waking and sleeping thought as Kate was beginning to. He tried to rationalise that moment in New York when in the middle of an important meeting his mind had wandered helplessly and he'd had the lightbulb inspiration of asking Kate to join them on holiday. How right it had felt.

He'd tried to tell himself that it was for Rosie as much as himself; he was becoming more and more acutely aware, as she grew older, of the lack of a solid female role model in her life. Yet he'd never introduce anyone into their intimate circle who Rosie wasn't completely comfortable with. When he'd mentioned asking Kate along on holiday to Rosie she'd been more excited about the prospect than she'd been about anything in weeks. The fact that they'd obviously bonded merely comforted him that he'd made the right decision. And he *did* genuinely feel grateful to Kate for stepping in to care for Rosie at such short notice. But he knew that for all his high-minded intentions a much baser desire lay behind the sudden impetus to ask her to come. He just wanted her in one place: in his bed, underneath him.

He recalled her obvious shock at the suggestion and felt curiously vulnerable before he quashed it ruthlessly. He had to wonder if this playing hard to get was just a game. Punishment for his earlier rejection? Or foreplay because she knew she was going to give in? A stab of disappointment ran through him; he didn't want that, but couldn't articulate why he couldn't accept that calculated behaviour from her when he might expect it from another woman. Conflicting emotions rose up, muddying the clarity of his thought, his intention.

One thing was clear: he wanted to keep Kate close until such time as he could let her go again, and he knew that day would come. He couldn't fathom any woman ever taking up that much space *for ever.* He'd never felt that way about anyone.

His conscience pricked. There had been one moment—that night ten years ago, when Kate had all but admitted she was a virgin. The realisation had tapped into something within him and he'd felt compelled to pull back, push her away. He'd found himself reacting from a place of shock—shock at how immediate and raw his response had been. And he'd been more curt than he had intended. The flare of wounded emotion in her eyes had seared through him, but after a moment it had been as if he'd imagined it.

And then her cool response had been all the proof he'd needed that she was exactly the same as every other woman. That momentary weakness he'd felt had been a lesson learnt— a lesson he'd needed in those months afterwards when he'd dealt with his duplicitous wife. If anything, what he'd experienced with Kate and subsequently with Stella had merely reinforced his own cynical belief system.

No, all he and Kate had was history—unfinished business. Thinking of how much he wanted her made him feel ruthless, and he never usually felt ruthless when it came to women. They didn't arouse such passionate feelings. Grim determination filled him as he refused to look any deeper into those feelings. Bed Kate and get her out of his system. There was nothing more to it than that. And if she said yes tomorrow she'd only be proving to him that all this was a playful front. And that was fine. It was all he wanted—wasn't it?

Kate lay on her back as the pre-dawn light stole into her bedroom, a tight knot low in her belly. She'd tossed and turned all night. And now she lay gritty-eyed, staring up at the ceiling.

Turmoil couldn't even begin to describe what she'd been going through in the wee small hours. As if she even had to *think* about Tiarnan's offer: of *course* she would not be going with him to some tropical island paradise to indulge in an affair. Yet, instead of feeling at peace with her decision, she was back in time and standing before Tiarnan in that library, with nothing but the firelight illuminating the room.

At the age of eighteen Kate, despite the fact that she'd been modelling on the international circuit for a couple of years and living in London, had still been unbelievably gauche and unsure of herself. But she'd learnt the art of projecting a cool, dignified façade from an early age, and she used it like an armour.

Kate had accepted Sorcha's plea to come and spend Christmas with her and her mother in Dublin; her own mother had been on holiday with a new husband. When Tiarnan had shown up unexpectedly for the family Christmas party, Kate's world had instantly imploded. She'd been in awe of him since he'd dropped her and Sorcha off at school one Sunday evening in his snazzy sports car. *All* the other girls in the boarding school had swooned that day. But Kate, as Sorcha's friend, had got to see a lot more of Tiarnan than the others. And as the years had progressed she'd developed a crush of monumental proportions.

The night of that party, after only seeing him fleetingly at his father's funeral some months before, and not for quite a while before that, to her he'd become even more handsome, more charismatic, with that cynical edge he still possessed today. Kate had been wearing a dress borrowed from Sorcha, far too tight and short for her liking, and had spent the evening avoiding Tiarnan's penetrating speculative gaze, trying to pull the dress down to cover her thighs. Feeling utterly over-whelmed, and not a little dismayed at her reaction to seeing him again when she'd hoped she would have grown out of such feelings, Kate had slipped away to try and compose herself.

She'd gone into the library, ran smack-bang into Tiarnan, and all good intentions had disappeared instantly. Her crush had solidified there and then into pure grown-up lust. But then something amazing had happened. Alone in that darkened room…looking into his eyes…she'd sensed instinctively that he was looking at her for the first time as an adult. She'd seen it in the quality of his gaze when he'd arrived to the party—it was what had made her feel so self-conscious.

Realising this had been headier than the most potent drink.

An electric awareness had sprung to life between them and she'd experienced a feeling of confidence for the first time in her life. A heady *female* confidence. The kind of confidence she faked for photographers and on the catwalk every day. She was tired of faking it. She wanted to *know* it. And she'd known that the only man who could teach her—who she *wanted* to teach her—was standing right in front of her. She'd known if she didn't seize the moment then, she never would. With that brand-new confidence something reckless had gripped her, and she'd stepped up to Tiarnan and boldly told him she wanted him. And then she'd kissed him.

Kate cringed now in the bed, ten years later, as it all flooded back. To have Tiarnan respond to her untutored kisses had been the most potent aphrodisiac. He'd pulled her close and she'd gone up in flames, pressing herself even closer to him. It had only been when his hand had found the hem of her dress and started to pull it up that reality had intruded for a rude moment. She'd instinctively frozen, becoming acutely aware of her lack of experience and the fact that a very aroused Tiarnan Quinn was about to make love to her. In an instant he'd pulled back and put her away from him with hard hands on her shoulders, looking down at her with glittering angry eyes.

Her heart thudded. So much had happened that night. Whatever romantic notions she might have entertained for a brief moment had been ruthlessly ripped apart within minutes.

She'd looked down, mortified and he'd ruthlessly tipped up her chin and asked brutally, 'Kate, are you a virgin?'

The flare of colour she had felt rising in her cheeks had told him her answer as eloquently as speaking it out loud. He'd spun away towards the fire, turning his back to her for a long moment. Their breathing had been harsh in the quiet room. She could remember how loudly her heart had been beating.

In that moment while he'd turned away Kate had struggled

to claw back some composure. Some semblance of dignity. The fact that he was rejecting her was blatantly obvious.

He'd finally turned back to face her, tall and proud, every line in his body rigid. Kate had forced herself to face him, and the coldly speculative gleam tinged with concern in his eyes had been an instant master class in making her realise just how naïve she'd been.

And then he'd said, 'Kate—look. I'm not sure what just happened—*hell*.' He'd run a hand through his hair and his expletive had made her flinch. His eyes had speared her again. 'I don't sleep with friends of my sister. You're just a kid, Kate, what the hell were you thinking?'

Tears had pricked behind Kate's eyes at the unfairness of that statement. Until just moments ago he'd been with her all the way... And then for an awful moment she doubted that it had even happened the way she'd thought. Had he in fact been trying to push her away all along, and she'd been so ardent she hadn't even noticed? A sensation of excruciating vulnerability had crawled up her spine and she'd called on every single bit of training she possessed. All the years of her mother instructing her not to show emotion, to be pretty and placid.

'Look, Tiarnan, it's no big deal. I just wanted...'

She'd racked her shocked and malfunctioning brain for something to say—something to make it seem as if she didn't care. As if kissing him hadn't been the single most cataclysmic thing that had ever happened to her. Because he was Tiarnan Quinn, and he didn't *do* tender kissing scenes with his little sister's best friend and she should have realised that...

She repeated her words and shrugged. 'I just wanted to kiss you.' She felt exposed and numb. Cold. 'I wanted to lose my virginity, and you...well, I know you, and it seemed—'

Tiarnan had jerked back as if shot, staring down at her with eyes as cold as ice. 'What? As if I'd do because I was handy and available? You don't pull your punches, Kate...'

His face was stonily impenetrable. 'Do you know, it's funny,' he said, almost to himself. 'I might have actually assumed for a moment that you were different…' He shook his head. 'But women never cease to amaze me. Even an innocent like you.'

He'd come close, making a violent tremor go through her whole body, before he'd casually picked up his dinner jacket from where *she* had pushed it off his shoulders onto the floor. His voice had been so cold it had made her shiver, her hands clench tight.

'Go and find yourself a boy your own age, Kate. He'll be much more gentle and understanding than I ever could be.'

And then he'd cupped her chin with his big hand, forcing her gaze upwards to his. She'd gritted her jaw against his fingers.

'And when you've finished with him, go easy on the others…you're undoubtedly a consummate seductress in the making. I've already met the mature version of the woman you'll undoubtedly become.'

And within a scant week of that soul-destroying little speech, before Kate had had time to gather the tattered shreds of her dignity, news had broken of Tiarnan's impending parenthood with his South American ex-girlfriend. Rumours had abounded of upcoming nuptials, which had shortly afterwards been confirmed. Evidently his most recent association with the dark beauty Stella Rios had resulted in more than a kiss goodbye. And, even more evidently, renowned playboy and bachelor Tiarnan Quinn was happy to settle down overnight and avoid the clumsy moves of a woman *like her*.

Kate sighed. Raking up the past was no help, but the memories were still so fresh, the hurt still like a deep raw wound. That night she'd attempted to play with fire and had been badly burnt. She'd been shocked at how deeply Tiarnan's cynicism had run. His easy cruelty had dealt her a harsh first lesson in allowing herself to be vulnerable. And the fact that he'd read her so wrong had hurt more than she could say.

When would she *ever* be free of his hold over her? Especially now that he'd made it obvious he still desired her? At least before she hadn't had to contend with being the target of Tiarnan's attention…and she knew how determined he could be. He hadn't made his fortune and become one of the most influential men in the world through lack of determination. Now that he knew her weakness for him he would pursue her with single-mindedness until she gave in. Until she was powerless before him.

A flutter of traitorous excitement snuck into her belly, cancelling out the knot of tension even as Kate tried to reject the accompanying thought—a mere dark whisper of a suggestion: *What if she gave in?* She immediately rejected the audacious thought outright, aghast that her sense of pride had even let it surface.

But it wouldn't go, staying and growing bigger in her mind with obstinate persistence. And with it came an awful feeling of rightness, of inevitability. A surge of desire flared in the pit of her belly, between her legs, all the stronger because she'd been so desperately suppressing it.

But what if she looked at it as Tiarnan was so obviously looking at it? He had no idea she'd never really got over that night—had no idea and never *would* know that he'd hurt her so deeply. He had no idea that she'd all but believed herself to have become frigid. And he had no idea that last night had proved to her that she wasn't frigid; she was just inexplicably bound to one man. *Him.* A playboy who could never give her the stability she needed, who would undoubtedly hurt her all over again.

Kate clenched her fists, a sense of anger rising at his implicit power over her. Maybe she needed to play him at his own game? Perhaps the only way she could ever truly get over Tiarnan would be to give in? Allow this seduction. Render his hold over her impotent by sating her desire. It had to be because that kiss that night had assumed mythical proportions in her head. Despite her reaction to him just last night, who was to say if it went further he wouldn't have exactly the same effect as every other man had had? Ultimately one of disappointment.

If she slept with him—if she got him out of her system and negated his hold over her, restored the balance of his initial rejection—perhaps then she could walk away, not look back, and find the peace and happiness she craved in her life. Find someone to love, settle down with.

She'd had a fantasy vision of the life she wanted to create for herself ever since she'd been a small girl and had realised that her mother loved herself far more than she loved her, and that her father cared only about his work—to the point where it eventually killed him prematurely. Her life would be as far from her emotionally barren childhood as she could get, and while she knew that a man like Tiarnan Quinn was never going to play the starring role in that scenario, was this in fact an opportunity to gain closure? His words last night came back to her: *Unfinished business.* Wasn't that all he was to her too?

For the first time all night, as dawn broke in earnest outside, Kate felt peace steal over her like a complicit traitor.

'Are you going to tell me what's *really* going on?

Kate sat down heavily on her bed and bit her lip. Her knuckles were white around the mobile phone she held to her ear. Her open suitcase, half packed on the floor, said it all, and she didn't have to look at the clock to know she'd already missed her flight to New York.

She closed her eyes. 'Tiarnan's invited me to go to Martinique with him and Rosie for a holiday, and I've said yes.'

'Yes, I know that, Kate.'

Kate's belly felt queasy. Sorcha *never* called her Kate unless she was upset.

Her friend continued. 'I've just been talking to Tiarnan, and—oh, I don't know—a few things aren't exactly adding up: like the fact that little more than a week ago my brother paid a fortune to kiss you in front of hundreds of people when he avoided a public display of affection even on his wedding day; like you're still in his house in Madrid and tomorrow you're heading to a tropical paradise together.'

'With Rosie too,' Kate quickly asserted—as if that could save her now.

'Kate Lancaster, please give me some credit.'

The hurt in her friend's voice was unmistakable, and Kate's heart clenched painfully.

'Don't you think it's always been glaringly obvious to me that you're never exactly overjoyed when Tiarnan is around? You close up tighter than an oyster protecting a pearl.' Sorcha's voice changed then, became more gentle. 'Look, I know something happened between you two all those years ago in Dublin.'

Kate could feel the colour drain from her face. 'Sorcha, I—'

Sorcha sighed audibly. 'It's OK, you don't have to say anything. I just knew…and when you never said anything I didn't want to push it. But I just… Katie, you were there for me when I needed you, and I always wished that you'd trusted me enough to be there for you too.'

Kate's stomach had plummeted to the ground. 'Sorch, I'm so sorry. I *do* trust you—of course I do… I just—he's your brother, and I was just so mortified. It wasn't that I didn't trust you…'

'OK, look, we can talk about it again—but right now just tell me: do you know what you're doing?'

What could Kate say? She felt a bubble of hysteria rise. She was lurching between excoriating confusion and being absolutely sure that this was what she should be doing every two seconds. When she'd gone down to see Tiarnan in his study, after he'd come home from dropping Rosie to school, all rationality had flown out of the window. Yet despite her early-morning revelations, she'd been so determined to resist the awful temptation to give in and bring to life her greatest fantasy.

He'd stood from behind his desk, tall and intimidating, and

so gorgeous that her mouth had dried up. Like watching a car crash in slow motion, she'd heard herself blurting out, 'You said that night that you don't sleep with your sister's friends—so what's changed?'

Instantly she'd cringed at how she'd given herself away so spectacularly, proving that she remembered every word he'd said.

Tiarnan had come around the desk slowly, to stand lethally close. His eyes so blue it had nearly hurt to look at him.

'Everything. You're no longer an innocent eighteen-year-old. You've matured into a beautiful woman and the boundaries I would have respected before around your friendship with my sister have changed too. She's married, getting on with her own life… Don't you want to do the same, Kate? Haven't you always wondered what it would be like?'

Hurt lanced her at his uncanny ability to strike at the very heart of her most vulnerable self. And the fact that what he said underlined the biggest understatement of her life had rankled unbearably.

'So I'm good enough to take to bed now, just to satisfy your curiosity, Tiarnan? From what I recall there were two of us in the room that night, and there was a significant amount of time before you called a halt to proceedings. To be perfectly honest, I don't think I *do* want to give you the satisfaction of filling a void in your memory.'

And right at that moment Kate had felt as if she really *did* have the strength to walk away. The pain of his rejection was vivid all over again—right up until Tiarnan had hauled her into his chest, captured her close and kissed her, turning her world upside down and all her lofty intentions into dust. Desire had quickly burnt away any remaining paltry resistance.

He'd pulled back finally, when she'd been pliant and dazed in his arms, and said mockingly, 'What about giving *yourself* the satisfaction, Kate? Can you be honest enough with yourself to do that?'

Shockingly aware of his arousal, and knowing with an awful sense of futility that she didn't have the strength to walk away, she'd just said shakily, 'If we do this, Tiarnan, it's going to be on *my* terms. This affair ends when the holiday ends…'

'Katie? Are you there? Did you hear me?'

Kate came back from the memory of the bone-shattering intensity of that kiss. 'I heard you, Sorch. I know what I'm doing.'

She just hoped she sounded convincing.

'Katie, you know Tiarnan almost as well as me. He's always been adamant that he's not going to settle down again. And I just don't want—'

'Sorcha.' Kate cut her off before she could go any further. 'Look, I know what to expect. I'm going into this with my eyes wide open. Please just trust me. It's something we both need to…get closure on.' She winced at how trite that sounded, even though they were exactly the words she'd used to rationalise all this to herself only hours before.

Kate heard a baby's mewl in the background.

'You'd better go, Sorch. Molly sounds like she's waking up.'

Sorcha finally got off the phone, grumbling about the fact that she should have noticed that there'd been more to the tension between Kate and Tiarnan over the years than mutual antipathy.

Kate sat looking into space for a long moment. She knew that she couldn't turn away from this now. She knew that this was the only likely way to even *begin* getting over Tiarnan properly. But she was very afraid that Sorcha was right: that as distant as she planned to keep herself from emotional involvement with Tiarnan, she was already fighting a losing battle…

CHAPTER FIVE

THE following day Kate followed Tiarnan across the tarmac of the airport in Madrid to his private jet. He was hand-in-hand with a still serious-looking Rosie. As he'd said, Rosie had welcomed the news that Kate was coming with them—much to Kate's relief—but she still couldn't quite figure out the tension between father and daughter. Tiarnan looked back at her in that moment, making Kate's breath catch in her throat. He was wearing jeans and a plain polo shirt which made him look astoundingly gorgeous.

'We're flying to New York. I'm leaving my plane there and we'll be taking a smaller plane down to Martinique.'

Kate just nodded and forced a smile. What she also knew was that, far from just leaving his plane in New York, he was leaving it to be used by the philanthropic organisation he'd set up, which covered a multitude of charities he chaired or had set up. It was a very public move he'd made some years ago, to try and discourage the unnecessary use of private aircraft. Kate also knew he took commercial flights wherever possible.

She cursed him under her breath, her eyes drawn with dismaying inevitability to the perfection of his tautly muscled behind in the snug and faded jeans. The man was practically a saint, which made it so much harder to keep herself distanced. But from now on that was what she had to be—distanced. She was a woman of the world, sophisticated and experienced. Not shy, gauche Kate who quivered inwardly at the thought of what lay ahead.

Once they were settled onto the plane and it had taken off, Kate was relieved to see Tiarnan take out some paperwork. She and Rosie set up a card game at the other end of the plane. They were served a delicious lunch, after which Kate and Rosie had exhausted all the card games they knew—so Rosie started reading and Kate went back to her seat to try and get some sleep.

Tiarnan glanced over at her and Kate noticed that he looked tired. Her heart clenched, and she had the bizarre desire to go over and sweep away all his paperwork and force him to relax. Her cheeks warmed guiltily when she thought of how she'd like to make him relax. Already that precious distance was disappearing into the dust.

His head gestured towards the back of the plane, a glint in his eye. 'You can lie down in the bedroom if you want.'

Kate shook her head and tried to stem the heat rising in her body, which had reacted to that explicit glint. 'No, it's fine. Rosie's in there reading; she'll probably fall asleep.'

He just looked at her. After a moment he shrugged minutely and went back to his work. Kate reclined her chair and curled up, facing the other way.

Eventually the tension left her body. She was relieved that since that kiss in his study he'd been the personification of cool, polite distance. For all the world as if she were nothing more than a family friend joining them for a holiday. She would have been scared off if he'd been any other way: triumphant or gloating. But Kate didn't doubt that Tiarnan was a master in the handling of women, and even though that realisation hit her in the solar plexus she was too exhausted after a couple of sleepless nights to feel enraged.

When Kate's body had stopped moving, and it was obvious she was asleep, Tiarnan put down his paperwork and looked over. A tight coil of tension seemed to start in his feet and go all the way to his head. He allowed his eyes to rove over her form, taking in the deliciously round provocation of her bottom as it stuck out, straight at him, encased in linen trousers through which he could see the faint outline of her pants. Her legs were curled up, shoes off. Golden hair billowed out across the cushion and her head was tucked down into her chest. He got up silently and took down a blanket from overhead, spread it out over her body. In profile her face was relaxed, with none of that wakeful watchfulness that she seemed to subject him to, her big blue eyes wary.

He'd had to fight to control himself since he'd kissed her in his study. He'd expected to feel a certain level of disappointment in her acquiescence, which was such a contradiction when all he'd wanted was for her to say yes. And yet she hadn't been coquettish, she hadn't been calculating. When she'd stood in front of him in his study, strangely defiant, she'd had faint bruises of colour under her eyes, and if anything he might have guessed that she'd spent a sleepless night.

He stood straight and looked down at her. A surge of possessiveness gripped him. None of that mattered now. What mattered was that she was here, and very soon he would be discovering all the secrets of that luscious body. He turned abruptly before he did something stupid, like kiss her while she slept, and went to check on Rosie.

Kate woke to the sound of heated voices. Rosie and Tiarnan. She sat up and felt thoroughly dishevelled. She pushed her hair back from her face as she heard Tiarnan's voice emerge from the bedroom at the back.

'Rosalie Quinn, I will not continue this discussion until you can talk to me in a civil manner.'

Kate looked around, and her eyes widened as she saw Tiarnan standing in the doorway with hands on hips, obviously facing Rosie. And then she heard a tearful, 'Go *away!* I hate you, Tiarnan. Why should I listen to you when you're not even my real dad?'

And then a paroxysm of crying started. The door slammed in Tiarnan's face. He sighed deeply and jiggled the knob.

'Rosie, come on…'

Then, as if he could feel her eyes on him, he looked around and saw Kate. He ran a hand through his hair and walked up the cabin towards her, dwarfing everything around him as he did so.

'I'm sorry—we woke you.'

Kate just shook her head. 'It's fine…is everything OK?' Patently it wasn't.

Tiarnan sat in his seat, tipped his had back for a moment. 'Not really, no.'

He looked at her then, and Kate felt speared by the intensity of his eyes and the pain she could see in the blue depths.

'I should be honest with you, Kate. Rosie—well, it's a little more complicated than just moving schools—'

Just then the captain's voice interrupted, to announce that they were approaching New York and to get ready for landing. Kate had no idea she'd slept that long.

After the steward had come to make sure they were all awake, Kate said softly, 'Do you want me to go and—?'

Tiarnan shook his head. 'No, I'll get her. It's not your problem, Kate, and I'm sorry you had to hear anything. I'll explain later.'

After a few minutes a white-faced and obviously upset Rosie came out with Tiarnan and strapped herself into her seat.

As they landed and went through the formalities to change planes, Kate did her best to be upbeat and chirpy, to try and take Rosie's mind off whatever tension was between her and her father. She'd said that Tiarnan wasn't her real dad. Kate had no clue what that could be about. Sorcha had never mentioned anything.

By the time they'd boarded a smaller yet equally luxurious plane for Martinique, Rosie was obviously wrung out, and after picking at a meal she let Kate put her to bed in a small cabin in the back. Kate stayed with her till she fell asleep, feeling a very inappropriate level of maternal concern.

When she emerged to take her seat again Tiarnan asked, 'Do you want a drink?'

Kate shook her head, and then changed her mind abruptly, 'Actually, a small Baileys might be nice.'

Within seconds it was being offered to her by the steward on a tray. Once they were alone again, she could feel Tiarnan looking at her.

She turned to face him, and finally he said, 'I've decided to go to Martinique now with Rosie not only because of the school closing but also because we both need a break, and our house there is her favourite place in the world. It always has been. It's where she gets all the maternal love and affection I can't give her.'

Or her mother, evidently, Kate thought to herself. But she said nothing. Tiarnan was looking into his glass, swirling the liquid. Outside the window beside him the sky was a clear blue, strewn with white ribbons of clouds.

He looked at her and smiled a small smile. 'Mama Lucille and Papa Joe are like grandparents to Rosie. They've been the caretakers of my house since before I owned it, and they have five children and dozens of grandkids—all around Rosie's age. When we go there Rosie can disappear for days and I know she's fine. She turns into something almost feral with all her adopted family... I'm hoping that perhaps—'

He stopped, and the word *adopted* struck her. Kate asked quietly, 'What did she mean about you not being her real dad?'

He looked at her, and something intensely bleak crossed his face for a second before it was gone, making Kate think she'd imagined it.

'I'm not.'

Kate shook her head, frowning. 'But you are. I mean—'

He shook his head and downed his drink. His jaw clenched.

'No, I'm not. I believed I was until a couple of years ago. And I'd probably have never found out if Rosie hadn't got ill and had to have some blood tests done.'

He glanced at Kate. 'It was nothing serious, but we found out that her blood type didn't match mine. That isn't unusual in itself, but other tests were done and, to cut a long story short, I found out that Rosie is not my biological daughter.'

Kate just shook her head, frowning. 'But if you're not, then—'

'Who is?' He laughed sharply. 'Take your pick. It could be any one of the three or four men that Stella slept with around the time we split up.'

'Oh, Tiarnan, I'm sorry.'

His mouth was a grim line. 'The others weren't as wealthy or well set-up as me, so when Stella found out she was pregnant she decided to make me the father. A gamble that paid off. She had all the evidence, doctor's notes, and the dates seemed to match up. And I, who'd never wanted to find myself in that predicament, suddenly discovered a hitherto unknown paternal instinct, a sense of moral responsibility to do the right thing, so I proposed to Stella.'

Kate felt as if a stake were being driven into her heart. She tried to keep her face as bland as possible, not to allow that pain to surface—the pain she'd felt as a vulnerable eighteen-year-old who'd dreamed for a second that perhaps Tiarnan Quinn might fall for her in the space of one kiss.

'Stella married me and milked that paternal instinct for all it was worth. And then as soon as Rosie was born she was off—back to her current lover. We divorced soon after, she got a nice settlement—and the rest, as they say, is history.'

Kate knew that was an understatement. Stella Rios had made a small fortune out of Tiarnan. It had been all over the news at the time. Her head pounded with questions: Had he loved her, though, despite that reluctance to settle down? Was that why he'd married her, apart from wanting to do the right thing? Had she broken his heart?

Kate's throat felt dry. 'When did you find out about the other men?'

Tiarnan closed his eyes for a moment and rubbed a hand over his face. 'When I confronted Stella with the fact that Rosie wasn't mine.' He looked at Kate again. 'I officially adopted Rosie as soon as I discovered the truth. Luckily Stella had signed complete custody over to me on our divorce. There was no way I was going to allow her any opportunity to use Rosie as some kind of pawn in an effort to get more money. Which was exactly what she did as soon as she realised that I knew. But thankfully by then Rosie was mine, and Stella knows well that taking on a small child would disrupt her hedonistic life-style, so she's never contested.'

Kate could see that, despite finding out Rosie wasn't his daughter, in every sense she obviously meant as much to him, if not more, than if she *had* been biologically his. It made her feel an ache inside. This wasn't the Tiarnan she was used to—calculating and ruthless and a little intimidating. This Tiarnan was far more human.

'I only allow Rosie to see Stella because she wishes it. Invariably she returns upset every time, but no matter what happens she always wants to go back.' Tiarnan shook his head incredulously, clearly not understanding the apparently mas-ochistic instinct of his ten-year-old daughter. 'Over a year ago I went to Buenos Aires to pick Rosie up from a visit. She over-heard Stella and I arguing…she heard every word…unfortu-nately it was all about the adoption. At first Rosie refused to come home with me, but when Stella told her in no uncertain terms that she wasn't welcome to stay with her any longer, she had no choice…'

Horror coursed through Kate that a mother could be so cruel. She put a hand to her mouth. 'Oh that poor, poor child.'

Tiarnan looked grim. 'And yet Rosie still goes back. Still wants to see Stella even though she's been so unutterably cruel.'

Kate shook her head. She could feel Rosie's pain acutely. In some ways it was similar to what she'd endured with her own mother for years.

Tiarnan looked bleak again. 'I haven't even told Sorcha yet because I don't want to rake up her own painful memories.'

Kate knew what Tiarnan was referring to. When Sorcha and Tiarnan's father had died, Sorcha had found out that she'd actually been born to the mistress of her father—his secretary. She'd died in childbirth, and Tiarnan's Spanish mother had taken Sorcha in as her own. But they'd never really got on, and finding out the truth had sent Sorcha into dark turmoil which could have resulted in a tragedy but thankfully hadn't. Unfortunately Sorcha and Tiarnan's mother had had an even more estranged relationship ever since.

Tiarnan's voice cut through Kate's memories. 'Rosie is punishing me for this…'

Kate looked at him and answered instinctively. 'Because she can. She knows deep down that you love her, so she's lashing out at you when she really wants to lash out at her mother, for rejecting her. She just wants her mother to love her…that's all.'

Tiarnan's mouth thinned. 'I hope you're right. I could cope with anything if I knew that for sure. It's been a tough year.'

Looking into Kate's eyes, Tiarnan had a sudden sense of being out of control. He'd only ever revealed the truth of his marriage to one or two people, and that had been out of pure necessity. His own sister didn't even know about Rosie. And yet here he was, blithely spilling his secrets to a woman whose presence in his life was solely down to the desire he felt for her.

As if to drive away his disturbing thoughts, and an unwelcome feeling of vulnerability, he reached over and with effortless strength pulled Kate from her seat.

She landed on his lap, off balance, her hands against his

chest. Breathless, she said, 'Tiarnan, stop—we can't…not here. What if Rosie—?'

'Rosie could sleep through a bomb going off.' He quirked a sad smile. 'I used to think that she got that from me…'

An unbidden wave of tenderness and compassion came over Kate, taking her by surprise. 'Well maybe she did in another way. Biological ties can be highly overrated, you know.'

A dark brow arched. 'You sound like you speak from experience. Anything you'd like to share? What skeletons are in *your* closet, Kate?'

She shook her head and ignored the dart of pain that struck her. Her skeletons were dull and boring. She thought of her stressed-out, harassed father and her vacuous, narcissistic mother. Kate hadn't seen her flighty mother, currently on rich husband number four, for nearly a year—and that wasn't unusual. She didn't want to allow that old familiar pain to rise now. It would make her think of her yearning to create a solid, loving family base. She couldn't think of that here and now, feeling so raw after what Tiarnan had just shared.

Kate became very aware of being cradled in Tiarnan's lap. And very aware of a shockingly hard piece of his anatomy. When he tugged on her hair to pull her face closer she was powerless to resist. She felt as if a layer of skin had been stripped away, leaving her even more vulnerable to him. She touched her open mouth to his, breaths intermingling and weaving together. Their tongue-tips met, retreated. Breathing and heart-rates increased. Kate could feel his other hand drag her body even closer, and in an instant the kiss had changed from tentative and exploratory to full-on passion, mouths fused, tongues dancing an erotic dance.

After long, heady seconds Kate could feel the whirlpool of pleasure threatening to suck her down. Tiarnan pulled back, his chest still hard against hers. She made a sound of frustration when he broke away. She felt flushed, dizzy, breathless.

Smoky blue eyes glittered up into hers. 'You're probably right. Now is not the time…'

Sanity returned, and Kate pushed herself away from his chest with trembling hands. 'No, it's not.'

She stood up unsteadily and wobbled back to her own seat, snapping her belt shut across her lap, as if it might afford her some protection from the man she would have allowed to make love to her sitting right there in the seat if not for the fact that he'd stopped. In that moment she knew she had to protect herself—had to make Tiarnan see that this affair was on *her* terms and had limits.

She took a deep breath and looked at him, forcing herself not to notice the way his flushed cheeks, tousled hair, the almost feral glitter in his eyes that connected to something deep inside her with visceral intensity.

'Tiarnan, look—'

'That sounds ominous.'

Kate cursed him. 'We need to talk about…*this.*' She cast a quick look back to the closed cabin door, even though there was no way anyone could hear their softly spoken words. 'This has to end when we return home.'

His eyes flashed. Kate knew he probably wasn't used to his lovers dictating terms. Well, tough. This was the only way she knew would be able to get through this. This would be her great indulgence. She knew better than anybody after those revelations that Tiarnan was not the marrying or settling down kind. Once these ten days were over she would be getting on with the rest of her life. No matter how hard. She had to. She couldn't contemplate another moment of this lingering pain.

She forged on. 'I mean it, Tiarnan. I don't want to add to Rosie's woes by causing her more turmoil.'

Tiarnan's whole body bristled at that. 'Neither do I, Kate. I wouldn't have asked you here in a heartbeat if I thought it might result in upsetting Rosie. She wants you here too, and she won't see anything to upset her. If she'd expressed the slightest doubt about you coming I wouldn't have asked you.'

Kate immediately felt chagrined. 'Of course not. I know you wouldn't do anything— But I'd just be afraid of her seeing…something.' How could she not, Kate wailed inwardly, when all she had to do was look at Tiarnan and feel herself going up in flames…

Tiarnan finally looked away, after a long, intense moment, and seemed to spot something out of Kate's window. He came out of his seat to lean over her. Kate squirmed backwards, terrified he'd feel the peaking of her nipples against his arm, the evidence of how easily he could turn her on.

He pointed at something. 'Look—there it is.'

Kate looked down and, sure enough, an idyllic-looking island of forested green rose out of the unbelievably azure water around it. Mountain-tops and peaks were visible through the clouds.

Just then the cabin door opened, and Kate felt Tiarnan tense. Acting on pure instinct, she took his hand for a moment and squeezed it before he stood up to greet Rosie. He flashed her an enigmatic look. Immediately she felt silly, exposed. Who did she think she was? His wife?

'I was just showing Kate Martinique. We'll be landing soon.'

Tiarnan was barely aware of Rosie ignoring him as she came and sat on Kate's lap, pointing things out to her through the window. He sat down and could still feel the press of Kate's fingers around his. A show of support. He'd never had that— never had that sensation of someone sharing his experience. It made him feel— He didn't want to think about how it made him feel. Or how it felt to see Rosie sitting on Kate's lap with such trusting ease, their two heads close together.

Kate's assertion that she wouldn't want Rosie to be hurt had made all sorts of hackles rise. *He* was the one responsible for his daughter's well-being and security, and he had the uncustomary sensation of having allowed himself and her to be put in a vulnerable position. With an effort, he let himself tune into Rosie's chatter to Kate about Mama Lucille and Papa Joe, and her best friend Zoe.

Still feeling exposed, and studiously avoiding looking anywhere near Tiarnan, Kate hugged Rosie's skinny frame close until she had to take her own seat. Kate hated that her heart ached so much for Rosie and Tiarnan's distress. She shouldn't be allowing them to get too close. But as the plane touched down in a bright tropical paradise, all she could feel was a bittersweet joy so intense that she had to shield her face with her hair, terrified that Tiarnan or Rosie might see it.

With the time difference, it was afternoon when they arrived. The sun beat down, and it must have rained shortly before as the ground was steaming. The air was heavy and humid, warming right through to Kate's bones and already making sweat gather at the small of her back and between her breasts.

A smiling young local man met them off the plane, with a small open-top Jeep, and Tiarnan drove it now on a narrow road along the coast. They were heading south, and Kate was happy just to take in the scenery and listen to Rosie chatting non-stop about everything and anything. It was good to see her so animated.

Before too long they came into a charming fishing village, Anse D'Arlet with a white church dominating the seafront and a long wooden promenade that stretched out over the water, where colourful boats bobbed up and down. Shops were strewn along the main street. Some of the buildings were crumbling and had a faded grandeur that just added to the appeal of this slow, peaceful-looking place.

'This is it—our local village.'

Kate looked at Tiarnan briefly. Even he already looked more relaxed.

Rosie was standing up behind his seat, pointing a finger, and she said excitedly, 'That's Zoe's house—there, Katie, look! Tiarnan, please can I get out and go see her now?'

Kate could see Tiarnan's jaw clench, and she felt his pain at Rosie's insistent use of *Tiarnan*. He looked for a moment as if he was going to say no, but then he slowed the Jeep at the bottom of a small drive and Rosie jumped out. Another small girl appeared, and the two started squealing and running towards each other. Tiarnan waved at the woman who had appeared in the doorway of the house, and Kate guessed it must be the little girl's mother.

He turned then and shook his head at Kate. 'See? We'll be lucky to get her back for dinner, but she'll want to see Mama Lucille…'

Tiarnan kept driving southwards out of the small town, and after a couple of minutes turned right towards the sea into an open set of gates that were wildly overgrown with frangipani and exotic flowers. They emerged from under a dense canopy of foliage into a small forecourt in front of an idyllic white-painted villa.

It was old colonial French-style, and had a wooden deck wrapped around it and what looked like a long balcony above, with an intricately carved railing. Shutters were painted bright blue, and everything looked pristine and lovingly cared for. A shape appeared in the open front door, and Kate saw a huge, buxom woman with the biggest, whitest smile she'd ever seen in her life.

Tiarnan had stopped the Jeep, and as he helped her out he smiled and said, 'May I present the inimitable Mama Lucille…?'

The woman came to the top of the steps and put her hands on ample hips. She looked from left to right. 'Where is my baby girl?'

Tiarnan took the steps two at a time and gave her a huge hug before standing back, 'Where do you think? She had to stop and see her partner in crime—*your* granddaughter Zoe. No doubt they're already driving Anne-Marie crazy.'

Mama Lucille shook her head and laughed a big belly laugh,

and as Kate came shyly up the steps behind Tiarnan she could see that this woman truly was some sort of universal earth mother. She looked ageless.

Mama Lucille set Tiarnan aside and put her hands on her hips again. 'And who is *this* vision?' She glanced at Tiarnan with a wicked gleam in her dark eyes. 'Is she an angel come to save us all?'

Before Tiarnan could answer, Kate stepped forward and smiled. 'No angel, I'm afraid—just Kate. I'm an old friend of Tiarnan and Sorcha's.'

Kate's innate humility struck Tiarnan forcibly. She was one of the most famous models in the world, but she had absolutely no evidence of an ego to reflect that; no expectation that people should *know* her. The realisation unsettled him for a moment, and he had to concede that Kate was surprising him—exactly as she'd done in San Francisco, when he'd imagined things going differently. He was somewhat belatedly aware that he didn't really know her that well at all, and with that awareness came a tingling sense of anticipation.

Kate was holding out her hand, but Mama Lucille waved it away and dragged Kate into her massive bosom. 'Any friend of theirs is a friend of mine.' She pulled back then and held Kate away from her slightly, looked her up and down critically. 'Are you a model, the same as that sister of his?'

Kate nodded.

'Hmph. Thought so. Too skinny—just like that other one— but I'd say she's bigger now, after the baby!' Mama Lucille guffawed again and pinched Kate's cheek. 'Don't you worry, angel. A few days of my cooking and we'll put some fat on those hips…'

Kate had to laugh as she imagined her agent's horrorstruck face if she arrived back a few pounds heavier, and with that came the familiar yearning to just let go and stop being so aware of things like her weight.

Before she knew it, Mama Lucille had disappeared in a flurry of movement, with a promise of some dinner in a couple of hours. A young girl with a shy pretty smile appeared and took their bags into the house.

Tiarnan took Kate by the hand. She would have pulled away, but he held her with easy strength, looking at her with an assessing gaze that made her toes curl.

'Come on, I'll give you the tour.'

Kate felt dizzy by the time Tiarnan was leading her upstairs. The house was completely charming. All dark polished wooden floorboards, white walls and beautiful old furniture. White muslin curtains fluttered in the breezes that flowed through open sash windows, with latticed shutters wide open. She'd seen a butterfly dart in one window and out through the next with a flash of bright iridescence. It was truly a home. Kate could imagine the doors always open, people coming and going all day, and yet it had a tranquil air that beguiled and seduced...

'Do Mama Lucille and Papa Joe live here too?' Kate asked as she followed Tiarnan up the stairs and tried not to look at his bottom. He glanced back and she coloured guiltily.

'No. Even though I've been trying to get them to move in for years. They're on the other side of the property. There's a back entrance, down by the private beach, and they live in the old gate lodge. Mama Lucille says she prefers it because there's not enough room for her family to come and stay, and it's the only way she and Papa Joe get peace and quiet to themselves.'

Clearly, from the warmth in his voice, Tiarnan was as crazy as Rosie was about this place and the people. It made Kate's heart do a funny jump in her chest. And what also made her heart feel funny was that the same impression she'd had on the plane: she'd never seen this more relaxed side of Tiarnan before. There'd always been something slightly aloof about him, distant and distinguished. Formidable. And here all that was being stripped away. *Distance—keep your distance,* she repeated like a mantra in her head, futile as she knew it was.

She got to the top of the stairs to see a wide open corridor, doorways on each side, and a huge window seat at the end with what she could imagine must be a spectacular view over the garden. Tiarnan was leaning nonchalantly against a door that led into a bedroom.

'This is your room.'

Kate looked at him warily as she passed him and went in. Her bag had already been deposited inside. The same lovingly polished floorboards were echoed in the antique furniture. Old black and white photographs hung on the walls. A huge four-poster bed was in the centre of the room, its muslin drapes pulled back. A small door led to a white-tiled bathroom with a huge stand-alone bath and shower in the corner. It screamed understated luxury. A pair of open veranda doors led out to the second level wooden balcony, along which trailed vine-like flowers of colours so vibrant it almost hurt to look at them. And beyond that lay the unmistakable clear blue waters of the Caribbean. This truly *was* paradise.

She turned at the open door and looked back at Tiarnan, her heart thumping heavily. 'It's beautiful. Really.'

He walked towards her with all the grace and danger of a dark panther, and Kate could feel her eyes grow bigger as he came closer. Her loose linen trousers and shirt suddenly felt constricting, but he just took her hand and led her outside and to the left, where she could see an identical set of open doors. He stopped at the entrance and Kate could see another room, a little bigger and obviously decorated along much more masculine lines. *His room.*

He didn't even have to say it. The understanding was heavy between them. Within this stunning house and these two rooms they were as effectively cut off and private as they wanted to be. He let go of her hand and looked down at her. Kate felt unbearably hot right then, and it had nothing to do with being in the tropics.

He gestured with his head back to her room. 'That used to be Rosie's room when she was smaller, so I could hear if she woke during the night, but she hasn't slept there for a few years. Her room is on the other side of the villa. This balcony isn't accessible except by these two rooms.' He took her hand and raised it to his mouth, kissing it briefly, his eyes searing down into hers. 'All you have to do is let me know…'

Kate gulped. 'Tiarnan, I…' She stopped. She couldn't fight the inevitable—couldn't *not* own up to her own desire. So finally she just said weakly, 'OK.'

Sudden trepidation assailed her. He must be assuming that she'd had plenty of practice in the last ten years, and while she hadn't been celibate, she hadn't exactly been swinging from the rafters either. He certainly wouldn't be getting the sophisticated seduction he was no doubt used to and expecting!

He let her hand go and stepped back. 'Why don't you rest up and settle in? Mama Lucille will be serving dinner in a couple of hours…'

He stood there, silhouetted by the sun, looking taller and leaner and darker than she could ever remember him being, and Kate felt almost paralysed by the strength of her desire. When she finally could, she just nodded, and turned and fled.

CHAPTER SIX

THAT evening Kate looked blankly at her clothes laid out on the bed. Luckily she'd been able to go shopping in Madrid to pick up some more things. Tiarnan had offered to buy them for her, but her withering look at that suggestion had made him throw his hands up and step back saying, 'Fine—I've just never known a woman to turn down a chance of a free shopping trip.'

Kate's hackles had risen—and a sense of having made a monumental error. 'Well, I'm not every other woman out there, and I can afford to dress myself—thank you all the same.'

Her mind returned to the present, but with a lingering after-taste of the jealousy she'd felt when he'd alluded to dressing other women. She forced it from her mind. She was well aware that she was going to be the latest in a long line of Tiarnan Quinn's conquests. He was nothing if not discreet about his lovers, and Kate knew that was to protect Rosie—but, coming from the world she came from, she was well aware of the gossip that told of the countless beauties he'd bedded over the years, all of whom had been left with extravagantly generous gifts. Kate vowed there and then that she would not be the same. No trinket, no matter how expensive, would be lavished on her at the end of this. Even the thought of it made her burn with humiliation.

She finally focused on the clothes in front of her again. What did one wear to dinner with the man who'd stolen your heart for what felt like all your life? Kate felt the colour drain from her face and she pressed a hand to her chest, feeling suddenly constricted. He hadn't stolen her heart. *He hadn't.* How could he have? She'd had a teenage crush that had culminated in the single most shattering moment of her life. That was all. She hadn't spent enough time with him to fall in love with him. That night had ripped away any rose-tinted views she might have had of love. And she certainly hadn't come close since.

She couldn't love someone like Tiarnan. He was too hard, too forceful. Too obviously driven to succeed—like her father. She'd always pictured herself with someone kind, gentle…unassuming.

This was just going to be a brief interlude. A completion of something that *she* had started a long time ago. She was doing this so that she could move on with her life and banish Tiarnan Quinn from all the corners of her mind in which he still lingered. She wasn't in love with him, she was in lust. That was all.

The constriction in her chest eased, Kate breathed deep. And finally managed to choose something to wear.

When she came downstairs and approached the door leading out to the wooden terrace at the back of the house a short while later, she could hear Tiarnan's deep rumble of a voice and Mama Lucille's infectious belly laugh. Kate felt unaccountably self-conscious all over again, and resisted the urge to smooth sweaty palms on the dress she'd chosen. It was plain and simple, as only the best designer clothes could be. She'd picked out something that helped her to feel covered up—a deep royal blue silk maxi-dress. She knew how lucky she was that because of her profession she'd never lacked for beautiful clothes, and she was glad of the armour now—as if she could somehow project an image that Tiarnan would be familiar with: an elegant and nonchalant lover.

But when she took a deep breath and walked out Tiarnan looked up. His eyes locked onto hers, and she immediately felt undressed, despite the ankle-length dress, and regretted pulling her hair back into a low ponytail, wishing she had it loose, to cover her face. The silk seemed to cling and caress her body with indecent eagerness. All nonchalance fled and the churning turmoil was back with a vengeance as every step brought her closer and closer to that glittering blue gaze that swept up and down her body, leaving what felt like a trail of fire in its wake.

For a second, as Kate walked towards him, Tiarnan's brain went completely blank and every coherent thought was replaced with heat. She was a vision in blue silk that seemed to waft around her body and yet cling to every curve with a lover's touch. He looked down, and his chest tightened with an indefinable emotion when he saw that her feet were bare. The heat in his brain intensified, and only Mama Lucille pointedly clearing her throat stopped him from turning into a drooling speechless idiot. Some of the most beautiful women in the world had appeared similarly dressed before him, for his pleasure, yet they had never had this paralysing effect on him. He managed to stand just as Kate got to the table, her delicate scent reaching his nostrils as he pulled out her chair and she sat down with a warm smile directed at Mama Lucille.

Her colour was high and she was avoiding his eye, making Tiarnan feel unaccountably flustered. He ignored Mama Lucille's explicit look, which seemed to bore a hole in his head, and thankfully she bustled off with her young assistant in tow.

Kate struggled to get her heartbeat and her breathing under control. The dress which had felt so appropriate now felt like the most inappropriate thing she could have chosen. When she felt sufficiently calm she flicked a glance to Tiarnan. He was staring at her with hooded eyes. Against her volition, her eyes dropped, taking in the snowy-white shirt, open at the neck, and the dark trousers. His hair was damp, as if he'd showered not long ago, and Kate could feel heat climbing upwards over her chest. She grabbed her napkin and clung onto it, twisting it under the table.

'Where's Rosie?'

Tiarnan's eyes didn't move from hers. 'She came back here earlier with Zoe, for dinner with Mama Lucille. Zoe's mother, Anne-Marie, collected them just before you came down. She's spending the night at their place. It's something of a tradition. She'll be back in the morning.'

Kate looked down for a moment. *They were alone all night?* Her heart was thudding heavily, unevenly. Right then she wished for Rosie's comforting presence, even with the tension between father and daughter. 'She's having fun, then…'

Tiarnan nodded. 'Yes. She's surrounded by people who love her like their own, and it's important for her to have that while she's determined to reject me.'

Kate looked at him, unable not to, touched deeply by his concern that Rosie feel loved even while she was determined not to accept love from him. In her experience parents either ignored their children or resented them. And yet he was doing his utmost to make sure Rosie was secure.

'You're a good father, Tiarnan.' She cursed herself for sounding so husky and trite. And cursed herself again when she could feel that armour she'd put up around herself crumble ever so slightly. In an instant he had smashed aside her assertion that he was a man like her father—too career-orientated to care about his daughter.

To her relief Mama Lucille returned with a steaming bowl, followed by Eloise, the girl who'd helped with the luggage and who Mama Lucille now introduced as one of her older grand-daughters. Kate got up instinctively to help, but Mama Lucille ordered her to, 'Sit! Let us serve you now.'

Kate watched as more plates arrived, with what looked like an impressive array of fish and roasted vegetables and rice and potatoes and salad. Her eyes were wide, watching as Tiarnan poured white wine into glasses so cold they still had mist on them.

'I've never seen so much food in my life.'

He took her plate and proceeded to heap it high with the succulent food, saying drily, 'Don't tell me you're one of these women who prefer to push a lettuce leaf around your plate and watch it wither and die rather than eat it?'

'No,' Kate said quickly, taking the plate he handed her. 'I couldn't think of anything worse. My problem has never been lack of appetite, it's stopping myself eating.' She grimaced for a second. 'Unfortunately, unlike your sister and presumably you too, I can't eat everything around me and stay the same size. All I eat has to come off again.'

Tiarnan fought down the urge to let his eyes rove over her curves. She was right. Where Sorcha was lean and athletic, Kate had a more natural voluptuousness, a sexy lushness. He picked up his glass and waited for Kate to do the same.

Kate was intensely aware of the way the dusk was claiming the setting sun, turning the sky smoky mauve. The breeze was warm and the sound of the sea came from nearby. Small flaming lights nearby lit up the table and surrounding area. It was idyllic.

Tiarnan held up his glass and said, 'I thought it would be nicer to eat out here. I hope it's not too rustic for you?'

Kate shook her head, mesmerised, and picked up her glass. 'It's perfect. I love it.'

He touched his glass to hers and it made the most subtle chime.

'Welcome, Kate, and *bon appétit.*'

'*Bon appétite,*' she mumbled, her face flaming, and she took a quick sip of the deliciously dry wine.

Tiarnan made sure she had everything she needed, and then proceeded to fill up his own plate impressively. Kate didn't doubt for a second that a man like him would have a huge appetite. When she thought of that, the heat which had begun to recede surged back. She groaned inwardly and then groaned out loud as she tasted a langoustine and it nearly melted on her tongue with an explosion of exquisite tastes.

'This,' she said, when she could. 'Is amazing.'

Tiarnan smiled and nodded. 'Mama Lucille's cooking is legendary. She's had countless offers to work for others, even from the best restaurants here on Martinique, but she's turned them all down.'

Kate smiled too, and picked up her wine glass. 'And no doubt you keep her very well…compensated?'

He inclined his head modestly. 'But of course. I look after everyone I love.'

Kate's heart clenched, and she speared some more food to distract him from what might be in her expression. Was he also talking about the way he compensated his lovers so well? Did he, on some level, love them all too? In that easy superficial way that some men did? Only to let them go easily when they got too clingy? Was he capable of truly falling in love?

'What about you, Kate? Would you like children some day? You're good with Rosie—you seem to have a natural affinity…'

She just about managed not to choke on her wine, and put down the glass carefully, a little blindsided by his swift change of subject. Normally, with such a question from someone else, her natural inclination to reply honestly that she'd never wanted anything more would make answering easy. But here, now, with Tiarnan, she had to protect herself.

She shrugged one shoulder and looked down. 'Yes, I've thought of it. What woman my age doesn't?' Her voice was light, unconcerned, but her womb seemed to contract as she battled a sudden vivid image of holding a dark-haired baby in her arms, Tiarnan's head coming close to press a kiss against the downy, sweet-smelling skin.

In complete dismay at her wayward imagination, and in rejection of that image, she looked up almost defiantly, feeling brittle. 'But not yet. I'm not ready to be tied down. I'm sure it'll happen some day, though, when I meet the right person.'

Tiarnan lounged back. Kate could imagine his long legs

stretched out easily under the table. In comparison she felt incredibly uptight and tense.

'And you haven't met the right person yet, I take it?'

'Well, I'd hardly be here now if I had, would I?' She cursed herself for letting him get to her, making her sound snappy. Tiarnan's eyes had become assessing. Looking deep.

He shrugged too. 'I wouldn't know, Kate. To be honest, it wouldn't surprise me in the least. Let's just say that in my experience women are perennially unsatisfied—either with themselves or their lives—and will do whatever it takes to relieve their boredom.'

'That's a very cynical view to have.'

He shrugged and took a sip of wine. 'When the first relationship you witness has deep flaws, it tends to colour everything else.'

Kate's prickliness dissolved in an instant. 'I know your parents didn't…get on.'

Tiarnan's mouth tightened. 'To put it mildly. I don't have to tell you what it was like… But if none of that had happened I wouldn't have Sorcha for a sister.'

Kate said quietly, 'The fact that your mother took Sorcha in as her own was pretty selfless.'

He made a rejecting motion with his hand. 'A selfless act which drove the wedge between her and my father, and ultimately Sorcha too, even deeper. My mother was—still is—a devout Catholic. She took Sorcha in more out of a sense of religious duty than anything else.'

They both fell silent for a moment, very aware of how that had caused such pain and hurt to Sorcha when she had found out. Kate knew instinctively that there was very little likelihood that Tiarnan would discuss this with anyone else—it was just because of who she was, and the fact that she knew already. Any intimacy she was feeling now was false.

Something rose up within Kate, compelling her to say quietly, 'I do believe, though, that it's possible.'

'That what's possible?'

'For people to be happy. I mean, look at Sorcha and Romain; they're happy.'

Tiarnan's face looked unbearably harsh in the flickering light of the candles for a moment. 'Yes, they are.' He sounded almost surprised, and then his voice became hard. 'I, however, learnt my lesson a long time ago. I indulged in the dream for a brief moment and saw the ugliest part of women's machinations, and how far they're prepared to go to feather their nest.'

Kate's heart clenched. He was talking about Stella, of course—and every other woman too, it would appear, by proxy.

Tiarnan looked into his wine glass, tension gripping him. He cursed himself again for allowing this woman to loosen his tongue, and forced down the tension. He looked up and caught Kate's eye, allowed himself to dive into the deep blue depths. He saw her exactly as she was: a woman of the world, successful, confident, single. Not afraid to take what she wanted. She was like him. Immediately he felt on a more even keel. He snaked out a hand and caught hers, revelling in the contact, the way her skin felt so warm and firm and silky. Revelling in the sensual anticipation.

'For people like us, however, things are different… We won't be caught like that, seduced by some empty dream.'

Kate's heart clenched so hard at that she had to hold in a gasp. She stung inside that he believed her to be the same as him. Ironically enough, out of his sister and Kate, Sorcha had been the more cynical of the two, constantly teasing Kate for her innate romantic streak, for her maternal instinct. Sorcha had been the one with the high walls of defence erected around her, and Romain had been the only man capable of gaining her trust, opening her heart…

Yet, despite her own largely loveless upbringing, Kate had somehow emerged clinging onto those maternal instincts and that romantic dream. And a very secret part of her was still doggedly clinging onto it, despite witnessing the cynicism of the man to whom she was willingly, *stupidly* planning to give herself, in the hope that perhaps it would cure her of this obsession. The fact that he believed her to be as jaded as he was surely had to be in her favour? Protection for when she would walk away? He would believe her to be in one piece, unmoved, moving on with blithe disregard to her next lover. And she would be, she told herself fiercely now. She'd be blithe if it killed her.

She wanted to ask him about his wife—ask if *she'd* managed to break through his cynical wall to make him believe in love for a brief moment. But even if she had, considering how she had deceived him about Rosie, it could only have reaffirmed his beliefs, made them even more entrenched.

Kate forced down all her questions and leaned forward to start eating again, even though her appetite seemed to have vanished. She smiled brilliantly.

'Well, then, we can rest easy in the protection such beliefs can offer us: no expectation, no disappointment.'

The words seemed to score through her heart like a serrated knife, they so went against her own personal philosophy. A philosophy she couldn't share with Tiarnan.

Tiarnan smiled lazily, eyes narrowed on hers. 'A kindred spirit. I couldn't have put it better.'

As Kate forced herself to eat and sip the wine, engage in conversation that moved away from darker topics, she told herself that at least now she was under no illusion that some kind of fairytale would happen here. Tiarnan was utterly content with his life and there was no way he was going to let in Kate to shake things up.

The plates were gone, Mama Lucille had bade them goodnight, and Kate had kissed her in thanks for the meal, making the older woman look embarrassed but happy. Papa Joe, her handsome husband, had come to collect her to walk her home. Being bowed with age didn't diminish his charm. He seemed as naturally friendly and happy as his wife, and they heard them laughing and conversing loudly in local French patois all the way down the garden path. Witnessing their happiness made Kate's conversation with Tiarnan over dinner feel all the more unbearably poignant.

The heavy perfumed air was alive with the sounds of insects. Kate felt almost painfully sensitive to everything. All too aware of what she yearned for and what she was prepared to settle for with Tiarnan. He reached out and took her hand, and predictably she tensed.

'You don't seem very relaxed.' He stated the obvious.

Kate shrugged and forced down her tangled thoughts of yearning. 'Despite what you might believe, I'm not used to being whisked halfway across the world to become a rich man's mistress for a few days.'

Tiarnan's jaw clenched. She kept talking about the time limit. And she certainly wasn't just a rich man's mistress. She was going to be *his* lover. Her words over dinner, her reassurance that she was like him, should be making him feel at ease, confident, and yet they weren't. Not entirely. He didn't trust her. And he didn't know why that rankled. What woman *did* he trust? He was used to not trusting women.

He drove away the questions. He had no need to question anything. Kate Lancaster was here, his for now, and that was all that mattered. They were wasting time. He studied her downbent head, the gleaming blonde hair, the satin smooth skin of her bared shoulders under the straps of her dress, the swell of her breasts…and he knew just how to drive away those thoughts, the tenseness which made ambiguous feelings run through him.

Tiarnan kept a hold of her hand and stood, tugging her up with him. Kate's eyes met his and the world seemed to stop turning momentarily. 'I know just what we need.'

'You do?'

Kate's voice came out like a squeak. She cursed her inability to sound insouciant when she needed to. He nodded, and started to walk back into the house, taking her with him, his grip strong and sure. Her legs felt like jelly. Panic started to rise up, strangling her. She had to tell him, had to say something. He thought she was something she wasn't...

'Tiarnan, I—'

He turned and pressed a finger to her lips.

'I'm taking you out.'

Confusion cut through the panic. The scarily vivid images of their naked limbs entwined on his bed faded.

'What? Where?'

He looked at her for a long moment, and then just said, 'Dancing.'

Kate's hand was still in Tiarnan's as he led them into a dimly lit bar not too far from the house. A throbbing pulsing beat of music enveloped them instantly, along with the heat of bodies and muted conversations.

He'd waited till she had put on some shoes and had obviously made a call, as an open-top Jeep with a smiling driver had been waiting for them outside the villa. He led her to the bar now, only letting go of her hand to put an arm around her waist and draw her in close. Kate saw the bartender spot him and come over with a huge smile on his face.

'Tiarnan, my man! It's good to see you.' The barman's openly curious and very flirty glance took Kate in with blatant appreciation.

She felt embarrassed, and very out of her depth. Tiarnan kept surprising her at every turn, and the thought that he might have read her trepidation and done this to somehow make things easier for her made her feel vulnerable.

'And your beautiful guest...'

For the first time in his life Tiarnan felt the intense spiking of jealousy as his old friend Luc looked Kate up and down with what seemed to be insulting impunity. He'd noticed every other man's head swivelling too, as they'd walked into the bar. Kate stood out like a magnificent bird of paradise.

Resisting the unfathomable urge to walk straight back out again, he forced himself to sound civil and say, 'Luc, good to see you too. We'll have two of your best rums.'

He looked down at Kate and was surprised to see her looking almost…self-conscious. He tugged her in closer and she looked up, a flare of colour racing across her cheekbones.

'Is that OK?'

Kate felt almost disembodied, looking up into Tiarnan's eyes. 'Is what OK?'

'Martinique rum—you should try it.'

She just nodded, still barely aware of what he was saying. Their solicitous host insisted on showing them over to a secluded booth with a view over the faded grandeur of the bar, which was open to the street, and the dark inkiness of the sea in the distance. They were in the ground floor of an old colonial building. The crowd were local, the music was a kind of sexy upbeat Salsa. And then it changed smoothly to something slow and *very* hot. Some of the couples on the dance floor certainly looked as if they were just moments away from disappearing to a dark corner where—

Kate willed down the intense blush she could feel on her face as she looked at the couples, and just then Tiarnan's hand cupped her jaw, turning her to face him. She felt feverish.

He shook his head, and a thumb moved back and forth across her cheek. 'Enchanting. I don't think I've ever seen anyone blush the way you do.'

Kate burned inside and out. The enormity of where she was and who she was sitting with was hitting her anew all over again. 'It's just my colouring.'

Their eyes stayed locked for a long moment, until Kate felt as if she was melting inside. Just as she was about to beg to be released from that intense gaze, Tiarnan suddenly broke it and looked away, making Kate feel absurdly bereft all of a sudden. She was a mass of contradictions and warring desires.

Tiarnan's friend approached with two glasses, and left again with a mischievous smile and a look that Kate didn't miss. When Tiarnan had introduced them briefly she'd thought he'd been uncharacteristically curt to the other man, but Luc didn't seem to mind. She took a sip of the dark liquid and coughed immediately, her eyes smarting.

Tiarnan quirked a brow and smiled. 'Strong stuff.'

Kate grabbed for some water and drank it down. 'You could have warned me.' She watched as Tiarnan took another sip himself, watched the way the strong column of his throat worked. At that moment the music changed back to an infectiously upbeat rhythm.

Tiarnan extended a hand across the table. 'Come on, let's dance.'

Kate shrank back with genuine fear. She could see couples dancing with effortless grace and style, making moves she could never even hope to mimic. She shook her head desperately, 'I can't dance, Tiarnan.'

He left his hand where it was.

'Seriously,' she said pleadingly. 'I'm really, really bad, I'll just embarrass you.'

He stood up and took her hand from her lap, pulling her up.

She tried to resist. 'I'll watch you dance with someone else—honestly.'

He wasn't listening. He pulled her remorselessly after him. Kate was having flashbacks to excruciating moments on other dance floors where she'd shuffled around, invariably much to Sorcha's hysterical amusement. Or memories of standing on various hapless men's feet and apologising profusely.

She tried to pull away again. 'Tiarnan, you don't understand. I've two left feet—just like my father. I've never been able to—'

Tiarnan turned and pulled her into his arms, and Kate shut up instantly at the feel of his body so close to hers, one hand low on her back and the other held high. She could feel Tiarnan's hips move sinuously against hers, his legs making hers move in tandem with his.

His voice came low near her ear, making her tingle, 'Just feel the beat—let it go through you.'

All Kate felt was boneless, with an indecent need running through her.

Tiarnan moved them apart and put both hands on her hips. 'See? Look at my feet. Copy what I'm doing.'

She could barely function. Tiarnan's broad chest and those lean hips were hypnotising her. She didn't know if what she was doing was anything like dancing, but she did feel the deeply sexy beat in her blood, and when Tiarnan turned her around and pulled her back against him, his arm across her midriff, she didn't even care that she couldn't dance. She had to close her eyes and try not to let out a low moan of pleasure.

Then the music changed again to slow and sexy. Tiarnan twirled her around with effortless ease and pulled her into him, so close that she could feel the imprint of his body all along hers. He tipped up her chin. Her head fell back.

'See? Anyone can dance.'

'I wouldn't go that far,' Kate said huskily, her eyes seemingly riveted to Tiarnan's mouth, and as if to prove her point she stumbled and stood on his foot. She looked up to see him wince slightly and smiled sweetly. 'See?'

'It'll take a lot more than standing on my foot to diminish this.'

His voice was low and dark with promise as he pulled her even closer, and Kate's eyes widened on his when she felt the hard thrust of his arousal just above the apex of her legs. The silk of her dress was no barrier to the size and strength of it.

Hot liquid seemed to pool southwards in answer to his body's calling. Her hand clenched on his shoulder, as if to stop herself falling.

'See?' he asked mockingly, his smile dangerous with sensual intent.

Kate could barely hold it together. A bone-deep tremor was starting to build up through her whole body. She felt Tiarnan's hand go to her neck, massaging the delicate skin, undoing her hair so that it fell down her back. A shudder of pure desire ran through her, making her move instinctively against him, eliciting a deep growl from his throat. She turned her face into his neck, her hand resting on the hair at the back of his collar. He brought their joined hands in close to his chest. Her lips were so close to his hot skin. The slightly musky smell was an overwhelming temptation to snake out her tongue and taste, just for a second. She could feel the kick of his pulse under her tongue and exhilaration fired her blood.

Tiarnan stopped dead on the middle of the dance floor and pulled her even closer, urgency in his movements. 'Let's get out of here.'

Kate could do nothing but nod silently. Now she knew she was ready. Now she knew that nothing could hold her back.

Everything happened quickly. The smiling driver took them home. Tiarnan took her by the hand and led her into the house and up the stairs. One or two dim lights lit the way.

All Kate was aware of was the burning need inside her, the prospect of fulfilment more heady than anything she'd ever known. Since the moment she'd stepped up to Tiarnan to kiss him boldly on the lips all those years ago it had never been enough.

So now, when he halted outside her bedroom door and turned to face her, saying with a low voice, 'Kate, I want you. But I'll wait if I—' It was the easiest thing in the world to step close and put a finger to his lips.

'So have me...I'm yours.' She couldn't play games, couldn't

deny the need that had given her the impetus to say yes to coming here. She'd been waiting for this moment for so long.

Tiarnan emitted a guttural sound of satisfaction and pulled her in so tight against him she didn't know if it was his heartbeat or hers she could feel thumping so loudly and heavily. His mouth seemed to hover over hers for a long moment, as if relishing the anticipation, the moment, and then, with one hand spearing her hair possessively, his mouth slanted down onto hers, and Kate gave herself up to the maelstrom that erupted instantly around them.

Without really knowing how they'd got there, Kate found herself standing in Tiarnan's bedroom, facing him. Both were breathing harshly. Her universe had contracted to this moment and this man. It felt utterly right, as necessary as breathing.

She held her half-removed dress to her chest, not even knowing how it had become undone, and with a deep ragged breath let it go. It pooled at her feet in a swirl of vibrant blue silk. She kicked off her shoes and stood before Tiarnan in nothing but lace pants.

'Come here,' he said throatily.

Kate moved forward and started to undo his shirt, fingers grazing and revealing dark olive skin covered in a smattering of dark hair. He was so masculine, and it resonated with something deep within her. Recognition of a mate. Her belly quivered. He hadn't touched her yet, and it was all the more erotic for that. Her breasts felt full and aching and tight, the tips tingling painfully. Kate pushed his shirt off his shoulders and down his arms, and it too joined her dress in a pool of white on the floor.

She trailed her hands down across his defined pectorals, felt his indrawn sharp breath as her fingers trailed lower. She looked down, and amidst the haze of heat that seemed to surround them saw the small cut where her knitting needle had stabbed him just a few nights ago. She traced it lightly, and then bent forward to press a soft kiss to it.

Tiarnan sucked in a breath at the feel of her lips and her breath there. Her hair fell over one shoulder, and when she stood again he looked greedily at her lush form in all its glory. The tiny waist, feminine hips, impossibly long legs…up again to surprisingly full breasts. He quite literally ached to touch her, but this sweet anticipation was too exquisite.

With a voice he barely recognised as his own because it was so full of raw need, he said, 'Undress me. Please.'

Kate looked up into Tiarnan's face. She read the restraint and silently thanked him for it. He was giving her time, letting her dictate the pace. Yet she knew if he threw her on the bed right now and took her with no further ado she'd be ready. She felt indecently damp between her thighs. With other men since Tiarnan she'd always felt self-conscious, awkward, but with him it felt natural, *right,* and that gave her confidence. She had the fleeting wish that she could eradicate all other experiences and make this moment her first time all over again…

Feeling unbearably emotional for a second, she stepped forward and reached up to put her arms around his neck, bringing her breasts into contact with his chest. A shudder of reaction ran through both of them, and it took all of Kate's strength to stay standing and say somewhat shakily, belying her outward show of confidence, 'I'll undress you—but first…a kiss.'

Tiarnan couldn't resist. He smoothed his hands over her slender arms, then down over the bare curve of her waist and hips, settling on her behind, drawing her close. He dipped his head and met Kate's mouth with his, and within seconds the flames of desire were igniting around them, their tongues dancing feverishly. Kate forgot about teasing and restraint. She strained upwards on tiptoe to try and get even closer, pressing herself against Tiarnan blindly, seeking more, seeking to assuage the urgent need building deep in her core.

Without breaking contact she brought her hands down between them to his trousers, found the opening, careless in her haste, dragging his trousers down impatiently over lean hips. His hands had gone under her panties, moulding the cheeks of her bottom, making her arch into him, thwarting her attempts to drag down his trousers.

'Tiarnan...' She almost sobbed with frustration, not even sure what was hampering her, only knowing that she didn't want to stop touching him for a second. To lose contact with that hot skin, that heavenly musky scent, would be like depriving herself of oxygen.

His hands came up to her arms and put her back slightly. She felt dizzy, and they were both breathing as if they'd just been running.

'Kate...' He sounded hoarse, surprised and slightly bewildered. 'How could I have denied myself this for so long...?'

With indecent haste he brought his hands to his trousers and finished what Kate couldn't do. Finally he stood before her, naked and proud, virility oozing from every pore. Kate looked down and her throat went dry as she took him in in all his glory. She looked up again, and even though the room was dark she could see the expression on his face, the look in his darkened eyes. Passion and desire blazed forth—*for her.*

She was feeling suddenly weak, and as if he sensed it Tiarnan took her hand and led her over to the bed, through the muslin curtains that had been drawn down to protect against the stinging night insects. Surrounded by the gauzy material, the bed was like a cocoon, an oasis of pleasure.

Kate lay back and watched as Tiarnan stretched over her. He smoothed back her hair and it felt unbearably tender. Then he looked down her body, and wherever his eyes rested seemed to throb in response. He cupped one breast and Kate arched her back, eyes widening in a mute plea. She heard a dark chuckle, and felt his breath feather on her hot skin before he took the turgid tip into his mouth and suckled mercilessly, inciting the most intense response Kate could ever remember. She was gasping, grabbing his shoulders, his arms, hands clenched tight around bulging hard muscles as his mouth moved from one breast to the other, torturing her with pleasure. And then he moved down, and down again. The breeze whispered over the wet tips of her breasts and her stomach, where his tongue had touched her.

He pulled down her pants, throwing them aside, and then with ruthless intent pulled her legs apart. Kate stopped breathing for a long moment, her belly sucked in as she watched Tiarnan looking at her with such intimacy that she almost couldn't stand it.

Rising desire drowned out her mortification. Instinctively she moved on the bed, hips lifting slightly. 'Please…' She wasn't even sure what she was asking for.

Tiarnan looked at her, his hands travelling back up her legs, coming ever closer to her centre, thumbs massaging the tender inner skin of her thighs. His hands stopped at the very top of her legs, thumbs resting on the curls that covered her. They started moving slowly, back and forth, seeking, exploring, kneading her flesh.

Kate sucked in a breath that felt like a sob. *'Tiarnan.'*

'What? Tell me what you want?'

As if it was the easiest thing in the world.

'I…' Kate began brokenly. 'I want you to touch me… I want you inside me…'

One hand moved, and Kate felt long fingers thread through the damp curls, exploring ever inwards until he felt her slick heat for himself. She felt his reaction run through him. His erection lay thick and heavy against her thigh. She moved restlessly.

'Like this? First I touch…'

And he did. He touched her intimately. Fingers moving in and out, testing her, drawing out her response, his thumb finding that small hard nub and massaging it until Kate's hands clenched in the bedsheets so tight that her knuckles were white.

She felt all at once helpless, wanton and insatiable. And mortified at how he was turning her into someone she didn't even recognise. He bent his head, his chest close to hers, brushing against sensitive breasts, and kissed her deeply, erotically, as his hand and fingers caressed her intimately.

But just as she could feel the elusive peak she'd rarely reached with anyone else come like a vision through the haze of desire Tiarnan broke the kiss and removed his hand.

'Now *you* touch…'

He brought her hand down to cover his shaft. Kate's eyes grew big and round, glued to his as she allowed herself to feel and explore as he had done. It was his turn to shift restlessly, colour slashing his cheeks as she moved her hand, tightened her grip, feeling the satin smooth skin slip up and down over the steel-hard core. She could feel their heartbeats thudding slowly and heavily.

When he looked down at her with tense jaw and fever-bright eyes she took her hand away, and shifted herself so that she lay under him. She spread her legs, opening herself up to his welcome heat and heaviness.

'Now… I want you…' She reached up and pressed a hot kiss to his mouth, her tongue slipping inside with seductive innocence for a moment before she said, '…inside me.'

Tiarnan had lost all sense of time and place. At the last second before desire sucked him under completely he reached for protection and smoothed it on with all the finesse of a novice. This scene was so reminiscent of a dream he hadn't even acknowledged. He could feel Kate move beneath him. Her hair was spread in a golden halo around her head, and her eyes, like two huge pools of blue, looked up at him. Her legs parted a fraction more, and because it was the most necessary thing in the world he slid his erection, which felt engorged to the point of pain, into her silken heat, and died a small death of pleasure at the exquisite sensation.

He felt her move her hips, drawing him deeper. Exerting extreme control, he slowly started to thrust in and out. His eyes were locked on hers. Twin flags of colour stained her cheeks, her lips were plump and red…her teeth bit them as she fought to keep her moans back. It was all Tiarnan could do not to explode there and then. Seeing her like this was a fulfilment of something he'd so long suppressed.

Their skin was slick with sweat, their heartbeats no longer slow and heavy but frantic. The tempo increased. Tiarnan could feel Kate's legs wrap around him, urging him even deeper, harder. The pinnacle came in a blaze of white light and pleasure so intense they both stopped breathing for a long moment, hung suspended in time. And then came the fall, tumbling down and down all the way, their bodies releasing and pulsing for an age as Kate accepted Tiarnan's weight onto her, wrapped legs and arms around him even tighter, binding him to her.

Tiarnan woke at some point and felt an empty space beside him. Immediately a low hum of panic gripped him that he did not like. He lifted his head. Dawn was touching the sky outside and Kate stood on the balcony, leaning on the railing looking out to sea, dressed in nothing but his white shirt. The outline of her body was silhouetted enticingly under the material. Relief surged through him—which he also did not like.

Tiarnan got out of bed. As if linked to him by an invisible thread, Kate stood and turned around, pulled the shirt together over her chest haphazardly with one hand. Her hair was tumbled around her shoulders. Tiarnan prowled towards her. She was the only thing filling his mind, his vision in that moment. Seeing her dressed in nothing but his white shirt should have been a cliché. But it wasn't. Plenty of women had dressed like this for him, as if in an effort to do the contrived sexy thing, and all it had incited within him was mild irritation. Right now, though, irritation was the last thing he was feeling.

What he was feeling was a surge of primal possessiveness rushing through him.

Kate stood straighter as he came closer, put her hands out behind her on the railing. The shirt fell open, revealing tantalising glimpses of the twin globes of her breasts and then, down further, the ever so soft swell of her belly and the apex of her thighs, where golden curls hid paradise. Tiarnan reached her and pulled her into him, his arms around her naked back under the shirt. Even though they'd barely slept all night, he was ready to take her again.

He felt her lift one leg to hook it around his hip…knew instantly that she was ready again too. It was the most powerful aphrodisiac. They didn't even make it back to the bed. Tiarnan slid into her there and then. And with the dawn breaking somewhere in the east, tingeing the sky with pink, he and Kate entered another realm of the senses.

CHAPTER SEVEN

KATE had never felt so lethargic in her life—as if every limb was weighted down with a delicious warm stone. She couldn't even open her eyes. Vague flashes of memory came back: her dress pooling at her feet; kissing Tiarnan until she had to break away to suck in air; his body moving into hers, taking her breath away all over again, slippery with sweat; Tiarnan drawing her on top of him and watching her face as she took him in, then flipping her onto her back, driving in and out with such exquisite and ruthless precision that she'd been begging for release, near to tears.

Kate tried without success to shut the images out. Heat was already flaring through her just thinking about what they'd shared. She remembered getting up at some point and standing on the balcony, as if to try and make sense of it all, and then she'd heard him get up and he'd joined her there. Within seconds of touching they'd been burning up all over again. She squeezed her eyes shut tight, as if that might block out the wanton image. She could vaguely remember him lifting her up into his arms…after that a bath…and then oblivion. An oblivion touched with the peace that came from a long-held desire finally fulfilled. Her somewhat pathetic concern that sleeping with Tiarnan might prove to be disappointing had been blown into the stratosphere.

Just then a sound came from somewhere near—a door opened, small feet ran in.

'Katie, Katie—come on, get up, sleepyhead!'

Immediately she was alert. She was in her own bed, dressed in the T-shirt and boxer shorts she'd laid out on her pillow the previous evening. Rosie and her friend Zoe were standing looking at her, holding back the muslin curtain that was around the bed. Kate sat up and pushed down the clamour of questions. Tiarnan must have put her to bed here and dressed her after the bath. Had she really been so exhausted that she hadn't even been aware?

Heat suffused her face, and she tried to hide it by throwing back the covers and climbing out of bed. She smiled at the girls, hoping they wouldn't notice her discomfiture.

'What time is it?'

Rosie rolled her eyes at her friend, who giggled shyly. They were both dressed in shorts and vest tops, feet bare. Kate could see a trickle of sand had followed them into the room.

'It's *really* late, Katie. Nearly midday! Come on—we're going to the beach. Tiarnan wouldn't let us wake you for ages. He said you were jet-lagged…'

The two girls ran out of the room again, shouting that they'd see her downstairs in ten minutes. Kate sagged back onto the bed and pushed her hand through her hair. The thought of seeing Tiarnan after last night made her tummy flip. Was it even real? Or had she dreamt it? But her body was the evidence. She was glad he'd had the foresight to put her into her own bed. She'd obviously been barely capable of moving. The fact that *he'd* managed to retain a cool measure of control and was clearly marking the boundaries between them made her feel vulnerable.

As she stood under the spray of her shower a few minutes later, Kate's movements suddenly halted. She remembered that moment on the balcony; they hadn't used protection. Tiarnan had been so careful to protect them up to that point, and she hadn't missed the horrorstruck look on his face when he'd realised. The pain of seeing how violently he'd castigated himself had led her to reassure him quickly that it would be fine—she was at a safe stage in her cycle. And she *was*. But still, it shocked her how easily they'd been careless, and he'd vowed vociferously to make sure it didn't happen again. She had no desire either, to risk bringing a child into a very temporary moment of madness. And the thought of what such a scenario would mean to Tiarnan made her go cold.

'Morning. Or should I say *afternoon?*'

Kate took a deep breath to steady herself against the bone-tingling effect of the deep, sexy drawling voice before she looked up from tying her flat sandals, sitting on the bottom stair. But she couldn't stop her heart beating wildly. Mortification twisted her insides anew as the enormity of what had happened hit her. She'd been so easy. She'd shown him with bells on how she'd hungered for him for years... She should try to hide that vulnerability from him. She had to somehow make him think he was just another in a long line of lovers. She had to protect herself from him.

Gathering all her training, that armour she'd perfected over the years, she looked up and steeled herself not to react to seeing him—but it was hard. He stood leaning nonchalantly against a doorjamb, dressed in a white T-shirt that strained across the biceps of his arms and faded loose khaki shorts. Battered sneakers on his feet.

She finished fiddling with her sandals and stood, self-conscious even though she was dressed similarly, in long shorts and a vest top. Perfectly respectable. She saw that they were alone and came close to him. Trying not to falter, she tipped her face up to his and said, *sotto voce,* 'Thanks for last night, I really enjoyed it.'

She saw his smile fade ever so slightly. A hard gleam came into his eyes and she wanted to gag. Those words were so meaningless, when she really wanted to say that the previous night had been the most exquisite experience of her existence. That she'd already stored away every single moment in her memory. But she had to remember who she was dealing with—*had to.* Or he'd destroy her.

He took her hand before she knew what he was doing and raised it to his mouth, pressing a kiss to the underside of her wrist, causing heat to flood her belly and her breath to catch.

'I enjoyed it too. I'm already looking forward to tonight.'

Kate's eyes were snared by his. She was terrified that he would see that she was putting on a desperate act. She smiled and it felt brittle. She could do this if she had to.

'Me too.'

Just then sounds came from outside, and they moved apart just as Rosie burst into the hall. 'Come *on,* you guys. We'll be late!'

Tiarnan bent down to pick up a big basket that seemed to be bursting at the seams.

'Where are we going?' Kate asked as Rosie hopped around, impatient to go.

Mama Lucille came into the hall then, wiping her hands on an apron, and dragged Rosie close for a big hug and kiss.

Tiarnan looked back at Kate as he dodged around Rosie and Mama Lucille. 'We're going to the beach with a picnic. Zoe's family will be there too.'

Kate followed them out to the Jeep, which was laden down with things. This was obviously a bit of a ritual for them, and she realised belatedly that it was Sunday. It must be a traditional family day out for the locals.

Mama Lucille surprised Kate by giving her a big expansive hug too, and then they set off, the two giggling girls in the back reminding Kate bittersweetly of herself and Sorcha when they'd been young.

Disconcertingly, as if able to read her mind, Tiarnan said while gesturing to the back, 'Remind you of anyone?'

Kate smiled. 'I was just thinking about that.'

'Thinking about what?' Rosie piped up from the back, proving that her ears were very keen.

Kate and Tiarnan shared a complicit smile, and Kate couldn't stop her heart feeling as if it was about to burst. But she turned around and started to tell the two girls stories about her and Sorcha when they'd been young.

That evening, when they were in a very bedraggled and sandy Jeep returning home as night fell, Kate knew she hadn't enjoyed a day so much in ages. She felt deliciously sunburned, her skin tingling in the aftermath of a day spent outdoors. They'd gone to a beach that was obviously a local secret as it had been empty but for them and Zoe's extended family, all Mama Lucille's children and grandchildren, nieces and nephews. She could see what Tiarnan meant. Rosie was as much a part of that family as their own kids—she could even see that there was a fragile and gradual thawing in Rosie and Tiarnan's relationship. She hoped that the holiday would prove to give Tiarnan the breakthrough he sought with Rosie.

Earlier in the day Kate had given up trying to keep track of everyone she'd been introduced to, and Zoe's mother Anne-Marie had taken her under her wing. She was a beautiful woman in her early thirties, who had three children including Zoe, the eldest.

They'd been watching an impromptu football game, with everyone chaotically involved, toddlers and all in the mix, when Kate had impulsively confided, 'I envy you.'

Anne-Marie had looked shocked. 'Are you mad? You'd give up a glamorous lifestyle travelling around the world to live with *this* kind of mayhem?'

But the other woman's sparkling eyes had told another story. Kate had felt her heart clench. She'd hidden the true extent of her desire to get out of modelling and settle down even from Sorcha. Somehow here, with this woman who was little more than a stranger, it had been easy to smile wryly and say with feeling, 'In a heartbeat.'

Anne-Marie had leant close then, and said conspiratorially, 'He's a good man.'

Kate had blushed immediately and realised to her horror that her eyes had been greedily following Tiarnan as he'd run bare-chested down the beach with the ball, a gaggle of children running after him, adults laughing. It was a world away from the austere image he projected to the world of finance and high-powered achieving. In truth, she was slightly shocked to see this side of him—and shocked at the feeling it caused deep inside her. A deep yearning for family, *love,* for belonging. With him. When she should be getting over him...

Kate tried to be cool. 'Oh, I've known Tiarnan for years. His sister Sorcha's my best friend. And, yes, he *is* a good man.'

Anne-Marie hadn't looked fooled for a second. She'd just said, 'He's never brought anyone else here, you know...and no man is an island.'

Kate's face had been burning by then, but thankfully Anne-Marie had deftly defused the situation and stood, reaching down to haul Kate up too.

'Come on—let's show the men a thing or two.'

Kate's attention returned to the present. It was just the three of them in the Jeep—Rosie sleepy in the back, Tiarnan driving. She snuck a look at his proud profile as he drove. Anne-Marie was wrong, Tiarnan most certainly *was* an island, and there was no room on it for her except as a temporary bed companion. The sooner she could come to terms with that, the better.

After dinner Kate offered to go and see if Rosie was tucked into bed. Tiarnan caught her hand to pull her back and said with a seductive drawl, 'I didn't bring you here to act as a nanny to Rosie.'

Kate looked down at him and her heart twisted. They'd all showered and changed as soon as they'd got back, and Tiarnan looked heart-stoppingly handsome with damp hair, in a clean shirt and worn jeans. His blue eyes were even more intense against the slight tan he'd already acquired in one day.

She pulled her hand free. 'Don't worry. I know exactly why I'm here, Tiarnan. We both do.'

Something in her voice or expression caught him and caused an ache in the region of his chest, but he had no idea why. He watched her walk out, her sexy cut-off shorts effortlessly showcasing her long lissom legs. She wore a peasant-style top and her hair was loose down her back, slightly darker as it was still a little damp. Her scent hovered on the air and he had to fight not to close his eyes and savour it.

Slightly irritated with himself for this moonstruck streak he wasn't used to, he turned back to the table and drank down the rest of his wine. Along with the heat of desire that washed through him in waves was a much more ambiguous feeling.

He'd expected Kate to suffer somewhat through the day, having to spend it *en famille*. But she had smiled and gelled with everyone immediately. She'd seemed to genuinely enjoy herself—and the rambunctious nature of Mama Lucille's family. He'd seen her talking to Anne-Marie, laughing easily, as if they'd known each other for years.

She'd been quite happy to muck in and help out with the food and children too, assuming a natural gentle authority which had taken him by surprise. When they'd been playing football he'd seen her go to pick up one of the smaller children who'd been accidentally knocked over without a moment's hesitation, and even though she didn't even know him, she'd hugged him close and kissed him better, so that by the time the father had rushed over the child had been clinging to Kate and playing happily with her blonde hair.

As if to distract his line of thinking from going down a dangerous path he had no desire to explore, he recalled her body in its petrol blue bikini. The other men had had the nous not to stop and stare, but he'd been aware of their interest when she'd first stripped off to go into the water with Rosie and Zoe and the others. Immediately he'd irrationally regretted bringing her with them, and not locking her up in the house or back in his home in Madrid. And yet her bikini had been no more or less revealing than Anne-Marie's, or any of the other women's…

Despite that, he could recall only too easily his intense relief when she'd put on her shorts and top again to come and play football. He'd been afraid that he wouldn't have the restraint not to insist that she cover up. He rationalised it: having slept with her only the night before, after such a long build-up, his desire still felt raw. He was just realising how hard it was to share her with everyone else so soon.

The lingering traces of that desire were making him hard again. He'd spent the day in a perpetual state of near arousal, taking frequent swims to disguise it. And he couldn't block out or forget that he'd been so hot for her last night, that for the first time in his life *ever,* he'd forgotten about protection. He hadn't even been careless with Stella Rios. She'd assured him she'd been on the pill, and even knowing that he'd insisted on using protection. But one time it had broken, and *that* had been her chance for convincing him he might be Rosie's father—especially after she'd revealed that she'd lied about taking the pill…

Tiarnan assured himself now that Kate was *not* Stella Rios. He would not be caught again. He forced himself to relax, and waited to hear her footfall coming back downstairs. He couldn't help thinking of that indecipherable expression that had flashed in her eyes just now, and her behaviour today. Most of the women he'd sought out for affairs in the past would have been clinging to him like a limpet, complaining vociferously about the rustic nature of the entertainment. Quite apart from the fact that he had to concede that he wouldn't have brought them here in the first place.

A feeling of vulnerability swamped him. Was he allowing Kate to play him? In a way that no other woman had done before? Not even Stella Rios?

Enough! Tiarnan chastised himself for his introspection. They were effectively alone again, and he could spend the night punishing her for making him feel so uncharacteristically vulnerable. He heard her coming back down the stairs and stood jerkily, his usual grace deserting him as he turned and went to meet her halfway…

Two days later Kate sat in the shade in the garden, knitting. No sound warned her she wasn't alone, so when she heard a softly drawled, 'I come in peace; I'm not armed,' she nearly jumped out of her skin. She looked up to see Tiarnan standing there, his hands up in a comic gesture of surrender, looking expressively at her knitting.

He'd taken her by surprise in more ways than one because, predictably, he'd been occupying her thoughts. In particular, vivid images of last night in his bed, and the moments of ecstasy she'd experienced in his arms. She felt as though he'd be able to see that straight away and looked down again, feeling cross, putting the knitting away.

'Don't worry—I'll restrain myself.' She knew she must sound cool. But it was the only way she could stem this constant state of heat she seemed to be in. Escaping for quiet moments was keeping her semi-sane. And she was also consciously trying to give Tiarnan time alone with Rosie.

He came and sat down in the wicker lounger chair beside her, long bare legs stretched out, making her eyes drop betrayingly to linger on their perfectly formed muscles. She couldn't help but remember how it felt to have those strong hair-roughened thighs between her own, and a quiver of heat made her clench her legs together. He was wearing his usual Martinique uniform of casual shorts and T-shirt, looking as relaxed as any local. Whereas she felt as tightly wound as a spring.

'I thought Rosie was with you?' Kate said, as much to know as in an effort to fill the silence.

Tiarnan had put his head back and closed his eyes. The dappled sunlight coming through the leaves of the tree above them caught his skin in patches. He was looking more tanned by the day, and with it more devilishly handsome.

He opened his eyes and looked at her, shaking his head, putting his arms behind it to cushion it. Supremely relaxed. 'She went into town to go shopping with Papa Joe.'

'Zoe...?'

He shook his head again. 'They're still in school here, so Rosie has to do without her partner in crime during the day.'

'Oh...' Kate felt unaccountably awkward. She still hadn't got used to dealing with Tiarnan during the day, after nights which were filled with such passion. She was slightly overwhelmed. And, if she was honest, she was afraid of spending too much time with him, getting closer, seeing even more aspects of his fascinating character.

He leant forward and reached out a hand. Kate looked at it suspiciously.

'Come for a drive with me. I want to show you something.'

Tiarnan could see the reluctance on Kate's face and irritation spiked through him. She'd been keeping her distance the past couple of days and he didn't like it. During the night she was undeniably his—more passionate than anything he'd ever experienced. But apart from that... It was as if there were two different Kates. She gave off an air of insouciance he knew and expected. And yet she wasn't constantly seeking his attention or moaning about the lack of civilisation. She was here knitting quietly in the garden. As much as he hated this compulsion to get to know her better, he couldn't ignore it. He hungered for her, and he realised now that he hungered just to spend time with her—a novel desire, and one that didn't sit entirely well with him.

'What about Rosie? Won't she be home soon?'

Tiarnan shook his head. 'Papa Joe is taking her over to the other side of the island afterwards to a market. They'll eat there and won't be back till late. Rosie's been to the place I want to take you a hundred times already. Come on, Kate. Or are you going to tell me that knitting is more exciting than taking a mystery tour with me?'

He quirked a brow. Kate's insides liquefied. How could she resist this man? She made a show of seriously contemplating for a moment whether she'd prefer to sit and knit the day away, and squealed when Tiarnan moved like lightning and put her over his shoulder, lifting her as if she weighed no more than a bag of sugar. She was wearing a relatively short sundress, and his warm hand was disturbingly close to the tops of her bare thighs and her bottom.

'Tiarnan Quinn—put me down this instant! What if someone sees us? Mama Lucille…'

She felt Tiarnan swat her bottom playfully and say loudly, 'Mama Lucille has seen plenty in her lifetime—haven't you, Mama? I'm taking Kate out for the afternoon. Don't worry about dinner for us.'

Kate's face burned and her fists clenched when she heard the familiar full-bodied chuckle and saw Mama Lucille's feet in their flip-flops pass them by.

She spied something out of the corner of her eye, put out a hand. 'Wait! My camera.'

Tiarnan obediently halted and retraced his steps, picking up Kate's camera which lay on a hall table. Then they were out through the front door and down to the Jeep, where he deposited Kate in the passenger seat with surprising gentleness. He handed her her camera before coming around and getting into the driver's seat.

They were pulling away from the villa within seconds, and Kate couldn't help a bubble of excitement rising within her. Tiarnan looked at her and smiled, and it was so carefree that she couldn't help but smile back. Her armour and her resistance were melting in a pool at her feet and there was nothing she could do to stop it.

She sat back in the seat and said mock-sulkily, 'I was quite happy knitting quietly, you know. This is meant to be a holiday.'

For a second Tiarnan had to reconcile that image of such domesticity with the woman he'd expected Kate to be. It was an anomaly he ruthlessly diverted his attention away from.

'I'm sure…' he said then, slanting her a mischievous look. 'I could see how fast you were knitting—feverishly, one could say, almost as if your mind was filled not with thoughts of casting on and single back cross stitches, but rather something more…elemental…'

Kate burned—because he was absolutely right. Though she didn't know what was more shocking—that or the fact that he knew any knitting terminology.

She turned to face him in her seat. The sea was an amazing backdrop behind him. 'Don't tell me you've had to put up with *other* women being more enthralled with knitting than you?' She opened her eyes wide, acting innocent.

He shook his head. 'You're on your own there, Kate Lancaster. No, it was my mother. You don't remember all those hideous Christmas jumpers we got every year, until Sorcha was discovered giving hers away to a homeless person?'

Kate laughed out loud. 'How could I have forgotten? Your poor mother was so insulted—and if I remember it had a lovely holly and mistletoe pattern, which I must say in her defence would not have been easy to do…'

Tiarnan smiled ruefully. 'I'm sure. I was just relieved that

Sorcha had unwittingly saved us from a lifetime of lurid Christmas jumpers.'

Kate was tempted to return with a quip that *she* could fill that gaping hole in his life, but stopped abruptly when she realised how it might sound. As if she expected to be a part of his life after this holiday was over.

He looked at her curiously, and she could feel that she'd gone slightly pale. 'What is it?'

She shook her head and smiled brightly. 'Nothing. Nothing at all. So—where exactly are you taking me?'

'Ah, that's for me to know and you to see.' He glanced at the camera nestled on her lap, her hands over it protectively. 'That looks pretty professional. I saw you taking pictures in the garden earlier…'

Kate lifted up the camera and looked at it. She felt self-conscious.

'The photographers at work told me which one I should buy if I was seriously interested in learning.'

'And are you? Seriously interested?'

Kate shrugged one slim shoulder. 'I've done some photography courses. Travelling around the world so much I get to see so many things, and I wanted to start documenting them… It's a hobby, I guess you could say.'

Tiarnan cast her a look. She was avoiding his eye, studying the camera. He guessed intuitively that she must be very good. She seemed to have the kind of personality that would be utterly respectful of anything or anyone she wanted to photograph.

They drove on in silence for a bit, and eventually Kate read out the name of the town they'd come into, where Tiarnan started slowing down.

'Saint-Pierre…'

Tiarnan stopped the Jeep and parked up, and they got out. He immediately came and took Kate's hand. She didn't pull away, and a surge of something went through him.

Her hand felt so good in Tiarnan's. She loved the way he was so tactile. With other men when they'd tried to maintain contact she'd always felt uncomfortable. She looked around curiously at the streets. It was a pretty enough town, but…

'What are you thinking?' Tiarnan looked at her intently.

Kate stood still. 'I don't know,' she answered after a long moment. 'It's weird. It's almost as if the buildings don't fit the town, or something…' A shiver went down her spine. 'And there's something eerie about it too…'

Tiarnan pointed at a mountain in the distance. 'See that?'

Kate nodded.

'That's Mount Pelée. In 1902 it erupted, and within minutes this town and its thirty thousand or so inhabitants were decimated. The only survivor was a man who was locked in a prison cell below ground.'

'Those poor people,' Kate breathed, and then looked at Tiarnan. 'It's almost inconceivable to imagine.'

He nodded, and noticed that she was shading her eyes from the sun with her hand. He felt a dart of guilt. He'd rushed her out of the house so fast she hadn't had time to pick anything up. He spied a shop across the road and led her there.

Two minutes later they emerged, and Tiarnan handed Kate a pair of lurid pink sunglasses, complete with pineapples on each corner, and a big floppy straw hat with a ring of fake flowers around the base.

She sighed and took them from him. 'Just what I've always wanted. To look like a clown.'

But she took them and put them on, and smiled up at him so beautifully that he couldn't resist taking her face in his hands and pressing a kiss to her lips. Only when someone wolf-whistled nearby did he let her go, slightly in shock at how turned-on he was already—and how easy it had been to kiss her like that when he normally had an absolute abhorrence for public displays of affection. He took her by the hand and led her away.

Kate's heart was beating quickly in her chest as she held onto the ridiculous hat and followed Tiarnan. That kiss had been so impromptu and so devastating. He'd taken her completely by surprise, buying the hat and glasses too. Right then she wouldn't have wanted their designer equivalent in a million years.

They walked for a bit, then came to the local museum where Tiarnan showed her the exhibits. Outside in the car park they looked down over the town. It was obvious where the lines of destruction still lay, despite the new buildings and life going on.

It gave Kate a sense of how fragile life was—how quickly everything could be ripped away. She felt as though she were falling off a high precipice. Unconsciously she gripped Tiarnan's hand tighter and he turned to look at her,

'OK?'

Kate tried to drive down the overwhelming sense of making every moment count with this man, because she knew now it would be all that she had, and she turned and looked up, pasting on a bland smile. 'You certainly know how to show a girl a good uplifting time.'

He smiled dangerously and drew her into him tightly. Kate held in a gasp at the potent feel of his rock-solid body against hers. The other tourists milling around them were forgotten.

'We'll discuss good uplifting times when we get home.'

'Promises, promises,' Kate said somewhat shakily, and Tiarnan let her go again, but kept a hold of her hand.

Later, eating ice creams he'd bought them outside a shop, they walked back to the Jeep. They stopped near the harbour wall for a moment, to finish eating, and something in Tiarnan's stance caught Kate's eye. He was looking out to sea, his profile so beautiful that she couldn't resist lifting her camera and taking a quick snap. He turned when he heard the shutter click and Kate smiled. 'For posterity,' she said. And felt inordinately guilty—because she knew it would be for *her.*

* * *

They took the road back the way they'd come, returning south, and Kate felt acutely aware of *everything*. Tiarnan turned left off the main road at one point and all of a sudden they seemed to be in the middle of a lush rainforest. Kate put out her hand as they drove, to try and touch the branches by the side of the road.

'This is so beautiful. I'd never have imagined this kind of scenery here.'

'Wait till you see what's up here…'

Kate felt a bubble of pure joy rise upwards within her as she watched Tiarnan drive against this backdrop. She was truly content, for the first time in a long time, and she wouldn't allow thoughts of the end of this holiday, and inevitably this affair, to cloud the moment.

They pulled up outside an impressive church and Tiarnan said, 'Remind you of anything?'

Kate looked up and gasped. 'It's the Sacré-Coeur!'

'A replica,' Tiarnan confirmed, and got out. 'Come on—there are some amazing views over Forte-de-France below…'

A short while later, as they drove back towards the coast, Kate's head was bursting with images—and a lingering sense of peace from the church that had been built as a smaller replica of the iconic Parisian landmark.

She could recognise the route now. They weren't too far from home. But Tiarnan surprised her by taking a winding road down towards the sea, and pulling in outside a beautiful old colonial-style house, half buried in thick bougainvillaea and hibiscus flowers. Martinique was certainly living up to its name as 'the isle of flowers'.

It turned out that the house was actually a converted restaurant, and when they walked in Kate wasn't surprised to see Tiarnan greeted like an old friend. As was the custom she was getting used to, she was greeted effusively, and they were led to a stunning white-clothed table in a wrought-iron balconied alcove that looked directly out to the sea and the setting sun.

Kate leant forward, a small frown creasing her forehead. 'Aren't we dressed a little...well, casually for somewhere like this?'

Tiarnan looked around then, and noticed a few men sitting with partners and looking at Kate with brazen appreciation. Jealousy rose swiftly. He turned back to Kate. She looked all at once so demure and so incredibly sexy that he had to bite back a completely irrational urge to tell her to cover up. And how could she, when he'd all but manhandled her out of the house earlier? Her hesitation before, in the garden, came back to him, made something inside him twist.

'You're fine,' he said gruffly.

She'd been a good sport today—happily wearing the ridiculous hat and glasses, taking snaps, eating ice cream at the side of the road. Once again he'd been hard pushed to think of any of his previous mistresses in those surroundings, happy to sightsee.

He gestured to her shoulders. 'You got a bit burnt today.'

Kate grimaced. 'Oh it's nothing.'

She looked at him with something almost like shyness in her expression, but Tiarnan had to reject that thought. It couldn't be. He wanted to keep seeing her as a cool, sophisticated woman of the world.

'It feels good, in all honesty. I usually have to be so careful of my skin. And my weight.' She rolled her eyes then, and imitated her agent's broad New York drawl.

'"Kate, honey, you're known for your porcelain skin. So don't gimme a heart attack and come back looking like me. I can take the sun. You can't. And whatever you do watch your weight. I'm always telling you, you don't have it as easy as the other girls, you're not naturally skinny. It's a shame, but we have our crosses to bear and yours is pasta..."'

She stopped and blushed when Tiarnan laughed out loud.

She knew he knew Maud well. She was Sorcha's agent too. Kate felt foolish all of a sudden. 'I'm sorry…Sorcha calls them my Maud monologues.'

He caught her hand, smiling widely. 'You mimic her brilliantly. I could have sworn she was here.'

Kate's hand tingled in his, and he only let go when a pristinely dressed waiter arrived and addressed Tiarnan in French while handing them menus.

Tiarnan replied fluently, and Kate made a face when the waiter left. 'No throwing of food allowed here, I'd guess?'

Tiarnan looked mock stern. 'Certainly not, young lady.'

Kate had to catch herself. She'd never have guessed she'd feel so at ease with Tiarnan, so comfortable. This day was in danger of becoming incredibly special, and she drove that thought down, to some deep and dark place. She took up the menu and made a great show of studying the indecipherable French.

After a long moment she heard an amused, 'Would you like me to translate?'

Drat the man. She had the grace to smile self-deprecatingly and put the menu down. 'Would you please?' she said. 'I don't particularly want frog's legs or snails.'

'So, the photography…tell me about it. Did you do a degree?'

Kate watched as Tiarnan speared a morsel of fish and ate it, and felt the familiar shame grip her. She nervously tucked her hair behind her ear.

'No…I couldn't do a degree because I never completed school…' She shrugged slightly and avoided his eye. 'I was already working in London and then New York…earning money…and then it was too late.'

She heard him put down his knife and fork. Compelled against her will, she met his eye.

'Kate, it's nothing to be ashamed of. I didn't go to college myself.'

She smiled tightly. 'Maybe, but in a world like this men are judged far less harshly than women if they've proved themselves in the interim—qualifications notwithstanding.'

He inclined his head and took a sip of wine. 'You're right. Unfortunately. But if it means that much to you why didn't you complete when you had a chance?'

'Like Sorcha, you mean?' Kate and Sorcha had both started modelling at the same time, but Sorcha had made the effort to get her Irish leaving certificate qualification, and had then had done a degree in psychology in New York.

Tiarnan nodded.

Kate shrugged again. How could she admit her even more secret shame, of constant years of her mother telling her that her looks were all that mattered and why should she worry about working? She took a fortifying sip of wine and looked at Tiarnan.

'You remember my mother?'

He nodded. He remembered a brash woman who had grated on his nerves—a woman who cared more for her appearance and her social standing than anything else. He also remembered that she would flirt outrageously with *him* at any given opportunity. He knew that on some level when Kate had approached him that night ten years ago he'd assumed she was of the same ilk as her mother—forward. And yet, despite her cool assurance after he'd put a stop to their lovemaking, he'd glimpsed a vulnerability that was at odds with her seemingly confident actions. He'd dismissed it that night and in the intervening years—especially as he witnessed her blooming into the stunning beauty she now was—and her cool exterior confirmed for him that she'd become accustomed to a certain kind of attention. But, despite all that, right now that vulnerability seemed to be back, and it jarred with his assessment of her character.

He tried to bring his focus back to the conversation, feeling as if he were treading on dangerous ground.

'How *is* your mother?'

Kate was glad to be stalled for a moment. She smiled tightly and looked at him. 'Oh, I'm sure she's fine. She's on a cruise with rich husband number four and blissfully happy, no doubt.'

Tiarnan frowned. 'You don't see her, then?'

Kate shook her head. 'Very infrequently. If she's shopping in New York for a few days or going to the shows... But in general she doesn't like to be reminded of her mortality, and I'm afraid that's what I do.'

Tiarnan winced inwardly. That didn't surprise him.

'My mother is a great believer in a woman surviving on her looks. After Sorcha and I were discovered by the model scout that day in Dublin she saw no real need for me to stay at school. I was never the most academic anyway, so in later years the thought of completing studies as an older student and failing was somewhat daunting.'

Tiarnan reached across and tipped up her chin from where she was studying the table. She felt excruciatingly exposed. She'd never admitted this to anyone. And now to *him* of all people? But with his hand on her chin she was forced to meet his gaze.

'Kate, you are most certainly not stupid, if that's what you're afraid of. You have an innate intelligence that anyone would recognise a mile away. And lack of qualifications hasn't stopped some of the world's most successful people from succeeding. I bet half the world-famous photographers you work with are self-taught.'

Kate gulped and reddened. Tiarnan had sounded almost angry.

As if he realised this, he took his hand away and said, 'Sorry...I just wouldn't want you to put yourself down like that.' He shook his head. 'Parents can be so cruel, and do so much damage.'

Kate felt a well of emotion rise up and had to blink away the prickling of tears. She put her hand over his and said huskily, 'Thank you for that. I know intellectually everything you say is right—and you're right about parents…' She smiled shakily, 'Rosie is lucky to have you for a father.'

He grimaced. 'You wouldn't think so at the moment. She goes out of her way to avoid me.'

Kate squeezed his hand. 'She'll come round. You'll see.'

Tiarnan just looked into the blue depths of Kate's eyes and felt unaccountably as if he were drowning.

That night when they returned to the villa Kate felt as though something had changed between her and Tiarnan. It felt dangerous. And yet heady.

She'd just come out of her bathroom, having washed her face, when Tiarnan appeared at her bedroom door. Her breath stalled in her throat and she felt her nipples respond with wanton eagerness. Aghast at her reaction, she reached for a wrap and pulled it on over her singlet and boxers, knowing it was slightly ridiculous to feel so self-conscious.

'Rosie wants to say goodnight to you.'

'Of course.'

Kate went to go out through the door, but Tiarnan blocked her way. His hands cupped her face and tipped it up, threading through her hair. He was huge, his shoulders blocking out the light, his face cast in shadow, and he looked so darkly handsome that Kate couldn't catch her breath again. Every part of her body reacted to his proximity.

'I enjoyed today, Kate—and this evening.'

'Me too,' she said huskily. The image of the sun setting over the sea beside them as they sipped wine and ate delicious food would be forever engraved on her memory.

He pressed the most fleeting and yet earth-shattering of kisses onto her mouth and said simply, 'I'll be waiting for you.'

Then he stood back and let her go.

Kate walked to Rosie's room on very wobbly legs, and when she got there she told Rosie all about where they'd gone. Rosie chattered about her day with Papa Joe, suitably satisfied that she'd missed Saint-Pierre, telling Kate that she'd been there, 'Like, *tons* of times.'

When Kate bent forward to kiss her goodnight, she said, 'Thank you, Rosie, for letting me share your holiday with you and your dad. This is such a special place.'

She was almost at the door when she heard a soft, 'Katie, did your daddy love you?'

Kate stopped dead and turned slowly. She could see Rosie's pale little face in the soft glow of the one lamp. She came back over and sat on the bed. 'What makes you ask that?'

The little girl shrugged. 'My dad—' She stopped and then started again. 'Tiarnan doesn't love me. I'm adopted…he's not even my real dad.'

Kate knew she had to tread carefully. 'Well, sweetie, my dad died a long time ago. I think he loved me—I mean, I'm sure he loved me…even if he didn't really show it.'

Rosie looked at Kate suspiciously. 'What do you mean?'

'Well, he was always very busy. He used to come home late at night, after I'd gone to bed.' She wrinkled her nose. 'And he was worried about work a lot, and money…things like that.'

Rosie looked contemplative for a moment. 'Tiarnan's busy a lot too…but he always tucks me in at night and takes me to school, and if he's away he calls me all the time.' Kate saw her bottom lip quivering. 'But it still doesn't mean he loves me. My mother doesn't love me either…not like Zoe's mum loves her.' A sob broke free and Rosie started crying in earnest, her little shoulders shaking.

Kate gathered Rosie up into her arms and let her cry it out, guessing she'd needed to do this for a long time. She rocked her back and forth, rubbing her back, her heart breaking for the child's pain and confusion.

When the crying had become big hiccupping sighs, Kate pulled back and smoothed Rosie's hair from her flushed face.

She got a tissue from the box nearby and wiped away her tears, made her blow her nose. 'Sweetheart, don't think that. Your dad loves you *so* much.'

'How do you know?' Rosie asked chokily.

Kate tucked some hair behind her ear. 'I know because he always talks about you, and he worries about you and tells everyone about you.' Kate took a bit of poetic licence and mentally crossed her fingers. 'And he's so proud of how well you're settling into your new school. How brave you are to make the change.'

Rosie's face twisted. 'He *made* me change schools and I've no friends now.'

Kate feigned shock. 'What? A stunningly beautiful and funny girl like you? Not possible.' She laid Rosie back against her pillow and then came down close, resting on an arm. 'Do you know? I had to change schools too, when I was just a bit older than you.'

'You did?' Rosie visibly perked up.

Kate nodded. 'And not only that I had to change countries as well. I was living in England, and after my father died my mum moved back to Ireland—right next door to where Auntie Sorcha lived. That's how she and I became best friends. And if I'd never moved country or changed schools I wouldn't have met her…and we wouldn't know each other and I certainly wouldn't know *you,* or be here now.'

'Wow…' Rosie breathed.

'It is hard when things change, but sometimes they change for the better. I bet you're going to have such good friends at the new school. You just have to give it a chance.'

Rosie was plucking at the sheet, looking down. 'Katie, my mummy doesn't want me to go and see her.'

Kate had to hide her visceral reaction. 'Rosie, I'm sure your Mummy loves you…but sometimes adults can be a bit confusing. It's not always easy to understand why they do certain things.' Kate took her hand. 'And you know what? You're lucky to have Tiarnan for a dad, because he loves you twice as much as any other dad.'

'What do you mean?' Rosie looked up with a wary light in her huge brown eyes.

'Even when he found out he wasn't your real dad he made sure to adopt you, so that no one could ever take you away from him. He wanted everyone to know you were his. And I know you still love him, even though you're angry with him.'

Rosie's face got red, and she looked down again.

Kate smoothed her hair. 'It's OK, sweetheart—really it is. Nothing you could do or say will make him stop loving you. He is always going to be there for you, no matter how angry you get, or if he annoys you or if you annoy him, because that's what fathers do.' Kate caught Rosie's eye and made a funny face, tweaking her nose. 'He didn't send you to a horrible nasty cold boarding school in the middle of nowhere, did he?'

Rosie giggled and shook her head. 'No… Katie, tell me a story about you and Auntie Sorcha in school—the one about the midnight feasts.'

Kate kissed her on the forehead and hugged her tight again for a second. 'OK. Just one story and then time for sleep?'

Rosie nodded and gave a big yawn, and by the time Kate was halfway through the first sentence the little girl's eyelids were already drifting shut.

When Kate walked into Tiarnan's room a short while later he lay sleeping on the bed, bare-chested, with the covers riding indecently low on lean hips. Even in sleep he dominated the space around him. She knew she should leave, go to her own bed despite what he'd said, but she felt so full of emotion in that moment she literally couldn't.

She dropped her wrap and went and curled up next to him. Automatically his arm came out and hugged her close to him with a vice-like grip, and Kate knew right then that all her attempts were for naught. Just like that day in the church in France. She could see through her own paltry attempts to protect herself, and she had the awful suspicion that they were failing spectacularly.

A couple of mornings later they were eating breakfast on the wooden terrace. Papa Joe was discussing the garden plants with Tiarnan, Mama Lucille was bustling back and forth, and suddenly Rosie appeared, dragging her bike up the steps from the garden.

'Daddy, can you look at my chain? It's falling off again,' she said.

Kate went completely still, and wondered if Tiarnan had noticed. He and Papa Joe stopped talking. Papa Joe walked away unobtrusively, with an expressive wink at Kate. Kate was about to take the hint and leave too, but Tiarnan shot her a look which told her to stay put.

He went and had a look at the bike and Kate's heart went out to him. He was trying to be so casual. He was fiddling with the bike, but even from here Kate could see the chain looked fine. And then Rosie said, ever so casually, 'Daddy, can we go hiking in the mountains today?'

He looked at Rosie. Kate could see that Rosie was avoiding his eye, scuffing her flip-flop off the ground, as if all this was normal.

Tiarnan's voice was husky. 'I thought you didn't enjoy doing that any more?'

Kate held her breath and to her relief Rosie said, 'I know, but I was thinking I wouldn't mind—and Zoe's in school so I've no one to play with.'

Rosie looked at Kate then and came over, jumping onto her lap to give her a big hug. 'Katie can come too! We can show her all the spiders' nests and things.'

Kate shuddered expressively, and made a face that had Rosie

giggling, 'Yuck! No, thank you very much. I think I can do without seeing where spiders live. I'm not good with creepy-crawly things. You can take pictures.'

Rosie jumped off her lap. 'Silly Katie—it's fun. But it doesn't matter. Me and Daddy can go this time, and you can come next time.'

And with that Rosie hared off into the house, shouting for Mama Lucille to help her pack a picnic for them. Kate's heart had clenched at Rosie's assertion of *next time*.

Tiarnan was standing looking stunned. In shock. He came and sat down and looked at Kate. 'I can't believe it. She hasn't called me Daddy in over a year.'

Kate shrugged. 'Children don't hold grudges for ever.'

He stood again and came around to her seat, hands on either arm of it, trapping her, eyes roving over her face, assessing. 'Why do I have the overwhelming suspicion this has something to do with you? You said goodnight to her for a long time the other night, and she's been unusually quiet these past two days…'

Kate shook her head. Tiarnan's voice had an edge to it that unsettled her. He didn't sound entirely happy with this development. She felt compelled to keep Rosie's counsel, knowing in her heart of hearts that it wouldn't help to divulge how upset she had been.

'We just talked, Tiarnan. She likes hearing stories about me and Sorcha in school. You should go and enjoy the day with your daughter.' Kate forced a smile and tried to shake off the sense of unease that she'd done something wrong. 'I've got a plan to bribe Mama Lucille for some of her secret recipes.'

Despite the fact that he still wasn't smiling, she could sense his relief and sheer happiness. The joy she felt for him scared her, and the realisation hit her like a thunderbolt: she was so deeply in love and bound to Tiarnan Quinn now, and to his daughter, that all she would be able to settle for in her life would be a very pale and insubstantial imitation.

Seeing him just now with Rosie, sensing his innate protec-tiveness, had rendered any lingering prejudice she might have had about him void. He was nothing like her father. He had a capacity for deep and abiding love, for putting his daughter first. Just no place for a woman or partner in his life… Desolation gripped her like a physical pain.

He spoke then, jerking her out of her reverie, and she was shocked that he didn't seem to see the emotions written all over her face.

'Are you sure you'll be OK here on your own for the day?'

Kate nodded emphatically. Suddenly she wanted nothing more than to be away from the pull of this man's orbit. 'Absolutely.'

Tiarnan seemed to search her eyes, as if looking for some-thing, and then he finally spoke, sounding very stiff and unlike the man who seduced her so ruthlessly every night. 'Very well. We'll be back later—don't wait up; it'll probably be late.'

Kate's sense of unease deepened and lingered right up until the moment she waved Tiarnan and an ecstatic Rosie off in the Jeep.

Late that night Kate found herself waking from a fitful sleep to see the powerful outline of Tiarnan's build as he leant non-chalantly against the doorframe leading out to the balcony, sil-houetted by the moonlight. Her first reaction was not of surprise or fear, just immediate joy, and a surge of desire so powerful she shook inside. She sat up.

'Tiarnan…' Her voice was husky from sleep and from that burgeoning desire.

Tiarnan looked at Kate and fought down the intense, nearly overwhelming urge to stop the clamour of voices that mocked him, silence them by going and laying her flat, stripping her bare, taking her so hard and fast that he'd have immediate satisfaction.

Despite the fact that today had proved to be a welcome turning point in his and his daughter's relationship, it had been overshadowed by the bitter realisation that he'd underestimated Kate. He'd put Rosie in an unforgivably vulnerable position. Since the other night, and before Rosie's *volte face* that morning, he'd noticed her introspection, seen how clingy she'd become with Kate, practically overnight. Without looking into it too deeply he'd been thankful that Rosie and Kate got on so well, and had noticed that lack of a central female figure in his daughter's life for the first time in a very concrete way. But that morning everything had been brought into sharp focus, and the time spent away from Kate and her seductive presence had provided the necessary distance for him to see things as they really were.

At first he'd tried to reassure himself that he was being ridiculous. But in his mind's eye all day he'd seen flashes of tender little moments between Rosie and Kate, the easy intimacy that had grown stronger each day, until he couldn't deny the evidence any more—not what it pointed to.

He couldn't *believe* he'd ignored his own instincts and that sensation of vulnerability he'd felt numerous times. He knew with an intense conviction now that Katie had been playing him masterfully all along. From the moment she'd looked at him in France and told him silently of her desire to the feigned reluctance to come with them on holiday and her false concern for Rosie. He'd played into her hands beautifully, all rationality gone in the grip of a lust so powerful he'd been rendered momentarily weak. But not any more.

He'd given her an opportunity and she'd adroitly taken every chance to inveigle her way in. He had no one to blame but himself. She'd admitted only the other night that she had no intention of settling down any time soon, and yet she'd obviously seen a way to assure herself a strong position as his mistress by using Rosie. And it was entirely his fault. He simply could not see another reason for her behaviour. His own mother and Stella had both proved to be woefully inept mother figures—

how could someone like Kate, an international model, possibly be any different? Especially with a child who wasn't even her own? Self-recrimination burned him deep inside.

Kate watched as Tiarnan straightened from the door and walked towards her slowly. Tension and that sense of unease was back with a vengeance. He stopped at the foot of the bed, his legs in a wide, unmistakably dominant stance. Arms folded. None of the teasing, lazily smiling seductiveness he usually displayed.

'We're leaving tomorrow.'

His words fell like shards of glass. Kate was completely non-plussed, had no clue as to what he was talking about or why it felt like a slap in the face.

'But…I thought we had at least another four days here? Has something happened?'

He shook his head, and then laughed harshly. 'You could say that. I've realised that I made a grave error of judgement in bringing you here.'

Pain lanced Kate, and she felt unbelievably vulnerable in her plain T-shirt, her head still a little fuzzy from sleep. 'What do you mean?'

Tiarnan came around, closer to the bed. Kate fought not to shrink back and looked up. The blue of his eyes was intense despite the dim light.

'I shouldn't have trusted that you wouldn't use Rosie in some kind of manipulative effort to gain a more intimate place in our lives—my life. A more permanent position. I can see now that that's *exactly* what you were doing in your own quiet little way.'

Suddenly Kate was wide awake. Without really thinking she sprang out of the bed to stand beside it, her heart hammering. 'What on earth are you talking about?' She shook because she was in such shock, so affronted. 'I would *never* use Rosie like that. How could you think such a thing?'

Tiarnan's face was harsher than she'd ever seen it. 'Because you said something to her the other night and she's now developed a sense of devotion to you that you've undoubtedly engineered for your own ends.'

Tiarnan thought again of the day he'd just spent with his daughter—her easy chatter about everything and anything that he'd missed so much, and how it had been interspersed with countless references to Katie this and Katie that. He'd had no idea that Kate had insinuated herself so subtly into their lives—and more importantly into Rosie's life. The child clearly had a case of hero-worship—no doubt fostered by Kate herself.

Kate drew herself up to her full height, unbelievably hurt that Tiarnan could think such a thing. And yet she knew she couldn't, *wouldn't* betray Rosie's confidence.

'I'm very fond of Rosie, and I'm flattered that she likes me. She's a very lovable little girl. But I would never foster intimacy with her just to get some kind of closer relationship with you, as you're suggesting.'

Tiarnan unfolded his arms and made a slashing gesture that forced Kate to take a step back. She'd never seen him look so angry, and realised that it was an intense anger at himself. Her heart ached in the face of his blatant mistrust, that he could believe that he had put Rosie in any kind of danger.

'There's a good reason I've never invited a woman into my life on such an intimate level. For you I made an exception, because we have a shared history and because you're not a stranger to Rosie. But it was a grave error, and it's one I'm going to rectify immediately—before Rosie can grow any more attached to you. I take full responsibility. I should never have allowed you to look after her in Madrid in the first place, or invited you here.' *Why had he thought for a second that she would be any different from any other woman?*

Kate folded her arms, willing the hurt from her voice. 'So you're going to banish me from your sight and from Rosie's presence? What about Rosie? What is *she* going to think if I suddenly disappear?'

He came close and put a finger under her chin to tip her face up. Kate clenched her jaw, refusing to let him see how badly he was affecting her.

'I've told Rosie that you've been called home for work. You can say goodbye to her in the morning. I'll escort you back to Madrid. I have some urgent business to attend to there for a couple of days, and then I'll return here alone to spend the rest of the holiday with Rosie.'

Anger rushed through Kate at his high-handed manner and she bit out, 'You don't have to escort me anywhere, Tiarnan. I'm not going to steal the silver on my way out. Need I remind you that I never wanted to come here in the first place?'

Tiarnan quirked his brow. His voice was like steel, reminding her of how intent he'd been on seducing her that night in San Francisco. It grated across Kate's nerves.

'I'll escort you because, as I said, I've business to attend to. And need I remind *you* that it took just one night to act out your charade of playing hard to get before you agreed to come here?'

Shame coursed through Kate. He was right. But it had been no charade.

Before she knew what was happening Tiarnan was pulling her close, reaching for the hem of her T-shirt to pull it up. Kate slapped his hands away ineffectually, incensed that he would think he could speak to her like this, accuse her of this, and still seduce her.

'What do you think you're doing?'

'I'm taking you to bed—which is what I should have remembered is the primary focus of this relationship.'

Kate pulled back within the tight band of steel of his arms, trying desperately to avoid his head as it lowered, his mouth intoxicatingly close to hers. She shook her head from side to side, felt Tiarnan catch a long skein of her hair, holding her head still.

'*No!* I won't do this. I don't deserve this, Tiarnan. It was your decision to ask me here. I did not manipulate you in any way. And I did *not* take advantage of Rosie.'

Her words sliced into Tiarnan with the precision of a knife, reminding him of his misjudgement once again. He drew back, but held her close. Angled his hips and moved them against hers so that she could feel his arousal. He saw the flare of helpless response in her eyes, saw it race across her cheeks in a blaze of colour. Triumph surged through him. He felt as if he was back in control.

'Well, then—if, as you say, you've no intention of using Rosie, and never wanted to be here in the first place, you can't possibly object to going home, can you?'

Kate stilled in her struggle, and felt an empty ache spread outwards from her heart. She might not have wanted to come here initially—but she had, and she'd seen a slice of paradise that had more to do with the family idyll she'd always craved and less to do with the stunning surroundings. But of course Tiarnan could never know that. So she hitched her chin and said, coolly and clearly, 'No. I couldn't think of anything I'd like more than to go home.'

'Good.' Tiarnan's voice was grim, and rough with barely leashed desire.

Kate heard it and her treacherous body responded. She knew at that moment that this was it. Once they returned to Madrid the next day she was going to walk away from Tiarnan and move on with her life.

So now, when he pulled her closer and his mouth found hers, she emitted a growl of angry, hurt capitulation, but she allowed him to sweep her along in the tide of desire that blew up around them because it would be for the last time.

CHAPTER EIGHT

THE journey back to Madrid was uneventful. Kate looked out of the window and saw that they were approaching landing. Relief should have flooded her, but it didn't—only heaviness. Tiarnan was immersed in paperwork and Kate was glad of the reprieve. She'd been terrified that he'd attempt to seduce her on the plane and that she wouldn't be able to hold her emotions back. She'd barely managed to hold them back last night after they'd made love and, despite the tension tinged with anger on both sides, Tiarnan had brought her to a point of such transcendence that she'd cried silent tears afterwards. He hadn't seen, though, and she'd feigned sleep, waiting for and willing him to return to his own bed, which he eventually had done, leaving her mortifyingly bereft.

The plane landed and the stewards escorted them out. Kate spied the car she'd ordered from Martinique waiting in the distance, and finally the relief she craved flooded her. Tiarnan's own car was pulled up by the steps. He gestured for her to give the driver her bag but she clung onto it. He frowned at her, a man clearly not patient with being made to wait for anything. He held out his hand.

'Your bag, Kate.'

Kate shook her head and backed away, looked over her shoulder to the other car. 'That's my car there, Tiarnan. I'm booked on a flight back to New York from here, I don't have much time.'

His eyes speared her and she quivered inwardly.

'Don't be ridiculous. You can stay with me until I have to return to Martinique.'

Kate smiled, and it felt brittle and false. 'Is that what you see happening? Now that I'm safely out of Rosie's way we can continue this affair until such time as you or I get bored?'

Tiarnan frowned even more deeply, an uncomfortable prickling sensation running over his skin. He wasn't used to women articulating his inner thoughts. That was exactly how he'd envisaged things going. He'd removed what he'd seen as a threat to Rosie from her life, which allowed him to continue his affair with Kate. He made a discreet gesture and knew that his driver had melted away into the car behind him.

He gestured with his hand again, and didn't like the sense of desperation gripping his innards. 'Come on, Kate. Let's not waste time.'

She shook her head again, more emphatically. 'No. I told you before this affair was only going to last for the holiday, and it's over now.' She forced the words out, even though they were like broken glass lacerating her tongue. 'Thank you for taking me. I had a nice time.'

A nice time? Tiarnan felt so incandescent his vision was blurred for a moment. He had the strongest, most primal urge to pick Kate up, throw her in the back of his car and instruct Juan to drive and keep driving until his head was clear of this gnarled heat.

'Kate, you don't have to act out this charade. I want you. But I'm not going to play games pursuing you all over the world. I'm quite happy for you to be my mistress. I just won't have you use Rosie as a pawn to get there.'

The pain was intense, but Kate forced herself to stay standing. 'I'm not playing games, Tiarnan. I don't do that. I meant what I said. This is over.'

The quiet intensity of her voice suddenly told him that she spoke the truth. And in that instant unwelcome and burning came the suspicion that he'd grossly misjudged her motives where Rosie was concerned. He couldn't deny that he'd acted out of a knee-jerk sense of panic that he'd done something wrong—that he'd allowed someone into their intimate sphere who could harm Rosie exactly as Stella had. The truth was, he'd simply never seen Rosie trust a woman so implicitly who wasn't either Sorcha, her grandmother, or Mama Lucille and her family…

Kate stood in front of him and she'd never looked lovelier. Her flawless skin had taken on a warm honey glow, and her hair had streaks of platinum among the blonde strands. She was dressed in a simple white shirt and jeans, and he noticed the straw hat she held in one clenched hand. It was the tacky hat he'd bought her in Saint-Pierre. Suddenly a memory hit him right between the eyes: the evening they'd returned from that outing she'd caught him about to throw it away, with the sunglasses. She'd grabbed them from him with surprising force and said, 'Don't!'

And then jokingly, as if to diminish it, 'I plan on showing them to one of my designer friends. You never know—they could inspire his next collection.'

But it was her eyes that had caught him. They hadn't been joking. They'd been deadly serious.

Right then, standing by his car, a lot of things seemed to be clicking into place. Everything that had happened between them seemed to merge into one memory, and he recalled how she'd looked at him when he'd pulled back from their kiss ten years ago—the light that had shone out of her just before he'd asked her what the hell she was thinking. He could see now that he'd forgotten how that light had dimmed…but the memory of her vulnerability was suddenly vivid.

He backed away, the compulsion to drag her off by her hair

curiously fading. And yet he felt empty inside. Twisted with conflicting emotions.

'Yes,' he said, not even sure what he was replying to. 'Thanks for coming with us, Kate, I'm sure I'll see you soon.'

Kate paled and she looked uncertain—as if she'd expected more of a fight, as if she were almost disappointed. 'Yes. No doubt. And, Tiarnan?'

He stopped and looked at her, feeling numb.

'Please don't feel that you have to give me anything…like a token… If you do, I'll just send it back.'

And then she turned and walked away quickly, that hat in one hand, her case in the other. Tiarnan watched as a driver leapt out of the other car and took her case, then waited till she sat inside and closed the door behind her. Then the car was pulling away and she was gone.

Two weeks later. The Ritz Hotel, Central Park, New York

'I'm afraid I'm not a very good dancer, William.'

Kate forced a smile at the man whose arm was far too tight around her waist as he led her to the dance floor through the throng. He was her date for the evening and, as for how getting on with her life was going, things were pretty dismal.

He breathed in her ear—far too close for her liking, 'I don't believe it for a second. It's impossible you can't dance well.'

Kate mentally told him, *You've been warned.* She'd been invited to this glitzy charity function by the honourable William Fortwin the Third, the pampered son of a well-known media mogul. And she'd come because she had to at least give him a chance. Now she wished she was anywhere but here. Her feet ached from working all day and her dress was too tight. She put it down to Mama Lucille's cooking, and then abruptly diverted her mind from that dangerous avenue of thought.

Her breasts felt almost unbearably sensitive too—and, come

to think of it, she felt sensitive all over, and bloated. It had to be down to her overdue period… She was practically bursting out of her dress, which wasn't a good thing as it was strapless and had a provocative slit to the thigh. She really didn't need William to have any more encouragement to look at her cleavage.

She sighed deeply as he swung her a little too enthusiastically onto the dance floor, and resolutely moved his hand back up to her waist from her bottom—*again*.

Tiarnan watched Kate move the man's hand from her bottom and unclenched his own hands a little. But everything else stayed clenched. He hadn't expected to see her here tonight; how many functions had he been to in New York over the years and never bumped into her?

And yet ever since he'd touched down in New York she'd filled his mind so completely that at first he'd thought he was hallucinating when he'd seen her. All thoughts of the business deal he was meant to be wrapping up were gone. And he had to concede now that she'd been filling his mind constantly in the last two weeks. Returning to Martinique and Rosie should have been a balm to his spirit. But it had proved to be anything but. It had seemed lacklustre, empty. Even his improved relationship with Rosie had failed to lift his spirits, and at every turn people had seemed to mention Kate and ask about her, ask when she might come back. She'd created an indelible impression in just a few days.

That sense that he'd misjudged her had been compounded even more so when Rosie had finally revealed what she and Kate had talked about that night. He could see now that Rosie had needed that outlet desperately—someone independent that she could confide in, someone who wasn't him. And from what he could gather Kate had reassured her with a gentle intuition that had done anything *but* take advantage of the vulnerable little girl.

He took her in. She looked stunning. Her dress was a champagne colour, and her skin glowed with the remnants of her tan even from where he stood. Her hair was swept up and kept in place with a diamanté pin, baring her neck, which made Tiarnan feel inordinately protective. There was something about her tonight that he hadn't noticed before—a kind of *glow*. She was undeniably beautiful, but it seemed to be radiating right out of her in a way he'd never seen before.

The crowd cleared for a moment, and Tiarnan saw the man's hand descend to Kate's bottom again—just as the thigh-high slit in her dress revealed one long shapely leg. It was too much. Restraining himself from physically throwing people aside, he went out to the lobby, where he spoke briefly to the receptionist and then went back into the ballroom.

As he walked towards her now, with one goal in mind, all the nebulous tendrils of revelation and doubt he'd felt that evening standing before her at Madrid airport were conveniently forgotten in the mist of this lust haze clouding his vision. Also forgotten was the fact that he'd felt that instinctive need to let her walk away. He couldn't fathom right now how on earth he'd let her go.

Kate felt a prickling on her neck, and as she apologised to William for what seemed like the umpteenth time she wondered if perhaps she was coming down with flu. Then she heard a deep drawling voice behind her, and would have fallen if not for the fact that she was being held in such a grip.

'She really is a terrible dancer—I'm sure you won't mind if I cut in.'

It wasn't a question, it was a thinly veiled threat, an imperative, and William Fortwin recognised a superior male when he saw one. He dropped Kate like a hot coal, much to her chagrin and relief.

'Of course. Here…'

And before she knew what was happening Tiarnan Quinn had smoothly inserted himself into William's place. Suddenly

Kate's evening exploded into a million tiny balls of sensation. Her head felt light, she no longer felt constricted…or she did, but it was a different kind of constriction. Shock rendered her momentarily speechless. Lust and heat were intense and immediate after a two-week absence. All efforts to forget about this man and his effect on her were shown up in all their pathetic ineffectiveness.

And with that shaming realisation, as if she hadn't done the hardest thing she'd ever done in her life just walking away from him two weeks ago, she allowed anger to rise. She would *never* forget the way he'd so grossly misjudged her, letting his innate cynicism distort her innocent friendship with Rosie. Or the way he'd let her walk away from him in Madrid and, even more shamingly, the way that despite all her precious efforts to self-protect she'd longed for him to haul her back to him and demand she stay. He'd morphed in an instant that evening from hot and astounded to cool and distant, and she'd been terrified that he'd seen something of her real feelings. Her eyes flashed what she hoped were real sparks.

'What do you think you're doing?' she spat. 'That man was my date.' This was punctuated with an accidental stepping on Tiarnan's toes. He didn't even wince.

'You need to dance with someone who can handle your lack of…shall we say…skill?' He quirked his beautiful mouth.

Kate saw red at his easy seductive insouciance. 'You can't just order him off like a dog.'

Tiarnan's mouth thinned. 'I just did. That man wasn't fit to clean your shoes and you know it. You would have put up with the dance, feigned a headache and insisted you had to go home alone.'

Kate gasped, aghast. It was exactly what she'd been planning on doing. She coloured, and Tiarnan looked triumphant.

She smiled sweetly. 'Well, then, you can save me the bother of saying the same to you.'

He didn't respond, just seemed to be transfixed by her mouth—which made her groin tingle and her breasts tighten even more painfully. She began to feel desperate. He had to go.

'*What* are you doing here? Or did you somehow manipulate it so that I'd be asked here on a date just so you could cut in?'

He didn't look in the least bit insulted, and Kate tried valiantly not to notice how stupendously gorgeous he was in his tuxedo, even darker and more dangerous-looking after the holiday.

'I'm here on business. But the business side of things paled into insignificance the minute I saw you across the room.'

The uncomfortable realisation struck him that the business side of things had paled into insignificance long before tonight.

Kate stood on his feet again, but he merely whirled her further into the dance floor. She had to acknowledge that along with a sense of exasperation that he was here was also—much more treacherously—an intense joy she couldn't deny. To be in his arms again was such heaven, and even more so when contrasted with her hapless date.

Kate struggled not to let her eyes close as she repeated in her head like a mantra: *Just get through the dance…just get through the dance.* She had the awful feeling she wouldn't have the strength to walk away from him again, even if he was cool and distant. A humiliating image rose in her mind of her clinging onto his feet like a whipped puppy.

And then he bent his head low and whispered with bone tingling intimacy, 'I want you, Kate. You've kept me awake for two weeks.'

Kate jerked back and looked up, her eyes growing wide. She was shaking all over—and inside. She felt so torn that she was close to tears, unbelievably raw at seeing him here like this, taken by surprise. As if sensing weakness, Tiarnan kissed the edge of her mouth fleetingly, his tongue making the merest dart of sensation against her lips. It was enough to set off a chain reaction of desire throughout her body so strong that she could only look at him helplessly and follow him, her hand in his, as he strode off the dance floor and through the crowd. Desire transcended everything, and it eclipsed Kate's need to self-protect.

He didn't hesitate or deviate for a second, as if knowing how close Kate was to turning tail and running. They got into the lift, neither one looking at the other, just at the numbers as they ascended. Kate's hand was still in a tight grip with Tiarnan's much larger one.

The lift came to a smooth halt and the doors opened with silent luxuriousness. Tiarnan led them into a plush corridor and took out a room key to open a door. Kate vaguely took in the sumptuous room, with its grand view over the darkened outlines of Central Park lit up by moonlight in a clear sky. The lights of the city glittered and twinkled.

But she didn't care about views or luxurious rooms or any of that. She only cared about Tiarnan, and the fact that he had to touch her now or she'd die. As if reading her mind he threw off his jacket with an almost violent movement—and then she was in his arms and his mouth was on hers. And it felt so right. So good. So necessary.

They were still standing. Kate kicked off her shoes. She felt Tiarnan snake a hand up under all the chiffon folds of her dress. She gasped against his mouth when he reached her pants. He pulled them down; she kicked them off, urgency making her clumsy.

She struggled with and finally tore off his bow tie, opened his shirt to bare his chest, reached down between them to open his belt and release him. All the while their mouths were fused, as if it was too much to break apart even for a second.

Kate felt the clip being pulled from her hair, and the heavy mass fell down around her shoulders. Tiarnan's hand luxuriated in the strands, massaging her head in an incongruously tender gesture amidst the passionate urgency.

She finally managed to pull down his trousers, freeing his

heavy erection. His hands were under her dress, lifting it up. Kate raised her leg and cried out when she felt Tiarnan lift her against the door and thrust up into her in one smooth move.

For a moment, as if savouring the intensity, neither one moved or breathed, and then, because it was too exquisite not to, they moved. Kate wrapped her arms around his neck and clenched her buttocks. Tiarnan let out a long hiss of breath. They moved in tandem, surrounded by nothing but their breathing and their frantic heartbeats as Tiarnan drove in and out, taking them higher and higher, his chest heaving against Kate's which felt unbearably swollen against her dress.

When the pinnacle came, it seemed to go on for ever. Tiarnan had to soothe Kate, tell her it was OK to let go, before she finally allowed herself to fall, let the release sweep her away. Tiarnan joined her, and when they were finally spent he buried his head in her neck. It had been fast and furious. Shattering.

After what seemed like ages, Tiarnan finally let Kate down. Her legs were unbelievably wobbly. She muttered something and went to find the bathroom, locking herself inside with relief while she tried to gather her wits and come to terms with what she'd just let happen.

Her mind was barely able to function, but uppermost was a need to protect and survive. She had to get away from Tiarnan. After a few minutes she stood and looked in the mirror. She was wearing more make-up than she normally would and was glad of it now. Somehow she'd had the wherewithal to pick up her pants and hair clip. With shaking hands she stepped back into her underwear and pinned her hair back up—a little untidily, but it would have to do. And then, taking a deep breath, she went back out to the suite.

She came out to see Tiarnan smile at her with sexy laziness, in the act of taking off his cufflinks. His trousers were open at the top, shirt undone. All her good intentions nearly flew out of the window. *Nearly.*

She called on the cool reserve that felt so alien and hard to muster now and said, 'I meant what I said in Madrid, Tiarnan. It's over. And that—' she looked accusingly at the door '—shouldn't have happened.'

'Well, it did,' he drawled, and indicated to the bed. 'I've got the suite for the night.'

Kate looked at the bed. She was angry, because a very big part of her was tempted to just give in, throw caution to the wind and indulge in another ten hours of bliss. But then when and where would it stop? She had to be strong—had to do this now once and for all.

She shook her head and stood her ground. 'No, Tiarnan. I'm not staying the night. Much as I might be tempted, it's not going to happen.'

He stopped what he was doing and looked at her. She didn't look as if she wanted to hang around. Irritation and frustration prickled under his skin. He wanted her already again. Painfully. Urgently. The frustration of the past two weeks still shocked him with its intensity.

He couldn't stop the impatience lacing his voice. He was a man used to getting what he wanted, when he wanted. 'Look, Kate, you want me—I want you. We're good together. What's the problem?'

Kate wanted to scream; was it always this simple for men? She answered herself: it was if they didn't have feelings invested. Tiarnan started to walk towards her and panic made her jerky. She flung out a hand. 'Stop! Don't come any closer.' She knew if he so much as touched her she'd be a mess.

He stopped and frowned.

'Whatever we are is neither here nor there, Tiarnan. I'm not in the market for an affair. I just won't do it.'

'Well, I wouldn't call what we're doing an *affair*—we know each other, we're friends…it's more than that.'

He didn't even trust her with his daughter. Sadness and pain gripped Kate. 'It's *not* more than that because you don't trust me, Tiarnan. But that's beside the point—because it's going to come to an end, isn't it?'

Tiarnan wasn't sure where this was going. 'Well, of course it will—at some stage. But does it have to be tonight? Right now?'

Kate nodded and held back a sob. 'I can't do this. With you.'

She started walking to the door. Before she got to it Tiarnan reached her and turned her around.

She looked up, stiff all over, feeling more constricted than ever. 'Please, Tiarnan—just let me go.'

A muscle clenched in his jaw. She could see the confusion in his eyes. And then he said, 'Tell me why—just tell me why you don't want to do this.'

She looked at him for a long moment and knew that there was only one way he would let her walk away. She would have to bare her soul. Even so, she asked, 'Do you really want to know?'

He nodded. Grim. Determined.

She pushed past him back into the room, putting space between them. She paced for a minute, and then stopped and looked at him, summoned all her courage. 'Because that night ten years ago took way more out of me than I revealed to you at the time.'

He frowned, his black brows creasing over those stunning blue eyes.

Kate continued, but every word was costing her an emotional lifetime. 'That night…I'd no intention of trying to seduce you. I…' She faltered and looked away, then back again. 'I'd had a crush on you for a long time, Tiarnan, and that night I thought I saw you notice me as a woman for the first time. I somehow got the courage to kiss you…and you kissed me back…'

'So…?'

Kate could see he was trying to figure it out. 'I guessed you believed I was more confident that I really was. But then, when you rejected me, I wanted to protect myself—pretend that I'd been in full control. I felt humiliated, and I hated that you might see how much it had meant to me.'

Tiarnan had the strangest sensation of the earth shifting beneath his feet, but he stayed standing. He'd had that instinct, but then when she'd seemed to sure…so mature…so cool… he'd doubted it. But he shouldn't have. It was the vulnerability he'd sensed in Martinique. And at the airport in Madrid, when it had compelled him to let her walk away.

He tried to cling onto something. 'What does that have to do with *now?*'

'Everything!' Kate wailed, throwing up her arms, taking him by surprise.

Colour was high in her cheeks. Her eyes sparkled like jewels and he felt a chasm opening up between them.

Her chest rose and fell with agitation. 'I've been aware of you for the past ten years, Tiarnan. Every time I've looked at you I've remembered that kiss. The pitifully few and far between men I've been with have all come a far distant second to the way I imagined *you* might have made me feel.' Her voice cracked ominously. 'How pathetic is that? They fell short of little more than my imagination. I couldn't even form a decent lasting relationship because the shadow you'd cast made everyone else pale in comparison.'

Her mouth twisted bitterly, making Tiarnan want to kiss the bitter line away, hating that he had caused it.

'Over the years I learnt to protect myself. I never wanted you to know how I'd failed to get over you. But at the christening that day it was so hard to stand there and witness Sorcha and Romain's joy and love with you right beside me…and then in San Francisco…I couldn't hide it any more.'

She shrugged again, and it made something lance Tiarnan's heart, but he couldn't move.

'I agreed to go to Martinique with you because I thought it might help…that by sleeping with you it might somehow make you fall off your pedestal. Reduce what we had shared to something more banal. But it didn't, Tiarnan. It's made things worse. I can't do this. And I would never have used Rosie in any kind of manipulative way. I *hate* that you would think that.' She shook her head and made for the door again.

Feeling panic surge, Tiarnan gripped her shoulders and pulled her around, tipping her chin up. Her eyes were closed. He grabbed her hands and brought them up, holding them tightly, manacled in his. 'Kate—look at me.'

She shook her head, and he could see her press her lips together in a desperate attempt at control. A tear trickled out from under the long lashes that rested on her flushed cheek. He felt weak inside. Utterly helpless. And like the biggest heel.

'Kate—please, don't cry. I owe you a huge apology. I'm sorry for accusing you of using Rosie. I can see how wrong I was.'

The full extent of his own cynicism hit him forcibly. It was so clear now. He'd lashed out as much in an effort to protect himself as Rosie, and the realisation disgusted him. Kate had just got too close too quickly. She opened her eyes then, and the naked emotion in their swimming depths put him to shame. But he couldn't let go of her wrists. He felt the frantic beat of her pulse and it reminded him of a caged bird.

In a hoarse voice filled with emotion she said, 'This is who I really am, Tiarnan, and what I really want: if I never had to stand in front of a photographer again to have my photo taken or parade down a catwalk I'd be ecstatic. My idea of a good Saturday night is staying in and baking bread. I like knitting—and I like to crochet if I'm really going out on a limb. I make homemade soup. What I want more than anything in the world is to find someone to love who'll love me back and to have babies with them—lots of babies—and raise a family. That's what I want and need. I've no idea if that's as a result of my emotionally barren childhood or conditioning or whatever. All I know is that it's what I want in the deepest core part of me.

I'm not the kind of person who can have an affair and not get involved. And I would never ask any of this from you because I know you've done it. You've got it. You're happy. But I'm not, Tiarnan, and as much as we might have *this*…' she jerked her head to the bed '…it's not enough for me.'

She pulled her hands to try and free them, but he held on with something like a death grip.

'*Please* let me go, so I can get over you and get on with my life.'

Tiarnan stood in silence, stunned to his very depths. Shocked. In awe of this passionate Kate—a different kind of passionate that he'd never seen before. A huge block prevented him from speaking. She was looking up at him defiantly, as if daring him to seduce her again, knowing everything he now knew. She'd give in if he just kissed her. He knew she'd give in. They both knew. It permeated the air around them. But how could he do that?

The revelations he'd acknowledged when he realised that she *hadn't* been a dim and distant memory for him throughout the past ten years seemed so pathetic now, compared to her feelings. He knew he couldn't even begin to articulate that without sounding as if he was making excuses. It would be like trying to placate her—or, worse, patronise her.

She looked so young at that moment, so beautiful. His instinct had been right that day at the airport when he'd seen her holding onto that ridiculous hat. He'd seen something momentarily unguarded in her eyes. He realised now that it had been her attempt to make the break.

She was right. She deserved her happiness. She deserved to find a good man who would love her the way she wanted to be loved and give her all the babies and joy she wanted. Something in him reacted forcibly to that image but he forced it down. He had no right to it. No right to feel jealous.

All of a sudden he felt tired and jaded and cynical. He'd been there and had been badly burned in the process. He had always vowed never to expose himself like that again. He had Rosie. He had Sorcha and her family. Kate deserved more. He had to let her go.

Kate dropped her head. She couldn't keep looking Tiarnan in the eye, seeing the myriad emotions as he finally came to the realisation, as she knew he would, that he wouldn't be able to get rid of her fast enough. She sensed it before it even happened. He dropped her hands from his grip and stepped back. He was letting her go again. And this time she knew it was for good.

She couldn't look up. 'Thank you,' she said faintly.

His deep voice impacted like a punch in her solar plexus. 'You deserve to find what you want, Kate. I wish you all the best.'

A couple of days later Tiarnan stood in his office in Madrid, staring out of the window with his hands in his pockets. The fact that he *never* stood staring vacantly out of the window was not something that impinged on his consciousness. His eminently professional assistant knocked on his door and came in. He didn't notice the fleeting look of alarm cross her face just before he turned to face her. 'Maria?'

She came towards him and held out a brown padded envelope. 'This came for you just after you'd left for New York. It's marked "Private". I didn't want to open it.'

Tiarnan took it and had a strange feeling. He dismissed Maria and turned the envelope over. On the back, in the same clear, neat writing as on the front, was a familiar New York address and the name K. Lancaster.

He sat at his desk and opened it. Out fell a sheaf of glossy black and white photos. With his hands none too steady he looked through them, becoming more and more amazed and seriously impressed. They were stunning, and all taken completely off guard: pictures of him with Rosie, pictures of Mama

Lucille and Papa Joe, moments snatched. And he hadn't even been aware of her taking the pictures.

There was another smaller envelope, marked for Rosie. Tiarnan couldn't help himself. He had to open it. So far there were no pictures of Kate. The photo that fell out was of Kate and Rosie making funny faces at the camera, which must have been on a timer. And on the back was a note.

Rosie, I miss you already. Please know that I'd love you to come and visit me any time, and the next time I'm in Madrid we'll go out for ice cream—I'll be looking forward to hearing all about your new friends. In the meantime take care. Love, Katie.

It was only after a long moment that he realised he'd been holding his breath. He carefully put the photo back into the envelope. He stood up abruptly and went again to the window.

He couldn't want her this badly—so badly that a photograph of her pulling a funny face made him feel weak. Grim determination settled around him like a weight. She was gone. He had to let her be. She was right. He had his life. He had Rosie. He didn't need anything else, didn't want anything else. Maybe if he kept repeating it he'd start to believe it.

CHAPTER NINE

Six weeks later. Madison Avenue, New York.

KATE huddled deeper into her long padded coat and wrapped her scarf tighter around her neck. It was coming up to Christmas, and the shops were alive and bright with decorations and lights. They twinkled merrily in the dusk. She felt removed from it all, though—she was in total shock. She'd just come from an evening clinic with her doctor. Her awful growing suspicion of the last few weeks was now confirmed. There was a reason the bloated feeling had never gone away, and a reason for the fact that her breasts were so sensitive it hurt to touch them. And a very good reason for the fact that she hadn't had her period yet.

She was pregnant.

Over two months pregnant.

She stumbled on the sidewalk and someone automatically put out a hand to steady her, Kate smiled her thanks and kept going. But she felt as though everything was starting to disintegrate around her. She had to get home. She unconsciously started walking faster, sudden tears blurring her vision, and looked down to avoid people's eyes. Right in that moment she'd never felt so alone in all her life.

On the one hand, despite the shock, she felt the pure ecstatic joy of being pregnant, and on the other hand she felt the sheer desolation of knowing that the father would only see this as a burden or, worse, as something planned to trap him in some way. How could he not when it had happened before?

Why, oh why, had she blurted everything out to Tiarnan that night? Kate had remonstrated bitterly with herself ever since. The only thing she could give any thanks for was the fact that she hadn't come straight out and told him that she loved him.

But, she reminded herself, she hadn't needed to. She'd all but prostrated herself at his feet.

Kate unseeingly followed the mass of humans who were walking down Madison Avenue, her mind and belly churning sickly. All of a sudden, out of nowhere, she hit a brick wall. But it was a brick wall with hands and arms, steadying her. God, she couldn't even manage to walk down the street without avoiding mishap.

She looked up to apologise and her world stopped turning. She had the absurd impulse to laugh for a hysterical moment, before cold, stark reality set in.

'No,' she breathed painfully. 'It can't be you.'

'Kate? Is that you?'

It *was* Tiarnan. Looking down at her with dark brows pulled over piercing blue eyes. In a dark coat. Kate cursed fate and the gods, and at the same time had an awful soul-destroying awareness of how impossibly handsome he looked. How was it that she'd managed beautifully for ten years to avoid him and suddenly he seemed to be around every corner? And yet even amongst the shock and despair of seeing him she couldn't control her body's response, the awful kick of her heart.

'Yes, it's me. Sorry, I wasn't looking where I was going.' She attempted to be civil, normal, and completely and conveniently blocked out the fact that she'd just found out that she was pregnant and that the father stood in front of her right now. An extreme urge to self-protect was strong. 'How are you, Tiarnan?'

He was still holding her, looking at her strangely. Almost absently, he answered, 'Fine. Fine…'

It was only at that moment that Kate noticed someone hovering behind him. A woman. A petite, very beautiful, very soignée brunette, who smiled icily at Kate. It was all the impetus she needed. She was raw with the news she'd just received. Too raw to cope with this.

She stepped away, dislodging Tiarnan's hands, and noticed for the first time where they were. Kate had bumped into Tiarnan as he'd been walking into a restaurant. The same exclusive restaurant outside which she'd bumped into him dressed as a French maid some years before. With another dark-haired beauty. He'd obviously reverted to type.

Before she could lose it completely there on the path, in front of the man she loved and his lover, she fled. Exactly as she'd done before. Except this time Tiarnan had seen her and recognised her. The humiliation was so much worse this time, and the awful irony of coming full circle was nearly too much to bear.

Tiarnan watched as Kate strode away, her bright hair like a beacon among the sea of anonymous people. He still felt the force of her body slamming into his, full-on. He still saw her upturned face, those huge eyes. She'd looked pale—too pale. And tired. Concern clutched him. And a sudden feeling of *déjà vu*.

'Tiarnan? Are we going in? And who was that woman? She looked incredibly familiar.'

Tiarnan finally noticed his date again for the first time. He'd only asked her out in some kind of pathetic attempt to regain something close to normal in his life, but he knew now that he'd just watched his only hope of being normal again walk away. When he'd held Kate steady for those brief moments just now he'd felt at peace for the first time in weeks. A deep sigh of relief had moved through him.

He tried to focus on his date. 'Melinda, I'm sorry, but something's come up. I'm going to have to cancel dinner.'

He was already urging her back to his car at the kerb. He heard a very piqued, 'It's *Miranda,* actually—'

He opened the car door and ushered the woman in with little finesse, saying to his driver, 'Please take Miranda—sorry, Melinda—wherever she wants to go.'

Tiarnan slammed the door and watched the car pull away with an inordinate sense of relief. He started walking in the opposite direction to the one Kate had taken; as much as he wanted nothing more than to go to her straight away, he knew he had to handle this carefully. Impatience and urgency coursed through him, but for once in his life he had to control it. He had some serious thinking to do.

Kate felt as washed out as a dishrag. It was as if hearing from the doctor that she was pregnant had kick-started her body to react, and morning sickness had arrived with a vengeance. She finally emerged from the bathroom with her hand on her belly, which was feeling hard and surprisingly big already, now that she knew she wasn't just bloated. But she knew why that was. Her mind just shied away from thinking too much about it at the moment.

She was finding it hard to process everything, and also the fact that she'd bumped into Tiarnan last night. The pain of seeing him with that woman was buried deep. She still couldn't even begin to think about how she was going to tell him…and Sorcha… A welcome numbness came over her and she knew it was some kind of protective barrier, stopping the pain and hurt from impinging too deeply. She gave up silent thanks that she didn't have to work today, and then her head hurt at the thought of breaking the news to Maud too that she was pregnant. Her lingerie contract would be out of the window—not that Kate would be sorry.

A knock came on her door, and Kate started. She couldn't deny the fact that after seeing Tiarnan in the street she'd half expected him to turn up at her door behind her. And when he hadn't…the shame of how much she'd wanted it and the pain that he hadn't had been indescribable. She reassured herself now that it could only be someone from inside the building, as the concierge usually rang up if there was a visitor. It was probably the super—or Mrs Goldstein from next door.

As she approached the door she pulled a cardigan from the chair by the door and put it on. She was only dressed in ancient sweatpants and an old T-shirt of Sorcha's.

She opened the door, and when she took in who was on the other side she could feel the colour drain from her face. Her hand tightened on the knob. She instinctively clutched the cardigan around her belly, ridiculously glad she'd had the foresight to put it on.

'Tiarnan.'

'Kate.'

For an absurd moment neither spoke. They just looked at one another. Kate heard Mrs Goldstein's door creak open, and a voice with a thick New York accent asked, 'Kate? Are you OK?'

Kate dragged her gaze from Tiarnan's and stuck her head out. Her heart was hammering, and she was very tempted to say *No, I'm not OK!* But she didn't. She just said, 'Fine Mrs Goldstein. It's just Sorcha's brother. You can go back inside.'

'All right, dear.'

Mrs Goldstein's door closed and Tiarnan said drily, 'Security system? Together with your knitting needles, I'd say you and Mrs Goldstein could pack quite a punch.'

For some reason Tiarnan's comment hurt Kate terribly. She bit her lip and tried to swallow past the huge lump in her throat. 'What do you want Tiarnan? I'm busy.' She knew she sounded choked and could see Tiarnan's eyes flash in response.

All of a sudden he looked incredibly weary, and Kate could see lines on his face that hadn't been there before. His eyes looked a little bloodshot. Even so, he was still absolutely gorgeous, and she firmed her resolve. Thankfully her composure seemed to come back slightly.

'Kate, can I come in?'

'I'd prefer if you didn't.'

'Please.'

Her composure threatened to crack again, and Kate felt the weight of inevitability fall around her like a cloak. She was pregnant, and she had to tell him sooner or later. In truth, she was terrified of facing this on her own.

Eventually she stood back and held the door open.

Tiarnan walked in, past her, and Kate had to grip the doorknob tight again and close her eyes momentarily as his scent washed over her.

When she'd gathered herself enough after closing the door, she turned to face him. He had taken off his long dark overcoat and she saw that he was wearing a dark sweater and jeans that moulded lovingly to his long legs and hard thigh muscles.

Immediately her belly felt quivery. She felt weak, and moved jerkily to sit on the couch, very aware of his eyes on her.

Kate was as prickly as a porcupine. Tiarnan's eyes drank her in hungrily as she sat down. Her hair was tied back in a high haphazard knot and he longed to undo it. She still looked unbelievably pale, making concern spike through him again. And she looked different, somehow. Even though her cardigan and sweatpants hid her body, he remembered the feel of her slamming into him the previous evening. Every curve and contour.

He felt himself stir to life and cursed. Now was not the time. He had to hold it together—but he couldn't help reacting like a sex-starved teenager. She looked somehow more bountiful, and despite her paleness, more beautiful than he'd ever seen her. It shone right out of her, just as he'd noticed in the ballroom.

'Tiarnan, what is it you want?'

Her husky voice caught him and his eyes met hers. He'd been ogling her like a teenager.

Where to start? Uncharacteristically stuck for words, feeling all at sea and more terrified than he could ever remember feeling, Tiarnan paced up and down, running a hand through his hair. How did he come out and say it? He wanted her—he wanted *it*—he wanted everything. For the first time in his life.

Kate watched Tiarnan pace and saw the look of torture on his face. For the first time she had the awful abject fear that this had nothing to do with *them*. Something else must have happened. She stood, and he stopped pacing and looked at her. She almost couldn't frame the words she was so scared.

'What is it? Is it Rosie? Did something happen? Is it Sorcha or Romain?'

He looked completely nonplussed for a moment, and then comprehension dawned. Kate realised she must have looked terrified, because he was beside her in an instant and sitting her back down, coming with her to sit on the couch.

He shook his head quickly. 'No, nothing's happened to anyone. They're all safe. I'm sorry, Kate, I didn't mean to scare you.'

Relief flooded her—along with the scary realisation that Tiarnan was too close and touching her. She moved back to the corner of the couch. He let go.

She kept silent, but inwardly she was screaming at him to just tell her what he wanted and then leave. She'd even forgotten about telling him of her pregnancy.

Finally he spoke, and it sounded as if it was being torn out of him. 'Kate, I want you.'

Her stomach plummeted. She stood up and moved away, crossing her arms. When would this torture end? She turned to face him. 'Tiarnan, I've told you. I can't do this. I know you want me.' Bitterness laced her voice. 'And you know I want you. But I'm not going there.'

A vivid memory of that woman's face last night outside the restaurant came back into Kate's mind's eye like poison seeping into a wound. Acrid jealousy burned bright within her. 'I'm sure that woman you were with last night can give you what you need.'

Tiarnan stood, and the pain on his face was stark. His hand slashed the air in a gesture of absolute rejection.

'Kate, I couldn't even remember that woman's name after bumping into you—and in truth I was hard pressed to remember it at all. That was my pathetic attempt to try and get back to what I knew, to pretend that you don't exist. To try and block out the fact that I haven't been able to stop thinking about you for a second, the fact that it's taken me weeks of torture to finally realise that I can't live without you. And to block out the fact that I've been haunted with images of you meeting someone else, falling in love with someone else, making love to someone else. Having babies with someone else.'

His eyes burned so intensely blue they held Kate in absolute thrall, unable to move or speak.

His voice sounded rough. 'I wanted to follow you home straight away last night, but I forced myself to wait. I knew that I had to come to you and make you believe what I said— believe that I wasn't just saying it to get you into bed. I was going to be calm, rational, but it's the last thing I feel now. I need *you,* Kate. I don't just want you. *I love you.* And I'm terrified that you won't give me a chance to try and prove to you how much I love you. I'm terrified it might be too late for you to give me a chance to try and make you happy, because I know you want to find someone else. You deserve someone who isn't tainted with mistakes from the past, with an already grown daughter…but I'm selfish, and I don't want you to be with someone else. I want you to be with *me.* For ever.'

Tiarnan's words seem to hang suspended in the air for a long time. Kate didn't know if she was breathing, and then she felt something in her belly quiver. Even though she knew it couldn't be the baby yet, it seemed to inject the life force back into her system.

All the pent-up emotion she'd been keeping down and suppressing for so long seemed to rush up. The fact that she'd all but bared her soul to *him* and yet he'd let her walk away. The torture she'd been going through. She took a jerky step towards Tiarnan, tears prickling, and was so utterly confused and overwhelmed that she hit him ineffectually on his chest, lashing out at the pain he'd caused her. He stood there and let her hit him again, and that made her even more upset. Because even now she couldn't bear to hurt him.

Tears blurred her vision completely and made her voice thick. 'How can you just come in here and say those things? *How?* It's not possible. You can't do this to me, Tiarnan. You can't just walk in and offer me everything I've ever wanted and dreamt of for ever like it's the easiest thing in the world. I've spent a long time getting over you. I don't need you. I've tried so hard to forget you. But now you're here, and you're saying…you're saying…'

She put her hands to her face in turmoil and despair, sobbing her heart out. She sobbed even harder when she felt strong arms wrap around her and pull her close, holding her so tight that somewhere a spark of hope ignited—and the very scary thought that perhaps she wasn't dreaming this. That maybe he had actually said those things and meant them.

Kate had never felt so exposed and raw and emotional in her life. Eventually the sobbing stopped, and she felt her hands being gently pulled away from her face. She was too weak and limp to do anything but look into Tiarnan's eyes, uncaring of how awful she must look. His eyes were full of concern, and something else she'd never seen. *Love.* Tears blurred her vision again.

With the utmost tenderness he cupped her jaw and wiped the tears as they fell with his thumbs.

He sounded tortured. 'Katie, sweetheart. Please don't cry. I'm so sorry for making you cry. I don't ever want to be the cause of making you cry again.' He went very still, and tipped up her chin so she'd look him in the eye. 'I can't bear to see you so upset. If you want me to leave, to walk away, then I'll leave right now.'

She could see the stoic resolve in his eyes. His jaw was clenched, as if to ward off a blow, and a muscle twitched. Kate wiped the back of her hand across her cheek, unaware of the heart-achingly vulnerable image she portrayed. She shook her head and then said softly, shakily, 'If I was stronger I'd make you walk away, so you know what it feels like… But the truth is I'm not that strong. I don't want you to go anywhere. I don't want you to leave my sight ever again.'

Tiarnan put his hands on her upper arms and Kate could feel them shaking. 'Kate, are you saying…? Will you let me try and make you happy?'

Kate finally felt a sense of peace wash through her, diminishing the pain, and with it came trust that this was real. She couldn't keep back a wobbly smile. She put up a hand and touched his jaw. 'Tiarnan, much as I hate to admit this to a man of your supreme confidence, unfortunately you're the only person on this earth who has the power to make me happy. I need *you* so much. I think I've loved you for ever.'

With an unusual lack of grace Tiarnan pulled Kate into him again, then took her face in his hands and kissed her with small feverish kisses saying, *'Thank you…thank you…'* over and over again.

Kate finally stopped him and took *his* face in *her* hands, pressed a long lingering kiss to his mouth. Desire swept up around them, all consuming. Tiarnan's hands roved hungrily over her form, down her back, her hips, her bottom, pulling her in close.

She felt her belly press against him, and had to gasp at the painfully exquisite sensation when he cupped one throbbing and too-sensitive breast. Immediately he pulled back, concern etched on his face.

'What is it?'

Sudden trepidation trickled through Kate. *The pregnancy.* She searched his eyes, terrified that telling him would burst this bubble. But she had to tell him and deal with his response— no matter what it would be.

She pulled back and his hands fell. But she took hold of them tightly.

'When I bumped into you last night I'd just been to see the doctor. That's why I was so distracted…'

Immediately tension came into Tiarnan's body. She'd been so pale. Her cheeks were flushed now, but it could be a fever. 'What is it? Are you OK? Is something wrong?'

She shook her head and said quickly, 'No, nothing's wrong. Everything is fine.'

She smiled shyly then, and all Tiarnan could see was tousled strands of hair falling around her face, her lips plump from his kisses. He wanted to kiss her again so badly, to hold her tight and never wake up from this moment.

He squeezed her hands. 'What is it, Kate?'

She bit her lip and looked down for a moment. Even before she spoke a trickling of awareness came into his body and his consciousness. He recalled how hard her belly had felt just now, how her breasts had felt bigger, more voluptuous. They were obviously sensitive. An incredible joy started to bubble through him even as she looked up and said the words, with naked vulnerability on her face.

'I'm pregnant, Tiarnan. I found out last night. Nearly ten weeks. It must have happened that first night in Martinique…'

Tiarnan could see her start to become nervous.

'I know I said it would be OK—and I really thought it would. It's entirely my fault.'

He immediately shook his head. Anything to stop her talking. He put a finger to her mouth, watched her eyes widen.

'Stop. It's OK. I know what you're thinking, and what you're scared of: that I'll think it's Stella Rios all over again?'

She nodded her head slowly.

'That it's too soon and I might not be ready for this news when we haven't even discussed it?'

She nodded again, her eyes huge and intensely blue.

'Well, don't be. I was halfway to guessing the minute you mentioned the doctor but said you were OK.'

Tiarnan led Kate over to the couch and sat down, pulling her onto his lap. He lifted a hand and kissed it, and then covered her belly with their joined hands, looked into her eyes. 'I never imagined a day when I would be feeling this way about anyone. I'm so in love with you the only time I feel normal or rational or sane is when I can see you and touch you. I've never felt that way about anyone—not even Stella. Never Stella. My association with her was always about the baby, about my responsibility to an unborn child. Stella and I never even consummated the marriage.' He quirked a smile. 'I used her pregnancy as an excuse to hide the fact that I didn't desire her any more. For some reason a blonde-haired blue-eyed witch I'd just kissed kept distracting me.'

His smile faded. 'I should never have rejected you so cruelly that night. The truth is that you'd shocked me out of every arrogant and complacent bone in my body. The desire I felt for you that night was urgent enough that if I hadn't realised how inexperienced you were and remembered *who* you were I would have made love to you there and then, like a randy teenager. I lashed out at that. And then, when you were so cool and blasé, I felt stupidly insulted that you weren't bothered.'

Kate felt pure joy rip through her at his words, at the acknowledgement that it had meant something more for him too. She saw the regret in his eyes, on his face, and smoothed the back of her hand across his cheek. 'We were both young—I was far too young.' She smiled ruefully. 'I don't think I would have been able to handle an experience so intense. And perhaps it's as simple as the fact that Rosie needed you. She wouldn't be in your life now if it hadn't been for Stella.'

Tiarnan felt subtle tension snake into Kate's body and her eyes clouded. He took her hand again. 'What is it? You're closing up on me.'

She shrugged and avoided his eyes. 'It's just that you've only just developed these feelings for me, and you never wanted more children, and I'm just scared… You changed so quickly on Martinique. It scared me how easy you found it to think the worst…'

He pulled her face back to his, forcing her to meet his intense gaze. 'It was easy because I'd never let another woman in so close before. For the first time since Rosie was born I put my needs first and assured myself that Rosie would be OK. When I saw the evidence of her trust in you I panicked. I was terrified I'd lost all sense of judgement and was about to let another woman take advantage of her. I didn't stop to think.'

Kate looked at him, searching as if to see whether she could trust him, and finally said, 'I believe you. I can see how it might have looked… But are you sure you're ready for a baby? You've always—'

He put a finger over her mouth, stopping her words. 'Kate, I've never wanted children again *with anyone else*. But now— with you.' He shrugged with endearing vulnerability. 'I feel like I've been given a gift. A chance to experience something I denied myself for a long time. My background and Stella Rios poisoned my attitudes. You've healed that. These feelings have been brewing for a long, long time. Seeing your desire at the christening that day was merely the catalyst. I've been aware of you all these years, even though I might have denied it to myself. I kept you strictly out of bounds. But you intrigued me with your studied indifference and your coolness. It was just a matter of time before I would have been unable to fight the urge to discover why I couldn't stop thinking about you. I've never felt that same desire for another woman until the moment we kissed again.'

Kate blushed furiously, and Tiarnan tenderly caressed her cheek and said wonderingly, 'Even now you can blush.'

She was still serious for a moment. 'What about Rosie? I mean, does she know about this?'

He nodded, smiling. 'It's one of the two things I did last night, while I tried to restrain myself from coming over here. I told Rosie I was going to come and ask you to marry me, and after she stopped squealing she said, "Does this mean you'll go back to normal now and stop being so crabby?" I assured that I would as long as you said yes, so she's been praying all night that you would say yes.'

He got serious then. 'She cares for you, Kate, and even more importantly she obviously trusts you enough to confide in you. You've already been more of a mother to her than her own mother has been her whole life. She has the picture you sent her in a frame by her bed. A picture I'm extremely jealous of, I might add.'

Kate flushed with pleasure and buried her head against his neck for a moment, hugging him tight. Relief and joy flooded her, because she knew she would never have been happy taking up such a big role in Tiarnan's life unless Rosie was happy too.

She pulled back and pressed a lingering kiss to Tiarnan's mouth. 'You can tell Rosie I said yes. What was the other thing you had to do?'

His eyes flashed in response to her yes, and his hands tightened around her. 'I had to ask Sorcha for her blessing, of course. She told me that if I hurt a hair on your head she'd break my legs—or words to that effect.'

'Great,' Kate grumbled good-naturedly. 'Everyone knew about this before me.'

He looked at her sheepishly. 'There's something else I haven't been able to get out of my mind. You're going to think this sounds crazy, but bumping into you last night made me think of it again. A few years ago I bumped into a girl outside that same restaurant—'

Kate groaned and buried her face in her hands. She mumbled from behind them, 'In a French maid's outfit?'

Tiarnan took down her hands and looked at her, shocked. 'That *was* you?'

She nodded and smiled. 'It was a hen night. I ran away. I was so mortified.'

He shook his head and laughed out loud, head thrown back. 'I thought I was going mad—turned on by some anonymous girl in a tarty costume. Do you realise that after that night I couldn't look at another woman for weeks...months? And at night all I could dream about was you, and wonder what the hell was going on?'

Kate smiled. 'Good! I'm glad I tortured you a little too. It's not entirely fair that I had to endure hearing about your endless parade of women down the years—'

Tiarnan suddenly flipped them, so that Kate lay on the couch underneath him. He undid her hair until it flowed out around her head. He ran a hand over her burgeoning breasts, causing her breath to catch, and down to her belly, caressing the growing mound.

Kate put her hand over his and felt the exquisite quickening of desire that only this man could engender. She pulled his head down and said throatily, 'First, before I kiss you all over your body to within an inch of your life, Tiarnan Quinn, I have to tell you something else.'

Tiarnan had already started kissing her, pulling her top up.

Kate stopped him and looked at him mock sternly. '*Wait.*'

She smiled, then brought his hand back to her now bare belly and looked at him with shining eyes. 'How do you feel about twins?'

He stopped and looked down at her, eyes widening in wonder. 'Seriously?'

Kate nodded. His hand tightened on her belly. An unmistakably proprietorial gleam lit his intense gaze, making Kate rejoice inwardly.

He growled softly. 'Tell me how much it's going to cost to buy you out of every job contract and campaign you're booked for—because you and our babies are mine now, and I'm not letting another person have the right to touch you or photograph you without my say-so.'

Kate smiled and revelled in his innate possessiveness. She shifted easily under him, feeling the heavy weight of his arousal pressing against his jeans. She moved sinuously. Colour stained his cheeks.

'Kate,' he said warningly.

She made a quick calculation and said a round figure. He paled slightly under his tan, but didn't miss a beat. 'I paid a fraction of that just to kiss you, so I figure it's worth it to marry you, to be the father of your children and live happily ever after.'

'Sounds good to me.' Kate smiled, and pulled him back down to where she wanted him for ever—in her arms.

EPILOGUE

Two and a half years later, Martinique

KATE stood in the dim light and looked lovingly at the two small sprawled forms in the big double bed, protected by a muslin net hanging from above. Dark-haired Iris was on her back, thumb stuck firmly in her mouth and sucking periodically. Blonde-haired Nell was on her front, arms outstretched, her head resting on one chubby cheek and looking angelic. Kate smiled. She'd been anything but angelic a few hours ago.

Pure joy rose up within her, and she had to press a hand to her chest to try and contain it. And then she felt a big solid presence behind her, strong arms wrap around her waist. She leant back into the familiar embrace and smiled wider when she felt firm lips press a hot kiss to her neck.

They were in the room that had been hers the first time she'd come to Martinique. Now it was a nursery for the girls. She heard Tiarnan whisper close to her ear, 'We'll have to put bars around the room. I caught Nell making a near-successful bid for freedom earlier.'

Kate stifled a giggle at the image.

Tiarnan took her hand to lead her out and back to their own room along the balcony. He was in nothing but boxer shorts, and Kate's eyes ran over him appreciatively. Tiarnan caught her looking. He stopped and pulled her into his arms.

'Why, Mrs Quinn,' he said mock seriously, 'I think I'm feeling a little violated by your very explicit look.'

Kate leant into him luxuriously, loving the feel of his body, and especially the way it was reacting. She wrapped her arms around him and pressed a kiss to his neck. 'I'm very sorry, Mr Quinn. I know how sensitive you are.'

He groaned softly when he felt her move her hips, bringing the apex of her legs into close contact with his rapidly hardening arousal.

Kate looked at him, revelling in the intimate moment. Revelling in the bliss to come and the bliss she felt every day. She took his hand to lead him into their bedroom.

He asked on the way, 'What was wrong with Rosie earlier? Apparently I "wouldn't understand".'

Kate looked back and smiled. 'It's nothing, really—just girlie issues. She likes one of Zoe's cousins, but he likes someone else…'

Tiarnan groaned, and said with feeling, 'I knew there was a reason I married you. I could never deal with all this puberty stuff.'

Kate hit his arm playfully and said something—but it was indistinct as they disappeared into the bedroom, and then everything faded into the beautifully warm and fragrant tropical darkness.

THE SAVAKIS
MISTRESS

BY
ANNIE WEST

Annie West spent her childhood with her nose between the covers of a book—a habit she retains. After years of preparing government reports and official correspondence she decided to write something she *really* enjoys. And there's nothing she loves more than a great romance. Despite her office-bound past, she has managed a few interesting moments—including a marriage offer with the promise of a herd of camels to sweeten the contract. She is happily married to her ever-patient husband (who has never owned a dromedary). They live with their two children amongst the tall eucalypts at beautiful Lake Macquarie, on Australia's east coast. You can e-mail Annie at www.annie-west. com, or write to her at PO Box 1041, Warners Bay, NSW 2282, Australia.

To two lovely ladies:
Marilyn and Lee
Thank you for all your support!

CHAPTER ONE

CALLIE'S heart thundered in her ears, muting the sound of their hoarse breathing. Hers and his, mingled together.

Aftershocks shuddered through her. Light flickered behind her closed lids, remnants of the white-hot ecstasy that had exploded through her moments ago. An ecstasy she'd never before experienced.

Who could have known?

She dragged in a breath and inhaled his spicy scent. Clean masculine sweat, musky skin and something indefinable that made her want to burrow closer into his bare shoulder.

She nuzzled his damp skin and was rewarded with a rumble of approval deep in the wide chest that cushioned her. One large hand slid gently over her hip, long fingers caressing her bare flesh, pulling her closer to his hot, slick body so she lay half across him.

Callie's breath puffed out in a sigh of astonished bliss. He was strong, tender and generous.

Everything she'd never had from a man.

Everything she'd learned not to expect.

He'd taken her to paradise. Teased and pleasured her until reality shattered in a conflagration of sheer bliss.

She'd never known such intense joy as when she'd soared to ecstasy in his arms. She'd always be grateful for the gift he'd given her today. The shared pleasure that connected her, however briefly, to him. That sense of linkage, even more than the physical delight, warmed her to the core.

She'd felt alone for so long.

From the moment she'd seen him row his dinghy from the gracious old yacht, his wide shoulders gleaming bare and golden in the sun, she'd sensed something different about him. Something special. He epitomised a masculinity so perfect it had sucked the breath from her chest.

She, Callie Manolis, who hadn't looked at a man with desire in seven years! Who'd thought she never would again.

For days she'd tried to ignore the stranger who invaded the seclusion of this private beach. Invaded her refuge. Each morning as she lay under the pine trees, spent from swimming, she attempted to focus on her book. But inevitably her gaze strayed to where he pottered on deck, fished, or swam in the clear waters of the tiny bay.

Even with her eyes shut she'd been aware of him. As he'd been of her.

Had he really needed to ask the way to the track for the nearest village? The sizzling gleam in his eyes told her he hadn't. But for once Callie had warmed to that wholly male glint of appreciation. It hadn't repelled or annoyed her.

He looked the way she felt when she saw him.

Ensnared by his dark, dark eyes, Callie had been like a swimmer adrift on the Aegean, cut off from reality. From her future plans, the pain of the past, even her distrust of men. What did trust matter in the face of this potent attraction? It was extraordinary yet stunningly simple.

Her lips curved against his skin. She couldn't resist the temptation to press a kiss there, tasting his salt tang. A sound between a growl and a purr vibrated from his throat, exactly matching her own sense of lazy triumph.

Perhaps sexual abstinence made this sudden passion so exhilarating. She was twenty-five and he was her second lover. Perhaps that was why...

Thought clogged as his hand moved splay-fingered down her leg. It circled, light as a wind-blown leaf, slipping between their bodies to caress her sensitive inner thigh.

Callie sucked in an astonished breath as the tingling started again deep inside. A jolt of desire pierced her, shocking her to full awareness in an instant.

Heat radiated from his touch as his hand strayed to the place where need had pulsed a short time ago. She gasped as he stroked her, tenderly yet deliberately. Stunned, she felt a shimmer of excitement ripple through her sated body like a rising tide.

'You like that?' There was lazy satisfaction in his deep voice. And a knowledge that told her he knew *exactly* how much she craved his touch.

He understood her reactions better than she. Callie was a novice at this but even a woman so inexperienced recognised a master of the sensual arts.

She flattened her hands on his chest and pushed herself up so she could look down into his face.

A smile lingered on his sensuous lips and his glittering eyes flashed an invitation. His unruly black hair flopped over his brow, in gorgeous disarray after she'd clutched it. Her gaze strayed past his solid jaw to the strong column of his throat. To the reddened patch on his neck.

Was that a love bite? She'd marked him with her teeth? Surely she hadn't been so wild.

'We can't,' she blurted out. 'Not again.'

One sleek black brow rose and he bestowed a slow confident smile that sent a buzz of pleasure through her.

'I wouldn't be too sure of that, little one.'

His questing fingers moved and her body trembled.

Automatically she clamped her fingers around his wrist, intending to drag his hand away. She needed to think. But she couldn't shift him. His arm was all hard bone and muscled strength. His touch was bliss.

'Yes,' he whispered, his gaze fixed on her with searing intensity. 'Hold me while I touch you.'

Callie's eyes widened at his deliberate eroticism. Her heart leapt. The melting warmth between her legs belied her instinctive denial and she squirmed.

After their desperate lovemaking this should be impossible. Yet the feel of his sinewed hand moving beneath hers was…

exciting. As was the burgeoning strength of his arousal against her thighs.

'No.' Her voice was breathless. She squeezed her eyes shut, trying to claim control of her wayward body. 'I have to go. I have to—'

'Shh, *glikia mou*,' he murmured in that seductive, black-velvet voice. He withdrew his hand to cup her face with callused fingers. He stroked the erogenous zone at the corner of her mouth she hadn't known existed till today. 'Relax and enjoy. There's no rush. Nothing more important than this.'

His hand slid to the back of her head and he pulled her inexorably down to meet his mouth. The kiss was long, languorous and seductive. Callie's resistance seeped away like sea water through sand. Her bones melted as her lips opened and he ravaged her mouth with sweet possessiveness.

How could anything so unprecedented feel so right?

'You can leave later,' he murmured against her lips, each word a caress. 'Afterwards.'

Afterwards. The word circled in Callie's hazy brain then disintegrated as she kissed him back. The remnants of self-control dissolved in the heat of rising passion.

It was oh-so-easy to give herself up to the luxury of his expert seduction. To throw away a lifetime's caution and live for the moment. To forget the real world and the harsh lessons she'd learned there. Just for a little longer.

Madness.

That was what it had been, Callie decided as she stood before the mirror in her guest room. Nothing else could explain the way she'd allowed herself to be seduced.

No, not *allowed*. She'd encouraged him, eager for the feel of his tall, muscular body against hers. Impatient to pursue the sensual promise she'd read in his eyes. Eager for the sort of loving she'd never had, and now, to her stunned delight, had experienced for the first time.

With a stranger.

Her eyes rounded and a shudder rippled through her at the

thought of what she'd done. She, the woman the tabloids had once dubbed the Snow Queen, had given herself to a complete stranger in passionate abandon! Not once. Nor twice. But three times, in heart-stopping succession.

Shock and shame flooded her as she remembered in exquisite detail.

Given herself! She grimaced at her reflection. She hadn't even had the grace to be embarrassed that he carried condoms when he'd come ashore today. All she'd felt was relief.

He had a swimmer's body, broad shoulders, slim hips, with long muscled limbs and the easy stride of a man at ease with his strength. The sort of body she'd seen on beaches at home in Australia a lifetime ago. Not what she'd expect on a tiny island off the tourist trail in northern Greece.

She knew gorgeous men. They left her unmoved. Their charm and good looks had never quickened her pulse.

The gossips had been disappointed as for six years she'd remained loyal to her much older husband.

Even the fact that her husband had desired her only as a possession to display and jealously guard hadn't driven her to seek consolation elsewhere. Alkis had been impotent and Callie had buried her libido as well as her emotions during their sterile, unhappy marriage. More, his sick jealousy and frightening outbursts ensured she kept men at a distance. She'd learned to brush off the importunate ones with a cool grace that had become her hallmark.

Never had she felt this fiery yearning when she looked at a man. Until today, just hours ago in the deserted private cove of her uncle's estate.

It had been a momentary insanity, brought on by worry for her aunt's health and stress from this duty holiday under her uncle's roof. By the release of unbearable tension after those dreadful last months with Alkis.

By a lifetime of being what her aunt would describe as a 'good girl', doing what was expected.

Callie's lips quirked in a humourless smile as she met her gaze in the mirror. She didn't look like a good girl now.

She'd done as her uncle insisted, donning a full-length gown, totally over-the-top for a family dinner. She'd piled her hair up and wore the flashy diamond pendant and bracelet set that was all she had left of Alkis' gifts.

But the formal clothes didn't conceal the change in her.

There was high colour in her cheeks, her eyes sparkled over-bright, her lips were plump as if kissed long and hard by an expert. And that look of secret satisfaction surely must betray her.

She should be mortified by what she'd done.

Yet, staring at the stranger in the glass, she knew an overpowering urge to flee. To forget the stuffy dinner her uncle had organised and race barefoot to the beach and find her stranger.

Her lover.

The man whose name she didn't even know.

But she could never do that. Callie had been trained too well. Ruthlessly she subdued the renegade impulse to ignore a lifetime's lessons and run to the man with whom she'd shared her yearning and her inner self.

She'd had her single afternoon of madness. Now it was over and she had to forget him before he swept away all her desperately won defences.

'I want you girls to make a special effort tonight.' Uncle Aristides turned the statement into a threat. He waggled a warning finger at his daughter, standing beside Callie. 'Especially you, Angela. Your mother's unwell again, so you'll stand in for her.' He spoke disapprovingly, as though Aunt Desma had planned to be ill.

Seeing the scowl wedge between her uncle's beetling brows and the miserable look on Angela's face, Callie swallowed a pithy retort. It would be her docile cousin who'd pay if Callie made her uncle angry.

'The evening will be perfect, Uncle. I've checked with the staff. The meal looks superb and the best vintage champagne is on ice. I'm sure your guest will be impressed.'

Her uncle was even more touchy than usual, lashing out furiously at any perceived problem. Poor Angela was already a bundle of nerves, anticipating an explosion.

'I hope so,' her uncle boomed. 'We have an important visitor tonight.' He emphasised the point with a wave of his hand. 'A *very* important guest.'

Callie's stomach sank with foreboding. What *did* he have planned? This was more than a family celebration for her twenty-fifth birthday. Diamonds and designer gowns weren't usual attire, even in this house where oppressive formality was the norm. He was up to something.

His eyes strayed again to Angela and Callie's curiosity twisted into a stab of anxiety. She knew exactly how ruthless her uncle could be, and how devious.

'Don't forget what I said, Angela,' he barked.

Angela's face paled. 'Yes, father.' At eighteen she had none of her father's brash confidence. Callie knew she found it a chore mixing among her father's associates.

Callie stepped forward. 'Tonight will be a success, Uncle. Don't worry, we'll see to it.'

If she had to dredge up every last ounce of patience to smile and listen to one of his cronies bore on about the iniquities of the government or the flaws of the younger generation, she'd do it. Anything to prevent an angry outburst that would force Angela further into her shell.

Aristides Manolis looked Callie up and down as if seeking to find fault. But six years of marriage to a rich man, of mixing in glamorous society, had given her the gloss to shine in any surroundings. And the experience to handle any social situation.

Dinner for four, even with the most demanding, querulous guest, would be no problem at all.

'You will be our hostess,' he said. 'But I don't want Angela fading into the background as she usually does.'

Callie found herself nodding in unison with Angela. She'd only been in this house five days and already she felt the old yoke of submission settling on her shoulders.

Could it really be just hours ago she'd lain naked in the arms of a man? Brazen enough to have sex with him in a secluded grove of pines by the beach?

As soon as her uncle strode from the room, Callie reached for her cousin's hand. It was cold.

'It'll be OK, Angela. I'm here with you.'

Trembling fingers squeezed hers and she felt her cousin's desperation. Then Angela pulled away, head up, back straight, the picture of elegant composure, as expected of the Manolis girls.

It was something the women in her family learned early. To conceal emotion. To appear calm and agreeable, an ornament and an asset to the right man.

The right man. Callie repressed a shudder of horror. Thank heaven that was behind her now. She need never again be the biddable possession of any man, much less a cruel control freak. The knowledge of her new-found independence still took her breath away.

Yet a sixth sense kept Callie on edge. Something was wrong. This wasn't pre-party jitters.

'What is it, Angela? What's the matter?'

Her cousin cast a furtive glance to the doorway. 'This visitor.' Her voice was a shaky whisper. 'Papa is arranging for me to marry him.'

'Arranging to marry?'

Callie's lungs seized as horror gripped her. The world spun chaotically and she grabbed the back of a nearby chair.

The years slid away. Once again she was just eighteen, Angela's age. She stood here, waiting alone for him to arrive. The man her uncle had informed her she had to marry.

Unless she wanted to destroy her family.

'Callie?'

Angela's voice pierced the fog of nightmare reminiscence. Callie blinked, clearing her blurry vision and strove for composure.

Another arranged marriage. Another disaster.

Callie groped for Angela's hand, knowing how much her little cousin needed her now. Remembering…

The sound of the men approaching sliced through her garbled thoughts. Her uncle's forthright tone echoed from the foyer but his guest's voice, though pitched low, was more resonant. It pulsed through her, tightening her stomach muscles with an illusion of familiarity.

She thrust aside the absurd idea. Angela's news had knocked her off balance. As had an unexpected afternoon of passion with the sexiest man on the planet.

How she wished she were with him now, rather than in this suffocatingly opulent room, facing another catastrophe of her uncle's devising.

Callie breathed deep. Angela needed her support. She couldn't give in to weakness no matter how shocked she was.

'Let's get through dinner then talk.' She aimed a reassuring smile at her cousin. 'He can't force you into anything. Remember that.'

Angela looked doubtful but there was no time for further conversation. The men were approaching.

Again the timbre of their visitor's voice caught at something inside Callie. Something that had awakened today beneath the sheltering pines and the sensuously heavy touch of a man. It made her pulse trip to a faster, rackety beat.

Ignoring the strange sensation, she stepped forward. She only managed a single pace before jolting to a stop.

Uncle Aristides wore a wide smile as he looked up at the man beside him, then turned to gesture expansively to the room at large.

'Well, my dears, here is our guest. I'd like to introduce a valued business associate, Damon Savakis.'

Time shattered in splintering, razor-edged shards as Callie saw their visitor. A flutter of reaction started high in her throat and her breath faltered. Her heartbeat raced as she took him in. Surreptitiously she snagged a quick, desperate breath, then another.

She stood frozen, staring as shock slammed into her.

Elegant. That should have described him. He wore his dinner jacket as if born to it, with a debonair grace that proclaimed his utter confidence. But the tailored perfection couldn't conceal the man beneath. A man who vibrated energy and authority. A man with the posture and physical perfection of a born athlete.

His face was breathtaking, a sculpted embodiment of male power and sensuality. Except for one thing: his nose sat slightly askew, as if it had been broken. That only emphasised his charisma and an undercurrent of raw masculinity. This was no charming lightweight, but a man to be reckoned with.

His eyes narrowed as he took her in, a glitter of appraisal barely veiled. That searing look did curious things to her insides.

Callie's mouth dried. Dimly she was aware of her uncle drawing Angela forward for an introduction.

Finally, far too late, she stepped forward, her hand out-stretched as she dredged up a polite greeting.

'How do you do, Kyrie Savakis? It's a pleasure to meet you.'

His warm hand engulfed hers. She repressed a shiver at the echo of memory that sped through her. Of a man touching her, far more intimately, only this afternoon.

She pulled back but his hold was firm and unbreakable, his look piercing.

Dampness hazed Callie's brow as, for an instant, panic flared. Her stomach churned and she gulped down a hard knot in her throat. Then a lifetime's training kicked in. She ignored the jumble of emotions whirling inside and pinned a meaningless smile to her lips.

Damon Savakis' eyes were dark. Darker than brown. Dark as a moonless night. Dark enough to sweep a woman into a whirl-pool of need and longing and hold her there till sanity fled.

Callie knew it because she'd seen them before. Had already experienced the heady invitation of that bold, sensuous gaze.

He spoke at last, his voice brushing across her skin in an intimate tone that made the hairs rise at her neck.

'It's a pleasure to meet you, Callista.' The words were trite, expected, polite. Nothing at all like the searing expression in his fathomless gaze.

Nothing at all like the lazy, sensual approval in his laughing eyes as he'd seduced her a few short hours ago.

CHAPTER TWO

CALLIE'S lungs emptied as his gaze piniomed her.

It *was* him!

There was a roaring sound in her ears, like a jet coming in to land. In the distance her uncle spoke. Yet here, close to *him*, there was nothing but the fire in his eyes. Its impact devastated her, obliterating all thought of what she should do or say. Leaving only a yearning so strong it consumed her.

He was to marry Angela?

Impossible. It was a mistake.

But her uncle didn't make such mistakes.

Callie wanted to smooth her palm along the sharp angle of his jaw to make sure he was real. She wanted to inhale the heady male scent of his burnished skin. She wanted…

No!

Her stomach cramped at the idea of explaining to her uncle how well she already knew his special guest.

This afternoon should have been a moment out of time, a once-in-a-lifetime fantasy. A passing aberration.

Now she was face to face with the man who'd persuaded her to shed every defence she'd used to keep the world, and especially men, at a distance. To keep herself safe.

In a moment of terrifying discovery she realised he had power, real, tangible power over her. She'd let him in, casting aside caution, opening her private, vulnerable self to him. Too late now to slam that door shut again.

This afternoon she'd unwittingly opened a Pandora's box of raw emotion and physical longing. Feelings she'd locked away seven years ago had sprung to life.

And now this hunger, this weakness couldn't be denied.

Hunger for a man who was here to woo her cousin.

What had Callie been to him?

Her stomach somersaulted in distress.

Desperate to break the bond of knowledge and need that pulsed between them, Callie turned, gesturing abruptly to the sofas. Her hand looked steady. Only she knew of the fine tremors running through her body.

'Won't you take a seat?' Her voice was cool, almost without inflection. She prayed that no one else noticed her brittle control over her vocal cords. Tension sank talons into the rigid muscles of her neck and shoulders.

'After you.' He inclined his head and raised his arm behind her back, as if to usher her towards one of the antique French lounges.

Centimetres separated his palm from the silk of her dress, yet she felt his heat, like a phantom caress in the small of her back. Instantly her spine stiffened.

'No, please. Let me get you a drink. What would you like? A cocktail? Wine, sherry? Or something stronger? We have ouzo, brandy…'

He watched her silently, as if he knew nerves made her babble. Gone was the heat in his gaze. Instead his look was speculative.

'Thank you. A whisky.'

Callie moved quickly towards the bar. 'And you, Uncle?'

'Brandy, of course.' There was a snap in his voice, but Callie barely noticed. She was too busy trying to control the trembling in her legs that threatened to buckle her knees.

Disbelief and shock clogged her brain.

She knew the name Damon Savakis. Who didn't? He ran a company that had interests across the globe, in everything from marinas to luxury-yacht production, from exclusive coastal resorts to shipping lines. His wealth matched his uncanny business acumen, his ability to strike at precisely the right moment, turning an ever greater profit. The pundits said he was sharp, ruthless and had the luck of the devil.

More, he was the Manolis company's biggest rival. Surely her uncle had spoken of him as a threat, not a friend?

Why was he staying in their cove on a beautiful but old yacht?

Had he known who she was all this time? She'd been on the family's private estate. But if so surely he'd have mentioned his connection to her uncle.

And his plans to wed Angela.

Unless he'd deliberately withheld the truth. Callie's breath caught.

Had he got a kick out of seducing her, while arranging to marry Angela? Had he laughed at how easy, how gullible she'd been? Did he enjoy watching her flounder for composure?

Bile rose in her throat as bitter memories surged.

Callie had too much experience of powerful men and their diversions. The way they used women. How had she been so stupidly trusting as to forget? Her first real happiness in seven years had been a betrayal.

She fumbled as she reached for the glasses.

'Here. Let me help you,' he murmured from just behind her. A long arm reached out to snag the corkscrew from her hand. 'You prefer wine?'

The words were innocuous, but his breath on her neck sent tingles feathering across her skin. His body behind hers evoked an intimacy that made every hair on her nape rise in anticipation.

Shame washed through her. She couldn't control her reaction.

Curtly she nodded and stepped aside as he uncorked the wine. She was crowded into the corner as he blocked her view of the room, separating her from the others. His heat enveloped her. Callie's nostrils flared as a familiar scent reached her: all male, all too evocative.

'So we meet again, *Callista*.' His whisper was pitched for her ears alone. Yet in that thread of sound she heard the echo of smug satisfaction.

She raised her eyes to meet his then wished she hadn't. They blazed like a dark inferno, scorching her face, her throat, her breasts, in an encompassing survey that told her he remembered this afternoon in vivid detail.

'You're obviously a very versatile woman. What role are you playing tonight?' Disapproval frosted his gaze and his words, making her shiver.

Callie faltered at the unexpected attack. 'What do you mean?'

He shrugged but the intensity of his stare belied the casual gesture. He watched her like a hawk sighting a fieldmouse. 'From wanton to well-bred society girl in an afternoon.' His lips pulled back in what might be a grimace of distaste. 'You look like butter wouldn't melt in your mouth. But just a few hours ago you were seducing a total stranger. Are you always this *adaptable*?'

Callie's vocal cords jammed at his calculated insult. It was true what he said, and yet…after what they'd shared, how could he be so disapproving? Why?

She hadn't been the only one hot and eager down on that beach. How dared he judge her?

'As adaptable as *you*, Kyrie Savakis.' The words nearly choked her.

For an endless moment their eyes meshed. Heat bloomed in her cheeks and she jerked her gaze away, only to find her attention snagging on his hand as he held the wine goblet out to her. He had a workman's hands. Long-fingered but capable, powerful. His grip on the delicate glass should have seemed incongruous. Yet nothing could be further from the truth.

He slid his index finger up the fragile stem then down again. Her mouth dried as she remembered the way he'd touched her nipples with that same finger. The way darts of sensation had rayed out from his touch, making her squirm with delight. The way she'd moaned into his mouth as he'd caressed her and discovered her intimate secrets.

Watching the slow, deliberate movement, feeling the heat of his scrutiny on her flesh made her feel vulnerable. Naked.

Impossible that her body should betray her so. Disgust filled her.

Hurriedly she took the glass from his hand, careful not to brush his fingers. She pushed a tumbler of whisky along the bar towards him.

He was too quick, his hand closing around the glass and her fingers in a grip that made her still.

'What are you doing over there?' her uncle grumbled. 'Callista, you mustn't monopolise our guest.'

'Coming, Uncle,' she called, trying to slide her hand from Damon Savakis' hold.

'What's the matter, Callista? Aren't you glad to see me?' His voice was as seductive as she remembered. As if she'd imagined his disapproval moments ago.

'As a friend of my uncle's you're welcome here,' she said through numb lips, desperately clamping down on the accusations and questions clamouring for release. What did this man want of her? It seemed impossible he was the same warm, exciting lover who'd given her the precious gift of intimacy and tenderness. A wholeness she'd never known.

Damon's eyebrows tilted down in the hint of a frown. His lips thinned a fraction.

'Not a very convincing welcome, *glikia mou*,' he whispered. 'I would have expected something a little *warmer*.'

A ribbon of searing heat curled through her at his endearment in that deep, rich voice. Her weakness horrified her. How could she respond so to a man who had no shame about seducing her while he was here to court Angela? Who chided her for her promiscuity yet played games of innuendo?

Today had stripped her emotionally bare. The experience had overwhelmed her. Physical pleasure had been a vehicle for much deeper feelings, even for a tentative, unexpected sense of healing.

Her stomach cramped so savagely she could barely stand. What had meant so much to her was a sick amusement to him.

At last she managed to slide her fingers from under his and reached for her uncle's brandy. She looked pointedly over Damon's shoulder, hanging on to control by a thread. She would *not* make a scene.

'If you'll excuse me, I'll take this to my uncle. It's time we joined the others.'

He didn't move. His eyes and his body held her trapped. He blocked her exit. She looked away, at the precise bow-tie on his perfect white shirt.

'Are you planning to visit me again tonight, Callista? To ensure I feel truly welcome?' His voice dropped to a low note that resonated through her very bones. There was no mistaking his blatant sexual invitation. The innuendo and exultation.

Panic welled. And distaste. She felt raw and vulnerable.

He'd deliberately tricked her, luring her into betraying her innermost needs and desires. Desires she'd never known before. Now he wanted to gloat. To turn her one bright, glowing slice of heaven into something sordid.

'Callista?'

She looked up into his shadow-dark eyes, catching the gleam of hunger there and a hint of amusement.

He thought this situation funny?

Instantly her spine straightened. Her chin tilted as indignation and hurt heated her blood. She'd had her fill of the malicious games men played. Of being a pawn, subject to a man's whim.

'You want the truth?' she whispered hoarsely. 'You don't belong here, *Kyrie* Savakis. The last thing I want is to be forced to share a meal with a man like you.'

She stepped forward, calling his bluff.

He had no option but to make way.

Yet the flash of surprised anger in his glittering eyes told her he didn't like it.

Tough! He'd had his little game at her expense. No doubt he'd got a kick out of seducing the woman the gossip mags had dubbed 'untouchable'.

Nausea churned in her stomach and an icy chill crawled through her. She'd believed today was precious. An oasis of warmth and comfort in a cold world.

Fool. Hadn't she learned better than to trust a man?

'That is the way you want to play, Callista?'

There was a warning edge to his tone. She ignored it.

'I don't *play*, Kyrie Savakis.'

She had a swift glimpse of narrowed, calculating eyes, of a chin jutting with masculine displeasure.

He was like the rest, expecting her to bow to his whims. But she was her own mistress now, free and independent.

Nevertheless her heart pounded as she walked past him. The sensation of his eyes on her bare back was like a lick of flame down her spine.

How was she going to survive a whole evening with him?

She had a sinking feeling that instead of her defiance dampening his conceit, he thought she'd thrown down the gauntlet.

He didn't look the type to ignore a challenge.

'No, thank you.' Damon shook his head as the servant proffered wine to top up his glass.

'Come, come, Damon.' His host waved an arm impatiently across the table. 'No need to be abstemious. It's not as if you're driving. Drink up, man.' He nodded to the waiter and watched as his own glass was filled with premium vintage champagne. 'You'll only find the best quality in this house.'

'I don't doubt it,' Damon responded. He looked from the uniformed servants clearing away plates to the ostentatious gold cutlery laid with such meticulous precision on the damask tablecloth. Not many people seeing the luxury in which Aristides Manolis lived would suspect how parlous was his financial state. How close he was to ruin.

Damon knew. Damon was the man whose money could save Manolis and his family company.

Or destroy it.

He'd worked his adult life for the day he'd have Manolis in his power. The need to acquire and then take apart his precious company piece by piece had driven Damon for years. Revenge for what this family had done to his would be sweet.

A flash of light caught his eye and he turned. Callista's necklace caught the light. A fabulous piece, white gold and several carats of diamonds. Yet it was too obvious for his taste. Too showy. A blatant statement of wealth.

She reminded him of so many other rich, spoiled women he'd known. It was the cost of the gems that mattered to them, not the merit of the design.

Looking at her now, in her exquisite couture gown, her expression bland, he couldn't believe her the same woman who'd seduced him so wantonly. That woman had revealed such vitality and innate sensuality. There'd been something honest about her abandon. Something warmly generous and, he'd almost believed, *special* about her.

He'd responded to her with a hunger that stunned him. He'd spent the hours since anticipating the next day. When, he'd vowed, he would learn more about the woman who intrigued him more than any lover he could recall.

How could he have been so gullible?

'You're admiring my niece's jewellery?' There was gloating satisfaction in his host's voice. He enjoyed flaunting what he had, or pretended to have. Any man who required two staff members to serve a meal for four was trying too hard to impress. 'It's quite something, isn't it?'

Callista looked up then, her face a polite, gorgeous mask. But when her gaze met Damon's he felt again that visceral pull, the drag of spiralling anticipation.

It infuriated him. He should be able to master this raw craving now he knew who and what she was. A pampered member of the Manolis family who'd targeted what she thought was a bit of rough on the side.

Her sensual abandon, her responsiveness had enchanted him on the beach. But from the moment tonight she'd stared at him with blank eyes and chilly hauteur he'd realised today's interlude had been just a jaded socialite's cheap thrill.

If not something more contrived.

He shot an assessing look from his host to Callista.

'The necklace is stunning,' he murmured.

His gaze followed the fall of diamonds on her pendant, the way they dipped into the valley between her ripe breasts, visible in the low-cut gown.

She knew how to show off her assets. The thought annoyed

him. Or perhaps it was the cool way she surveyed him with those amazing green eyes that infuriated him. He wasn't used to women, particularly women he'd made love to so thoroughly, being indifferent to him. Or telling him he was unworthy to share their table.

One taste of her had left him craving more. He'd planned to look for his siren lover tomorrow. Now he discovered his fantasy woman was nothing but a spoiled rich girl who was ashamed of what they'd shared.

Ashamed of him.

That idea scored his pride, uncovering old wounds he thought he'd buried a lifetime ago. His slow-burning anger ignited at her dismissal, and at the fact he even cared.

Perversely her cool-as-a-cucumber air ignited his desire. He couldn't resist a challenge. Not while she tried to put him in his place like a dirty secret. As if, despite his wealth and power, a blue-blooded Manolis wouldn't sully her fair skin by letting a man with his working-class roots touch her again.

'Alkis' taste was always excellent, wasn't it, my dear?'

'He certainly knew what he wanted, Uncle.' Her voice was crisp and uninflected, as if she discussed tonight's meal rather than the thousands of euros of gems that dripped down to her breasts. She took her wealth and her life of pampered indolence for granted.

'Alkis?' Damon queried.

'My husband.' Her eyes dropped in an expression that might have been demure if not for the flamboyant glitter at her slender neck, ears and wrist.

Her husband. The syllables thrummed in his ears. Something hard and cold lodged in his belly. Fury sizzled along his veins.

He should have guessed. She was a bored society wife, looking for a little diversion. That was what today's escapade had been.

She'd used him.

Unbidden, memories crowded thick, of the days before he'd made his money. When his only assets had been his determination and his flair for commerce. And his looks. Rich women had clustered round him then, eager for adventure, the thrill of walking on the wild side.

As if he'd swallow his pride to be any woman's plaything.

'Your husband isn't here with you?' Damon reined in brewing anger and self-disgust at having given his libido free rein without checking exactly who she was.

Wide eyes lifted to meet his across the table. They were the colour of the sea in the secluded cove where his yacht was moored. The sea whose lapping waves had muffled the sound of this woman's cries of ecstasy as she found release in his arms.

For a moment he felt again that illusion of oneness they'd experienced as their bodies joined. He'd felt more pleasure with her than he could remember with any woman.

That alone stoked his distrust. And his disgust that he'd fallen for the fantasy she projected.

'My husband died some months ago, Kyrie Savakis.' A chill shuttered the momentary warmth in her eyes.

Too late, Callista! She might act the ice maiden now but he'd already discovered the sensuous fire that blazed inside.

Her passion today hadn't been the by-product of grief for her husband. There'd been no shadowy spectre between them, no yearning for the past. Just untrammelled lust.

A merry widow indeed.

'My condolences,' he said and she inclined her head fractionally. She was so aloof. Not a trace of bereavement or even regret. Damon wondered what sort of female could lose a spouse and not feel anything. Instinct told him, whatever she concealed with that cool expression, it wasn't a broken heart.

'Alkis always chose the best,' Manolis boomed. 'Those diamonds are of the finest quality.'

'Really?' Damon leaned forward as if to get a better look. 'They're quite unusual.' If it was unusual to expend a fortune on something so gaudy. 'I don't think I've ever seen anything to match them.'

'They were made to order. Callista, give our guest a closer look. No need to stand on ceremony, girl.'

'Uncle, I'm sure he doesn't really want to see—'

'On the contrary,' Damon cut across her. 'I'd very much like to see them up close.' If the Manolis clan was vulgar enough to flaunt its apparent wealth, he was happy to take advantage of the fact.

He watched a swift unreadable glance pass between Callista and her silent cousin. Then she rose and walked round the table towards him.

Her exquisite body shimmered seductively and his groin tightened. Lamplight caught thousands of tiny silver beads on her dress. Each step accentuated her lithe lines and sultry curves in a shifting play of light. His muscles tensed with the effort of sitting still and not reaching out to touch. To claim her as, even now, he hungered to do.

When she stood before him he caught a waft of scent that he knew retailed for an exorbitant price. He'd bought some as a parting gift for his last mistress.

He got up, annoyance flaring as he realised he preferred the fresh, natural fragrance of her bare skin this afternoon. The artificial scent masked that.

Yet it served to remind him the woman he'd met earlier, the woman he'd been drawn to, was a fake.

Callista stood, her breasts rising and falling rapidly, making the stones flash and glitter. To his mind she'd look better without them. Just bare golden skin to match the dark-honey hair piled up in a chic style behind her head.

Damon reached for one drop earring. She trembled and the stones scintillated. The fine hairs on her arms stood up, signalling her awareness of him. It couldn't be a chill on a night so warm. Damon's body stirred, attuned to her tension.

He enjoyed the knowledge that she wasn't as calm in his presence as she appeared.

'Remarkable,' he murmured, stepping in so his body almost touched hers, as if to view the heavy pendant. Instead his eyes traced her décolletage. His palms itched as he remembered the bounty of her breasts in his hands.

'They are, aren't they?' Manolis' voice had a self-congratulatory ring. 'Alkis always got his money's worth.'

'I'm sure you're right.' Damon stared into her sea-green gaze, close enough now for him to note again the gold flecks that had dazzled him earlier.

What had her price been?

He'd realised now, remembered the story. A pity he hadn't made the connection earlier today. His enquiries about the Manolis family had revealed only a daughter, no scandalous niece.

This was the woman who at nineteen had been the talk of Athens when she married a rich Greek-American more than old enough to be her father. She'd cashed in her youth and good looks for his wealthy lifestyle and prestigious name, selling herself as a trophy wife.

Damon had been in the Pacific at the time, finalising work on a luxury marina complex. On his return everyone had talked of the match. Now he knew why. Callista was stunning, one of the loveliest women he'd met.

His lips twisted wryly. Like her name, Callista was most beautiful. But that gorgeous body hid a strong mercenary streak. A heartlessness that had enabled her to sell herself for a life of pampered luxury.

Deliberately he turned away, catching the startled gaze of the other woman present. 'But sometimes it's not fabulous jewels that are most alluring,' he said in a low voice. 'Sometimes a more natural style is the most attractive.'

He caught the sound of a hastily stifled gasp beside him. Callista would be used to holding centre stage at the expense of her quiet cousin. She must have read the insult in his words.

'You're right, Damon. Absolutely right.' Manolis boomed in that over-hearty voice as Callista resumed her seat on the other side of the table, her face expressionless. 'Sometimes true beauty is more subtle.'

Subtlety wasn't a trait Damon's host possessed. There was no mistaking his eagerness as he extolled his daughter's virtues, as if she were a thoroughbred in an auction ring. Nor could Damon miss the younger girl's embarrassment as her father's bluff en-comiums continued so long.

Damon's eyes narrowed as he sized up the situation.

Did Aristides think he, Damon Savakis, who could take his pick of women, would be interested in a shy little mouse who couldn't even look at him without blushing? Under her father's watchful gaze she stumbled into halting conversation of the blandest sort. Then Manolis began blathering about the importance of family connections, of trust between those who had personal as well as commercial interests in common.

Damon's lips firmed. So that was the way the wind blew. Manolis hoped Damon would fix his interest on his host's daughter.

The man was mad.

Or, perhaps, more desperate than he'd realised. Did he know Damon intended to dismantle his company?

Damon's gaze flicked to Callista. If their passion had meant anything she couldn't be happy about her uncle's matchmaking plans. Yet she looked regal and unruffled, if a trifle stiff. Her message was clear: she'd had her little adventure but now it was over.

Had she acted on her own behalf when she offered herself to him today? A rich woman looking for a tumble with what she thought was a working-class lover? His mouth tightened in distaste. He'd met the sort years ago.

Or had Aristides Manolis planned her convenient visits to the isolated cove?

The notion had been at the back of Damon's mind from the moment he'd found her here, glittering from head to toe like some provocative Christmas gift. The suspicion had made him lash out at her when he arrived, even as he crowded close, unable to keep his distance.

Had Manolis discovered Damon's early arrival to enjoy a low-key, incognito break while recuperating from flu? Had Manolis decided to soften him up before the negotiations began, using his niece as bait? It was the sort of underhand ploy he'd expect from a man like him.

If so, Manolis had miscalculated badly. While she didn't mind slumming it with a stranger for hot sex, obviously her aristocratic pride revolted at having to socialise publicly with a man with working-class roots.

Anger seethed beneath Damon's skin.

Had she bartered her favours to help her uncle, just as she'd bartered her body for a rich husband?

Disgust was a pungent bitterness on Damon's tongue.

Manolis was desperate. Soon Damon would take over the Manolis family company, lock, stock and barrel. The notion warmed the part of his soul that, despite his enormous success, could never quite let go of the past.

There would be satisfaction in crushing Aristides' pretensions and obliterating him commercially.

He was minded to leave and delegate the negotiations to his lawyers. Only curiosity had prompted him to come. He remembered the awe with which his parents had spoken of the Manolis family that employed his father and grandfather. The company that had finally destroyed them.

Times had changed and the mighty had fallen. Now Damon was the powerful one, the man whose word could make or break this family.

Nothing he'd seen tonight made him feel anything but contempt for his hosts.

And yet…he looked at Callista, felt the slide of her cool gaze glance off his face as she turned to her cousin. Her lips tilted in a half-smile that made his stomach tighten and his breath catch.

Whatever her motives, she'd used him, played him for a fool.

His male pride demanded satisfaction. Damon Savakis was used to calling the shots, not being manipulated.

Yet even now his body hungered for hers with a raw, aching need. This wasn't over. It couldn't be over while he still felt this tide of desire.

He decided in that moment to accept Manolis' offer of hospitality and stay on. Not because the commercial negotiations demanded his presence.

It was business of a much more personal nature he intended to pursue.

CHAPTER THREE

'WHAT do you mean my trust fund is frozen? It can't be.' Only by a supreme effort did Callie keep her voice steady as she stared at her uncle across his over-sized desk. 'I inherit the day I reach twenty-five. That's today.'

He didn't meet her eyes.

That was a bad sign. Usually Aristides Manolis bullied his way out of answering awkward questions. The fact that he didn't attempt it this time set alarm bells ringing. Plus he'd gone to such lengths to avoid a private conversation all week. Finally he'd summoned her to his study after they'd farewelled Damon Savakis.

She shivered despite the sultry air wafting through the open windows. Damon Savakis was someone she didn't want to think about.

Her nerves were raw from an evening of stilted conversation with the man who'd alternately treated her with polite conde-scension and devoured her with his gaze. The man she'd actually trusted for a few short hours.

'On your birthday, that was the plan,' her uncle said, shifting a silver letter opener. 'But circumstances have changed.'

Callie waited, every instinct alert. But he refused to continue.

'No, Uncle. Not a plan. It's the law.' She took a calming breath. 'My parents set up the trust when I was a baby. Today I inherit the estate they left me.'

She had precious little left of her parents. Memories and a

well-worn photo album. When she'd come to live with her Greek relatives, a grief-stricken fourteen-year-old from the other side of the world, her uncle had brusquely informed her that her parents' home would be sold with its contents. It was an unnecessary luxury, he'd declared, storing furniture. Better to plough the proceeds into the fund she'd inherit.

Callie had arrived with only a suitcase and her new lime-green backpack. The one her mum had bought for the sailing holiday they'd planned.

A jagged shaft of pain shot through her, drawing her up straight. Even now memory of that loss had the power to hurt.

'You'll get your inheritance, Callista. It will just take time to organise. I had no idea you'd be in such a rush to access the funds.' His voice had a belligerent, accusing ring. 'What about the money Alkis left you?'

'Alkis left his fortune to his children, as you well know. I'm sure that was covered in your negotiations over my marriage.' A tinge of bitterness crept into her voice. She cleared her throat, determined not to get sidetracked. 'What was left I spent paying his debts. Which is why I want to sort this out. I need the money.'

Callie had plans for her future but she needed her money to achieve them. She'd sell the last of her gaudy jewellery when she left here and put the cash to good use, starting a small retail business. She'd make her own decisions and run her life without interference.

She'd learned her lesson. The only way to be happy was to rely on no one but herself. She knew what she wanted and nothing was going to stop her achieving her goal.

For the first time in years she felt energised and excited, looking forward to the challenges, hard work and satisfaction of building something of her own.

'Perhaps I should just call the family lawyers and—'

'No!' The word was a bellow that made her pulse jump. Her uncle wrenched his tie undone and slumped back in his chair. 'You were always headstrong and difficult. Why can't you wait instead of badgering me about this?'

Years of practice kept Callie's face impassive though her blood boiled. Headstrong! Over the years she'd allowed the men in her life to lead her from one hell into another. If anything she'd been too submissive, too stoic. She'd had enough, starting now.

'Clearly I'm distressing you, Uncle,' she said in her coolest tone. 'Don't disturb yourself. I'll go to Athens tomorrow and sort out the legalities myself.'

There was something akin to hatred in his glare. 'It won't do you any good. There's nothing there.'

Callie felt the blood drain from her face. Her uncle never joked, especially about money.

'Don't look at me like that,' he snarled. 'You'll get it. As soon as this deal with Damon Savakis is finalised.'

'What's he got to do with my inheritance?' The freeze she'd felt earlier clamped tight round her chest.

'The family company…hasn't been doing well for some time. There have been difficulties, unexpected labour and resource costs, a market downturn.'

Strange the downturn affected only the Manolis company when rival ones, like Savakis Enterprises, were booming. Aristides Manolis wouldn't expect his niece to know that. He thought the women in his family empty-headed and incapable of understanding even the rudiments of business.

'And so?' Callie sank into a chair, grateful for its support. Her knees felt like jelly.

'So when the deal with Savakis goes through, this…temporary cash crisis will be rectified.'

'No, Uncle. Even if the deal succeeds, that doesn't explain my trust fund.'

Aristides' fingers tightened on the paper knife with barely repressed violence. His gaze slid away. 'Things were so difficult with the company; I had to find a way to keep it afloat. A temporary measure to tide us over.'

A burning knot of emotion lodged in Callie's throat, choking her, making it difficult to breathe. She squeezed her eyes shut, hearing only her desperately thudding pulse.

How many times would this man betray her?

Why had she naïvely believed that finally, for the first time in her life, things would work out right?

Greed and betrayal. Those were the constant themes in her adult life. You'd think she'd have learned to expect them by now. Yet the shock and hurt, the disbelief, were as overwhelming now as they'd been each time she'd been victim of a man's duplicity.

Wearily she opened her eyes and gazed at the mottled face of her dead father's brother. The one man who, above all, she should have been able to trust.

'You stole my inheritance,' she whispered.

'Callista Manolis! Recall your place! Now that your husband is dead I'm the head of your family.'

'I know who you are.' She thrust aside the panic, the distress, the sheer pain of this ultimate betrayal. 'And *what* you are.' His eyes bulged but he said nothing. 'I thought you'd have more pride than to steal from your own family.'

His fist smashed down on the desk but Callie didn't even blink. 'It wasn't stealing. It was a temporary redistribution of funds. You wouldn't understand—'

'I understand you're a thief,' she said, holding his gaze till he looked away. 'As my trustee you were supposed to behave legally and ethically.'

Callie battled rising fury. She was tempted to report him to the authorities, now, tonight. To see just one of the men who'd used her for their own purposes brought to book.

But the thought of her cousin and her dear aunt stopped her. Justice would hurt them and it wouldn't get her inheritance back.

'The money will be available soon.' His voice was as close to pleading as she'd ever heard it. 'With interest. When this deal goes through.'

'You're expecting Damon Savakis to bail you out of strife?' Hysterical laughter bubbled up inside her. 'His reputation is formidable—as a winner, not for compassion to rivals. He has no interest in helping you.'

'But we won't be rivals.' Aristides leaned forward, his plump hands splayed on the polished wood. 'If my plans go as I expect, Damon Savakis will be more than a business associate. He'll be a member of the family.'

* * *

The sound of voices at the poolside stopped Callie in her tracks. Her cousin Angela and Damon Savakis. No other man could unsettle Callie with the low rumble of his laughter. His deep tones made something shiver into life in the pit of her stomach.

Only yesterday, with her face pressed to his broad chest, she'd felt his lazy amusement bubble up and emerge as a deep chocolate caress of sound. Through a haze of sensual satiation it had made her feel vibrantly alive.

Her fingers clenched as desire pulsed again.

She was a fool. He'd used her for cheap amusement in the most calculating way. She'd taken him at face value, believing he, like she, had been blown away by an attraction too strong to be denied.

She suspected with Damon Savakis nothing would ever be simple.

His behaviour last night punctured that foolish daydream. He'd found her amusing. Her confusion and distress had added spice to the evening. How piquant, having his lover and soon-to-be-fiancée together.

She knew his reputation for meticulous attention to detail. Impossible that he hadn't known who she was on the beach. Members of the Manolis family would have been basic research.

But he'd kept his identity a secret, enjoying the joke on her. Seducing the woman dubbed the Snow Queen must have been diverting to an appetite jaded by over-eager women. Watching her squirm last night had been a bonus to a man who revelled in power.

The sort of man she detested.

She straightened her shoulders.

'Good morning, Angela. Kyrie Savakis.' She bestowed a brief smile as she approached the table where she and Angela often shared a meal. No chance now of a private chat. They'd missed their opportunity last night when Uncle Aristides called her to him. Afterwards Callie hadn't found Angela. She hated to think of her alone and distressed.

'Sorry I'm late. I didn't realise we had a guest.'

'Kyrios Savakis is staying with us for a few days,' Angela said quietly, sending a shiver of apprehension down Callie's spine.

A few days! This got worse and worse.

'He arrived for breakfast.' Angela sounded calm and relaxed, a perfect hostess. Only someone who knew her well would realise her discomfort, her fingers busy pleating the linen tablecloth, her body a fraction too poised.

Callie's heart stalled as guilt smote her. She hadn't thought of her poor, shy cousin acting as hostess alone. She'd slept late after a night grappling with what her uncle had conceded about their bleak financial situation. Reliving the horror of discovering Damon's identity and true character.

'Your uncle kindly invited me to sample more of your hospitality,' a deep voice murmured from across the table.

Did she imagine a wry emphasis on the last two words? As if he referred to a service she might personally provide?

He couldn't be so crass. Could he?

Slowly Callie turned to face him, ignoring the escalating thud of her pulse.

He looked disgustingly self-satisfied. Like a man whose appetites had been sated. Callie was horrified at the drift of her thoughts. She forced a smile to her lips, hiding her shudder of reaction as she drank in the sight of him.

Despite her anger, he looked good enough to eat.

If you had a taste for danger.

He wore a white shirt open at the throat, designer jeans and an expression that proclaimed him utterly at home as he leaned back in his seat.

'I was about to show Kyrie Savakis the guest bungalow,' Angela explained.

The guest bungalow? Thank heaven. At least they wouldn't share a house.

'Please, call me Damon. Kyrie Savakis makes me feel like I belong to your father's generation. There's no need for formality.'

But there is, Callie thought, sliding a glance at Angela.

Even after a night coming to grips with her uncle's outrageous plot, Callie couldn't suppress horror at how history repeated itself so appallingly. Her skin crawled. It was a nightmare that he'd use such a scheme a second time.

'Thank you, Damon. Please call me Angela.'

'Angela.' He bestowed a brief smile then turned to spear Callie with his dark, questioning gaze.

'Technically speaking, you *do* belong to another generation.' Callie said before he could speak to her. 'You're in your late thirties, aren't you? Angela is just eighteen.'

Dark brows inched together, then his lips quirked in what looked suspiciously like humour rather than annoyance. 'I'm thirty-four, since you're wondering,' he murmured.

'Really? So—er—young?' Callie arched her brows as if in surprise. She knew when he was born. She'd looked him up on the net last night. He was too old for Angela. As well as the years between them, there was a gulf of experience and expectation that would never be breached. Callie knew it from bitter personal experience.

'Old enough to know my mind, Callie.' The sound of her name on his lips sent a shock wave trembling through her, like the silent aftermath of a sensory explosion. 'May I call you Callie? Or would you prefer Callista?'

She'd prefer neither. Both were far too intimate, especially when he used that smoke and velvet tone guaranteed to seduce a woman out of her senses in thirty seconds flat.

Yesterday just the sound of his voice and the slumberous promise in his eyes had her eager for his touch.

'I…' It was on the tip of her tongue to tell him to use her full name, when she caught Angela's anxious gaze. 'Of course, call me Callie.'

She was only Callista to her uncle, who managed to invest the syllables with disappointment and disapproval.

'Thank you, Callie.' His ebony eyes gleamed with a light she couldn't interpret. His expression sent awareness tingling through her blood. It took a moment for her to realise Angela had turned to talk to one of the staff.

'Would you excuse me?' She rose from her seat. 'There's a phone call I need to take.'

Callie saw the blush on Angela's cheeks and knew Niko must have rung. The son of a local doctor, he'd loved Angela for years. He was building his tourism business, hoping to win Uncle Aristides' approval for their marriage.

Callie knew better than anyone Aristides would never countenance his daughter marrying a local boy, no matter how decent or how much in love they were. Money and status were what mattered to her uncle.

Her gaze shifted to Damon Savakis, lolling in his seat sipping coffee. She felt anxiety shimmy down her spine, knowing what Aristides planned for his daughter.

With those dark good looks and air of leashed power, Damon could model for a pasha of old, accustomed to sumptuous luxury, sensuous pleasures and unquestioning obedience. He'd devour poor Angela in one snap of his strong white teeth then seek amusement elsewhere. As he'd found it yesterday, seducing Callie then playing games of innuendo through the long evening while she squirmed and suffered.

One sacrificial lamb in the family was enough! Callie had performed that function for the Manolis clan years ago. They couldn't demand another.

She refused to watch her uncle ruin his daughter's life with an arranged marriage as he'd ruined hers. Especially when Angela had a chance for happiness with an honest, caring man. That sort of man was as rare, in her experience, as a snowstorm on Santorini.

'Don't hurry, Angela. I'll look after our guest.'

'That sounds promising.'

'Pardon?' Callie turned to find Damon surveying her with a smile that didn't reach his eyes.

'I like the idea of you,' he drawled, 'looking after me. What did you have in mind?'

Heat danced in that calculating expression. His gaze trawled down to her jade top gathered in a knot below the bust, and lower to her bare midriff. Fire blazed over her skin as if he stroked his callused palm over her flesh.

Only yesterday…

Callie shoved back her chair, ignoring the juice she'd poured. 'Showing you the guest bungalow,' she said in a voice that was almost steady.

When he looked at her that way she couldn't prevent the surge of reaction as her body came alive.

She wished she'd worn something other than lightweight trousers and a skimpy top. If she'd known he was here she'd have opted for a full-length tunic dress. But the gleam in his eyes told her it would have done no good. He remembered what she looked like naked.

Just as she remembered him.

He stood, his long, athletic frame unfolding from the chair. She had instant, dazzling recall of how he'd looked yesterday, all burnished skin and honed, hard-packed muscle.

She drew a shuddering breath and looked away, trying to control the riot of hormones clamouring for gratification.

'Ah, Callie, is that all?' One long finger traced the side of her neck and she jumped, jerking out of reach. 'I'd hoped for something a little more…intimate.'

'You—' she sucked in a ragged gasp '—are pushing your luck!'

She lifted her chin, summoning the veneer of composure she'd perfected over the last few years. Ruthlessly she ignored the effervescent sensation of burgeoning desire and strolled to the edge of the terrace, back straight and face composed. It horrified her to discover how difficult it was to don her defensive armour. Only when she had her voice under control did she pause.

'The guest quarters are this way.'

Damon watched her precede him down the lawn. Her hips swayed seductively and his hungry gaze focused on the delicious curve of her *derriere*, shown off perfectly by tight white trousers. Had she worn them to tease? Even in the bright sunlight he saw no panty line to mar the snug fit of cotton against flesh. Did she wear a thong or was she naked beneath the trousers?

Heat roared through him in an infuriating surge. Wasn't it

enough she'd kept him awake all night? He'd been angry at how she'd used then rejected him, yet needy for another touch, another taste of her gorgeous body. Even the fact that she'd snubbed him hadn't doused his libido.

'Are you coming?' She stopped and half turned, showing her patrician profile. Even with her hair in a high pony-tail she looked as if she'd stepped from the pages of a glossy magazine, the sort his mother enjoyed. Beautiful, privileged people leading beautiful, privileged lives.

Privileged himself now, with more money and power than a man could ever need, still Damon felt the gulf between himself and such people. It was a gulf he'd consciously created, resisting the artificial lure of 'society'.

He enjoyed his wealth, made the most of what it bought him and those he cared for, but he'd vowed never to succumb to the shallow posturing and brittle selfishness of that world. He'd seen enough as a kid when his mother cleaned villas owned by some of the country's wealthiest families. When as a teenager he'd worked there and learned first-hand about the morals of the upper classes.

Damon was proud of his roots, unashamed that he'd succeeded by hard work and perseverance, not inherited wealth. He'd long ago learned the high-class world of the 'best' people hid an underbelly of greed, selfishness and vice. The last thing on his agenda was attraction to a woman who epitomised that money-hungry shallowness. A woman who'd inherited the Manolis family values.

The fact that he still wanted her annoyed the hell out of him.

'I'm right behind you, Callie.'

He strode to where she waited, mirroring her body with his. He was close enough to feel warmth radiate from her. He leaned forward, head inclined to inhale her scent.

If he'd hoped to discomfit her he was disappointed. With a swish of her pony-tail she led the way in a long-legged stride, riveting his gaze. It took a moment to realise that instead of the rich perfume she'd worn last night, the scent filling his nostrils was the intoxicating fragrance she'd worn yesterday: sunshine and musky, mysterious female.

Lust jagged through him, a blast of white-hot energy.

It confirmed the decision he'd come to last night—there was unfinished business between them. She couldn't brush him aside like some nonentity when she'd had her fill.

'Your colouring is unusual.' He followed her, eyes on the swing of dark-honey hair as it caught the light. He'd picked her for a foreign tourist when he'd first seen her.

She shrugged. 'Maybe I dye my hair.'

'Ah, but Callie, we both know you don't.' The golden-brown triangle of hair he'd uncovered when he stripped away her bikini bottom yesterday had been the genuine thing. 'I've seen the proof, remember? Up close and personal.'

He let satisfaction colour his voice and wasn't surprised when she slammed to a stop ahead of him.

For a moment she stood still, her shoulders curiously hunched. Then she swung round and met his gaze. Not by the slightest sign did she reveal embarrassment. Her eyes were the colour of cool mountain water, her expression bland. No doubt she was free and easy enough not to feel discomfort discussing personal details with her latest paramour.

What a merry dance she must have led her husband. Had he died trying to satisfy her? Or had he been forced to watch her with younger men who gave her what he couldn't?

'Just as I know your colouring is black as sin,' she murmured. 'So what?' Her brows rose as if she was bored.

'It's uncommon for Greek women to be so fair.' He stepped close enough to see the smatter of gold shards in her irises, like spangles of sunlight amongst the green.

'Half Greek. My mother was Australian.' Her words were clipped, as if he'd delved into something private. He waited for her to continue. 'Besides, some people here in the north have fairer colouring. All the Manolis family are the same.' Her gaze settled on his dark locks as if disapproving.

'Your cousin's hair is brown. There's no comparison.'

He watched her open her mouth as if to shoot off a riposte, then stop herself. She shrugged and turned away. 'Now, if I've satisfied your curiosity—'

'Not yet. Tell me,' he drawled, 'why keep me at arm's length? Surely after yesterday I'm entitled to a little more warmth. Are you one of those women who need the thrill of a secret assignation to fire her blood? Are you turned on by the possibility of being found *in flagrante delicto*?'

Callie stared at the sprawling bungalow a hundred metres down the path and knew it would be a miracle if she made it there with her temper and her composure in place.

Fire her blood, indeed!

Yet she shrank from the suspicion that maybe he was right. Maybe the thrill of desire that had swept her doubts and defences away yesterday was a result of their anonymity and the unspoken daring of their actions.

She shut her eyes, remembering the delicious excitement as he'd walked towards her through the dappled shade, his eyes never leaving hers so she felt the tug of his powerful personality like a living force. Without pause or hesitation he'd pulled her into his arms as if she belonged there. She'd welcomed each caress with a fervour that frightened her now.

Nothing had ever seemed so right, so perfect.

Callie snapped open her eyes. She'd given him too much already. She wouldn't let him toy with her while he played games of one-upmanship with her uncle. While he decided whether to take her cousin in a cold-blooded business deal.

She was done with being a pawn in any man's machinations.

'You're not *entitled* to anything from me.'

She fixed him with the cool look she'd perfected long ago to hide desperately churning emotions. Alkis had had no patience with emotion in his wife. Retreat behind her façade of indifference had been a hard-won but necessary survival skill.

'I disagree. After yesterday your attitude is downright unfriendly.'

Damon paced closer. She had to lift her head to hold his gaze. His heat curled round her like an invitation. The scent of soap, sea and healthy male enticed her till it was an effort not to reach out needy fingers for one last caress.

Callie slid her hands into her trouser pockets lest she be tempted to do something insane like touch him.

'Yesterday is over.'

'But what we had needn't be.' His low, seductive voice pierced her brittle façade. He made her yearn again for the delicious torment of his touch.

That terrified her.

'It's over,' she repeated, wishing she believed it.

'And if I'm not ready to end it?' His look was arrogant.

'There was nothing to end.' The words tumbled out. She had to concentrate on slowing down, maintaining her calm. 'We had sex. That's all.'

'Just sex.' His brows winged up and she thought she saw fury blaze in his eyes. Then the moment was gone and his face was unreadable. 'Is that what you specialise in, Callie? Hot sex with strangers you forget the next day?'

Her skin crawled with embarrassment and rage. Yet she knew better than to show it. She let her gaze drop to his shoulders, his wide chest, the powerful length of his arms and legs, then slowly up as if she were used to inspecting the finer points of a sexy male body.

'I could say the same for you,' she said, silently cursing the dry mouth that made the words come out too husky. 'You got what you wanted yesterday. End of story.'

'You're wrong, my fine lady. It's not the end at all.'

A tremor ran through her body, drawing each muscle tight with…anticipation? Excitement?

No! She refused to play his games of seduction and temptation. Yesterday had been a terrible error of judgement. She'd broken every precept, her own moral code, for a few hours' passion. It had been momentary insanity.

She should have guessed nothing was as pure and simple as it had seemed at the time.

'Believe me, Kyrie Savakis, it's over. Why not move on?' Callie had no doubt by nightfall he'd find another woman eager to become a notch on his bedpost. As she had been yesterday. Her chest constricted painfully.

'Because I'm a man who gets what he wants, *glikia mou*. You've whetted my appetite and I want more.'

His lips curved in a hungry smile that sent fear trickling down her spine.

'I want you, Callie. And I intend to have you.'

CHAPTER FOUR

WHAT the hell had got into him? Even as the words emerged from his mouth, Damon questioned his sanity.

She wasn't the sort of woman he wanted in his life.

Nothing he'd learned about her was positive.

Except for the ecstatic, uninhibited way she responded to sex. In that department she packed enough punch to flatten even his formidable self-control.

The unvarnished truth was once with Callie Manolis wasn't enough. Despite his scruples and his anger he wanted her. Still. More. Again.

He cursed his weakness but couldn't pull back. His need was primal, stronger than reason.

Her eyes widened. Her mouth sagged and he fantasised about plundering it with an urgent kiss that would lead to other, more satisfying activities.

'Your threats don't frighten me.' Yet her voice was husky. She *was* frightened.

Or turned on. Damon's body tensed on the thought.

'No threat. A promise.'

'You have no hold over me.' She lifted her head and bestowed a blazing look, like an Amazon queen, defiant and proud. 'I run my own life. *No* man tells me what to do.'

She gestured to the bungalow at the end of the path. 'I'm sure you can find your own way, Kyrie Savakis.' Then she turned and left him. She strolled easily as if she'd done no more than dismiss a servant.

No one dismissed Damon Savakis.

Yet he silently applauded her nerve. Not many people stood up to Damon.

She fascinated him. He wanted to smash past her poise and warm her body with his till the heat consumed them both.

He tucked his hands into the pockets of his jeans rather than haul her into his arms and force her submission with a direct, passionate assault.

That would be too easy, too crude. He wanted the satisfaction of her coming to him, begging for his attention.

In twenty-four hours Callista had become more than a challenge. She was fast becoming an obsession. Despite her disdain. Despite who she was. Or perhaps because of it.

Old anger stirred. His grandfather and his father had slaved for the Manolis family, wrecking their health for little pay. His grandfather had worked himself into an early grave. When Damon's father died in an industrial accident in the Manolis shipyards his mother had received condolences, a company representative at the funeral and none of the compensation she was entitled to. Lawyers had exploited a loophole to absolve the company of responsibility. As if it wasn't a matter of conscience and honour. As if his father's death had been another entry in a ledger.

Damon had directed his anger into his quest for success, ensuring his family was never again as vulnerable as when he was fifteen, the eldest of five fatherless children.

Was it any wonder he enjoyed watching Aristides Manolis scamper to please him? Or revelled in the idea of Callista Manolis, so dismissive, bending to his will?

Her damnable coolness set the seal on her fate.

Damon would make her confess her desire. He'd take her again, just long enough to have his fill. Then he'd dump her, leaving her craving more. Craving what she couldn't have.

Callie walked up the hill, resisting the instinct to run. The knowledge that he watched her gave her courage not to flee. That and the fact that her knees trembled so hard it was a supreme effort to move at all.

She felt his hot, possessive gaze like a touch. That proprietorial sweep of her body with eyes so black she fell into oblivion whenever they held hers. Despite her fury her traitorous body was alive with fizzing awareness.

She'd given herself blithely, not realising the danger.

Now she couldn't escape until she sorted out her inheritance. Without that she couldn't realise her dream of establishing a small business and supporting herself.

That dream had kept her going through the cruel years of marriage. It had given her hope. It was too precious to give up. Yet all she could do now was pray her uncle's deal went through and, miraculously, Damon rejected his matchmaking.

She stumbled to a stop as realisation slammed into her. Only Damon's money could save her plans for the future.

Thank God he had no idea. He was unscrupulous enough to use her vulnerability against her.

The sound of weeping interrupted her thoughts. Following it, she came to a secluded grove. There, to her dismay, she found Angela huddled on a bench, shoulders hunched.

Callie froze, memories swamping her.

Déjà vu. Seven years ago she'd come here to sob out her broken heart when the love of her life betrayed her. She'd thought nothing could eclipse her pain and disillusionment.

How naïve she'd been. That had just been the beginning.

'Angela! What is it, sweetie?' She hurried forward and wrapped an arm round her cousin's unsteady shoulders.

'It's Papa,' she sniffed. 'He knew I'd been talking to Niko. He was furious.' She slumped and Callie drew her close.

'He's forbidden you to see Niko?'

Angela nodded.

'Go on.' Callie's heart was leaden. She'd hoped it wouldn't come to this. Her uncle had let slip last night that Damon hadn't yet agreed to the marriage.

'He won't listen, doesn't care that Niko and I love each other.' Angela wailed. 'He says I have to save the family and the company.'

Callie's arm tightened.

'I tried to reason with him.' Angela's voice was ragged and

Callie's chest squeezed, knowing what it had cost her cousin to stand up to her bullying father. 'I said Damon wouldn't be interested in me. I'm not glamorous like you. That only made him angrier. He said Damon wanted children with someone obedient and docile. Someone from a good family to connect him with the right sort of people.'

Callie cringed at her uncle's prejudiced views. As if Damon needed marriage to secure his place in society! His authority and massive wealth gave him entrée wherever he cared to go. Her uncle was a troglodyte.

But in one thing he was right: men still bartered wealth to possess women. Her uncle had cashed in on Alkis' obsession with Callie to shore up the family coffers last time he'd mismanaged the company. Callie had been naïve enough to fall in with his wishes, for the good of the family. She'd thought her life over at eighteen and hadn't realised the yoke she'd put around her neck, marrying a man as cruel and controlling, and as insecure as Alkis.

'Papa said a man took a wife to bear children and make life comfortable. That Damon would look elsewhere for…for…'

'Shh, Angela. It's all right.' Bitter fury surged in Callie's veins at her uncle's callousness, treating them like pawns. At the ruthless men who joined his devious games.

'But it's not. If I don't obey we'll lose everything. The house. Everything. And Mama is so sick, more than Papa realises. If she needs treatment…'

Angela sat up, breaking Callie's embrace. Her face was pale and set, despite the tears tracking down her cheeks.

With a last hug Callie let her arm drop, watching Angela's drawn face with foreboding. Despite her quivering mouth there was resolution in the tight angle of her jaw.

'You're not alone, Angela. Remember that. I'll help.'

'But what can you do? What can either of us do?'

Callie stood and reached out a hand. Angela let Callie pull her up. 'Don't give up yet. We'll find something.'

Whatever it took she'd find a way to save her cousin.

She couldn't let Angela endure what she, Callie, had. She'd walk over hot coals to prevent it.

Callie's lips thinned in a grimace of determination.

She'd get down on her knees and beg Damon Savakis, if that was what it took.

'Thank you, Callie.' Damon accepted the cold drink, deliberately encircling her slim fingers.

She jumped and sticky juice cascaded over their hands.

Her nerves were frayed, he saw with satisfaction. Her touch-me-not composure crumbled after days playing hostess to him. The business could have been concluded in a few hours but Damon had let Manolis drag out discussions, since it meant having Callie at his beck and call.

At first he'd thought she'd run. He'd been ready for a chase. Instead the hunt had become a slow siege, a war of attrition. With each day the flicker of hunger in his belly grew to a blaze as he sensed her defences weaken.

She tugged her hand. Damon didn't release her but got up from the poolside chair, fingers still wrapped around hers.

'Sorry,' she murmured, her gaze skating from his then back again. 'I've spilled it. I'll go and get a cloth.'

'No need.'

'But I—'

'Let me.'

He lifted their linked hands. Gold sparked in her sea-green eyes and beneath the high-necked silk top her breasts rose and fell rapidly. As rapidly as his shortened breathing.

He shifted his hold and bent his head, licking the juice from her thumb, her forefinger, the sensitive V of flesh between them. A judder ran through her. Only his iron-hard grasp stopped her dropping the glass.

Her taste was sweet and salt and feminine musk. The scent of her skin like summer. Instantly his hunger escalated to a desperate craving. Too late he realised his mistake. The taste of her sent him spinning out of control. He was rigid with the force of swelling desire.

'Don't. Please.' Her voice was low but he couldn't miss the quiver of unsteadiness.

A bolt of something like guilt or even pity cleaved through him, making him frown. What had happened to the Callista he knew—all ice and fire? Her self-possession slipped and he glimpsed a different woman behind the façade.

That was what he wanted, wasn't it? For her to surrender and admit she wanted him?

Yet looking at her averted profile, reading the fine lines of strain around her mouth and the smudge of tiredness beneath her eyes, he knew a moment's doubt.

'Callie,' he murmured, drawing her closer.

'Callie, can you help? I—' Angela's voice came from the terrace and Damon turned as the younger girl approached. Her eyes were huge as she took in the pair of them. Belatedly Damon released his hold. Instantly Callie shifted away. 'I'm sorry; I just wanted to check something.'

'Hi, Angela. No need to apologise.' Damon smiled. He liked the girl despite her puffed-up father. She reminded him of his youngest sister, timid with strangers but delightful.

Callie hurried to Angela, drawing her away. She shepherded the younger girl, her arm raised as if to protect.

Damon frowned. He'd seen that gesture before. It had taken this long for him to notice, for whenever Callie was near he didn't think clearly.

Now he watched and wondered, his brain clicking into gear. He recollected how regularly Callie appeared when he and Angela were alone. How she often sat between them.

Why?

The women conferred about a projected dinner party. As if aware of his regard, Callie raised her head and something sparked in her eyes. She excused them and ushered Angela ahead of her into the house.

Could it be that, despite her hoity-toity attitude, Callie was jealous of the attention he gave her cousin?

He turned and paced the length of the pool.

Or had he been right the first time? Was she trying to protect her cousin? The idea nonplussed him.

He'd never be a threat to a sweet girl like Angela. The girl was probably a virgin and far too young. He didn't seduce innocents. Life was less complicated with lovers who understood long term relationships weren't on his agenda.

When the time came to think of marriage he…

Damon stilled.

Was that it? Aristides Manolis' plan to interest Damon in marriage to his daughter? The idea was nonsense. As if he needed help choosing a wife! As if Angela would suit him!

Then he remembered the look on Callie's face as she urged her cousin inside. Could she really believe he was interested in marrying Angela?

Suddenly so much made sense.

A smile of satisfaction spread across Damon's face.

He had her.

He knew the chink in Callie's armour. All he had to do was apply a little pressure.

'Just who I wanted to see.' Damon's voice was low and intimate. The hairs on Callie's neck rose in instant awareness. 'We need to talk.'

It didn't matter that he held her in contempt. Or that he threatened the fragile peace of mind she'd built up since Alkis' death. A force stronger than reason or pride held her in thrall to Damon Savakis.

Who'd have thought desire could be so strong? In her inexperience it had seemed far more—as if in the seclusion of the pine-shaded beach, she'd connected with the only man in the world who was…right.

Her lips thinned. She'd always been too naïve. She should have stopped believing in fantasy long ago.

Slowly she turned. After a morning in her aunt's sick room, Callie had sought the secluded platform at the end of the garden. She'd hoped its view over the village and the sea beyond would help her find the peace she'd lost.

He wore a crisp white shirt and tailored dark trousers, a jacket slung over one solid shoulder. He looked serious, a man to be reckoned with.

He'd been with her uncle for hours. What had they decided?

'I'm leaving soon,' he said, stepping close.

Callie's hands tightened on the balustrade. Relief, not dismay. She told herself she *wanted* him to leave.

'I hope you've enjoyed your stay.' She turned, unable to hold his stare. Instead she gazed at the distant harbour.

'Your family's hospitality has been most…generous.' His odd inflection sent unease skimming down her backbone.

A vessel in the harbour, a tiny blue-hulled boat, chugged towards the open sea. Callie wished she could be on it, sailing safely away from Damon. Her lips twisted. Just the idea of going on board a small boat made her stomach cramp with fear. She couldn't even fantasise about her escape!

'So generous that I'm considering strengthening my connection with your family.'

She should be relieved. If the deal was favourable she might get her inheritance. Yet, turning to see his satisfied expression, she had an awful suspicion it wasn't so simple.

'With a merger?' She held her breath.

He draped his jacket over the railing then leaned, arms splayed. He looked like a man who commanded all he surveyed.

Disquiet thrummed through her. Her uncle had invited a powerful predator into their midst and foolishly believed he could keep the upper hand. Instinct told her Aristides Manolis had badly underestimated Damon.

'Not necessarily.' Was that a hint of amusement? 'I'm considering something more personal.'

Callie's fingers clenched round the rail in spasm.

'Your cousin is a lovely young woman.' There was a purr of satisfaction in his voice that made Callie's hackles rise.

He wasn't serious! He didn't need marriage to a Manolis to cement his place in society. The idea was farcical.

'I don't see the connection,' she said through clenched teeth.

'Don't you? Odd, I thought you quite astute.'

She cast him a surprised glance then looked away.

'Angela will make someone a fine wife,' he mused. 'She has the qualities a man looks for in a permanent partner.'

'What? Timid, eager to please and biddable?' She couldn't keep the sarcasm from her voice. She'd learned what men wanted. Someone to shore up their egos and obey their whims. They didn't look beyond the surface to the woman beneath. Much less recognise her needs.

'Trust a beautiful woman to be so scathing of another.'

'That's not what I meant! I—'

'I'm surprised you don't know your cousin better. I was going to say Angela is intelligent, amiable and generous. Pretty too in her quiet way.'

'She's too young for you,' she blurted out. 'Far too young.' Defiantly she confronted him. The impact of his gaze, so intense, so penetrating, dragged the air from her lungs.

One eyebrow, dark as night, rose speculatively.

'You can't be serious,' she hissed.

'Why not? A man reaches the stage when he wants a woman to come home to.'

'I'm sure you have no problems finding women eager to wait up for you.'

His lazy smile set her teeth on edge. 'You're right. But I'm not talking about casual sex. I'm talking about the mother of my children. A man wants to pass on his name, his genes, his fortune to the next generation.'

Callie had become used to such attitudes since moving to Greece in her teens. Yet the cold-bloodedness of taking a wife simply because it was time to settle down irked her.

'You want a brood mare.'

'More than that.' His expression was amused. 'I require someone to be my hostess too.'

'Why tell me?' she asked flatly.

'You're an intelligent woman. You know your cousin. Your opinion interests me.'

She regarded him through narrowed eyes. There was a catch somewhere. 'It wouldn't work. Angela doesn't want to marry you. She's in love with someone else.'

No male with any pride would stomach the idea of his woman pining for another. Hadn't Alkis' obsessive jealousy arisen from the false belief Callie would seek the passion he couldn't provide in another man's arms? He'd made their lives a misery and their marriage a cruel prison because of it.

Damon merely smiled, like a hungry wolf sizing up its next meal.

'She's eighteen. Of course she fancies herself in love. She'll get over it. Any husband worth the name would see to that.' He straightened, shifting his weight. Callie was struck anew by the sheer masculine charisma of his tall frame. If any man could turn the head of a susceptible teenager it was him.

'You don't understand.' Callie turned and paced, unable to stay still. 'They're really in love. This is genuine.'

'At her age? It's puppy love.'

Callie opened her mouth to argue then snapped it shut. At eighteen she'd been head over heels in love with Petro, a clever, older law student. She'd believed it a grand passion, a once-in-a-lifetime thing.

Callie had been an ugly duckling who'd never felt at home in Greece, or with her new family, and still grieved the loss of her beloved parents. She'd spent four years struggling to fit in where everything, from the language to the customs, was foreign. She'd barely scraped a place at university and had been pathetically grateful when a dashing older student found her attractive.

How easy to seduce her, a gawky eighteen-year-old virgin. Callie had dreamed of happily-ever-after in his lean embrace. Until the day Uncle Aristides descended like Zeus thundering down from Mount Olympus. He was enraged at paying so much money to dispose of a fortune hunter.

Petro had left with never a second glance. Once he had funds at his disposal he'd gone back to his girlfriend.

So much for his protestations of undying love.

Callie had been heartbroken and distraught. Easy prey for her uncle's scheme with his crony, Alkis.

'Callie?'

Damon's baritone dragged her back to the present. She

blinked and found she'd wrapped her arms round her torso. Slowly she unwound them and stood straight, looking at a point near his collarbone.

'Angela deserves the chance to marry the man she loves.'

'Don't tell me you believe in romantic love?'

She shrugged, trying to don an air of insouciance. She felt too brittle. As if her façade of control might splinter.

'For some. For Angela.' Not for herself. She'd given up that fantasy long ago.

He dismissed her argument with a single slashing gesture. 'I don't see a problem. Especially with your uncle onside. Between us we can overcome any doubts she has.'

All warmth leached from Callie's body. She knew her uncle's tactics too well. The mixture of blustering threat and heartfelt appeals for the good of the family.

At Angela's age Callie had succumbed and agreed to marry the polite older man who'd payed court so graciously. Too late she'd learned her husband's old-world charm hid a cruel and unstable disposition.

The knowledge filled her with desperate resolve.

'No! You can't. You mustn't.' The words spilled out and she took an involuntary step towards Damon, one hand outstretched in her urgency.

'Mustn't, Callie? You're not in a position to dictate to me.' Damon towered over her, eyes glinting with challenge.

Her hand dropped as fear swamped her. How could she win against this man? What weapons did she have to thwart him?

'Once you're married you're tied permanently.' She'd bet Damon would see a failed marriage as a personal failure. 'Are you ready to settle down and devote yourself to one woman?'

'Why?' Heat flickered in his eyes. His stare was so intense it grazed her cheeks. 'Have you changed your mind about our affair?' He closed the space between them, forcing her to retreat till the balustrade dug into her back.

'No! I just—'

'You just decided you didn't like your little cousin doing well for herself.' Damon's lip curled derisively and Callie's heart dived. She'd never overcome his bias against her. 'You don't like being overlooked. I bet Angela has lived in your shadow for years.'

'That's not true!' Callie had never wanted centre stage. Only Alkis' determination to show her off had propelled her into a social sphere where she'd learned, painfully, to hold her own, despite the barbs and whispered gossip. She looked at Angela and saw herself at eighteen: quiet and far too vulnerable. 'Angela's not a rival, she's—'

A disparaging flick of his hand silenced her. 'I'm not interested.' He paused, eyes pinioning hers. 'Although…'

'Although?' Her hands wrapped around the railing as she straightened. Was he having second thoughts? Hope blossomed.

'One thing might make me reconsider,' he said slowly, one hand rubbing his jaw.

'Yes?' She took a half-step forward before slamming to a halt, suddenly far too close to his big body. His heat shimmered through her, his scent reminding her of intimacies she tried hard to forget.

Damon reached out and cupped her chin with his palm. Her body responded with a thrill of excitement that drew every nerve to attention. Slowly, oh, so slowly, his thumb slid across to her mouth, swiping deliberately across her bottom lip and tugging her lips apart.

She fought to keep her eyes open against the surge of physical longing his touch evoked. Callie's fingers clenched into fists at her sides, the breath catching in her chest till she felt lightheaded.

One caress, one touch, did that!

'Yes.' His sibilant stretched out in a hiss of satisfaction as he lowered his head.

She should move. Pull away. Run! But her feet were glued to the spot, her will to resist eclipsed by a flood of remembered pleasure.

'Come to me tonight, Callie. Give me one night and I'll say no to marrying Angela.' The sensuous burr of his voice enthralled her. She had trouble focusing on his words.

His eyes burned dark fire as she stared up into his bold face. This close she saw the way his fine-grained skin began to darken along that chiselled jaw. Not by so much as a blink did he betray emotion. There was just that all-consuming sensuality, drawing her closer.

Stunned, she felt her will soften, her body sway towards him, drawn by the force of a desire she couldn't conquer.

Then her brain clicked into gear. His words percolated through her hazy thoughts. She jerked her chin from his hold, stepping back carefully as if expecting him to lunge for her.

'And if I don't?'

His smile disappeared. His eyes narrowed as anger sparked. 'What do you think?'

'I think you're some piece of work, Damon Savakis.' Callie wrapped her arms round herself, as if to stop the sudden pain that engulfed her. For a moment she'd hoped he felt a little of the magic she'd imagined between them. The reality of his outrageous proposition was too cruel. 'This is a sick game you're playing.'

'No game, Callie. A simple deal.'

'You think you can *buy* me?'

He shook his head. 'Don't play innocent. It doesn't suit you.' He raked her with a searing stare that burned her flesh. 'You've been bought before, remember? When you married your late un-lamented husband.'

The horrible truth was like a blow to the solar plexus, winding her and cramping her stomach.

That was different, she wanted to scream. I didn't care about anything then because I thought my life was over. I was hurt and vulnerable and I believed I was saving my family. If only I'd known the mistake I was making.

'But you're asking me to…give myself for your pleasure.'

Damon folded his arms. The movement accentuated the muscles in his arms and chest, and his air of lazy confidence.

'No need to be melodramatic, Callie. I'm not asking you to do anything you haven't done, *and enjoyed*, before.' His mouth pulled wide in a smile of satisfaction that sent the blood tingling through her body.

'That's not the point!' Callie was so furious, so appalled she felt like landing a punch that would bend his arrogant nose completely out of shape.

Her anger was heightened by the knowledge that he was right. She'd enjoyed every moment of their intimacy.

'Then what is? You don't want me to marry Angela. Very well, I'm willing to compromise. I'll take you instead, on a strictly short-term basis. One night. That's all I want.'

He'd never consider *her* as a marriage candidate. He'd want someone pure, innocent and gullible for that role.

Callie's mouth quirked in a humourless smile. That was one thing she'd been saved: a marriage proposal from another arrogant lord-of-all-he-surveyed tycoon.

'What's so amusing?'

'Just relief you're not offering anything permanent.'

His eyes widened, then he jerked his head up in denial. 'Don't hold your breath. A single night will be sufficient.'

'Thank heaven for small mercies,' she muttered. Her pride smarted at his dismissal. But despite her anger heat flared under her skin as his gaze trawled her, slow and assessing. As if remembering how she looked naked.

Was this how slaves felt in the ancient markets, scrutinised by buyers? His glittering appraisal left Callie exposed and vulnerable. Yet a tiny, renegade part of her thrilled, knowing he desired her.

'You're bluffing.' She straightened her shoulders.

'I don't waste my time with bluff.' He paused as if weighing her mood. 'Tonight's my last night here. That's your deadline. Come to me tonight, stay as my lover and the deal will go through without a marriage contract. I'll even allow a fair settlement on the Manolis family.'

He watched her with glittering eyes. 'Tonight,' he repeated. 'I'll be waiting.'

'You'll wait a long time.'

His sensuous lips curved in a smile that did nothing to allay her fears. 'In that case I'll look forward to seeing you dance at my wedding.'

CHAPTER FIVE

DAMON strode across the living room of the opulent guest bungalow, swung round and paced back the way he'd come.

Eleven o'clock.

She wasn't coming.

Hell! He'd been so sure. Certain that at last he'd find respite from the voracious hunger that gnawed his vitals, distracted him from work and kept him from sleep. He speared his fingers through his hair, frustration rising.

He wasn't used to losing. Couldn't remember the last time he hadn't got his way in an important negotiation. And this, for reasons he couldn't fathom, was important.

Callista Manolis got to him as no woman ever had.

She should leap at the chance to share his bed, hoping for the expensive trinkets a man as rich as he could buy her.

But that wasn't her game. She'd sold herself in marriage once. No doubt she was angling for another cushy, long-term position. She set a high price on her favours.

Except when she pursued a little casual distraction with someone she thought unimportant, someone she could use briefly then discard. As she'd used him at the beach. She'd been warm and wanton in her pursuit of pleasure. So uninhibited he'd plunged headlong into a passion that far surpassed any of his recent liaisons.

He slammed to a stop, frustration rising in a tide that tightened every muscle. At dinner tonight she'd worn a dress designed to drive men to the edge of sanity, hinting at barely concealed feminine treasures. He'd taken it as a sign of her capitulation.

Instead the vixen had been toying with him.

He lunged for the sliding glass door and hauled it open, needing fresh air. He strode out to the flagstoned terrace then catapulted to a stop.

She was here.

His breath stopped as relief swamped him. It came in a rush so overwhelming he clutched at the door. Dimly he registered amazement at the intensity of his reaction.

His heart accelerated to a restless, arrhythmic beat as he watched her pick her way down the path from the main house, holding her long skirts up around her ankles.

Fire glittered on her breasts and round her wrist. She'd worn the diamonds again. But it wasn't jewellery that fixed his attention. Each time she passed a glowing uplight on the path it turned the fabric of her dress translucent, hinting at her seductive form.

The gown was long, white, gossamer-fine gathers of fabric designed to look like an ancient Greek dress. Fine gold cords crossed at her waist and below her breasts, defining luscious curves and a slim figure. The neckline plunged so deep she couldn't wear a bra. The silken swish of fabric as she moved was designed, he hoped, to indicate the absence of underwear.

Damon's hands itched to reach for her. He remained where he was.

Let her come to him.

'You decided to accept my offer.' He kept his voice firm, devoid of the raw satisfaction that would betray his pleasure. He would show no vulnerability to this woman.

'How could I resist such an alluring proposition?' The words came low and husky in the darkness, drawing the tension in his belly tighter. Yet even in the dim light there was no mistaking the jeering twist of her lips.

She still feigned distaste. Did she never give up?

She stepped onto the terrace and stood a few metres away, hands concealed in the folds of her dress, chin up, expression glacial. Yet that mask of disdain couldn't conceal everything. Her breasts rose and fell quickly, making the diamonds at her cleavage shimmer.

She wasn't the ice maiden she pretended. Soon she'd thaw for him.

'So what is this?' He waved a disparaging hand at her long dress. 'Your virgin-sacrifice outfit?'

Her lips curled in a tight smile that didn't reach her eyes. 'Hardly. You made it clear it wasn't an innocent you wanted. I thought that's why I appealed—because I've got such *vast* experience with men.'

Callie held her breath, amazed at her temerity in baiting him. She didn't know whether to be horrified or glad she still had strength to trade insults with Damon Savakis. Part of her cringed at what she was doing. The impulse to flee kept her poised for flight.

The idea of agreeing to this cold-blooded arrangement made her stomach churn and her mind revolt. She was so inexperienced she could count on the fingers of one hand the number of times she'd been with a man.

Her as a billionaire's plaything for the night!

Yet she had no choice. She couldn't, wouldn't turn her back on her cousin. No girl deserved to have her life blighted as Callie's had been in a contract marriage. Not where all power rested with an older, powerful husband who saw his wife as a chattel, not a real person with feelings.

That thought steadied her nerves.

'You look stunning,' he murmured. 'You know how to dress to please a man.'

Bitterness twisted in Callie's belly. Alkis had chosen this, as he had all her evening dresses. He'd selected expensive outfits that showed off his wealth and too much of her flesh. Though impotent, her husband had enjoyed making her flaunt herself, despite her protests, or perhaps because of them. He got a perverted kick out of parading her half-naked before other men. As if their thwarted desire compensated for his own inability to consummate the marriage.

He'd revelled in the sight of their tongues hanging out as they undressed her with their eyes. But it hadn't stopped him lashing out at her in private for supposed infidelities.

Oh, she knew all about dressing to please a man. That was why she hated this dress. It made her feel tainted.

'I thought you'd appreciate the dress.' He was like the others, interested only in her body.

'Tell me,' he purred in a voice that rubbed like velvet over her bare flesh, 'are you wearing anything under that?'

Callie's forced smile froze on her lips as a shiver of trepidation swept through her.

Fear threatened to puncture her carefully constructed mask of indifference. For this wasn't like before, when they'd come together in a joyous rush of mutual desire. This was something beyond her ken. There was an edge of danger to this situation. He looked so…predatory, as if he wanted to gobble her up with one snap of his jaws. There was nothing warm or gentle about the hunger in his face.

A *frisson* of stark panic sped down Callie's backbone.

'Would you prefer it if there wasn't?' Surreptitiously one slim heel slid back on the flagstones, till she realised what she was doing and forced herself to stop.

She'd made up her mind to do this. If she didn't please Damon it would be disastrous. This way her family would retain their home and Angela would be free to marry Niko.

Only Callie would be stripped of her dignity, and her privacy. Her mind shied frantically from the thought.

Yet after all she'd endured, she'd survive this. One night. *One long night.* Then she'd be free.

'I like the idea of you coming to me naked beneath the glitter and the haute couture.' He shrugged. 'But it doesn't matter. I'm sure you'll find a way to satisfy me.'

Callie's throat closed on a spasm of horror. How long could she keep up the pretence of indifference? Already she was torn between the desire to curl up and hide and the need to have him show again the tenderness that had obliterated all her defences.

No! She couldn't think like that.

Tenderness wasn't on Damon's agenda. He looked alert, aware, hungry. His stance was a hunter's, ready to attack.

'Aren't you going to invite me in?' He'd been silent so long her nerves stretched thin.

'Of course.' He stood aside and gestured for her to precede him into the lamp-lit sitting room. 'Welcome.'

Said the spider to the fly. Callie shivered at the carnivorous edge to his smile. Her steps were reluctant but she forced herself forward.

If she didn't do this she'd regret it for the rest of her days. She *would* rescue Angela. As she'd wished so often someone had stepped in years ago to save her from making the worst mistake of her life.

That knowledge gave her the strength to slip past him, chin up, eyes straight ahead. She faltered as she caught his scent, warm and intoxicating, and felt a whisper of desire shiver into life. But anxiety extinguished it as she stepped into the shadowed room.

She felt movement behind her and shuffled a couple more paces forward.

The sound of the door sliding closed made her scalp prickle. To her overwrought imagination it was as loud as the thud of a cell door. She licked dry lips then wished she hadn't as Damon stopped beside her, his gaze zeroing in on her mouth.

'Would you like a drink?' He gestured to the bar.

'No. No, thank you.' That would only prolong the agony of waiting. Better to get this over before her craven urge to run sabotaged her intentions.

He stopped before her, eyebrows raised. 'No? So eager, Callie. I like that. I like it very much.' With one hand he tilted her chin so she met his ebony eyes. They gleamed with a heat that scorched her right to the soles of her feet in her high-heeled sandals. The stroke of his finger along her jaw evoked memories of pleasure she'd almost forgotten in her anger and distress.

Maybe…maybe this wouldn't be as hard as she thought. If he'd sweep her into his arms, kiss her with the same passion they'd shared once before, perhaps she could forget she was selling herself to him. That she had no choice.

But even as her eyelids fluttered in expectation of his next caress, his hand dropped and he stepped back.

What now? Why had he stopped?

'You want me to make this easy for you. Don't you, Callie?' The words hung between them as the silence lengthened.

Yes, she almost screamed at him, her nerves raw with the tension crawling through her. Please, please, just…

'But, given your condescension and your cold treatment, I think it's time you made the first move.'

Callie's jaw sagged and she snapped it shut as a surge of vibrant emotion straightened her weakening resolve.

'You want your pound of flesh, is that it?' She spoke through clenched teeth.

His lips twitched. 'You could say that, *glikia mou*.' His firm mouth, so beautifully sculpted, curled up into a smile that made her want to smash something. Preferably him.

'So what did you have in mind?' Already she dreaded the answer.

'You're my mistress now. I'm sure you'll think of something. Why don't you just seduce me?'

Seduce him! She had no idea where to start. When they'd made love there'd been little thought involved. It had seemed so natural, so right, she didn't remember a conscious decision to give herself to him.

Tentatively she reached out, screwing up her courage as she lifted her hand to his face. But she moved too late. Her hand touched air as he stepped away and sank onto a long sofa. Nonchalantly he spread his arms along its back and stretched his long legs, crossing one ankle over the other.

'Go on,' he urged, for all the world as if he anticipated a show!

Did he expect a striptease? Wrath heated her chilled body at his deliberate show of power.

How like Alkis he was in his smug superiority. Something like hatred clawed at her chest, tightening her throat. But it helped. Now her hands were rock-steady as she jerked out the rhinestone pins holding her hair up.

Moments later her hair slipped down, a concealing weight around her shoulders and breasts. Callie let the pins fall.

'And the diamonds.' His face was unreadable but his voice sounded curiously thick. 'I don't want you coming to me wearing another man's diamonds.'

His proprietorial demand reinforced her contempt. He thought by possessing her body he had a right to control *her*. She unsnapped the bracelet and tossed it onto the marble coffee-table. Her earrings followed, splashes of scintillating light in the lamp-light. Callie raised her hands to the clasp of the necklace and caught Damon's look as it raked her face and upthrust breasts.

A shock of sensation jolted her out of her fury. A shock of something almost like excitement.

She dropped the necklace to the table and discovered she was breathing hard, as if she'd run here instead of tottering on ridiculously high heels. She stepped out of the delicate slingback sandals and her feet sank into the luxurious pile of the carpet.

Still he said nothing, just watched her with eyes that glowed with an inner fire.

No time for second thoughts. She'd committed herself. Head up, back straight, she paced towards him. He didn't move except to tilt his head, the better to watch her.

He really was a manipulative bastard. He enjoyed this power play. She sensed it even though his face remained granite-hard.

The realisation gave her the strength to sink onto her knees beside him on the sofa. She twisted a little, her leg aligning with his thigh, so solid and warm and unmoving. Without giving herself time to think she reached out and cupped his jaw in her hand. His skin was hot and smooth. So smooth she wondered if he'd just shaved. Had he been so sure she'd come to him?

Of course he had. He held all the cards.

Anger spurred her on. She leaned in and kissed him, full on the mouth. He didn't move. Didn't respond. His lips were warm and uncooperative. She tried again, this time pressing closer, her

tongue flicking across the seam of his mouth. He didn't open it
for her.

Callie clasped his face in both hands, caressing him slowly.
She pressed kisses to the corner of his mouth, along his jaw and
up to his ear, grazing her teeth along flesh that tasted of that
unique spicy tang she remembered from a week ago. A shiver
of pleasure, an echo of heady excitement, raced through her,
tightening her skin. She inhaled his scent as she nuzzled his neck
and a wave of dizziness hit her.

She edged closer, pressing herself to his solid heat. Her hands
slipped down to the collar of his shirt, swiftly unbuttoning till
she could slide her fingers, her hand inside. Crisp hair and steamy
skin met her touch as she smoothed her palm across his firm
pectoral muscles.

A dart of pure heat pierced her, arrowing straight to her
womb, and lower, to the juncture of her thighs, as heady
memories of sensual pleasure swamped her.

Again she kissed him, urging him, silently pleading with him
to let her in. To reciprocate. This wasn't about his challenge any
more. She felt that telltale surge of desire deep within her at the
touch, taste, scent of Damon. It felt suspiciously like…coming
home.

Despite her anxiety, her anger, her disappointment, there was
a truth about this, about her and Damon together, that was more
powerful than logic or pride. The realisation swamped her, flat-
tening her defences.

Her trembling fingers worked frantically at the remaining
buttons, ripping his shirt open to bare his torso. Callie sighed her
pleasure as she slid down, exquisitely aware of the friction
between their bodies as her breasts, covered only by thin silk,
moved against his broad chest. Darts of fire lit the darkness
behind her closed lids as she experienced again the raw power
of sensual need.

She licked his collarbone, then swept urgent kisses down his
sternum. He tasted as good as she remembered.

Following instinct, she licked one firm nipple, then tugged it
lightly between her teeth. He shuddered and she let her questing

hands mould and stroke the powerful contours of his chest. Did his heart beat faster? It pounded against her palm as she slid her arms round him.

He was so big, so superbly made that her pulse ratcheted faster in awareness of all that restrained masculine power. She remembered how he'd used that power so wonderfully, so tenderly to make her come alive in his arms.

Fire danced in her veins and need shimmered through her, drawing every nerve-ending awake and aware.

Callie rose, nipping his jaw, his chin, kissing his mouth with an insistent urgency that threatened to spiral out of control. She speared her hands through his thick hair, holding him captive as she teased, tempted and silently implored him to respond. That was what she needed, what she craved.

She sagged against his chest, breasts sliding against him. Sparks of pure delight flared from the contact. The heat built, urging her on.

Hurriedly she slid a hand to the waistband of his trousers, fumbling to undo his leather belt.

His mouth moved beneath hers. Yet he didn't return her kiss.

'At last,' he drawled. Callie sat back on her heels as his tone penetrated the haze fogging her brain. His glittering eyes held her captive.

'I thought you'd forgotten *I'm* the one you're supposed to pleasure. Not yourself. You'll have to improve your technique, Callie, or I might change my mind about having you. Perhaps I should take your little cousin as my wife instead.'

It was a douche of icy water, shocking her out of her stupor.

Callie's skin crawled as she realised what had happened. In a few short moments she'd forgotten everything about why she was here: his callous demand, her subservient role, the degradation of giving *herself* like a commodity in a business deal. Unbelievably all that had been obliterated by a force so strong it terrified her.

She'd succumbed to a primal, inexplicable need. The need for *him*. It shattered everything, even her pride, to smithereens. All that remained was a compulsion so strong even now she felt it pulse and rage in her blood.

She'd been completely out of control while he…

Shame and hurt and rage warred, forming an ice-cold lump of misery in her chest.

How had it happened? Through years of unhappiness, of occasional desperation, only control, her ability to withdraw inside herself, had kept her strong. It was how she had survived.

His hands thrust hers aside, making short work of his belt. Callie heard a zip slide down, then he spread both arms again along the sofa, the image of supercilious impatience. She scooped a lungful of air, transfixed by his arrogant stare.

In the gloom his expression looked familiar. The hard line of his mouth, the cold glint of his eyes. So had Alkis looked as he berated her for her failings, chastised her for not pleasing him in some way, or accused her of infidelity.

She'd escaped one manipulative man only to fall prey to another.

The searing, life-affirming heat of desire she'd felt seconds ago seeped from her body as ice-cold splinters of horror ripped through her.

What had she almost done?

Unbelievable that she'd hungered to give herself to this man! And all the while he'd felt nothing but impatience for her inexpert caresses.

Something shrivelled inside. If she did this, she'd lose what little was left of her hard-won self-respect. That was all she'd salvaged from the last six years.

In a surge of desperate energy she propelled herself back off the couch and onto legs that wobbled uncontrollably.

'Well?' He raised one interrogative brow. 'I'm waiting.'

She opened her mouth but no sound came. She slicked dry lips, ignoring the flicker of interest in his gaze. He sat with his clothes open, his arms splayed. He looked every inch the arrogant sensualist, awaiting his pleasure.

The thought nearly choked her.

Callie took a step back, then another.

'What are you doing?' The lazy boredom disappeared from his voice. His tone sharpened.

ANNIE WEST

Fear spiked. Fear that, even now, she couldn't quite conquer the urgent desire that drew her back. Even arrogant and impatient Damon Savakis wielded a power that made her tremble with feminine weakness. That shamed her.

A second later Callie spun round and wrenched open the door. She grabbed her long skirts in her hands and raced pell-mell up the path, terrified that at any second his hard hands would curl round her shoulders and yank her back.

Gravel bit her bare feet, her hair streamed behind her and a sob tore from her constricted throat. She stumbled but kept running, her breath sawing desperately in her throat.

She'd only just escaped the degradation of a loveless marriage to a venal, cold-hearted man. She *couldn't* deliver herself into the hands of another like him.

It was asking too much.

Damon stared in disbelief at the pale figure flying up the hill, long skirts billowing about her as she ran.

He stumbled to his feet, cursing his lack of co-ordination. He could no more catch her up than he could fly. His body was in lock-down, gripped in the stasis of a sexual arousal so potent it hurt to move.

Hell! It hurt to breathe.

Damn his vitriolic tongue. His need to assert his dominance. Dominance! His mouth compressed in self-disgust.

He'd been putty in her delicate, sensual hands. Only determination to make her pay for her condescension, for the burning frustration he'd suffered, had lent him strength not to plunder her mouth and her body instantaneously.

Pride demanded he remain unresponsive to begin with.

He'd gripped the sofa so hard in his effort not to respond that his fingers were numb. The upholstery was probably shredded. She'd bewitched him and he'd fallen into a helpless state of immobility, muscles frozen in stunned disbelief.

Damon had reached breaking point. He'd been about to ravish her luscious mouth when she fumbled at his belt and relief spiralled through him. Just as well she hadn't touched him lower or he might have embarrassed himself. He was more explosively aroused than he'd been since his teenage years.

That realisation had given him the bare strength to meet her eyes and lie bald-faced about how she made him feel.

He'd never relinquished power to any woman. The realisation that she, of all women, had turned the tables with just her kisses and her slow caress of his bare torso, scared the hell out of him.

He'd lashed out, trying to redress the imbalance of power. Now look where that had got him!

Cursing himself for a fool, he did up his trousers and walked stiff-legged to the door. The winding path was empty. Callie was long gone.

Unbelievably, for the first time he could remember, Damon had overplayed his hand.

It was late when Callie emerged next day. After a night of no sleep she'd spent ages concealing her pallor and puffy eyes with make-up.

Had Damon left for Athens? Had he changed his plans and announced he'd marry Angela?

Callie bit her lip and faltered to a stop on the stairs. Her chest constricted, misery swamping her. She'd failed Angela. Guilt burned a hole in her belly.

Despite her determination, her vaunted self-possession, she'd let Damon frighten her into failure. It almost didn't matter that she'd pay a personal price now. He'd be furious enough to screw the Manolis family for every penny and she'd never get back what her uncle had stolen.

But that was only money. She'd find a way to pursue her dream, even if it meant years of delay. She *would* support herself and lay to rest the taunting echo of Alkis' voice telling her she was good for nothing but show. He'd belittled her brains, her ability and almost succeeded in breaking her. But she'd prove him wrong. Prove her worth to herself.

The thought of Angela, trapped in a marriage that would destroy her happiness, her very soul, ripped Callie apart. And her aunt, diagnosed with a heart condition, who'd lose her home if the deal didn't go ahead.

Callie had just discovered that bombshell this morning as she looked in on Aunt Desma. The results of the medical tests had come through. Her aunt put on a brave face, but the prognosis was serious. She needed quiet and professional treatment. Not to be uprooted from her home. Not to deal with her husband's volcanic temper if he lost everything.

It was the stuff of nightmares.

Guilt swirled inside her. She'd had the power to save them all, to placate the man who held their futures in the palm of his hand.

She'd failed them.

'Callista!' Her uncle's voice echoed up from the vestibule. 'There you are. Come here immediately. You're needed.' She peered over the railing to see him bustle back into his study.

Reluctantly she forced herself down the stairs. Was Angela's marriage a *fait accompli*? Or had Callie's actions last night scuppered the deal completely? If Damon was as incensed as she suspected, had he pulled the plug on the merger?

No, business would always come first with Damon. He wouldn't let a woman get in the way of profits.

Her uncle turned as she reached the doorway. His brow was puckered but his unctuous smile sent a shiver of revulsion down her spine.

Damon had done it, then—announced his intention to wed Angela. Callie's stomach cramped so violently she grabbed the door to hold herself upright against the pain.

'Come in, come in. It's time you turned up. We've been waiting for you.'

'For me?' She stepped over the threshold and slammed to a halt when she saw his companion, leaning back in an easy chair. Damon Savakis, large as life and wearing an impenetrable expression.

'Of course.' Aristides Manolis seemed ill-at-ease. 'Damon and I have sorted out the business side of things. But there are personal matters to be resolved.'

'Personal?' The word was torn from her lips. Surely that

meant a wedding. Callie swung her head, searching for her cousin. The study was empty but for the men.

Damon's mouth curved in a slow smile. Something hot and possessive flickered in his eyes.

The door closed behind her with a snick that sounded like the clang of a prison door.

CHAPTER SIX

DAMON watched Callie's stiff posture and wary eyes.

Quite an act. She looked almost apprehensive.

As if she didn't know her uncle had spent the last hour haranguing him about his intentions, trying to manoeuvre him into 'doing the right thing' by the woman he'd compromised.

Disgust rose as Damon thought of their cleverly orchestrated ploy.

He'd been genuinely remorseful for his behaviour last night. There'd been no excuse, not even the confusing welter of emotions Callie created inside him.

After a lifetime protecting the women in his family he understood how appalling his behaviour was. He'd spent a sleepless night berating himself for arrogance, stupidity, his bloody ego. To distress her so…

He'd arrived at the house early, needing to see her.

That was when he'd learned the whole scene had been a charade. Manolis and his niece had set him up. *Again.*

Manolis had taken the tone of disappointed host and strict guardian. He'd seen Callie enter the house last night. She'd been distraught, he'd said, adding a reference to her dishevelled state, her lack of jewellery and shoes.

It was a new experience for Damon, being wrong-footed by his own actions.

A niggle of conscience reminded him that, as far as the world was concerned, he'd acted reprehensibly. Society's rules,

his obligations as a guest, his own sense of honour all damned
his behaviour.

Except Callie was no victim. Manolis had pulled out all the
stops. Throwing his daughter at Damon in hopes of a marriage
to secure financial security. And, as back-up, a dirty little scheme
of blackmail. From the moment Callie had given herself to her
tearful flight, it had all been a con to entrap him. She'd played
the role of distressed victim last night.

Fury sizzled in Damon's veins. He'd never been so gullible.
He should have been more cautious dealing with an unscrupulous old fox like Manolis.

Instead he'd let desire cloud his judgement. In that their cheap
ploy had worked.

His pride screamed for payback.

Damon interrupted Manolis as he wittered on about resolv-
ing the situation. Damon would resolve it, but not the way this
pair intended.

'I'll talk to your niece alone.'

Manolis objected but Damon cut him short.

'It's too late for a chaperone.' Damon met her snapping gaze
and wondered if she'd ever been a naïve innocent. She was perfectly suited for the role of *femme fatale*. 'Your niece is a widow,
not an inexperienced teenager.'

Callie shut the door carefully behind her uncle. She pressed
clammy palms to the wood, trying to centre herself. Between her
uncle's words and Damon's steely glare, she felt dazed and
cornered, her pulse tripping unevenly.

'What game are you playing?' She swung round to confront
Damon where he slouched in an armchair.

One eyebrow rose indolently and her fingers curled into fists.
She longed to shatter his superior air.

'Game? You accuse *me* of playing games?' Never had Damon
looked so remote, yet Callie knew what she'd heard.

'What's this about us marrying?'

Her uncle couldn't be serious. Just the words froze her blood.
Her stomach dived in distress. The sangfroid she'd clung to

so desperately deserted her. She pushed away from the door and paced, unable to keep a lid on churning emotions.

'What's wrong, Callie? Having second thoughts? Or do you feel cheated I haven't grovelled on one knee?'

Callie couldn't imagine Damon grovelling. Yet the idea of him on his knees before her made her feel hot and unsettled. Abruptly she paced to the window.

'I want to know what you're up to!'

'According to your uncle I'm satisfying honour and obligation by making an honest woman of you.' His face was unreadable, his words sharp. Her eyes narrowed on his rigid shoulders and tight jaw.

'It was Angela you talked of marrying.'

'So it was.' His expression didn't alter.

Her hands curled into fists of frustration. 'You don't want to marry me! You said so.'

He crossed one leg over the other, surveying her as she paced the room. He said nothing.

'I'm not—'

'What? A virgin?' He smiled and instantly fire sparked in her veins. 'It's not a prerequisite these days. Besides, our sexual compatibility is proven.'

'There's more to marriage than sex!' She turned her back on his penetrating gaze and stalked to the window.

'Ah, there speaks the expert. Tell me, is that what held your previous marriage together? Sex?'

Callie spun back, her hair flaring around her shoulders. 'My marriage is none of your business,' she hissed as poisonous memories swarmed to the surface. It was as if he knew all her weak points and delighted in prodding them. With every challenge, every snide remark, he stripped her bare and vulnerable.

'You don't even like me,' she whispered, focusing on a point in the distance.

The walls pushed in. Claustrophobia choked her.

Marriage! To another controlling male! Over her dead body.

The sound of slow clapping jerked her round. Damon's mouth twisted in a jeering smile as he straightened.

'Congratulations, Callie. If ever you decide to work for a

living you'd be a huge success on the stage. You got that distress and confusion just right.'

'What are you talking about?' Callie felt she was walking on sands that shifted beneath her feet.

'Your display of reluctance is a little overdone. I know you and your uncle concocted this plot to snare a rich man to salvage the family fortunes. But I refuse to fall in with your plot.'

Callie frowned. 'There was no plot.'

'Your uncle just happened to be in the right spot at the right time to see you looking the picture of compromised virtue?' His eyes flashed. 'Give me credit for some sense.'

Numbly she shook her head. 'I don't want to marry you.'

'Just as well. Marrying you is the last thing on *my* mind.' He spat the words as if tasting poison.

Yet as she watched his expression changed.

'But I want you, Callie.' His voice vibrated with repressed passion. The stark hunger in his eyes sent incendiary sparks through her tense body. 'And now I'll have you. On my terms.'

'Terms?' It was a strangled whisper.

'In my bed. But the stakes have just got higher.'

He *couldn't* want her if he believed that of her. 'I don't understand.'

'After the…inconvenience of your little farce, I've decided I want more than one night. You'll be my mistress, at my beck and call, for as long as I desire.'

The sizzle in his eyes gave a whole new meaning to the phrase beck and call. The breath whistled from her lungs as his intentions sank in.

'But my uncle—'

'What? He's old-fashioned enough to be distressed at the notoriety of his niece living as my mistress rather than my bride?' His dark eyes snapped. 'Tough. The pair of you should have thought of that before you tried to manipulate me.'

'I didn't—'

'Don't waste your breath, Callie. Those are my terms.' He steepled his hands under his chin. 'Accept them or face the consequences.'

Her limbs stiffened at the threat in his dark velvet tone. Her mouth dried. 'What consequences?'

Damon uncurled his body from the seat and paced towards her. Each deliberate step reinforced the sensation she was being stalked. Backed against the window, she had nowhere to run. Her hands splayed on the cool glass behind her.

'You think I'd let you make a fool of me then walk away unscathed? You're not that naïve. I can break your uncle like that.' The click of fingers near her ear made her jump.

'Refuse me and I ruin him in a hostile takeover. I owe the Manolis family *nothing*. On the contrary,' his lips flattened to a grim line, 'the Manolis debt to *my* family is too long outstanding.'

Callie's eyes widened at the burr of deep-seated anger in his voice. He sounded, and looked formidable. She couldn't doubt he meant every word.

'Or,' he continued, 'I could temper my annoyance by taking sweet Angela for myself and leave your uncle at least the appearance of dignity.' Damon thrust his head forward aggressively, obliterating her illusion of personal space.

'Either way you lose. Your dear departed husband didn't leave you more than a pittance and that's already gone. Perhaps he'd discovered you weren't an ideal wife.'

His sarcasm barely penetrated. Callie's stomach hollowed as memories crowded. Of Alkis' accusations and threats. Of the nightmare life she'd led, unable ever to satisfy her husband's expectations.

'You had me investigated?' He must have, to know Alkis had left his money to his children by an earlier marriage. Callie had thought herself beyond outrage, but a new shaft of pain sliced through her. She felt violated, knowing some investigator had pried into her life.

Was there no end to this nightmare?

'Only a cursory report into your current assets,' he said as if invading her privacy was nothing.

'Well,' she drawled, summoning the last of her fading strength, 'that's all right, then.'

His bark of spontaneous laughter echoed round the room. 'I see we understand each other.' He placed one hand on the wall beside her head, blocking her in. His heat enveloped her; his warm breath caressed her forehead.

'The time for playing is over, Callie. Come with me now, today. It's your only choice.'

Panic gripped her as she felt her avenues of escape cut off. She had too much experience of ruthless men to doubt for an instant that Damon would deliver on his threats.

Last night she'd run, unable to give herself cold-bloodedly to him. But escape had been an illusion. She'd have to face even that mortifying ordeal. Her heart sank.

Callie shuddered at potent images of Damon demanding her submission, Damon making her body sing like an instrument tuned only to his touch.

At least Alkis hadn't possessed her body. But with Damon there'd be no escape, no privacy. Instinctively Callie knew she couldn't survive a long-term relationship with him. His will was too strong, her physical weakness for him like a Trojan horse planted deep within the last bastion of her defences. Who knew what damage her destructive craving would do to her fragile sense of independence and self-worth?

Her only hope was to keep this short-term.

Determination and weary acceptance seeped through her, strengthening her spine.

His face was close when she raised her head. So close her heart thudded as awareness rippled through her.

'I have your word you'll leave Angela out of this?'

'You have it.' A gleam in his eyes betrayed his pleasure. No doubt he was planning ways to enjoy her surrender. Callie re-pressed a shudder at the knowing, intent lick of heat in his gaze.

Her tongue was clumsy as she capitulated.

'Very well. You can have your revenge. I'll go with you.'

'I thought we were taking the big ferry.' Damon heard a thread of what sounded like anxiety in Callie's voice and shot her a look as a servant took their bags from the four-wheel-drive and went ahead.

In the shade of the pine grove her face gave nothing away. It was a stiff mask, leaving him to speculate on that tiny betraying quiver at odds with her appearance.

Yet nothing could dim his satisfaction. Ever since she'd given in to his ultimatum two hours ago, anticipation had sizzled in his blood.

He intended to enjoy this liaison to the full.

'Do I look the type to travel on crowded ferries?'

Callie's shoulders lifted in a tight shrug. 'It's either that or a helicopter to the mainland.'

'Why bother when I have my yacht? We can be private aboard *Circe*.'

Damon took her in slowly, from her blonde head to the white top, pale yellow trousers that cradled her neat curves and low-heeled sandals. She looked fresh and alluring in a way that had nothing to do with mercenary schemes. She looked…innocent.

His mouth thinned at the absurdity. She was an expert in playing up to male fantasies. Last night's charade had proved her anything but innocent.

She knew how to tease a man's libido. And his conscience.

He hadn't been privy to her conversation with Aristides Manolis this morning, but he'd heard her uncle's bellowed disapproval. Manolis was chagrined his plan to snare Damon in marriage hadn't worked. Seeing the barely contained fury in the older man's eyes later, Damon knew an unexpected admiration for Callie. No little innocent could handle such a bully. Callie was savvy and determined. Quite an operator.

'But…' She paused and gnawed on her lip. He zeroed in on the movement, heat building in his belly even as his brain filed away that surprising hint of nerves for later consideration. 'We'd get to Athens faster if we flew.'

'Who said I want to return quickly? I told my assistant to cancel my appointments.'

Damon's gaze travelled appreciatively down her slim body. They were near the place where they'd discovered exactly how much pleasure they could give each other. Memories rose hot and close, tugging at his control.

But he wanted the luxury of his own bed when he had her again. Despite his anger at her plot, it was desire not revenge that fired his blood now.

'I'm looking forward to a *leisurely* trip,' he murmured.

She blinked but said nothing.

He'd swear she'd been about to blurt something. Curiosity stirred. The idea of Callie saying anything unguarded intrigued him. Even in anger she gave little away. Except when she'd argued so passionately that he shouldn't marry Angela. Then he'd known for sure she was genuine.

'Isn't *Circe* up to your standards?' The yacht, just visible through the trees, was a rare vintage classic.

He'd spent a fortune refurbishing *Circe* to the most exacting standards of a man used to the best. Callie probably preferred an ostentatious cruiser over gracious lines and perfect craftsmanship. Her jewellery revealed a flashy taste rather than an appreciation of beauty.

'*Circe* is glorious. Only a philistine would think otherwise.' Callie shot him a look that mixed surprise and scorn. 'It amazes me that a man obsessed with takeovers and revenge recognises quality when he sees it.' She turned on her heel and headed away from him.

Damon surveyed her. The clench and release of her sexy bottom as she walked drew a sigh of appreciation.

'How you stayed married so long with your sharp tongue is beyond me, Callie,' he said to her retreating back. 'I bet you didn't make allowances for your husband.'

He paused, intrigued, as she stopped and slowly turned. Her face was set in lines of rigid hauteur, her body preternaturally still. Had he hit a sore spot?

When she didn't immediately respond he continued, surprised at his need to know more. 'Did you give him the cold shoulder too?'

'I've told you, my marriage is none of your business.' She drew herself up straight, perfectly erect, perfectly poised. So damnably perfect to look at it was hard to believe she was so conniving.

'Why don't you talk about it? Because you're ashamed of the way you treated your husband? Don't try to tell me you're sick with grief. You're not mourning him.'

She paced towards him. Fury flashed in her eyes.

'I suppose you'd prefer I dressed in black and retire quietly for the rest of my life.' Her lips curled in contempt. 'It must be upsetting to realise a woman can get on just as well without a man in her life.'

'You admit it? You weren't in love with him?' Triumph warred with disgust as he took in her supercilious expression. 'Is that why you don't use your married name? Why you reverted to Manolis? Because he meant nothing to you?'

Damon knew an insane desire to stamp his presence deep in her psyche, make her feel so much her life wouldn't be complete without him.

If possible the chill in her gaze deepened. Her eyes were glacial pools that would suck the heat and the life from a man unwary enough to venture there.

'You're not sentimental about keeping your husband's name?' he prodded. 'Or about the man who shared your bed for all those years?'

Damon waited for her excuses, but her mouth stayed fixed in an unyielding line.

She really was a piece of work.

'So,' he murmured, 'you didn't love him. Not surprising when he was so much older than you. He must have been, what, twenty years your senior? More?'

'Thirty-five.' Her lips barely moved on the words.

'Thirty-five years older than you.' Damon whistled. 'It must have been a challenge, summoning the enthusiasm to make love to a man so much older.' The image of Callie, sprawled naked and beautiful, letting some grizzled codger do what Damon had done with her, turned his stomach. Acid rose in his throat. 'Did you lie back and think of all his lovely money you could spend?'

Silence enveloped them. A stillness so thick he could almost reach out and grasp it. Yet she didn't move. Didn't even blink.

What would it take to unsettle her? He *knew* that behind the frozen façade was a flesh-and-blood woman whose physical passion matched even his.

'You know nothing about my marriage,' she said finally. 'You're not even original in your insults. There's nothing you can say about my marriage that hasn't been said before.' She looked as if she didn't give a damn. 'You don't know me,' she added.

'I know all I need to know. I remember in perfect detail. Every sigh, every moan, every passionate response. You couldn't get enough of me.'

Damon stepped near, raising his hand as if to caress her cheek, stopping with his palm centimetres from her skin. Static electricity sparked between them, tickling his hand and igniting his libido.

He watched her sway the tiniest fraction, as if drawn irresistibly to his touch. She felt it too, the tug of desire, stronger than ever. Satisfaction warmed his belly.

Soon he'd have what he craved. Then, when *he* was satisfied, he'd resume normal life, free of this net that bound him tight. Even his fury at the stunt she and her uncle had pulled barely mattered. All that mattered was the extraordinary intensity of his need for Callie.

Their gazes meshed then she stepped away, her face set in a frown of displeasure and confusion that did nothing to diminish her vibrant beauty. His hand dropped.

'You're fantasising, Kyrie Savakis—'

'It's Damon, remember?'

She shrugged, a jerky movement that told him all he needed to know about her awareness of him, of them.

'Contrary to what you think, not all women are placed in your path solely for your amusement.'

'You mean you have some other purpose?' he jibed. 'Apart from socialising, and shopping, and attending a charity function or two?'

His sisters would have his hide if they heard him, and his mother. But he was too busy watching her reaction to his deliberately outrageous comment to care. He was determined to make her lose her cool.

Eyes like jade daggers speared him. The confusion in her expression disappeared, swamped by indignation. For what seemed a full minute she glared, till he felt the heavy, anticipatory thud of blood pound through his body.

'Congratulations,' she said finally, inclining her head. 'You know,' she mused, her voice soft enough that he leaned forward to catch each syllable, 'you're everything I'd expect of an arrogant Greek tycoon. And then some. Thanks for warning me what to expect.'

Without waiting for a response she turned and strolled down the path, her casual gait deliberate provocation.

Damon felt emotion rise to the surface as he digested her words. He had to bite down hard to stifle a bark of appreciative laughter.

Little viper. Did she really think her words could sting him? Yet he had to hand it to her, she didn't back down or sulk when challenged. She'd looked him in the eye and told him what she thought. Did she know how appealing that was?

Damon's curiosity stirred, as well as his libido. The more time he spent with Callie the more she intrigued him. She might be shallow and conniving, but she had backbone and a gumption that appealed.

She was more than a sexy bed partner. She was an enigma he was determined to crack.

CHAPTER SEVEN

THE deck shifted beneath Callie's feet. Automatically she adjusted her stance to its gentle roll. It was second nature, like riding a bicycle.

That didn't stop the *frisson* of panic sliding down her spine. She fought to suppress it.

Damon thought her shallow and unprincipled. She refused to let him think her a coward too. Surely she could conquer this phobia till they reached the mainland.

Once she'd have revelled in being aboard a sleek beauty like *Circe*. She slid her hand along a lovingly polished surface. It felt familiar. Smelled like memories of long-lost summer afternoons. Nostalgia welled and with it piercing memories of a simpler time. When she had been loved and loving. When the future had seemed bright and beckoning. Before she'd learned about cruel obsession and manipulation.

'Alone at last.'

Callie jumped and swung round to see Damon watching her. Reflective sunglasses hid his expression.

Her uncle's staff were heading ashore after depositing their luggage and supplies.

'Wishing you were with them?' His voice was sardonic.

How she did! Instead she confronted twin horrors: her phobia of small vessels and giving herself to the cold demands of a man bent on stripping her pride and self-esteem.

Her lips tightened in a mirthless grimace. If this didn't kill her she must emerge stronger.

'Why don't you show me around?' If she kept busy maybe she could conquer the worst of her fear.

His eyebrows rose. 'Of course. Follow me.' He led the way to the stairs, peeling off his shirt. Bare-chested, he looked the way he had the first time she'd seen him. The sun lovingly glinted off toned olive skin that rippled with strength.

Callie's throat dried as she followed. If only he was the sort of man she'd first thought him—generous, teasing and tender. A man she could trust.

'Do you usually sail alone?' She forced the question, refusing to dwell on fantasy.

'No. Usually the *Circe* is full to the brim with family.'

'Your family?' Callie froze on the top step. He *couldn't* be married!

He turned but in the gloom at the bottom of the stairs she couldn't read his expression.

'I'm the eldest of five and the last to hold out against matrimony. There's usually someone wanting to come out with me. I'm even adept at stopping toddlers falling overboard.'

The ripple of unexpected amusement in his tone sent heat slanting through her. Callie had a vision of Damon wearing nothing but long swim shorts, cradling a dark-haired child in his arms. The image was unaccountably appealing. Maybe he was different with his family. Less driven, able to trust.

That was none of her business. Callie firmed her jaw and followed him, eyes widening at the luxury she found.

'It's stunning,' she breathed, pivoting to take in the elegant furnishings and state-of-the-art equipment. The interior was a stylist's dream, a harmonious marriage of old-world charm and modern functionality.

'I'm glad you approve.' Strangely, she detected no sarcasm. He'd removed his sunglasses and scrutinised her through narrowed eyes. She allowed herself the pleasure of absorbing her surroundings. How she'd love to be commissioned to fit out a yacht like this. Maybe one day, if her home-furnishing business really took off…

'The only complaint so far is my mother's. That I didn't put in an oven large enough for a triple batch of moussaka.'

'Your mother sails with you?' That didn't fit her perception of him as a ruthless tycoon, isolated by his self-importance, busy with business and seductions.

He shrugged and smiled. The first real smile she'd seen since the day they'd come together down by the shore. Its impact was like an incendiary flare deep inside.

'It's in the blood. I come from a long line of fishermen.'

'Then your father must enjoy sailing too.'

A stiffening of his body warned her she'd overstepped the mark. 'My father is dead.' The words rang with a cool finality that didn't brook further questions. 'Come. I'll show you the rest.'

Their few moments of unexpected truce were at an end. And with it Callie's momentary ease. Tension gripped her shoulders as she followed Damon.

Several hours later, watching the sun set across the liquid-silk Aegean, Damon was puzzled.

Callie had confounded his expectations. No sooner had she climbed aboard than she'd slipped off her sandals, obviously aware of the need to respect *Circe*'s timber decking. She seemed completely at home on board. He'd seen her slide her hand along the timber and brass fittings as if she too relished the vessel's superb craftsmanship.

He'd put her to work and she'd anticipated his instructions. She was no stranger to sailing. Real sailing. Not lounging on a floating resort.

Yet her usual grace was lacking, her movements cramped and stiff. Unease tugged his conscience but he'd stifled it, suspecting some new trick.

Now, with the yacht anchored in the lee of a tiny island, Damon stretched. He hadn't seen her in an hour. She was below, preparing their meal.

Heat coiled in his belly as he strode across the deck.

The cabin was dim. She hadn't put on a light. He catapulted downstairs and strode through the lounge, intent on finding her.

His body thrummed a heavy, urgent beat. Food could wait.

No sound of her in the galley. Damon paused, frowning as he took in the food on the counter. She hadn't got far with her preparations. Would she insist they make for port so someone else could deal with the chore of cooking?

He stalked towards the other cabins and almost tripped.

She was huddled on the floor in the semi-darkness, her back braced against one wall, her arms wrapped around knees drawn hard into her chest.

'Callie?' His voice was a hoarse croak of surprise as fear spiralled through his gut.

Not by a flicker did she register his presence. Her eyes stared but she didn't see him. She seemed…cut-off. Foreboding speared him as he saw her faint rocking movement.

Something was very wrong.

He hunkered beside her, touching her hand. It was icy.

'Callie, what happened?' Urgency welled. That sightless stare worried him.

He raised his hand to her face. Her cheek was too cool, and wet with the tears that dripped unheeded from her chin.

Damon's chest clamped at the sight of such patent distress. This was no act.

Warmth. That was what she felt. Heat enveloping her.

She'd been so cold. From the moment Damon had casually declared they'd travel on his yacht. The chill crept in, spreading like a frost till finally she hadn't been able to pretend to be strong. Till icy fingers of fear and ancient pain wrapped around her heart and squeezed tight.

Callie had tried to be brave, forcing herself to climb on deck and appear unaffected. Each movement had tested her determination as she obeyed Damon's instructions and tried to douse her rising panic at being aboard.

She hadn't set foot on a yacht since she was fourteen. Not since…

Callie burrowed closer to the wondrous heat, needing it as a starving man craved sustenance. If only she could blank out the memories.

Vaguely she realised the cold had started long before the sight of the yacht moored and ready to carry her onto the treacherous sea. It had sunk into her bones years ago. When Petro had used and betrayed her. When Alkis had kept her in a travesty of marriage that excluded normal human interaction.

She shuddered as pain ripped through her. The pain of loss and betrayal. The hurt she'd bottled up so long.

'You're safe now. You're all right.' The low burr of words penetrated the fog of her distress.

Safe. It sounded wonderful. The heat intensified, curling around her. She sank into it gratefully.

A rhythmic movement lulled her body. Gradually her muscles eased, leaving a dull ache in place of screaming tension. She felt heavy. Exhausted.

It took a long time for her to realise the soothing rhythm was the caress of a hand, rubbing up and down her back. That it echoed the thudding near her ear. A muffled heartbeat.

Damon.

With an enormous effort, like a half-drowned diver struggling to the surface, Callie broke through the enveloping stupor. She began to take note of sensations.

She was cradled in his arms, surrounded by the living heat of solid muscle and bone. Her head was tucked in under his chin. To her horror she realised she never wanted to move from this cushioned comfort.

He smelt of sunshine and the sea, of the potent salty tang of a virile male.

Callie sucked in a breath. He must have found her huddled where she'd cowered as her defences crumbled. She'd needed to catch her breath, regroup and strengthen herself to ignore the distress that had sideswiped her so devastatingly.

Nothing like this had ever happened before, even in her darkest days. Her pulse thundered at the idea of him finding her.

'Callie?' The hand at her back halted. After a pause it resumed its soothing motion.

She considered pretending not to hear. But she couldn't play the coward.

'Yes?' she whispered, her voice raw and thick.

A silent shudder rippled through his big frame and she heard him exhale. In relief or annoyance?

No doubt he'd come below anticipating their next bout of verbal sparring. Or perhaps the surrender of her body.

Dread carved a hollow inside her. She wasn't ready for that.

'What happened?' His voice was surprisingly gentle.

Reluctantly Callie opened her eyes. They were in the master cabin. She recognised the wide fitted berth they sat on and the brass-edged portholes high in the walls.

Her breath stopped and she jerked back in his arms, realising the implications.

His bed. His mistress. His pleasure.

That was why he'd come to find her, to consummate their arrangement. Despite her determination to deliver what she'd promised, Callie couldn't stop the instinctive kick of repugnance at the idea of a cold-blooded coupling as he'd demanded last night.

One long arm roped round her shoulders and hauled her close, fitting her to him again. His heat enveloped her, from his steely thighs beneath her legs to his powerful chest and shoulders supporting her.

'Nothing happened.' The words were slurred, her voice unfamiliar. She had the oddest sensation of distance, even from her own body.

'You usually sit on the floor for a good cry, do you?'

Sarcastic wretch! She hadn't cried in years. Callie searched for a tart rejoinder but her brain was too muzzy.

'What is it, Callie? What's wrong?' One large hand cupped her jaw, his thumb swiping tears from her chin, across her cheek. But there was nothing sexual about his gesture. It was simply… comforting. Her eyes flickered and her head lolled. His heart beating beneath her ear mesmerised her.

'Don't go to sleep on me now.' His hand firmed on her jaw.

'I'm not sleepy.' But she felt strangely lethargic. 'I don't know what's wrong with me,' she blurted out. The wobble in her voice horrified her and she tried to rise. He held her still with an ease that would have frightened her if she'd been thinking clearly.

'Did you injure yourself?' He paused, letting the words sink in. 'I couldn't find a wound.'

She found it easier to respond to his brisk, impersonal tone. 'No. Nothing like that. I just…'

'You just…?'

'You're going to have to tell me,' he added in a conversational tone when she said nothing. 'I'm not going anywhere till I get the truth.'

Callie's lips twisted. Much he cared for the truth. He preferred his own skewed view of people.

'Callie…' No mistaking the warning in his tone as he tilted her chin up. She jerked her face free, letting her hair, loose now round her shoulders, curtain her features. She stared across the cabin, fixing her gaze on a porthole.

'I…don't like yachts.' Callie felt a sliver of grim amusement at that bland explanation. She just had to get close to a vessel like this to become queasy with terror.

'You don't like them?' His voice gave nothing away. At least he'd dropped the sarcasm.

'I…avoid them.' Understatement of the century. For eleven years she hadn't been on anything smaller than a massive, multi-level inter-island ferry. Even that was a test of her nerves, leaving her shaken and sick to her stomach.

'You get seasick?'

She shook her head.

'Not seasick. So it's something else.' He wasn't going to let up till he'd prised the whole story from her. 'But you're a sailor, a good one.' Callie blinked in surprise at his praise. 'You didn't learn your way around a yacht by staying ashore.'

She hitched her shoulders. 'I used to sail as a kid.' Some summers she'd spent more hours on the water than ashore.

'And then?'

She dragged in a breath, knowing she couldn't escape this. He wouldn't let her go and he wouldn't settle for prevarication.

'My parents died when their yacht foundered in a storm off the coast north of Sydney.' Callie's view of the porthole misted but she kept her voice more or less steady. 'They'd gone to assist another craft in distress. In the end both yachts were lost.' A lump the size of the acropolis rose in her throat and she had to pause before continuing. 'There weren't any survivors.'

'How old were you?'

'Fourteen.' So long ago yet right now, aboard the gently swaying yacht so much like the one her dad had refurbished, the grief was as fresh as it had been then.

Maybe if their bodies had been recovered, if she'd been able to say her goodbyes instead of being whisked off to Greece by her uncle, who'd decreed that attending a memorial service would only upset her further…

'I'm sorry.' The simple, apparently sincere words, sliced through the silence. Callie turned to meet his eyes.

She'd expected impatience, derision even, at the childish fear she'd been unable to shake. Her uncle had no patience with her phobia. She was just thankful Alkis hadn't been aware of it, as he'd preferred flight to sea travel. Callie could imagine the vicious delight he'd have taken in exploiting her weakness.

But Damon's eyes held nothing but regret. She blinked, absorbing his sympathy.

'Thank you.' Callie tugged her gaze away, her breath an uneven gulp in her raw throat. She was perturbed at the illusion of warmth, of connection that sparked between them. Her emotional meltdown must have shorted something in her brain, making her imagine things.

'You should have told me before we came aboard.'

She shrugged. It hadn't occurred to her. Men, in her experience, didn't let a little thing like female nerves stand in the way of their plans.

How could she have known she'd react like this?

She'd thought she could master her fear. But the feel of the yacht beneath her feet had been the last straw after days strung out with tension. Damon's demands and manipulative methods had resurrected memories she'd worked hard to repress, of Alkis and their awful sham of a marriage. Of a misery so intense she'd thought she might die of it.

The extremity of her grief, welling up through her very pores, had stunned her.

'Why didn't you tell me?'

She turned. He looked sincere. But that meant nothing. She raised an unsteady hand, swiping tears from her cheeks.

Callie hated that he'd seen her so vulnerable.

'Why hand you one more weapon to use against me?'

Damon's lungs constricted as he read the sincerity in her drowned eyes. She meant it!

A splinter of pain pierced his chest as he watched her withdraw into herself again.

She thought he'd stoop so low? To use her genuine fear, her grief over her parents' death, to his own ends? It was one thing to play on her desire to keep her cousin from him, another to plumb such depths.

Shock tore through him.

He remembered the loss of his own father. Remembered too well its impact on his mother and siblings. The desolation and the grief. No decent man would use such emotions for his own gain.

Damon was a hard man in business, but honest. With women he was generous.

Pride revolted that Callie thought so little of him.

Suddenly this wasn't about the give-and-take game of awareness between a man and a woman. Callie referred to a different sort of battle. An ugly one with no holds barred.

What sort of men had she mixed with to make her believe he'd use her grief against her?

Her uncle was a selfish opportunist, but she'd faced him down only this morning.

Who else? Her husband? Men she'd known during her marriage? Had her lovers been so unsavoury? Had they used her in some way, rather than being fodder for her rapacious desires as he'd assumed? The notion stirred protective anger.

A sliver of doubt stabbed him as he thought of his ultimatum. The power he'd wielded to make her come with him.

It was something he'd never done before—threaten a woman into his bed. Logic told him he was simply turning the tables on her. She'd connived and now it was his turn. She was facing her just deserts.

Yet he couldn't repress a shiver that felt like guilt as she huddled in on herself.

'Come here.' His voice was rougher than he intended as he stripped the covers and lifted her onto the bed.

Wide eyes met his before she jerked her head away. Her mouth compressed in such misery his chest squeezed.

He swung her legs up so she lay in the bed. Seconds later he'd shucked off his shoes and lay beside her, drawing the covers over her. He slid his arms around her and pulled her close so her head rested on his collarbone.

She needed warmth and comfort.

Something other than his libido surfaced as he cradled her. He wanted to take care of her.

He'd feel the same about anyone in these circumstances.

Callie lay rigid in his arms.

After an interminable time she moved. Fingers tickled his throat and he swallowed down the surge of need that threatened to swamp him.

This was no time for sex.

Then he realised what she was doing. She'd fumbled his top shirt button open and was working on the next, her hands a delicious torment on his over-heated skin.

'Stop!' He clamped his palm over her hand and reared back so he could see her properly.

She was pale, her eyes enormous in her tear-washed face. Even her lips were pallid. But she'd stopped crying and there was a determined set to her mouth.

'What are you doing?' he demanded.

Her gaze slid to where he held her captive. Only now did he register the fine tremor in her fingers. He stroked them with his thumb, aware of their fine-boned fragility.

'Delivering on my promise.' Her voice was a husky wisp of sound, barely audible.

'Your promise?' He frowned, his mind still grappling with the evidence of her vulnerability and his body's inevitable response to her tentative caress.

'I promised myself to you. As your mistress,' she added as if she hadn't been clear the first time. 'You wanted—'

'I know what you promised,' he growled, thrusting her hand away as if stung. The reminder of their agreement, now, with her so patently vulnerable, made their deal seem tawdry.

Surely she couldn't believe he'd demand she give herself here, now, when she was in such a state.

Surprised eyes met his. Grimly he tugged her close, pulling her head down to his shoulder. So he didn't have to look into those bruised green depths.

Heat scorched him from the soul out. Guilt engulfed him.

'Close your eyes and sleep, Callie. This isn't the time.'

CHAPTER EIGHT

'YOU have a beautiful home.' Callie gazed across the broad curve of the horizon pool to the indigo sea and the darker bulk of the mainland beyond. The peace of the tiny island enveloped her. After the shock of her emotional meltdown yesterday this was balm to her soul.

If only she could be alone to enjoy it.

Her skin prickled and she knew he watched her. Reluctantly she turned. He sat just a metre away.

His eyes snared hers and remarkably she felt again the illusion of connection with him she'd experienced the first time.

'I'm glad you approve. I didn't think it would be to your taste.'

His gesture encompassed the mansion behind them. Not a modern construction as she'd expected but a lovingly restored home with a history of its own. It had elegant long windows, full-length shutters, a pantiled roof and delicately poised balconies. Inside, as on his yacht, Damon had blended grace with modern convenience.

Callie's gaze followed the line of the house to an unfinished building in a similar style, connected by a glazed walkway that surprisingly worked, rather than detracted from the original villa.

Damon was expanding, using the centuries-old house above its private bay as his centrepiece.

Callie liked his approach.

'Just like you assumed I wouldn't like the *Circe*?'

'My mistake.'

Callie blinked. In years of marriage she'd never once heard

Alkis admit to an error. Even to something so trivial. She grimaced and swallowed some wine. It slid like nectar down her throat. Only the best in Damon's home.

'My uncle's taste isn't mine.' He probably thought she'd inherited Aristides' love of over-the-top decoration.

Just as he'd assumed she was conniving and unscrupulous like her uncle.

'So I'm discovering.' Damon's gaze slid over her, taking in her simple, stylish dress in cream and bronze. The colours suited her but there was no cleavage on display.

She lifted her chin. 'Disappointed?'

'Intrigued.' The banked heat in his gaze revealed a familiar hunger. And something more: curiosity.

No wonder. He'd got more than he bargained for when he took her aboard his yacht. She cringed at the memory of that episode. He'd seen her at her most vulnerable. Yet to her amazement he hadn't taken advantage of that.

Callie had woken from a dreamless sleep this morning to find Damon had sailed overnight to the mainland and organised a helicopter flight to his island.

He'd saved her the distress of staying on his yacht. When she'd tried to thank him he'd brushed aside her gratitude as if he'd done nothing at all!

More, he'd rejected her fumbling attempt to initiate intimacy. Instead he'd simply held her till she slept. The memory of his steady heartbeat soothing her, his strong arms protecting her, his scratchy chin moving against her hair as he spoke, created a tiny unfurling bud of warmth deep inside her.

There'd been no chastisement for her weakness, no rant about the inconvenience she'd caused. Instead she recalled his brusque tenderness as he'd rocked her to sleep. Damon had been patient and practical, as if dealing with a mistress's phobia were commonplace.

She couldn't fathom him, morphing from cold-blooded manipulator to carer in the blink of an eye. She'd never have believed it possible.

Who was Damon Savakis, really?

'Is your family from this island?' The intensity of his stare unnerved her. Polite conversation was better than silence when he watched her every move.

At least watching was all he'd do, for now. This morning she'd had to explain, red-faced with embarrassment, that her monthly cycle had begun early. Damon hadn't batted an eyelid, no doubt used to such discussions with live-in lovers.

She didn't have to please him in bed. Yet.

'No, we're from the south. From the Peloponnesus.'

'So why here?' Nerves forced her to continue.

He shrugged and she was reminded of him, bare-shouldered onboard *Circe*. Heat rippled through her and she looked away.

'I'd sailed here and knew the island. It's an easy commute to Athens by chopper or even speedboat.'

'You travel every day?' He'd left her here all day, alone but for his unobtrusive staff. Presumably he'd spent the time working, despite his plan to take a few days off.

Of course, that was before he'd learned his new mistress was inconveniently unavailable for sex.

Why spend time here in the meantime? Nothing could have reinforced more clearly her place in his world. She served just one purpose.

'This is a holiday retreat. My principal home is in Athens. But I thought you might appreciate the peace here.'

Just like that Damon pulled the rug out from under her assumptions. He'd come here so she could recuperate?

Heat flushed her throat and cheeks. Mortification warred with gratitude and surprise. 'I… Thank you. That's very kind of—'

'Besides,' he spoke again, cutting off her clumsy thanks, 'I wanted to check how the build was progressing.' He gestured to the extension beside the original villa.

Callie pressed her lips together. Either he didn't want her thanks or she fitted neatly with his existing plans. She had no idea which. With Damon all her certainties crumbled.

'I make it a point to keep a personal eye on all important matters.'

'Like visiting my uncle when you took over his company?' The words were out before she could regret them.

'Precisely.' Damon's mouth firmed as he watched the distant view.

'Do you oversee every deal?' He was a billionaire with a reputation for decisive action. Surely he delegated some negotiations to his staff.

'Ah, but that was more than a business deal.' His lips twisted in a grim smile. 'That was personal.'

'How?' As far as she knew her uncle had never met Damon before this week.

Slowly he turned to face her. His expression made her quiver. 'He didn't tell you.' It was a statement, not a question, almost as if he spoke to himself. 'Both my grandfather and father worked in the Manolis shipyards.'

Callie felt the slide of premonition down her backbone, like the touch of an icy finger.

'My father died in an industrial accident there.' He spoke in a monotone. But she saw the angry glitter in his eyes.

'I'm sorry.'

Again that shrug of wide, powerful shoulders.

'Your uncle was in charge of the company by then and his lawyers saw to it my mother didn't get compensation. She barely got enough to cover funeral costs.'

Callie gasped at such callousness. But she could believe it of her uncle. He was all for screwing money out of the business any way he could. Empathy for workers was a foreign concept to him.

Remorse stabbed her, carving through her chest.

With his action Aristides had tainted the company her father had helped expand. He'd tainted their family. No wonder Damon expected the worst of them. Of her.

'Acquiring Manolis Enterprises was payback. Is that it?'

Silently he nodded.

'How long have you been planning your takeover?'

'Since the day the lawyer bullied my mother into relinquishing her claim for compensation.'

Silence stretched, a taut wire between them.

All this was about revenge? Even his pursuit of her? Carefully she placed her glass on a nearby table as her hands began to shake. Her pulse pounded frantically.

How better to triumph in his victory over her family than to rub their noses in her weakness for him? No wonder he'd targeted her for seduction. She'd been collateral damage in his quest for vengeance.

The tentative warmth and gratitude she'd begun to feel leached away in the face of his calculating actions.

'You don't really want me,' she whispered. 'You want retribution.'

His ebony eyes gleamed as he surveyed her.

'Wrong, Callie. I have my payback. But make no mistake. I want you too.'

Eight days later Damon emerged from the pilot's seat of his chopper and strode from the helipad to his villa.

As usual, he was eager for his first glimpse of Callie.

Today the business with her uncle had been finalised. Contrary to his original plans, Damon had settled a generous sum on Manolis. The memory of Angela's tentative smile, the knowledge of Callie's worry for the sick aunt she rang daily, had played on his conscience. Instead of stripping the family bare of assets he'd acceded far more than he needed to.

He grimaced. He was getting soft.

His family told him his protective instincts were too strong, that he took his responsibilities for their welfare too seriously. Now he found himself going out of his way to provide for his arch rival's womenfolk!

But the worry pleating Callie's brow whenever she got off the phone, her obvious concern for her relatives, touched him. In that she was genuine and he respected her for it.

Besides, Angela and her mother shouldn't suffer for Manolis' behaviour. Hadn't Damon slaved for years to protect his mother and siblings from the fallout of that man's machinations?

Strange how, after years plotting revenge, the reality was tempered by other considerations.

Yet he was satisfied with his decision.

He'd even decided to salvage what was left of Manolis Industries, building it into his own vast enterprise so it became profitable once again. Only a fool would destroy something with such innate potential.

He pushed through a side-door and bounded up the stairs, anticipation firing his blood.

He hadn't seen Callie since dawn, when he'd held her close and done nothing to assuage the ravening hunger to possess her again. For over a week now he'd kept his distance, insisting only that she share his bed. He had no intention of letting her establish herself in another room.

Each night had been a torture of thwarted desire, but he refused to give up the pleasure of sleeping with her. Even though he did precious little sleeping!

Her reaction aboard *Circe* had stunned him. He hadn't realised her vulnerability.

Nor had he counted on the twinge of guilt that assailed him about his tactics in getting her to himself. Despite the underhand blackmail stunt she'd organised with her uncle, he had a sneaking idea he'd lowered himself to their level in forcing her hand.

Yet grief for her parents didn't absolve her of how she'd lived since she was old enough to sell herself to a rich old husband. Or try to trick Damon into marriage.

She was simply more complex than he'd supposed, her mercenary gloss hiding doubts and fears, like anyone else.

Nevertheless, as he entered the corridor at the top of the stairs, he knew he wanted more. He didn't want Callie giving herself because he demanded it. Because he'd blackmailed her by playing on her fears for her cousin.

He wanted her to come to him because she wanted him.

He reached the door to the master suite and he heard running water. Damon slammed to a stop.

His groin hardened as his imagination presented a picture of Callie in glorious detail. Her hair would be like dark honey, slicked over her shoulders and down the sweet arch of her spine.

Her thighs, belly and breasts glistening with water. Her hand moving slowly, soaping tender, sensitive skin.

A groan of anticipation filled his throat.

Damon reached out and turned the door handle.

CHAPTER NINE

CALLIE secured the plush bathrobe at her waist then bent to towel-dry her hair.

These last eight days in the luxury of Damon's private estate had given her plenty of time to think. Yet thinking got her no further forward.

She hated the way he'd forced her into this arrangement. Yet she'd seen glimpses of a better man hidden beneath the surface. A man who, despite every expectation, had gone out of his way to look after a woman he saw as his enemy when she was in distress.

The size of the Manolis family debt to his weighed heavily on her conscience. She could even understand, after dealing with her uncle, how Damon believed she'd tried to trick him in a plot to secure a wealthy bridegroom.

And running beneath all her ponderings lay the swift, dark channel of desire. Strong as rushing water, deeper than she cared to test. It blindsided her too often, especially when Damon held her in his arms every night, spooned in front of him or nestled across his chest. Each morning she'd wake to find they'd snuggled closer in sleep. His thigh between hers, his hand on her breast, her mouth on his warm throat.

Horrified by the way her body accepted his, she feigned sleep till he got up to shower ready for the office.

But nothing stopped the memories of a time when his touch had been magic to her starved senses.

When the time came and he demanded sex, would she resent his domination? Or would she welcome it?

Her indignation and defiance had wilted. Or was it just that today's news had sapped her strength? After a long discussion with her lawyer there was still no news of the trust. Her plans to start her business were indefinitely on hold. She couldn't rely on her uncle to hold to his promise.

Callie gritted her teeth and rubbed her scalp harder.

No! She wouldn't give up. She *would* make her new start. As soon as she was free of Damon she'd find herself a job and start saving. She—

Callie's hands stilled, tightening like claws against her scalp. A pair of large, bare masculine feet appeared in her line of vision.

Her heart pumped faster and her breasts rose and fell as her breathing turned shallow. The movement reminded her that beneath the towelling robe she was naked. Her skin contracted in shivery awareness of her vulnerability.

Adrenalin shot into her bloodstream. Suddenly every nerve was on alert.

Slowly she lifted her head. Dark trousers, superbly fitted over long, powerful legs, planted wide in an attitude of assurance. Pockets bulged where his hands rested, obviously at ease. Trim waist, flat stomach. A powerful chest beneath a tailored shirt.

Callie's heart nosedived as she saw the top buttons of his shirt open, his tie missing and the taut, anticipatory smile on Damon's beautifully sculpted lips.

His eyes blazed heat that spilled over her, stoking her temperature till her cheeks were on fire.

You're mine.

No need for words. His proprietorial expression said it all.

The towel dropped from Callie's nervous fingers and she bent, scrabbling to pick it up.

He stepped towards her and she backed, holding the damp towel in front of her, a token barrier.

'You're home early.' Her voice was a nervous whisper that matched the rising panic deep inside.

She'd told herself she'd go through with this, no matter how cold and demanding he was. He couldn't damage her pride any more than it had already been savaged. At least his arrogant demands would help her retain her contempt.

But there was a vast difference between theory and reality. Try as she might she couldn't conjure the cool persona she needed to keep him at bay.

Or silence the voice inside that purred in expectation of his caresses.

The reality of Damon in the flesh, a threat and a promise, sent her pulse skittering.

'Yes.' His eyelids lowered, giving him a sensuous look that made Callie's limbs grow heavy. 'I wanted to see you.'

Her eyes widened as he opened the cuffs of his shirt.

'I've been thinking about you all afternoon.'

His voice dropped to a deep, ultra-masculine burr of sound that made the fine hairs on her arms stand up. Her nipples peaked and she crossed her arms as if that would prevent her reaction.

'I…wanted to see you too,' she blurted, following the dexterous path of his long brown fingers as they flicked open every shirt button.

He raised one brow. 'Really?'

'Yes. My things have arrived. The belongings I left at my uncle's.'

He nodded then shrugged out of his shirt, tossing it onto the linen basket.

Callie tried to focus on the fall of fine silk, but her gaze swung back to Damon. His chest was bare: tanned, muscled, perfect. At the sight of his naked torso her stomach coiled tight and hard. She saw the fuzz of dark hair spread across his pectorals and arrow down his belly and remembered the feel of it teasing her nipples as they'd rocked together, moving as one.

'There's quite a bit of stuff,' she choked out, looking away, holding herself rigid. 'I haven't got a home base yet.'

She no longer had a home in the US and her uncle had refused to store anything of hers. He was furious that she'd stymied his plans for a Manolis-Savakis marriage.

'That's OK.'

Damon stepped closer, his hands at his belt. Callie backed up till she felt a wall against her spine.

'It's all been put in the bedroom at the far end of the hall. I thought—'

'I said it's OK. Keep your things there as long as you like. You can use that room as your own.' He paused. 'Except that you'll sleep with me.'

The flash of fire in his eyes confirmed he wasn't thinking about sleep. His expression made her defences crumble on their foundations.

Callie had an awful feeling if she let him close now she'd never be able to erect another barrier between them. The force of his personality was too strong.

'Do you want the shower?' she babbled. 'Let me just put this towel back then I'll get out of your way.'

Callie turned and stumbled to the towel rail, berating herself for her lack of coordination. Her prized composure, even her determination not to show any weakness, had deserted her.

Blood pounded in her ears as she fumbled to hang the towel over the rail. Finally she managed it then tightened the belt of her robe, assuring herself it was secure.

She was turning to leave, desperately searching for something, anything to say that would distract Damon from sex, when a sound made her freeze.

Running water.

Callie spun, then reached to grope for the rail as shock rippled through her.

Damon leaned into the massive double shower, adjusting the temperature of the spray. He'd stripped off the last of his clothes. He was completely, breathtakingly naked.

From this angle Callie saw the long sweep of his back and the heavy weight of his shoulders and muscled biceps as he reached for the taps. His thighs were solid, muscled and powerful. His buttocks tightly rounded.

She stood, rooted to the spot, unable to shift her gaze.

The solid planes and curves of his body made a magnificent picture.

She'd forgotten just how breathtaking he was. But her body hadn't. She felt the telltale softening between her legs, the anticipatory buzz of awareness, the revving heartbeat and knew she had to escape. Fast.

For, she finally realised, it wasn't Damon Savakis she feared. It was her own treacherous frailty.

He made her respond to him in ways she'd never dreamed possible, made her feel—

'Callie.'

His voice stopped her as she sidled to the door. It was a velvet promise of pleasure that tugged her eyelids to half mast and weighted her unsteady legs.

Just that one word weakened her resolve!

He stood before her, naked and unashamed. Fully, gloriously aroused, Damon Savakis was something to behold.

Callie's knees trembled as she stared. There was no escape. The faint scent of musk made her nostrils flare in the damp air. From his skin or hers?

Dark eyes scorched her mouth, her throat, everywhere they roved.

Her gaze dropped as he reached for something, a packet. He tore the corner and, eyes never leaving hers, fitted a condom, his movements quick and assured.

There was something incredibly erotic about seeing him, proud and ready for her. A surge of excitement scudded straight to her womb and tingles erupted deep inside.

His gaze claimed her. The melting warmth of her body was proof that physically she was his. He'd imprinted himself on her, awakening longings and desires she'd shelved long years ago. Now those longings centred on Damon.

Panic pulsed. Would she always feel this answering tide of hunger when he looked at her?

It wasn't the calculating stare that chilled her to the bone. It was the warm, smoky invitation she'd read in his eyes that first time.

An invitation to pleasure…and something even more powerful that lured her, heedless of everything but the need to respond.

'Callie.' The word whispered through her, tugging at her senses. He reached out and took her tie belt in his hand, yanking so the material fell away.

A hiss of breath sighed in her ears as he watched her robe swing loose.

He stood as if frozen.

Callie experienced a surge of impatience. Why didn't he follow through? Touch her? Claim her?

Callie tried to summon indignation, outrage at being made to give herself to him. But nothing came. Only a buzz of excitement at the prospect of intimacy with Damon. It was just as it had been the first time.

Magical.

'Do you want this?'

It took long seconds before she made sense of his words.

'Callie. Do you want me?'

He was *asking* her? No hint of force. Just the compulsive pressure of her own desire.

Damon was handing her the power to say no. Making it *her* decision!

Callie swallowed a sob as contradictory, unexpected feelings overcame her.

Tomorrow she'd regret this. But right now the honest truth was she wanted this as much as he. It felt as if she'd always wanted this, wanted him.

'Callie!'

He stepped back, his face paling as his hands clenched at his sides. She almost cried aloud at his retreat.

With difficulty she swallowed a knot of welling emotion.

'Please.' Her voice was a mere croak of sound. 'Yes.'

That was enough. Instantly he stepped close, palming the heavy robe from her shoulders so it puddled at her feet.

His eyes blazed, fever-bright, as he raked her from head to toe. Instinctively Callie crossed an arm across her breasts and another down over the juncture of her thighs.

But she no longer felt modest. No longer felt like the person she'd known for the last twenty-five years.

Damon had changed her irrevocably.

His knee nudged her thighs as he backed her into the warm shower, his hands sliding to her wrists then skimming up to her shoulders. Excitement sparked where he touched, exploding with an intensity that snatched her breath.

This felt so right.

'Damon.' Even under the steady thrum of water, her hair plastered to her ears, the word sounded like a plea. Needy and bewildered. Callie reached out and clasped his slippery shoulders, needing support. More, needing to touch him with a desperation stronger than anything she'd known.

She craved his strength, his power, his ability to satisfy the hunger that devoured her so completely.

There was no thought now of compulsion or blackmail. This was as simple, as elemental as desire between a man and a woman could be.

'Glikia mou.' Damon nuzzled her neck, her collarbone, and shock waves tore through her, making her body jerk and tremble beneath his touch.

'I want you.' There was freedom in the words. A freedom she'd never expected.

Callie slipped her hands across his shoulders to his slick hair, clamping her fingers against his skull and drawing him down towards her.

Bliss as he opened his mouth to her. His lips moved sensuously. His tongue laved the inside of her mouth, caressing and teasing and satisfying with slow, erotic strokes. Long, hard fingers bracketed her cheeks and jaw, holding her still as he tilted her face for better access.

Callie's eyes closed. In the rich darkness colours exploded as their kiss grew from languorous to hungry. From hungry to desperate. Damon's chest crushed her so exquisitely she rubbed against him, revelling in the slippery friction.

Deep in his throat Damon growled and slid his arms round her, holding her still. His tight embrace was perfection.

She felt him everywhere, from his tongue, warm and seductive against hers, to his hand clasping her bottom, drawing her higher so her soft belly pressed against his steel-hard erection.

Heat coiled and she melted, butter-soft and ready for him. Her fingers slid through his wet hair, seeking purchase as she pressed close.

'Damon, please.'

She needed him.

Water sluicing on her breasts and belly made her eyes snap open. Damon still held her but he'd stepped away, allowing the spray to cover her. Callie reached to pull him close, beyond caring that it was her doing the begging.

Obsidian eyes met hers and she dragged in a breath as shock ripped through her. She barely recognised the man before her. His face was stripped bare of softness. The stark angles of his bones, the rigid line of his jaw and the inky black slash of his brows painted a portrait of raw hunger. Of a need that matched her own.

Callie's heart squeezed for the pain mixed with pleasure she read there. Instinctively she reached to cup his face, to offer the comfort of a kiss, but he moved too fast.

One moment he was there, staring down with the eyes of a tortured man. The next he'd dropped to his knees, hands spanning her waist as he suckled her left breast.

Her moan of ecstasy shuddered through the cubicle as he drew out pleasure so sharp she thought she'd faint. She cradled him, arching forward to meet his lips, his tongue, his teeth. Delight speared her and she shook, grateful for the wall at her back, hands propping her up.

Then he moved once more, nipping tiny erotic bites at her waist and belly that sent flashes of electricity jagging through her. Callie's head thudded against the tiles as weakness invaded her very bones.

Too late she realised his intentions. Broad hands pushed her thighs apart. Her eyes widened as she felt his hot breath between her legs.

'No!' Her head jerked forward and she met his arrested gaze. 'Don't.'

For a moment her brain seized, absorbing the sight of him there, kneeling like a supplicant before her. Heat twisted in her chest and her heart thundered.

'No?'

She shook her head, her hands pushing at his shoulders. Her reaction was purely instinctive.

'I don't…' Her words petered out under his unwavering stare. How gauche she must seem in her inexperience. 'I haven't ever…'

His gaze seared hers as the water cascaded around them, drumming on the tiles. His expression was unreadable.

'Then allow me.' He waited only a second for her response but it stuck to the roof of her mouth, like her tongue.

Then it was too late. Damon leaned in and nuzzled her in that most secret place. Sensations assailed her: sharper, more acute than she'd ever experienced.

Callie's fingers curled into claws as his tongue flicked out and traced a fiery path of ecstasy right at her core. She shuddered and clung to him, dazzled by the intensity of what he made her feel. Again and again. She couldn't breathe, couldn't think. Could only sag back against the tiles as rivulets of fire burned through her, igniting the most exquisite reactions. She'd never dreamed…

'Damon. Please…' Her keening cry choked into silence as, like a red-hot lava flow, the momentum of pleasure built to an unstoppable surge.

Her knees gave way as sensation exploded, racking her body with wave upon wave of delight.

She shuddered and collapsed, sated and trembling as aftershocks of pleasure reverberated again and again. Her mind was a dazed whirl at this stunning new experience. At the gift he'd given her.

Hazily she was aware of Damon moving, holding her close, his solid body warm against hers. She sank against him, boneless in his embrace.

'Thank you,' she whispered against his broad shoulder as another aftershock hit her. Her words were slurred.

'It was my pleasure.' His voice was a deep rumble she felt through her chest as he held her to him.

But he didn't let her sink into oblivion. A moment later the suck of his mouth on her nipple shot exquisite pleasure through her, echoing the pulse of her fading climax. She jerked in his arms, zapped by a jolt of electrical current.

'And it's not over yet,' he said as his hands circled her waist and lifted her off her feet.

Callie's eyes snapped open as she felt slippery tiles at her back again. She looked down into fever-bright eyes, a furrowed brow and a mouth drawn in a tight line of concentration. She barely had time to register that she was no longer standing when he stepped close, under her.

'Lift your legs,' Damon ordered in a hoarse, unrecognisable voice.

Gripping his shoulders, Callie complied, her knees encircling his hips as he lowered her, with excruciating slowness, till they joined.

Her breath stopped on a gasp of astonished delight.

She'd thought herself sated. Yet even that lightning bolt of ecstasy hadn't satisfied her as this did—the two of them together as one, inextricably whole.

Callie leaned in, wrapping him closer. She was open to him and part of him so completely. Emotion welled, filling the hollow place where fear and defiance and loneliness had resided so long. She wanted to please him as he had her. She wanted to give him—

The abrupt, urgent rocking of his body against hers blasted thought from her brain. Instinctively she clung tight, curving herself round him to counter and enhance each hard thrust. His hands slid down to clamp her hips and he sank his teeth against her neck in a tender bite that sent rockets of heat corkscrewing into her veins.

Callie's eyes were closing as a shadow of movement across the room caught her eye. In the far mirror wall she saw Damon, all superb male power, his buttocks clenching with each upward surge. His biceps huge and solid as he held her. Pale legs encircled his dark skin, pale fingers grasped his wide shoulders.

Together they looked…they looked…

One final potent thrust and the conflagration engulfed them both.

A roar of triumph rent the air. Damon pulsed urgently within and her muscles contracted hard, welcoming and encouraging.

Sensation erupted as she rode the powerful wave of pleasure with her lover.

She clasped him close, their hearts thundering together, completion shuddering through them, binding them as one. Callie knew moment after moment of purest joy, then awareness began to slide and she slumped against him.

Eventually, dimly she became aware of the drumming sound ceasing, of the pounding water ending. Still she clung to him, not wanting to dispel the magic encompassing them.

Gentle hands, strong hands moved against her. Plush, warm towelling enveloped her. A voice murmured in her ear, drawing her back to reality.

'Relax your legs, Callie.' Firm pressure forced her to unlock her ankles and let her legs slip down. Taut muscles groaned at the release of pressure and she trembled.

Her feet touched the ground but she couldn't stand. She was sinking out of his hold when powerful arms scooped her high against a chest that still thundered, like her own.

'I'm sorry,' she mumbled. 'I can't seem to—'

'It's all right, *Callie mou*.'

She lifted weighted lids to see Damon watching. He wore an expression she barely recognized: tenderness mixed with puzzlement. And more that she was too weary to comprehend.

Her lips curved as rare peace filled her. She turned her face into him. Her palm rose to the slick warmth of his chest.

Then the world slipped away and all Callie's cares with it.

CHAPTER TEN

CALLIE woke alone.

It was early morning, judging by the light rimming the curtains. She swept the bed with her hand. It was warm from Damon's body. His spicy scent mingled with the musky fragrance of sex, making her weak, remembering.

Emotion catapulted through her, feelings so potent yet so jumbled they barely made sense. Through the long night they'd been lovers. To her overwrought senses, her befuddled brain, it seemed *lovers* was the right word. That they'd shared more than mere sex.

There'd been tenderness, a generous warmth that had transported her back to that magical afternoon on the island, when the whole world had seemed brighter because of Damon. When for the first time everything had seemed *right*.

Was she fooling herself again?

Callie forced drooping eyelids open, as if morning light could oust the fantasies lingering after a night of bliss.

She ached in places she'd never before ached. Her body was replete, her limbs heavy. Yet energy zinged in her veins as never before. She wanted to leap out of bed and dance, to climb a mountain top and shout her joy.

In Damon's arms she'd felt…cherished.

Callie stared at the indentation on the empty pillow beside hers. What did it signify?

Her burgeoning happiness fizzled as if doused in cold water.

It didn't take a genius to work it out. It meant he'd had what he wanted and now he was getting ready for the day ahead. A day in which again she had no part.

All that had changed was this time, instead of making do with an embrace that left them both unsatisfied and on edge, Damon had enjoyed her body to the full. Several times.

She meant nothing to him but carnal pleasure. And of course, an added twist to his revenge on the Manolis family.

She satisfied his ego.

She'd spent years satisfying her husband's ego.

Yet Damon was infinitely more dangerous than Alkis. Damon got closer to her long-buried emotions. He'd stripped away the façade behind which she hid, the veneer of cool sophistication that concealed the needy, vulnerable woman.

It was just imagination, hormones, forbidden fantasies that made last night seem special. She couldn't let that cloud her determination to remain aloof and preserve herself from the devastation he'd inflict if she let him close.

She had to do what Damon did so well—separate sex and emotion. Compartmentalise her life and keep her feelings locked away. *He'd* never suffer romantic daydreams about her.

Callie marshalled her resolve. She would be strong. Damon would never realise how profoundly he'd affected her.

How for a short time he'd reawakened naïve, girlish dreams of happily-ever-after with a man who seemed perfect for her. Caring and patient when she was in pain. Tender yet powerful and outrageously seductive in bed.

Spinning threads of wonder and ecstasy that stopped her thinking straight.

Allowing her control. The right to choose. She blinked furiously. How precious that had seemed last night.

Yet there'd *been* no choice. She'd been utterly ensnared by his potent seduction. Unable to escape. And he knew it.

The man she'd fallen for was a fantasy. He was *not* Damon. She had to remember that.

Callie would go her own way as soon as she could. Carve a

future for herself. Despite her lack of qualifications or work experience, she'd find a job and save. No matter how many years it took she'd earn enough to start her business, achieve her dream. She'd live her own life.

It would be all right.

Why, then, did her eyes mist with hot, prickling tears as her hand slid over that empty pillow? Why did her lip wobble so she had to bite down hard to keep it still and stifle the wrenching sob of pain that rose in her aching throat?

This was what she'd feared. Not the physical intimacy, though she'd known moments of doubt last night as Damon led her down paths, to experiences that were completely new. It was the sense of being swamped, overwhelmed by a force stronger than herself, that threatened to steal her identity.

The force binding her to Damon was stronger than blackmail. Her craving for tenderness had become a shackle, tying her to a man who would never care for her.

Callie would resist it. She refused to be a victim any longer.

Damon whistled softly between his teeth as he towelled his hair. Even the cold shower, necessary to keep his libido in check long enough to get out the door to the office, hadn't doused his buoyant mood.

She was his. At last Callie was his. She was as delicious as he remembered.

More. She was…more.

He'd never felt so jubilant after a night with a lover.

His hands stilled as the thought flashed into his brain that Callie wasn't like his previous women.

He ignored the idea. It was simply the result of supreme sexual satisfaction. Sex had never been this good. Callie was more than anything he'd ever imagined.

It had been tempting to stay in bed, consigning his morning's meetings to oblivion.

Far too tempting.

Damon prided himself on his willpower. He hadn't got where he was by getting sidetracked. He didn't intend to start now.

Especially when, for all her sweet abandon, he knew remaining would be a measure of her power over him.

No woman had that sort of power.

He turned to drape the towel over a rail then froze as a thought lodged. He felt more pleasure, more excitement finally having Callie where he wanted her than at acquiring Manolis Enterprises. That had once loomed above him like an unreachable goal.

A woman, *this* woman, meant more than the goal that had sent him into business all those years ago.

Hair prickled his nape and a twist of something like apprehension coiled in his belly.

Impossible!

Swiftly he dressed, holding at bay the subversive snippets of thought that threatened to distract him.

How his lust for business success had faded this last year or two. Outstripped now by his lust for one woman.

No! He wasn't a one-woman man. Not yet. Not till the time came to settle down and start a family.

How Callie had been everything he'd expected, yet different. Unexpected. In some ways almost innocent.

Could it be? After years of marriage? After the way she'd come to him the first time: so easy and uninhibited?

No, it was a tactic she'd used to excite him. Her apparent surprise and inexperience in the shower just showed she could pander to a man's fantasies—playing the role of shy ingénue to complement her obvious sensuality.

Yet his hands slowed on his shirt buttons, remembering the look on her face as he'd knelt before her: trepidation mixed with excitement.

She'd acted like an inexperienced virgin.

He knew for a fact she was anything but that.

Deftly he tucked in his shirt and reached for a comb. The surge of heat in his groin, the warmth in his chest slowly dissipated.

Had she conned him again? Didn't she know he wanted her just as she was? The *real* her. Not some carefully constructed persona like the one she'd created at her uncle's behest.

He preferred she didn't play such masquerades. He was a straight-down-the-line sort of guy. That was what he expected from her. Honesty. Was that too much to ask?

'There's no need to pretend you're asleep.'

Damon's voice came from too close. Callie had hoped he'd leave her, apparently sleeping, when he departed. She needed time to pull herself together before she faced him.

Perhaps he wanted to gloat. Men enjoyed revelling in their triumphs.

For a fleeting time she'd thought perhaps with him it could be different.

Reluctantly she opened her eyes. He stood beside the bed, fully dressed, his hair sleek from the shower. He was tall, dark and utterly gorgeous.

Her throat closed on a convulsion of emotion and her chest ached as if too full. She wanted to stroke her finger down the proud, skewed line of his nose, taste the heat of his lips with hers, feel his hands on her body.

His next words remedied that desire.

'Every morning you pretend not to be awake when I leave. That stops now.'

Guilty heat shot through her, yet she said nothing.

'I refuse to be ignored. Especially in my own bed.' His lips curled in a satisfied smile. 'Especially after last night.'

Suddenly Damon looked like a particularly hungry, particularly dangerous cat. And Callie felt like a tiny cornered mouse. She shuffled back from the edge of the bed, sitting up and drawing the sheet over her naked breasts.

She should have dressed while she had the chance.

He stepped closer till he was up against the bed, looking down.

'A kiss would be an excellent way to say goodbye before I leave for the office.'

Yet his deep voice, his hooded gaze told her he was considering more than a kiss.

He wanted her again.

In the light of day that scared her more than ever. His passion sucked her under, obliterating every defence she had. It made her vulnerable.

'Is that part of the job description for mistresses?' Defiance was her only defence.

His head jerked back, his shoulders stiffening as his lips turned down in displeasure.

'After what we've shared, you would begrudge a kiss?' Anger underscored his suddenly cool tone.

'No.' Callie's defiance ebbed.

It was a losing battle, trying to resist Damon when her body clamoured for him. What she wanted was to melt in his embrace and let him seduce her away to that fantasy paradise they'd discovered together.

She looked around for a robe but there was nothing to cover her nakedness. Instead she tugged the sheet loose and pulled it round her as she rose to her knees.

Damon's palm was warm on her cheek, his breath sweet temptation against her lips as she stretched up towards him.

She wanted this as much as he. It did no good to pretend otherwise. Her heartbeat accelerated in anticipation.

'Better, much better,' he murmured. 'But there's no need for the display of false modesty.'

His other hand curled round the sheet at her breasts and yanked. Horrified, she grabbed the fine linen and sat back on her heels, securing the cloth tightly around her.

'What are you talking about?'

An expression she couldn't read flitted across his face. His mouth hardened.

'You needn't pretend to be so innocent. I don't need games like that to pique my interest.'

His eyes glittered, scorching a trail down to her empty belly and lower, where an insidious pulse of excitement started beating.

'I'm not playing a game,' she responded, bewildered. 'I don't know what you mean.'

Abruptly Damon sat on the bed and reached out to her, his hand cupping her chin so she couldn't evade him.

'You act like you've never let a man see you naked.'

'Is it a crime to feel modest about baring my body?' Indignation snaked through her.

'All I'm saying is you can drop the pretence. I know who I took on when I accepted you as my mistress.'

Despite the warmth of his hand against her skin a chill engulfed her. That sounded remarkably like an insult. As if he was magnanimous admitting her into his presence.

'You've lost me.' Her chin tilted higher.

He jerked his head up impatiently, his hand dropping away. Yet his gaze held her snared like a bird before the hypnotic eyes of a deadly predator.

'Last night you pretended you'd never had oral sex. That you were inexperienced in quite a few things.'

Despite the disapproval in his eyes, Callie didn't miss the flare of heat as he remembered what they'd done together in the bathroom and here, in his wide bed.

Embarrassment was a swirling wave engulfing her, making her skin glow.

She wanted to look away but hiding wasn't the answer.

'As it happens, I hadn't. Is that a crime?'

The shock on Damon's face would have been ludicrous if it weren't so insulting.

What did he think she was?

Then she remembered exactly what he thought of her—some unprincipled socialite whose time was spent shopping and having affairs.

The last of the sweet, piercing joy she'd discovered as Damon made love to her through the night splintered and vanished.

Good, she decided over the soundless keening of her bruised soul. It had been a mirage anyway. Better she face that fact now than spin hopeless dreams.

'I told you, there's no need to act the innocent.' His jaw jutted belligerently. 'If I want you to play games in bed I'll let you know. In the meantime, don't lie. I don't like it.'

'I'm not lying.' Her voice trembled with an indignation so

fierce she strove to control her larynx. 'I did what you wanted, didn't I? That's enough.'

More than enough. The bliss she'd found in his bed was tarnished. She felt unclean.

'And I find your attitude insulting,' she added between clenched teeth. Bad enough when he'd misjudged her before. But now, after the intimacies of last night, the pain of his mistrust carved right through her.

She'd been right not to read too much into what had after all been just sex.

The trouble was the experience was still so overwhelming for her. She hadn't been able to shake the ridiculous idea that there'd been something special about the connection between them.

Damon was probably just as 'special' with all his lovers, she realised bitterly.

Yet she felt betrayed.

'*My* attitude?' He rose to his feet so swiftly she got dizzy. He towered over her, dominating the bed, but at least now he wasn't so close that he overwhelmed her. 'I think you need to consider your own first.'

'What, do I need to consult some *Mistress's Handbook of Etiquette*? I suppose I've broken an unwritten rule.' Callie found refuge in sarcasm, hoping to hide the raw hurt of his accusations.

'Don't tell me I didn't satisfy you,' she jibed before he could respond. 'That would be a lie. You were *well*-satisfied. Several times.'

Even if she *was* incompetent as a lover, his expertise had more than made up for it. In her naïvety she'd assumed her eagerness had pleased him as it had that first time on the beach. Clearly she'd been wrong.

'What are you saying?' He crossed his arms over his chest. Even in a dark silk shirt and tailored trousers he looked dangerous, as if civilisation was the thinnest veneer to the untamed, primitive man beneath. 'That I seduced an innocent that day on the beach? Even after you'd been married for six years?' His expression of disbelief made her bristle. 'I don't believe in fairy stories, Callista.'

His tone, his attitude, the echo of her uncle's disapproving use of her full name: it was the final straw.

After years bottling up the truth and the pain of her disastrous marriage, it was too much. Raw fury, white-hot and overwhelming, rushed through her, obliterating all else.

Deliberately Callie turned and made a production of plumping up the pillows behind her. Then she leaned back, feeling his eyes on her but pretending not to notice.

'Don't worry,' she purred in the deadly saccharine tone that only true disgust could conjure. 'I didn't claim that I came to you a virgin. Someone else had that pleasure.'

She paused, remembering with a jolt just how little the gift of her innocence had meant to her first lover.

The first man to betray her.

A tremor of dark emotion ripped through her and she folded her hands tighter across her breasts, angling her chin in what she hoped was an unconcerned attitude.

'However, I'm not quite the tart you imagine. My sexual history isn't quite as…adventurous or as extensive as you seem to expect. I haven't had a lover in a long time.'

'Lover…husband, don't play semantics.' Damon's gravel tone indicated his displeasure.

'I mean…' she paused and turned to meet him eye to eye. By rights he should burst into flames and shrivel up before her, such was the concentrated dislike in her glare '…my husband was impotent. The marriage was never consummated.'

She let him absorb that for a moment.

His eyes widened and sparked with surprise.

'And,' she continued, with the perfect, cut-crystal diction of outraged virtue, 'I was faithful to my marriage vows. Unlike the women you apparently mix with, I never took a lover to my bed while I was married.'

The silence thundered with the rush of blood in her ears, with Damon's unspoken questions and the echo of her words.

'You ask me to believe all that?' His voice had a hoarse edge that told her she'd finally unsettled him. But she was beyond feeling triumph at such a petty victory.

'Frankly, Damon, I don't care what you believe. You accused me of lying, so I set the record straight.'

Let him think what he liked. She was beyond caring.

After years of her being pilloried as a gold digger, and by her suspicious husband as an adulteress, it was incredibly liberating to blurt out the truth.

A burden lifted from her shoulders, as if by sharing just that one aspect of her disastrous marriage she shed some of the cramping pain that had filled her for so long.

Maybe forging a new start would be easier than she'd imagined. Perhaps she just had to reach out and grasp what she wanted. She shifted her gaze to the new daylight edging the curtains.

The thought gave her courage.

'Since it seems I don't satisfy you, Damon, I think we should end our arrangement.' She darted a sideways glance, taking in lowering dark brows and his preternaturally still form. He looked as if he'd had the shock of his life.

'I've given you what you wanted,' she continued. 'I kept my part of the bargain.'

She pressed back against the pillows. Once she was away from here, once she'd escaped the coils of desire that ensnared her when Damon was near, she'd start anew.

'I'll leave today.'

Tousled blonde hair framed her face and flirted around her breasts and bare shoulders. Wrapped in a sheet, looking thoroughly bedded, she shouldn't wield the authority she did.

Yet she was breathtaking: far too sexy yet curiously austere.

As superb as a warrior queen, issuing a royal decree.

His libido leapt into overdrive. He'd never before come across a woman who had that delicious combination of decisive, demanding female with a take-no-prisoners attitude and warm, seductive lover.

There was a power about her, a potent vitality that had been missing earlier. Even at her most haughty, sparring verbally with him over the past few weeks, she hadn't been this mesmerising.

Guilt engulfed him. Was she telling the truth? Instinct said she was. That he'd ruthlessly pursued a woman who, though not innocent, was far from the sexually experienced partner he'd assumed.

That didn't negate her manipulative plot with her uncle or her mercenary first marriage. Though if she'd spent her married life without her husband in her bed that perhaps explained her breathtaking enthusiasm for sexual pleasure.

But it altered the situation enormously.

Had Damon demanded too much? Too fast? He'd been insatiable and had given free rein to long-thwarted desire.

Yet despite her occasional hesitance, she'd been willing. So willing just the thought of her in bed threatened to blow the lid off his control.

More, the knowledge that what they'd shared was somehow right…more right than anything he'd had with any woman, overcame his pangs of conscience.

He couldn't let her go. Not yet.

'You're not going anywhere.' His voice was thick with the desire that filled every pore, strained every sinew.

She swung her head round, staring at him with the eyes of a seductress, a sorceress. Surely she'd bewitched him. Desire consumed him, obliterating all else.

No evidence now of any vulnerability in her. Not the innocent nor the anguished woman he'd held in his arms aboard the *Circe*. The woman who'd evoked all his protective instincts.

The memory of her last night, the sight of her now, proud and defiant and alluring, ripped the oxygen from his lungs.

'I beg your pardon?'

Damon's lips quirked in appreciation. She really did have attitude. So superior. So irresistible.

'I said you're not leaving.'

Even the moue of surprise on her soft pink lips tugged at his control. Had she really thought she'd leave after one night in his bed?

She was either incredibly naïve or playing some deep Machiavellian game.

He spun on his foot and paced the room, facing his doubts and his conscience.

'That's not for you to decide.'

He turned back to find her sitting taut and straight, her chin notched haughtily, her eyes blazing.

His belly tightened and some alien sensation stirred deep in his chest.

He *couldn't* let her go.

'Isn't it?' He paused, waiting as she digested his purposeful tone.

'But I delivered on my end of the bargain!' She leaned forward, eager to press her point.

His eyes dropped to the hint of cleavage visible as the fisted hand securing the sheet moved. With a supreme effort he returned his gaze to her face.

'You were to be my mistress for as long as I want.' He walked towards the bed, tugging at the tie that suddenly seemed too tight around his neck. 'And I still want. One night is barely a deposit. We'll discuss your plan to leave in a few months.'

Why this unholy pleasure in baiting her? The fire in her eyes ignited a flame of expectation that swamped the last of his scruples.

No other woman, ever, had affected him like this.

She froze, her mouth working as if lost for words.

'Too bad.' Her eyes narrowed and she pressed back against the bed head. 'One night was more than enough for me.'

Through the taut silence her eyes held his defiantly. Finally her lashes dropped and her gaze skated to the windows on the other side of the room.

Not so poised and certain, then.

'I don't want you,' she said in a voice that was too high, too light. Telling this lie didn't come easily. 'I never wanted you. And your ego won't allow you to force an unwilling woman to stay in your bed.' That note of triumph only stirred his fighting spirit.

'Liar,' he whispered as he dropped his tie. Of course she wanted him. Her eyes widened as she followed the movement. 'You don't convince me, Callie. You won't leave.'

'Why shouldn't I?' Her expression turned arctic. 'Are you

threatening to chase after my cousin again? You're big on threats, aren't you?'

Damon shook his head. He had no desire to become Aristides Manolis' son-in-law.

'No threat required, princess. This isn't about Angela. This is about you and me.'

A smile hovered on his lips as he approached.

She swallowed hard, her eyes on him as he paced to the base of the bed.

'You want me. You want to stay here, with me.' His gesture encompassed the vast, rumpled bed. With his other hand he flicked open the top button of his shirt. And the next. And the next.

Somewhere down the row her mouth opened a fraction and her eyes darkened to a deep emerald glow.

Damon shucked off his shoes and stripped off his socks.

When he straightened she'd moved further away, hands clenching the sheet to her collarbone.

'What are you doing?' Definitely a wobble in that voice now. She held herself like a monarch, oblivious to the actions of commoners like him. But her eyes gave her away.

Ah, Callie. Why fight it? Why not admit that, for now at least, he was the man who fired her blood and ignited her senses? The man who could give her everything she desired.

Excitement surged as he remembered her claim that he'd been the only man in six years. The thought thrilled his masculine ego.

As if she'd kept herself just for him.

Madness. She'd done no such thing. But that didn't stifle his pleasure.

'What am I doing? Proving you wrong, lover.'

He shrugged out of his shirt, noting the way her gaze followed the movement.

Not so aloof now, princess.

His belt slid to the floor as he climbed onto the bed. Slowly he prowled its length on hands and knees. Callie's eyes rounded as she shrank back.

His knees straddled her feet, her legs, her thighs. Still she glared back, a study in aristocratic disdain. But he had her measure now. He knew that behind the façade pulsed a heart as hungry for passion as his own.

The knowledge was immeasurably exciting.

Callie was exciting.

His heart drummed a staccato beat as he felt her warmth beneath him. He breathed deep, inhaling the fragrance of sweet female skin and the sultry scent of sex.

'You won't change my mind.' She blurted the words out, but they were a poor camouflage. Her nipples peaked like succulent fresh berries beneath the sheet. Her chest rose and fell with her rapid breathing.

'You want me, don't you, Callie?'

She shook her head, her lips a flat line.

He contemplated a frontal assault, kissing her till she capitulated. But that wasn't enough. He wanted the words. He needed to know her hunger matched his.

Braced above her but not touching, he lowered his head and pressed an open-mouthed kiss on the pleasure point where her neck met her shoulder.

She jerked beneath him.

Damon grazed his teeth across the spot and was rewarded with a judder of response. He watched her skin prickle and repeated the caress. The rhythm of her breathing altered, its tempo rattling out of control.

'Say it, lover. Say you need me.'

Callie sidled away. He prevented her simply by sliding his hand under the linen to cup her warm, full breast.

A bolt of energy sheared straight to his groin. He wondered if he had the control to manage a slow, persuasive seduction when every hormone screamed the need for haste.

Callie turned him into a man he barely recognised.

Her breath sawed as he kissed along her shoulder and back to her neck.

'Say it, Callie. Or walk out the door.'

He moved his hand, tracing his fingertip in spiralling circles towards her nipple.

She gasped as he tugged the sensitive point.

The sound of her, the feel and scent and memory of her stiffened his body to breaking point. Just like that.

What had been intended as erotic torment for her was torture for him too.

'I—'

'Yes, Callie?' He pressed another kiss to her collarbone then across her rapidly working throat.

'I…need you, Damon.' Her voice was deliciously hoarse.

His heart stuttered as slim, delicate fingers caressed his shoulders, slid down his chest, exploring across, up and then inexorably down.

Relief shuddered through him.

Damon slanted his mouth hungrily over hers, sinking into her generous depths like a sailor coming home to port after a long and dangerous odyssey.

He'd expected triumph when she capitulated. But the surge of warmth and overwhelming tenderness that enveloped him at her welcome was new.

For an instant it teased his mind. Then, inevitably, he fell into the pleasurable oblivion of Callie's loving.

CHAPTER ELEVEN

'THANKS for your hospitality, Damon. It's been a profitable meeting. And a delight getting to know you, Callie. I'll enjoy returning the favour when you visit.'

Callie smiled. 'It was lovely meeting you too, Paulo.' She watched the older man shake hands with Damon, surprised to discover how much she liked Damon's associates and friends.

This business lunch at Athens' picturesque Mikrolimano Harbour had revealed Damon as a relaxed and attentive host, as well as an astute entrepreneur.

There'd been wealthy businessmen and their partners, most now leaving the marina for the fleet of limos that would take them to their destinations. None had been in a hurry to go. All valued Damon's opinion and friendship.

'My pleasure,' Damon responded with an easy smile. 'We'll look forward to taking you up on your offer.'

They were going to Brazil? Callie shot a startled glance at Damon.

He sent her an unreadable look. 'I need to fit in a visit to South America in the next few months.'

Callie digested that. They'd been together several weeks. Callie still reeled at the intensity of their relationship. Surrendering to Damon hadn't been the punishment she expected. It had been mutual pleasure. No winner, no loser. Just the pair of them caught in a conflagration of desire.

Callie was alternately scared and delighted by the passionate woman his loving had revealed. But she'd assumed a passion that flared so brightly would burn itself out in time. Wasn't that why Damon never stayed with any one woman? Because eventually he tired of her?

But he was talking about months into the future.

Could she survive months with him and emerge unscathed? Already she found herself wishing for more. Wishing to understand the complex man who delighted her in bed, but remained an enigma outside of it.

'And you'll bring Callie? Excellent.' Callie turned to find Mariana, Paulo's gorgeous, dark-haired wife beaming at her. 'That will give me a chance to show you some of the places I told you about.'

Her smile was genuine and Callie responded automatically. She was still surprised at the warmth with which she'd been greeted by Mariana and the other women today. In her experience beautiful women with wealthy partners were more likely to be suspicious of potential rivals.

'That means shopping,' Paulo groaned theatrically. 'She'll ruin me yet.'

Mariana turned and gave him a playful punch in the arm then kissed his cheek.

Callie was dumbfounded at the pang of envy she felt as she watched the older couple. Her experience of marriage had put her off the institution. Especially as so many of her late husband's friends were in unhappy relationships: mismatched couples brought together by greed, duty or convenience.

For years she'd dreamed only of freedom and independence. But watching Mariana and Paulo…

'You'll enjoy yourself, Callie.' Damon's deep voice interrupted her thoughts. 'Paulo's home is the last word in luxury. And we'll visit my resorts. Sybaritic pleasure guaranteed.'

He thought that was what she wanted? She opened her mouth to disabuse him, but the words crumbled on her tongue as he reached out. One finger stroked a wisp of hair behind her ear then slipped down her cheek, under her jaw line, to nudge her chin up. Suddenly he was only a kiss away.

His eyes blazed with an intensity that had been missing moments before.

The fine hairs on her arms rose and a tingling started deep in her belly as she remembered his lips moving against hers. The swirl of fire as his tongue found hers and desire spiralled out of control.

'Come, Paulo. It's time we left.'

Startled, Callie dragged her gaze from Damon's and turned. Embarrassment warmed her cheeks as she met Mariana's understanding smile and heard Paulo chuckle.

'Very well, woman. We have matters of our own to see to, eh?' He waggled his eyebrows so obviously Callie had to stifle a smile.

He shepherded his wife to the door of the luxury cruiser's main cabin. 'By the way, Damon, do you still have that dog?' There was a sparkle in Paulo's eyes.

'What would I do with a dog? I travel too much.'

'She didn't die after all?' Mariana sounded upset.

'Of course not.' Paulo looped his arm around her. 'She wouldn't dare. Not after Damon took her under his wing.'

Intrigued, Callie looked from one to the other. 'What dog?'

'Just a pup,' Damon said brusquely. 'It was injured in a car accident.'

'The poor thing was being trained as a guide dog,' Mariana added, 'when a speeding car hit her. We were the next car along and Damon stopped to help.'

'Which meant hours finding a good vet and sorting things out with its owners,' Paulo added.

'Sorting things out?'

'They wanted to put her down,' Damon said gruffly. 'Just because she had a leg amputated. I arranged to take her.'

'Buy her, don't you mean? And pay the vet bills.'

'Easy to do, Paulo. I'm not exactly short of cash.' Damon looked as if he wanted to change the subject.

Mariana leaned forward and gave him a motherly pat on the cheek. 'You did more, Damon. You took the poor animal home yourself.' She turned to Callie. 'And when he found how long the waiting list was for trained companion dogs he endowed a new breeding facility and training program.'

Fascinated, Callie watched Damon's cheeks darken. He looked embarrassed.

'One of your projects to set the world straight,' Paulo murmured. 'You're always trying to make things right.' He looked at Callie. 'You'll find it's a fixation of Damon's.'

'You exaggerate as usual, Paulo. You'd have done the same if I hadn't.'

'So what did happen to the mutt?'

Damon shrugged. 'My nephew took a fancy to her and she bonded with him.' He rubbed his chin, his expression rueful. 'Only he insists on bringing her sailing. Keeping a four-year-old and his three-legged dog from sliding off a slippery deck has its challenges.'

Paulo barked with laughter and clapped a hand on Damon's shoulder. 'I knew you hadn't got rid of it. I just wish you were this soft in our business negotiations.'

'So you could fleece me? I'd like to see the day.'

After more farewells Callie watched Damon escort their guests ashore.

He was passionate, single-minded and ruthless in getting what he wanted. Yet Damon had an unexpected tender streak. He'd comforted her aboard *Circe*. He'd organised a chopper to take them to his home, understanding her fear of sailing.

What sort of self-absorbed tycoon cosseted the woman he'd blackmailed into his bed? Adopted a maimed pup? Went out of his way to fund a guide-dog centre?

She didn't understand him. She'd thought him cruel, relentless, motivated only by a desire for revenge and a taste for sensual pleasure. But there was more to his character.

Donating to charity didn't make him a saint. Alkis had supported charities, but on the advice of accountants, only to minimise tax. Never because he was moved by their cause.

She watched Damon walk back aboard and felt an overwhelming need to understand him. To know where she fitted in his world.

'What did Paulo mean about you trying to set the world to rights?'

He paused then sauntered across the room.

'Paulo exaggerates.' He met her enquiring gaze and she knew he wasn't going to elaborate. Instead the look in his eyes was intent, making her feel suddenly too warm, too vulnerable.

She hurried into speech. 'You were pleased with today's lunch? With your meeting?'

In her experience men were easily distracted by what interested them most—their plans to increase profits and prestige. If today's lunch was any indicator, Damon had reason to smile.

He shrugged and she couldn't help but follow the movement of his rangy shoulders.

'The discussions went well. It made a pleasant change to meet on board rather than in an office. Plus there was a lot of interest in this latest cruiser design.'

His nod encompassed the vast cabin with its aura of wealth. From the impossibly plush carpet to the exquisite marquetry woodwork, sleek, modern design and equipment, the room was the perfect setting for a billionaire.

Yet Callie remembered how Damon had looked, his hair rumpled by a sea breeze, his feet bare on the decking of *Circe*. As if he belonged. As if he enjoyed the unfettered freedom and simplicity of the grand old yacht.

Part of her hankered to experience that moment again. She'd felt for a short, incredible time that, with Damon's support, she might even conquer her fear of sailing.

'How about you, Callie? Did you enjoy yourself?' His question took her by surprise. He sounded genuinely curious.

'It was fun. They're nice people.' She'd enjoyed herself more than at any social engagement during her marriage.

What was different? The people? Damon's friends had none of the brash self-importance of Alkis' cronies. And the man at her side? With Alkis she'd always felt restricted, judged, undercut by his disapproval. With Damon…

'You were a hit today,' he murmured, his expression intimate. 'The men in particular were impressed and very jealous of me.' His smile was all male triumph.

Her mouth primmed as a cold, all too familiar weight dropped in her chest.

So that was why he'd invited her. She should have known.

He'd invited her to be his hostess, to entertain the women while the men discussed business then help him look after their guests over lunch. She'd felt a spurt of pleasure that Damon valued her assistance. He must have some respect for her, even if only for her social skills.

How pathetic to cling to such a crumb!

The gleam in his eyes told its own story. Things weren't so simple. She remembered the quickly veiled interest in several pairs of masculine eyes today, and the way the single men went out of their way to engage her attention.

Damon had been playing a game of one-upmanship, displaying his latest acquisition. His mistress.

The metallic tang of disappointment filled her mouth.

She should have guessed. To him she was a possession. For a while, enjoying a discussion with the women about house design and furnishings, she'd almost forgotten.

Damon didn't want her for her mind or personality. It was her body—the way it looked and how it could satisfy his needs—that counted.

'I think Rafael would have tried to steal you away if given half a chance.'

Damon's eyes bored into her, waiting for her reaction. What did he expect? Pleasure? Excitement?

He moved in a world where rich men acquired and dropped beautiful lovers on a whim. Where women prowled for wealthy protectors and men held ultimate power.

Her stomach churned. She'd had a taste of independence when Alkis died but now she was caught again in that net of male domination.

'You were the most beautiful woman here.'

Callie raised her eyebrows.

She had no illusions about her appearance. Her eyes were nice but her mouth was too wide and her nose too long. Only good posture prevented her looking gangly, despite her curves. Most of her allure was artificial—clothes, attitude, bearing. Her eye for colour and design helped her create an illusion of beauty.

For six years she'd been a possession displayed to prop up her husband's ego and even, she'd discovered later, to lure potential targets for his commercial plans.

She'd been paraded, slavered over and treated like a brainless mannequin. The memories were bitter and raw.

The last thing she needed was compliments on her looks.

She spun on her heel, pacing to the sideboard and the champagne flute she'd barely touched. Swiftly she tilted the crystal to her mouth and swallowed. Effervescent bubbles cascaded over her lips and burst on her tongue. They obliterated the taste of disappointment, though they couldn't quench her simmering resentment.

A few months of freedom and she'd foolishly allowed herself to forget her place in a rich man's world.

'Are we celebrating?' Damon's warm velvet voice caressed her bare neck. A shiver rippled across her skin as she registered the invitation in his tone. He stood so close his heat encompassed her. His musky salt scent invaded her space.

His lips brushed her nape once, twice and she melted. Despite her fury she trembled at his caress.

The flute landed on the wood with a click.

'No. I was just thirsty.'

A hand on her arm made her turn.

She found herself skewered by a dark, unrelenting gaze that sliced to the core of her.

'What's wrong, Callie?'

'I may be your mistress, but I don't like being made to feel cheap.'

'Cheap?' His eyes narrowed and he stepped close, filling her personal space with his big body, his spicy scent, his vibrating anger. 'Someone insulted you? Who was it?'

Callie shook her head, taken aback by his sudden wrath. He looked positively dangerous.

'No one.' She backed a fraction to find herself jammed up against the sideboard. 'I meant the way you invited me here just to show me off as your latest plaything.'

Damon's eyes sparked fire but his words were soft. 'You think that's why I invited you?'

'Why else? Up till now my place has been in your bed. Now you're busy gloating over how jealous your friends are.'

'You read all this from my comment about them admiring you?' He frowned.

She lifted her shoulders in a tight shrug. 'It's how men are.'

'Not this man.' It was a muted growl that made the hairs on her arms prickle. 'I don't need the jealousy of others to prop up my ego.' He thrust his face forward till his banked fury enveloped her. 'You're confusing me with someone else.' There was no mistaking his sincerity, or that he felt insulted. 'Your husband perhaps?'

Callie looked away. The memory of Alkis and his controlling ways was still too strong.

'I don't discuss my marriage.' Pushing that hurt aside was the only way she'd kept going.

'Yet you judge me because of his behaviour. Is that it?'

Callie kept her gaze fixed on the view of the harbour, intimidated by his righteous indignation.

'Didn't it occur to you that I invited you because I wanted you with me? Because I like having you beside me?'

Startled, Callie froze.

'Because I thought my guests would enjoy your company, which they did. And because I thought you'd enjoy theirs.'

Slowly she turned her face up to his.

He looked angry. Impatient. Sincere.

'You look for insults where there are none.'

'I'm sorry,' she murmured, thrown by his intensity, feeling guilty and foolish at her suspicions. 'I enjoyed today. Thank you. Especially meeting Paulo and Mariana. They have such a strong relationship.'

He tilted his head to one side. 'You sound surprised.'

Callie's lips twisted ruefully. 'Happy marriages are a rare commodity.'

'Including yours?'

She sighed. He just didn't give up. 'Including mine.' Callie sidestepped, gaining precious space. She didn't want to talk about Alkis. 'It's nice to see a couple so devoted.'

'My parents were like that.' Damon surprised her with the personal observation. 'And my siblings are all happily shackled.'

'You sound very close.' Maybe if she'd had a sister or brother she'd still have that sort of special bond with someone who loved her.

Damon stepped nearer. 'My sisters say too close. That I'm overprotective, that before they married I always tried to arrange their lives.'

'Whereas now you have to divert your energies into saving stray dogs?' Or settling an old score with the family who'd wronged his. Was that what Paulo had meant about him ensuring things turned out right?

'Not *all* my energies.' His voice was a silken skein of suggestion as he stroked her cheek, brow and lips.

Instantly Callie's eyelids lowered and she swayed close, drawn by the desire that pulsed between them. Each time it was the same—something she couldn't fight. A hunger that fed on itself, growing stronger by the day.

'I should go.' Her voice was husky. 'I have an appointment in the city.' She needed to prove to herself that she retained some shred of self-control.

His hand stilled. 'An appointment?'

'With my lawyer. I'd prefer not to be late.'

'Ah, I thought you'd dressed conservatively.' He gestured to her honey-beige suit, aquamarine camisole and high heels. 'But I like it.' His smile sent her pulse racing. His hand dropped to her lapel, sliding along the fabric.

'Is there some legal problem?' His question surprised her. She shrugged, half her attention on his wandering hand.

Today's meeting was to discuss her non-existent trust fund. She'd heard nothing from her uncle about her inheritance and her calls to Angela had centred on Aunt Desma. At least in that respect there was good news. The doctors had hopes she'd respond well to medication.

'Nothing I can't handle.'

Impenetrable eyes surveyed her so thoroughly she felt as if he stripped bare all her secrets.

'When is the appointment?' The liquid heat in his eyes told her he had plans for the afternoon that didn't include meeting with lawyers.

'In less than an hour.'

Damon's hand dropped, feathering past her breast in a stealthy caress that caught her breath. He stepped back.

'All right, then. Let's go. I'll drop you.'

His withdrawal stunned her. She'd expected him to ignore her plans and seduce her. Here. Now.

Disappointment fizzed.

He extended an arm and waited till she reluctantly tucked her arm in his.

For one instant she experienced a mad urge to lean against his solid bulk and blurt out her problems, as she had that day on his yacht.

Then logic kicked in, a savage blow to the solar plexus that sucked the air from her lungs.

Damon Savakis *was* her problem.

Damon strode quickly to the bedroom.

'Callie?' Still that fillip of excitement got him whenever he came home.

'Callie?' He entered the master suite and paused, disappointment crashing into him when he found it empty. She wasn't as he'd fantasised, in the sunken tub, waiting for him.

Since they'd moved to his Athens apartment she spent most days out on business of her own. She wasn't exactly secretive but she didn't offer information and after the little he'd gleaned about her marriage he didn't push. She was opening up to him only slowly.

He knew her spark of extra animation coincided with her trust fund becoming available.

He smiled. It was good to see the way she'd blossomed. She'd been gorgeous before, but now, with this inner glow of excitement, she was irresistible.

Damon headed down the hall. Maybe she was in the room she'd converted into an office. He knocked. Silence. He hesitated.

He'd never entered the private space where her belongings were stored.

Finally he turned the handle. It wouldn't be the first time she hadn't heard him because she was listening to earphones. There was that memorable time in his private gym. She'd been working out in tight shorts and a skimpy top, oblivious to his arrival, and he'd…

Damon stopped as the door swung open.

He had a hazy memory of the room as it been, designer-styled cream chic.

The memory vanished as vibrant colours caught his eye, lush, rich and inviting. He frowned, *feeling* a difference in the atmosphere.

Stepping into Callie's room was like stepping into another world. One alive with her presence.

The pristine monochromatic style of his modern apartment suddenly seemed soulless as he gazed around this space.

The bed was pushed into the corner to make space for a massive draughtsman's desk. The cream coverlet was piled with cushions in purples, greens and blues that made him think how much he wanted to make love to her here.

More cushions beckoned on a low sofa. On a glass coffee-table was an arrangement of lilies, their scent reminding him of Callie's skin as they made love, sweet and musky.

On the walls were a series of…he didn't know the word. Hangings? Embroideries? Massive artworks of fabric and beads in the colours of the sea. They depicted the ocean in moods ranging from pearly calm to steely grey and dangerous, all finished with exquisite stitching.

He stepped close, drawn to one that depicted a pine-fringed beach with water the colour of Callie's eyes. He could almost reach out and touch the sea.

A squiggle of gold in one corner caught his eye. C.M.

Callie's work? Could it be?

He moved back, stunned. Callie had done this? He went from one piece to another. On each were the same initials.

Callie said she sewed. But she'd been so reticent he assumed she made little doilies like those his mother sewed.

Astounded, he pivoted. These belonged in a gallery.

Why did she hide her talent like this?

Curiosity got the better of him and he moved to the vast desk, taking in catalogues, business cards of artisans who worked in glass and wood and timber. Swatches of fabrics. And beside them a much thumbed folder. A business plan.

Damon was so engrossed he didn't feel a qualm about sitting down and leafing through the document.

Half an hour later he flexed his shoulders and leaned back in the chair, closing the last page.

What a mystery his lover was.

She had outstanding talent. Even he, a philistine when it came to the decorative arts, recognised her genius for creating mood and sensation through her fabric scenes.

Her business plan for an upmarket home-furnishings boutique was careful and well thought out. She'd made a few potential mistakes, but had done a professional job.

Where had she learned about starting a business? Her husband? Unlikely. Yet she'd acquired the skills she needed.

She was some woman.

Pride warmed him at her determination to start her enterprise. It reminded him of his own drive to learn and succeed in business.

He glanced round the room, bright and welcoming and warmly sensuous. Like Callie.

He reached out and brushed his hand across a padded box upholstered in silk, with a beaded flying fish leaping across the top. Instinctively he knew Callie had made it. His hands curled around its soft edges, its glittering decoration.

Sitting in her space, Damon felt the warmth, the vibrancy, the secret something that drew him to Callie as to no other woman.

She'd turned his ideas about women on their heads.

Like the day at Mikrolimano when she'd entertained his guests. He'd known she'd be the perfect hostess. He hadn't hesitated in asking her, though he'd never invited any previous mistress to do so.

Nevertheless he'd been curious about her response to so much male interest. She'd been friendly but not too friendly. She'd spent most of her time laughing with the women and seemed almost oblivious of the stir she caused till later when she'd snapped at him.

Because she thought him like her husband? Something about her marriage was at the heart of her reserve.

For Callie wasn't the woman he'd first thought.

Prickly, independent, intelligent, fabulously responsive. She never pandered to his ego. She'd stood up to him time and again. She continually refused his gifts. She engaged his mind as well as his libido.

Callie was anything but a calculating man-eater.

She turned him inside out. For the first time he was no longer focused solely on the next merger, the next business triumph.

He wanted more. More of Callie.

CHAPTER TWELVE

'YOU mustn't let business take up all your time, Damon! Say you'll come to Kefalonia.'

The woman's gilded nails wrapped around Damon's sleeve and tugged him into contact with her over-abundant, unnaturally firm breast. It was as enticing as cuddling up to an overblown beach ball.

She turned scarlet lips up and her extravagant perfume closed like a fog around him.

'It will be a very select house party, Damonaki,' she purred, leaning still closer, as if her spouse wasn't just on the other side of the crowded theatre foyer. 'My husband won't be there till the weekend but I'll devote myself to entertaining you. Privately,' she added suggestively.

Her talons gripped tighter and he read the acquisitive glitter in her eyes.

Revulsion rose.

A swift glance at the throng around them made him swallow the curt retort hovering on his lips.

'I won't be available next week. Besides, my companion—'

'Callista Manolis?' He noted the barely restrained jealousy in the bottle-blonde's tone. 'She doesn't run your life. Not a strong, decisive man like you.' Her knee edged up his thigh. Bile filled his throat.

'Or,' she tilted her head speculatively, her mouth slackening in an expression of breathless excitement he found abhorrent, 'if you bring her we could have some fun. The three of us together.'

'I'm afraid that won't be possible.' The cool, cut-crystal tone interrupted before he could give voice to a pungent, earthy response.

He slid his arm free and turned towards the newcomer.

'Callie,' he murmured appreciatively. The sight of her, elegant and sexy in a high-necked, bare-shouldered black dress, was like a sip of pure spring water after swallowing something toxic.

Damon reached out and she slipped her hand into his. Warm, supple, it fitted perfectly. He was growing accustomed to this sense of rightness, having her with him.

'Damon and I have plans for that week,' Callie said, looking down from her superior height.

'You don't know which week we were discussing,' the other woman said. Her stiff facial muscles tightened more as she stared up at Callie.

Callie favoured Damon with a brief, knowing smile that made his heart drum faster. Even here, now, at this premiere event, he responded to the promise in her gold-flecked gaze.

'All Damon's weeks are booked up,' Callie asserted. 'Aren't they, Damon?'

Surprise transfixed him as that sultry, bedroom voice emerged from Callie's pink-glossed lips.

The only time he heard that tone was when they were alone and he'd driven her to the extremity of pleasure. Instinctively his body tightened.

'If you say so, *glikia mou.*'

He enjoyed the novelty of her playing the vamp. Usually she was reserved at events like this. As if the company of A-list celebrities and their cronies wasn't her style.

He leaned close and inhaled her fresh scent. It reminded him of sunny days and long, languorous loving.

Was she jealous? Was that why she'd appeared at his side?

The idea pleased him immensely. Though he had her in his bed every night and the passion between them was a palpable force, part of her remained steadfastly closed to him.

He chose lovers who understood he wanted no emotional entanglements. But with Callie he found himself wanting more than physical gratification. The realisation unsettled him and he shoved it aside.

'Well,' huffed the other woman. 'Far be it from me to come between a happy couple.' Her eyes flashed. 'But don't forget, Damonaki,' she pressed close again, her mouth a wet pout, 'you're welcome any time. You'd find my hospitality memorable.'

She turned and undulated her way through the crowd.

Instantly Callie's hand tugged, as if to be released. He firmed his grip. Anger simmered in her green stare.

'Nice friends you have, *Damonaki*.' She didn't conceal her disgust, almost spitting out the ridiculous pet name. Yet she stood straight and proud, as if unfazed by that gross little scene.

'Jealous, lover?' Her lips flattened and he relented. 'The rescue wasn't necessary but thanks. One day her poor sot of a husband will find her propositioning someone and there'll be hell to pay.'

'He doesn't know?'

Damon shrugged. 'Probably. But if it's under his nose he'll have to do something about it and break a lifetime's habit of ignoring what he doesn't want to see.'

Was it any wonder he despised so many of society's 'best' people?

'Are you ready to go?' Looking at her in that dress made him want to strip her out of it. It was time they were alone.

'Don't you want to stay?'

Damon's lips firmed. For all Callie's abandon in his bed, his shower, on his sofa or even, on one memorable occasion, on his vast dining table, it was he who initiated intimacy. She still maintained that air of aloofness.

It tried his patience, even as it turned him on.

He released her hand, his fingers sliding over her wrist to the sensitive pleasure point at her inner elbow. She shivered, her nipples peaking through the silky fabric as he caressed her.

'Let's go home.'

Home. Damon's huge penthouse *had* become home. More than Alkis' soulless mansion had been.

That was what had changed, Callie realised as Damon ushered her out to the waiting limo, his arm protective around her.

The deep freeze at her very core had begun to thaw.

Damon had done that. He mightn't trust her fully, might view her as a source of convenient sex, but he was more generous than any man she'd ever met. Generous with his time and himself, in ways that, to a woman used to being dismissed as an ornament, made something warm and soft burgeon inside.

Her weakness for him terrified her but she couldn't break away. Hadn't been able to since the morning he'd challenged her to walk out on him.

Callie was hooked on the passion blazing between them. It made her feel bliss.

More, it made her feel she was no longer alone against the world.

Damon wasn't generous as her husband had been, with easy gifts that proclaimed his ownership. Callie had made sure of it, refusing his offer of a designer dress, a glittery trinket from an exclusive jewellery house.

She would live within her means.

The recent, wonderful news that her trust fund had been restored fed her determination not to depend on a man's money again. More, she'd prove to herself she was capable, that she amounted to more than a woman whose sole accomplishment was as a man's trophy. She was hard at work on her plans, investigating commercial locations and sourcing products.

The suddenness of her lawyer's news still stunned her. She could barely believe her uncle had restored what he'd stolen. Had her lawyer pressured him somehow?

Her relationship with Greece's most eligible tycoon was based on sex, not profit. It still shocked her that she wanted him so badly, so constantly, but she found a curious dignity in their arrangement. An equality.

Both were victims of an attraction they couldn't resist.

Damon had been piqued and curious when she didn't live up to her reputation of grasping money-grabber. His first gift, an oyster silk negligée that shouted 'mistress' with every stitch, had resurrected her fury at being manipulated into his bed.

That argument had ended with the silk in shreds and Damon smiling with feral pleasure as for the first time she took a dominant role in lovemaking. He'd looked up at her, moving above him as the world spun in kaleidoscope colours, and huskily threatened to buy her lingerie every day.

Callie's lips twitched at the memory.

Even her pride couldn't force her to relinquish this passionate relationship. Especially since she enjoyed being with Damon. He made her feel good about herself. Amazing when he'd originally forced their relationship and she'd wanted to hate him!

'What are you smiling about?' Damon tugged her close on the limo's back seat, his arm around her shoulders, his fingers a warm imprint on her bare flesh.

Desire ignited. It erupted, a tangible force, shooting darts of heat to her breasts and womb.

She put her hand on his muscled thigh and felt a judder of reaction as Damon's muscles tensed.

In this they were equals. Her smile widened.

'Nothing important. Tell me,' she turned to look him in the eye, 'who was that woman? Not an old flame?'

She was too old for Damon with her surgically enhanced face. She was vulgar. She was wrong for him in so many ways.

'You've got to be kidding.' His mouth twisted. He lifted her hand to his mouth, licking across her palm and up her wrist, creating an earth tremor of rapture.

Callie's mouth slackened and her pulse accelerated. She leaned nearer, grateful for the privacy screen between them and Damon's driver.

'I didn't think your taste ran to anything so obvious.'

Damon cradled her hand to his face. Her heart kicked as his tongue swirled at the centre of her palm. Hot wires of tension snagged tight inside and her eyes fluttered closed.

'And you know all about my taste in women.'

Callie's eyes popped open to meet his impenetrable stare. She couldn't tell if he was serious or sarcastic.

Too late she realised she'd left herself open to a hurtful retort. Hadn't he accused her once of being obvious in her efforts to attract him?

Her fragile sense of well-being cracked.

'You intrigue me,' he murmured. 'Once I would have lumped you in the same group as her, with the morals of an alley cat.'

Callie stiffened and jerked her hand away, but he recaptured it easily, holding it between both of his.

'She's always on the prowl for fresh meat, a new lover she can corrupt with her tawdry charms.'

Numbly Callie shook her head, waiting for him to make a cutting remark about her own character. She should be inured to jibes. Hadn't she parried them endlessly before?

Yet after the intimacies of these recent weeks, the idea of such ravaging scorn cut her to the quick.

'They sicken me, the rich bitches who get what they want, no matter the cost to others.'

Damon wasn't looking at her. He stared at the streets of Athens, still crowded at this hour. Callie sensed it wasn't the city he saw. His thumb rubbed absently over her knuckles.

Curiosity stirred.

'She's not discreet,' she ventured. But the stares and wordless invitations directed at Damon by other women were often blatant.

No wonder he was so arrogantly certain of his attractiveness. He could have his pick. And every flashing-eyed stare made Callie's hackles rise.

He was hers.

She wasn't sharing.

Callie blinked, stunned at her vehement possessiveness.

'Discreet?' His snort of disgust brought her abruptly back to the present. 'Why be discreet when you can use wealth to smooth out any…inconveniences?'

'Damon?' His harsh expression scared her. He looked so angry. 'What is it?' Her fingers wrapped round his, tugging till he looked at her.

'Nothing,' he said at last. 'She reminded me of someone, that's all.'

Dark eyes held hers with an intensity that stilled her to immobility. He tilted her chin so he could see her face. She trembled under his intense scrutiny.

'What is it?' she whispered.

'We're almost home.' His voice held a sultry promise of pleasure and something more. 'Then we can talk.'

Since when had talking been the main item on Damon's agenda?

Twenty minutes later Callie sat alone on the shadowy rooftop terrace with its multimillion-dollar view across the city to the coast. The sweet scents of exotic flowers wafted from the exquisite penthouse garden.

She held a glass of sparkling water. Her bare feet were curled under her on the outdoor lounge and she still wore her black dress, the jersey soft and comfortable.

It was one she'd designed herself. She'd felt inordinate pride when Damon complimented her on her appearance.

Alkis had almost had an apoplexy at the idea of his spouse wearing anything 'home-made', no matter how exquisite. He couldn't see her creative flair, only the notion that anything she accomplished must be second-best.

As for starting her own home-wares and design boutique! He'd deemed it far beyond her limited female abilities.

Silently Callie lifted her glass in a silent toast.

To her new venture.

To being her own woman.

To no longer being classed as second-best.

'Sorry.' Damon's voice came from behind her, sending a shivery trail of awareness down her spine. 'It was an urgent call from California but it's sorted now.'

'That's all right.' Callie shrugged. 'I was enjoying the quiet.'

Without him. Was that the implication?

Damon frowned, wondering if she'd prefer to be alone.

He stepped into her line of vision, his heart contracting at the vision she presented. Her dress was simple and sexy, her hair up, emphasising the slender column of her throat, and she wore no jewellery. Yet her eyes were brighter than emeralds, her smile more alluring than pearls.

The flight of fancy should have made him scoff. A lifetime's experience had proved no woman, particularly an indulged woman from a privileged family, deserved to be put on a pedestal.

Yet Damon's cynicism foundered. He *knew* she was more than she'd seemed.

The time had come to unravel the secrets she hid.

'What are we toasting?' He raised his glass of wine.

Her lips curved in a secret smile that clenched his belly in a spasm of primitive ownership.

Sexually she was his.

But he wanted more. He was greedy for her in so many ways.

'New beginnings.' She touched her glass to his.

'To new beginnings.'

He sat with his back to the glow of the city lights. He'd seen that view many times. Tonight his focus was the enigmatic woman before him. He was determined to keep his distance until he had answers.

'Tell me why you married.'

Her head jerked and her eyes rounded.

'I don't talk about my marriage.' Frost coated her voice.

'I know. I want you to tell me anyway.'

'Why should I?' Her chin jutted.

'Why shouldn't you?' he countered, leaning forward, his elbows on his knees, his glass clasped in both hands. 'You're not protecting anyone, are you?'

'No,' she said after a moment's hesitation.

'Then what have you got to lose?'

'It's private.'

Ah, there it was, the serene expression of queenly disdain. It proved he was on dangerous ground. Instinct told him the secret of the real Callie lay buried in the circumstances of her marriage.

He didn't need to understand her to bed her.

He didn't need to understand her to revel in the heady bliss of the best sex of his life.

Yet still he needed to know.

Callie was more than the latest woman in his bed. Even that realisation couldn't deter him.

He didn't do serious relationships. But with Callie he needed more than a simple physical relationship. The knowledge had gnawed at him for weeks.

'You're afraid to tell me. Is that it?'

'Why should I pander to your curiosity?' Glittering eyes stabbed him. He watched her defences go up, just as they had in her uncle's home. Only he'd been too angry to see there was more to her attitude than pride and superficiality. That there was hurt as well.

This time he wouldn't react to the challenge. Though his body stirred at the idea of harnessing all the resentful energy quivering through her and directing it into passion that was hot and erotic and satisfying.

From the moment he'd found her huddled and grief-stricken on his yacht, the need to know more had grown. He'd felt her pain. There was so much more, unresolved. It had just taken him a while to realise it.

'Why are you scared?'

Predictably she met his gaze squarely. 'I'm not.'

'Don't you know what they say about sharing painful experiences so they don't fester and take over your life?'

Is that what had happened to Callie?

'We toasted new beginnings. You have to let the past go before you can make that new beginning.'

'Spare me your pop psychology.'

Yet her eyes narrowed, her mouth pursed, as if she considered the idea.

Silence stretched for long minutes, broken only by the distant hum of traffic. Damon watched her intently, alive for the slightest relaxation in her rigid posture.

'I'll tell you,' she said at last, looking stiffer than before. 'On one condition.'

He raised an eyebrow. 'Yes?'

'You answer a question of mine.'

'Done.' His reply was instantaneous.

He sat back, sipping his wine. Better not to crowd her. Yet his scrutiny was intense as he waited, watching her fiddle with the glass in her hand.

'I married for my family,' Callie said eventually, looking beyond him to the city.

'In what way for your family?'

'My uncle promoted the match. Alkis was an acquaintance of his.' Her voice was devoid of emotion. Eerily so.

'You married because your family thought it a good match?' He couldn't believe they'd consider a thirty-five-year age-gap wise.

'My uncle did.' She paused and gnawed her lip in the first overt sign of stress she'd revealed. Then the words poured out in a rush. 'The company was in financial difficulties. They were facing ruin. Uncle Aristides said that without Alkis' support the family would lose everything. But Alkis would only help if he could have me.'

'Your husband made you part of a *business* deal?' Damon's skin crawled at the notion. 'And Aristides agreed?'

The idea of her being given in marriage, a bonus to sweeten a contract, sent wrath surging through him. Acid burned his mouth and his fingers tightened around the glass. He'd like to tighten them around her uncle's flabby neck.

'Yes.'

'The bastards.' There was no question she was genuine. It was there in her anguished eyes and the tight curl of her lips. After living with her for weeks he knew this had the ring of truth. Far more believable, now he knew her, than her vamping an older man to win a fortune.

She was one of the least avaricious women he knew.

'You can say that again.'

'Your uncle bullied you into it.' It wasn't a question. He knew enough about Aristides Manolis to imagine how he'd threaten a young girl to get what he wanted.

'That's how he operates,' she murmured. 'My first love affair had ended badly and I was too wrapped up in that to put up much resistance. I felt I'd be responsible if my aunt and cousin ended up homeless.'

Curiosity about her lover sidetracked him until he realised the broader implications of her statement.

'Manolis just tried it again.' Damon put down his glass before he broke the stem; such was the fury rising within him. 'He tried to sell his daughter to sweeten our negotiations!'

Damon's fury exploded at the notion of being part of such a scheme, however unwittingly.

He'd dismissed the idea of such a match as wishful thinking by Manolis. Had Callie's cousin been under the same intimidating pressure to marry a wealthy man? It made Damon feel unclean.

'He wanted to force Angela too?'

She looked at him curiously. 'Of course.'

Damon leaned back, remembering Angela's diffidence, her nervousness. He'd put it down to natural timidity, but perhaps it was fear of failing to please him, or worse, fear that she'd have to marry him.

He catapulted to his feet, a tide of rage sweeping him along. How had he been so blind? He'd used Callie's protectiveness of her cousin to get her into bed, not for a moment realising the girls had genuine reason to take the idea of such a marriage seriously. That it had happened before.

He'd played on what he thought were Callie's unfounded fears and jealousies.

Christos! It must have been like history repeating itself for Callie, watching her uncle try to bring off another business coup by selling his daughter for profit.

He swung round. She looked calm in the moonlight, her face devoid of expression. Now he knew her he understood she concealed her pain. Pressure built in his chest, squeezing his lungs till his breath jettisoned in a rush.

He'd hurt her, unknowingly playing on what must be deep wounds from the past. He cringed inwardly at the accusations he'd made about her marriage. And the way he'd threatened so glibly to marry Angela if Callie didn't give herself to him.

'I'm sorry.' The words were such a strangled burr he had to repeat himself. 'I'm sorry, Callie. I had no idea. I was too busy finding fault and fighting lust to see what was in front of me.'

'You didn't know,' she said finally, shrugging, but she couldn't deceive him. The tense set of her shoulders, the line of her mouth belied her insouciance.

'I hurt you.' He stepped close, till she looked up and met his eyes. There at last he saw a flicker of something other than stoic control.

'I didn't see how serious Manolis was about his plan to marry me to Angela. Didn't realise the pressure he was applying to Angela. And to you.'

Callie scrutinised him as if she could read in his face whether he was genuine.

'You didn't deserve the way I treated you.' Understanding the full implications iced his bones. Never had he treated a woman so badly.

'No, I didn't.' She slumped back as if the fight had left her, or the effort of maintaining her composure was suddenly too much.

He sat beside her and took her limp hand in his.

'I behaved like an arrogant bastard too.'

Her lips curled in a lopsided smile that tore straight through him. 'You did. You were appalling.'

Yet she let him hold her hand between his palms without pushing him away.

'As bad as Alkis?' he couldn't help asking. Now he saw his actions in a new light. Circumstances and his own outrageous behaviour bracketed him together with the man he'd despised for pursuing a nubile young trophy wife.

His breath stopped as he awaited her answer. For whatever there was between them—sex, excitement, even a strange, raw relationship built on moments of connection like this—Damon wasn't ready to end it.

He wasn't ready to relinquish her.

'Nothing could be as bad as that.'

The quiet vehemence in her clipped words sliced through his thoughts. Her hand balled into a fist in his hold. What the hell?

'Why not?'

Glittering eyes focused on him. In the moonlight he saw brilliant tears well and cling to her lashes.

That curious tight feeling in his chest struck again and his hands tightened around hers.

'My husband was a manipulative, suspicious control freak. Mental cruelty was his speciality.' She drew a deep breath. 'I'm glad he's dead.'

Before Damon could respond she spoke again.

'I don't want to talk about him. But you owe me an answer.'

She halted, looking down at their linked hands then up again in a sidelong glance that told him she'd chosen her question carefully.

'Tell me. Who did the woman tonight remind you of?'

CHAPTER THIRTEEN

DAMON flinched at the abrupt change of subject. His grasp loosened, allowing her to slide her hand free.

He didn't want to talk about this.

It was too private, even now too raw.

He met her unwavering stare.

He owed her. He'd trampled through Callie's traumatic past, hauling to the surface long-buried pain and fear. Because he *had* to know what made her tick.

Now he understood. At least enough to piece together some of the betrayal and disappointment she'd suffered.

Six years with a man she didn't love or respect. With a man she abhorred. Yet she'd played the role of devoted spouse and affectionate niece rather, he guessed, than hurt the ones she loved: her aunt and cousin.

He heard enough snippets of phone conversations to know Callie rang them often, keeping tabs on her aunt's health.

Callie Manolis was the opposite of what he'd believed her. Strong, principled, stoic, with an integrity that shone.

Completely different from the woman she asked about.

Callie watched Damon withdraw as silence enclosed them.

For the first time she'd been honest about her marriage. Not even with Aunt Desma had she come clean about how awful it had been. Her aunt would have blamed herself for not stopping the wedding.

Callie's emotions were muddled. The old negative feelings surfaced. Yet she had a confused sense of something positive emerging from the morass of regret, anger and self-doubt.

It had taken all her strength to hold her own against Alkis' attempts to undermine her confidence. Damon's apology, so direct yet so obviously real, was like a brisk breeze, chasing away the tattered storm clouds of old pain.

Such a simple thing, an apology. But the first one Callie had received for any of the trauma inflicted by the men in her life.

It felt momentous.

Had he been right about sharing the past to make a fresh start?

Callie doubted it was so easy. But she felt better, as if some of the hurt she'd carried so long had healed.

And she felt…trust.

Damon wasn't the amoral opportunist she'd thought. He'd been shocked by her story.

She'd had glimpses of a man who might be far more, far better than the egotistic, power-hungry shark she'd thought him. Now she had proof.

Relief lightened her very bones. She was tied to Damon in deep, inexplicable ways, not just by sexual passion. For the first time she dared hope her feelings weren't self-destructive. That he was a man worth trusting.

He raked a hand through his hair, his face set in grim lines that told their own tale.

Instinct had been right. Some woman in his life had left her mark indelibly.

Did he trust Callie enough to share that secret?

Or had trust been a one-way street?

She held her breath as she waited for him to brush off her question with a glib reply.

'Leta Xanthis.' The words were a grating whisper. 'She reminded me of Leta Xanthis.'

'Leta…?' Callie frowned. The name was vaguely familiar.

'I forget. You didn't grow up in Greece.' His voice was terse. 'She was wife to the most powerful media mogul in Europe. Her beauty and glamour made her a household name.'

Callie nodded. 'She's dead, isn't she?'

'A drug overdose. It caused quite a stir.' Damon sounded as if he were reading a boring news item, not talking about someone he'd known.

Callie watched his mouth compress, his brows furrow. His hand speared again through his hair.

'Was she a friend of your family?'

He snorted. 'Hardly!' His head jerked back in obvious disgust and he shot to his feet. Energy sizzled through him as he paced to the railing on the edge of the terrace.

When he swung back his face was in shadow, the glow of city lights and the moon behind him.

'We didn't mix with the likes of her. She'd have been outraged.' He drew a slow breath. 'When my father died my mother supported us by cleaning houses for rich families with coastal villas.'

Callie heard the ripple of anger in his words. Damon was a proud man. It would have scored his pride to see his mother toiling for others in such a way.

'How old were you?'

'Seventeen. I'd dropped out of school and worked as a handyman and gardener on the same estates. But I didn't earn enough to support the family. My mother still had to endure years of grinding toil.'

Regret laced his tone. Obviously he'd felt he should have been able to step straight into his father's shoes and support the whole family.

'Leta Xanthis owned one of the villas?'

His head reared up as if Callie had interrupted deep thoughts.

'Her husband did. He rarely visited and she used it for entertaining.' He almost spat the last word, the venom in his voice so patent that Callie shivered, rubbing her hands over her arms.

'She knew your mother?'

'She wouldn't notice the woman who scrubbed the toilets or cleaned the filth after her orgies.'

Orgies? Surely he exaggerated.

'But she did notice the kid who came to trim the shrubs and look after the pool.' His words were bitter.

Callie sat up straight as his meaning sank in. 'She came on to you? When you were seventeen?' How much older had she been?

'Don't be so shocked.' Callie hated the world-weary cynicism of his tone. 'Leta came on to anything in trousers. She wasn't the only one. I learned early all about the carnal appetites of rich women with too much time on their hands.'

'She seduced you?' Callie choked on the words.

'No. But that only made it worse. I became a challenge. To her and her friends. What had become occasional visits to the villa grew more frequent, till finally she lost patience and found someone new to target.'

No wonder Damon had a low opinion of socialites. Even as a teenager he must have been breathtakingly handsome. If rich women had thrown themselves at him, it was no surprise he was jaded. Or that he didn't trust women who lived off wealthy husbands while amusing themselves with lovers.

Which was how he'd viewed her when he met her in her uncle's home.

The tension eased from Callie's shoulders as she realised his readiness to believe the worst didn't stem from anything she'd done but from a lifetime's mistrust.

Hadn't she felt the same repugnance at the shallow games played by Alkis' friends?

The sight of Damon turning to pace the length of the garden drew Callie to her feet. He was stiff with tension.

'Damon?' She took a step towards him then faltered as he slammed to a stop, one hand braced on a column supporting a pergola of scented flowers. Callie thought back to his last words and foreboding filtered through her.

'Who did Leta target instead?'

Even from here Callie saw the spasm rack his body before his unnatural stillness resumed. Whatever had happened, this wasn't easy for him.

No easier than her revisiting her time with Alkis.

'My sister.' The words bit like bullets from a machine gun. Callie's throat closed in horror.

'Sophie had come with me one afternoon while I made

repairs. I needed another pair of hands and Sophie was always eager to help.' He paused, then continued in a rush.

'One of Leta's boyfriends saw her and wanted her. Leta wasn't above pandering to his whims. She got Sophie alone and invited her to a party that night. But it had to be a secret. Unfortunately my sister was in a rebellious phase and thrilled by the invite. She was sixteen and too innocent to know what to expect.'

Callie pressed a hand against her churning stomach. She wanted to tell Damon to stop, but the words stuck.

'We didn't realise she was missing till late. One of the younger girls woke and noticed she wasn't in bed.'

'You went looking for her?'

Of course he had. The role of protector was ingrained in him. She'd heard it in his voice as he described his family circumstances. Callie had experienced it first-hand on his yacht when he'd cared for a distraught woman.

'I was almost too late.' The words grated out. Instinctively Callie closed the gap between them, needing to offer comfort. She stopped within reach of his taut, looming frame. He radiated tension. She felt it shiver through her.

'What happened?'

'He'd drugged her, or maybe it was alcohol. Whatever, she was out of it, lying there with her pretty dress rucked up high and…'

Callie wrapped her arms around Damon's waist, holding him close. The thunder of his heartbeat against her ear and the sound of his raw breathing filled the night. He was wound so incredibly tight.

'He didn't see me till I smashed his face in.'

His muscles quivered beneath her hold, reliving the moment of violence. Satisfaction coloured his voice. Callie couldn't blame him. Her hands had clenched in sympathy.

He heaved a mighty sigh and she felt those muscles ease a fraction. 'I ran foul of Leta's other guests, who didn't like me leaving with the prettiest girl there. But eventually we got away.'

Callie tilted her head and saw him rub absently at the skewed line of his nose.

'That's how you broke your nose? Saving your sister?'

He looked down, his dark brows slanted, his eyes flashing with remembered fury.

'All that mattered was getting her out. A couple of black eyes and a bloody nose meant nothing.'

Callie shivered at the idea of a lone, teenaged Damon taking on a bunch of older men, primed by alcohol. It couldn't have been easy. It must have been downright dangerous.

She lifted her hand and stroked the sharp angle of his jaw, feeling the faint graze of stubble tickle her palm.

'What's that for?'

Callie shook her head and let her hand fall. 'Nothing.'

He was so matter-of-fact about saving his sister he wouldn't understand the sudden surge of sympathy and admiration that welled within her. The softening deep inside that made her want to cling to him.

Maybe only a woman who'd never had a protector could feel so choked up by the story of his rescue.

'What happened? Were they charged?'

'No. My mother thought a court case would traumatise Sophie. We were sacked and threatened with the law if we showed our faces on the premises.'

Indignation fired Callie's veins. 'That's outrageous! How could they threaten you?'

'It was their word against ours. Leta was wealthy and powerful. I found new work in a place where I could learn about making money and beating that type in the only way they understood—with even more wealth and power.'

'And Sophie? Is she all right?' Callie rested her head on his chest. His arms encircled her.

Warmth that had nothing to do with shared body heat and everything to do with emotional connection spread through her. Damon's acceptance, his honesty about his past meant so much.

'Sophie's fine. She's one of Athens' leading lawyers.' Pride vibrated through his voice. Callie heard his smile without seeing it.

'She lives here?'

'Most of my family live close.'

Yet Callie had never met them.

Because she, a Manolis, wasn't good enough? Or because she was only temporary? A knot worked in her stomach.

Then he moved and her train of thought dissolved. He slipped his hand through her hair, tugging her head back so she stared up into his fathomless eyes.

Something sparked between them. Something vivid and strong, like the erotic charge of passion they'd experienced from the start. But it was more. The echoes of their pasts, their raw emotions, the trust they'd shared, made this deeper and more powerful.

His gaze stripped her bare. As if he saw her naked, not her body, but herself. Callie Manolis, the woman who'd spent her adult life hiding behind carefully constructed defences, keeping the world at bay and herself safe from further harm.

She saw a man of honour, integrity and compassion. Impatient, quick to judge and eager to have his own way. But his honesty and caring made him unlike any man she'd known since her father.

Was it possible she'd found a decent man? Someone she could genuinely, wholeheartedly care for?

Callie had fought not to relinquish her barriers in the face of his steamroller tactics. But now she'd capitulated and instead of surrender this felt like victory.

Excitement blazed as his head lowered. His breath caressed her face, teasing her lips.

'Damon.' It was a cry of pure longing as her hands snaked up and dragged his head down.

The world lit to a blaze of glory as he claimed her lips, engulfed her being with his. He surrounded her, his arm a steel bar at her spine as he bent her back. Willingly she complied, trusting him to keep her from falling as he took her to heaven with his deep, drugging kiss.

Starbursts exploded as Callie gave herself up to ecstasy. There was no shame in surrender. Just acceptance.

Peace.

Pleasure.

For Callie had done what she'd never dreamed possible. With every last scintilla of hope and trust and courage within her, she'd fallen headlong in love with Damon Savakis.

CHAPTER FOURTEEN

CALLIE coiled her hair behind her head and pinned it. Soon Damon would be home and she wanted to look her best.

She grinned at the woman in the mirror. He'd appreciate how the scarlet fitted dress clung to her curves.

Callie revelled in the effect she had on him. No longer was she repulsed by the feel of hot male eyes on her. Not when that male was Damon.

She'd come a long way. From a wary, damaged victim hiding fear and pain behind a cold shell of detachment to a woman ready to trust a man. Enjoy being with a man.

A woman ready to embrace her future.

A future with Damon? Her pulse quickened. She hoped so.

Before him she'd given up trusting men. Yet he'd smashed her defences till she opened up to him.

How far their relationship had moved. They were bound by more than ties of physical desire. There was respect and caring as well as mutual delight.

For the first time in seven years Callie was happy.

Surely he reciprocated at least some of her feelings? Enough to build on? Increasingly he was interested in her, in her thoughts and plans, listening attentively as she described her first tentative steps into the commercial world. As if what she had to say mattered.

Did he have any idea what a balm that was? To feel as if she and her project was really important?

Callie had to keep reminding herself Damon bought and sold multimillion-euro businesses as easily as she designed an appliquéd hanging. Yet in these last few weeks he'd questioned and challenged her, almost as enthusiastic about her plans as she.

For the first time since she was eighteen the world seemed a rosy, promising place. With Damon beside her she felt capable of anything.

She, the girl who'd barely scraped a place at university, who'd struggled with her studies. Who'd been shown time and again her only value was decorative, or as a lever to financial gain. After years of Alkis' snide remarks and mind games, Callie felt free, capable, independent. This sense of power, of self-worth, was heady.

As heady as the joy of having Damon in her life.

The phone rang and she reached for it eagerly. It was probably Angela with an update on her wedding plans.

Only last week Uncle Aristides had stunned them by agreeing to Angela and Niko's marriage. Angela could have married without his blessing, but his threat to keep his wife from visiting their daughter's home once she was wed had stymied the idea. Now everything was turning out right.

'Angela?'

But instead she heard her lawyer's crisp tones. Excellent news, he said.

'Are you absolutely certain about this?' she asked after he explained his reason for calling.

'Absolutely. The manager of the new complex confirmed it in person. She said your venture is just the sort they want in their building. So much so that they're willing to offer a reduced rental for the first eighteen months.'

Callie rubbed her forehead. She might be inexperienced but even she knew that exclusive new retail complexes did *not* cut their rent for an untried business. She'd queried the rent, guessing it would be far beyond her capacity to pay, but unable to resist checking out the most desirable new location in the city.

'What sort of reduction are we talking about?'

The figure made her head spin. She groped for a chair and sank onto it. He described a peppercorn rental.

Callie drew a deep breath and tried to marshal her thoughts. 'There's a mistake. Why would they make such an offer?'

The silence on the other end of the line stretched out. When he spoke again the lawyer's voice was stiff, as if with embarrassment.

'I understand your current…relationship was a factor.'

'My relationship?' He could only mean Damon. 'I don't understand.'

'You do know that Savakis Enterprises owns the building?'

No. She hadn't known.

'And you think the manager is trying to curry favour with the CEO by giving his…girlfriend a special deal?' The notion seemed far-fetched.

Again that pause before answering. 'My understanding is that the offer was made on the CEO's instructions.'

Damon had ordered the manager of the most exclusive retail development in the city to lower the rent? She shook her head. He was interested and supportive, but he was, after all, a businessman. Why take on such a risk?

'Are you certain?'

'Absolutely.' He cleared his throat then paused. 'Kyrios Savakis has taken an interest in your affairs before. Given your relationship, I thought you were fully aware of that.'

'What sort of interest?'

'Your inheritance. You know there was some irregularity about accessing the funds your uncle managed.'

'I know all the circumstances.'

'Forgive me, but perhaps not all. The balance of your inheritance was topped up by Kyrios Savakis.'

What? Callie's head spun.

'Damon paid the money? Not my uncle? Are you positive?'

'Completely. I understand he was eager to rectify the loss. Technically the money came via your family's company, but the source was most definitely Kyrios Savakis. Of course, I didn't divulge your personal circumstances but he was remarkably well-informed. He wanted to set things straight.'

The phone shook as Callie's hand began to tremble.

Set things straight.

That was Damon's specialty, wasn't it?

She thanked her lawyer in an unsteady voice and hung up.

Damon had provided the inheritance her uncle had stolen. He'd gone to extreme lengths to help her establish her business in a place that almost guaranteed success.

Because he loved her?

She hiccoughed on a bubble of disbelieving laughter. No, not that. He cared for her, enjoyed intimacy with her, but he'd never spoken of anything long-term. It was she, so needy, who yearned for more.

He'd been furious when he learned of her past and guilt-ridden about the way he'd forced her into a relationship. She'd even wondered if his initial interest in her tiny business might be driven by the need to make up for his earlier attitude and show he wasn't like her husband.

Had remorse driven him?

Set things straight.

That was how they'd met. Because he needed to make her family pay for what it had done to his. Settling the score.

Was he setting things straight now because he felt guilty about forcing her to be his lover? He'd been stunned by the truth of her circumstances. He knew he'd hurt her, compounding the damage done by Alkis and her uncle.

She remembered Paulo's words about Damon needing to fix things. His strong sense of responsibility.

Did Damon see her as a victim who needed protection? A problem to be recified?

Her heart squeezed as the suspicion grew. Was that behind his interest and support that she'd so treasured?

Damon felt *sorry* for her?

In the mirror her face was stark white, her lips a slash of scarlet that no longer looked sexy or alluring. Her mouth looked like a clown's painted grimace.

She lifted her hand and wiped the lipstick off with the back of her hand. It smeared like blood across her cheek.

'Callie?' A surge of anticipation quickened Damon's step as he crossed the penthouse foyer. Energy sizzled through him, and, amazingly, a hint of nerves. He hadn't been this excited since his first business coup.

Today was another red-letter day. An even more important one, if the tumult of adrenalin in his bloodstream was any indication.

He patted the small package in his breast pocket, assuring himself of its safety.

Everything was arranged.

He'd contemplated an intimate dinner for two in his apartment. Then he'd decided tonight was an occasion to be celebrated more traditionally. He smiled, thinking of his siblings and their families gathering now at his mother's house, agog to hear his news. The scent of succulent home cooking would fill the air and the rich sound of laughter.

Callie would like that. And they would like her.

But first, a private celebratory toast. His housekeeper had assured him everything would be waiting as instructed.

He stepped into the sitting room and halted, his pulse revving as he saw the slim figure in red at the window, her back to him.

His heart crashed against his ribs then slowly took up a more normal pace. She did that to him every time.

Callie. *His woman.*

A burn of satisfaction warmed his belly. He was doing the right thing, there was no shred of doubt. His decision had been simple. She was the one he wanted.

His gaze swept the elegant room and he realised that without Callie it would be soulless and unbearably empty. Callie's presence made it a home.

He shook his head. He had it bad.

So bad he didn't even care!

Damon strode to the ice bucket that cradled a superb French vintage champagne. Swiftly he uncorked the bottle and poured the delicately hissing contents into waiting flutes.

Only then did she turn.

Damon smiled and held out a glass.

'Here you are, *glikia mou.*'

Glittering eyes met his. He saw her tension, felt the quiver of her fingers as she accepted the glass. She'd sensed tonight was important. Had she guessed how important?

His eyes swept her long dress, gleaming ruby fire in the lamplight, tiny sparkles scintillating as she moved.

She'd dressed to please him. The knowledge pumped the blood faster in his arteries.

'You look gorgeous. Good enough to eat.' The rush of lust was inevitable. But for now he tamped it down. There'd be time later. All the time in the world.

His eyes rose to her face and he paused. Callie looked different. No lipstick. No glossy red to match her gown.

Because she knew he'd kiss it off? Damon eyed her lush pink mouth and realised he preferred her like this.

He took a step nearer, excitement building.

'*Callie mou,*' he murmured, his voice surprisingly husky.

He glanced at the wine in his glass, the tiny vibration on its surface betraying his unsteadiness.

Damon stood straighter, meeting her green stare with a smile that felt just a little ragged. He wasn't used to being anything except totally in control.

'We need to talk.'

'Yes.' She inclined her head fractionally and he was struck by her poise. How it contrasted with his sudden ridiculous anxiety.

He hadn't rehearsed what he'd say. He was a persuasive speaker and he knew what he wanted. It hadn't entered his mind that finding the right words might be difficult. But then what practice had he at this? It was new territory.

'About the future.'

'Good.' Her lips pursed. He watched her heft a deep breath and his gaze strayed appreciatively to her breasts. His hands itched to reach for her. 'I wanted to talk to you too.'

She paused, her eyes skating away from his. 'I've decided to leave.'

Damon watched her lips move, heard the words but couldn't believe what he was hearing.

His heart lurched then began pounding triple time.

'I can't see the humour in your joke, Callie.'

She turned to stare out at the city lights, presenting her perfect profile. It looked carved out of cool marble.

'I'm not joking.' Her voice was a low whisper. She lifted her glass and drank. Not a delicate sip but a long draught, her throat working almost convulsively.

Blindly Damon reached to put his glass on a nearby table before it cracked under the pressure of his grip.

'You're not leaving.'

Women didn't leave him, ever. He'd always been the one to end relationships. But more. This was *Callie*. The woman he'd selected for his own. The woman he wanted in his life permanently.

Wanted? He *needed* her.

He paced closer then froze as she shrank away from him.

His spine crawled as she turned to face him and he saw the blind look in her eyes. She looked…shattered.

'Why? Because it doesn't suit your plans?' There was an edge to her voice he hadn't heard in months. Not since they'd developed a rapport, an understanding. A relationship.

What was going on?

'What's happened, Callie? What's wrong?'

'It's time to move on.' Her chin tilted higher. 'I don't belong here. It doesn't feel right.'

Feel right? It felt wonderful! She'd changed his life and he couldn't imagine it without her. Didn't want to try.

'I won't let you go.' The words shot out before he had time to consider them. He was functioning on raw gut instinct as he reached out and curled a hand round her slim waist. Nothing felt so right as holding Callie.

'I thought you'd given up threatening me.' The tiny hitch in her voice was like a blow to his belly.

'Callie! There's no threat. Don't you trust me?' He'd worked so hard to overcome the damage he'd done. Worked to build her trust in him after his earlier reprehensible actions. He thought they'd moved past that, even though guilt still scored him for the way he'd treated her.

Again she lifted her glass and swallowed. 'As much as I trust any man.'

Her words speared his conscience.

'*Callie mou…*' he sidled closer, slipping his arm round her '…you can trust me.'

Tension vibrated through her body.

'You're a good man, Damon. But I don't belong here. I don't belong with anyone. I prefer to live alone.'

'You don't mean that.' He took the glass from her hands and put it down. Then he wrapped his arms round her and pulled her stiff body towards him, revelling in her softness against him. 'We're good together, Callie. You know we are.'

'Sex.' She shrugged and turned her head to avoid his kiss. Instead his lips grazed her ear. Instinctively he bit gently on her lobe and felt her shiver in response.

'See how you respond to me?' Triumph stirred in his belly. 'You don't really want to live alone.'

'I'm tired of being your mistress, the woman who's not even good enough to meet your family. I'm one of the enemy, remember? A Manolis.'

'That's not true!' How had she got it so wrong? 'They don't think like that. I was the one intent on retribution, not them. As for not being good enough, you couldn't be more wrong.' He thought of his siblings gathering to welcome her.

'There just never seemed a right time…' His words petered out as he realised she was right; he'd kept her from his family. At first because he didn't trust her, then out of habit. He never paraded his short-term lovers before his mother. Then, as he'd become more absorbed in his feelings for her, he was too greedy to share her. He'd wanted Callie all to himself.

Until now, when he'd finally realised how important she was to him. That she was the one woman he *would* introduce to his mother.

Callie's hands pressed at his chest, trying to push him back. But it was only as he saw her blink back tears that he relented and stepped away. His arms dropped to his sides, empty without her.

'That doesn't matter,' she murmured, clearly lying. He felt her hurt and cursed himself for his stupidity. 'What matters is that I don't want to stay indefinitely till you feel I'm able to stand on my own two feet.'

She wrapped her arms around herself as if cold. 'I'm quite capable of looking after myself.'

'What are you talking about?' Frustration filled him and the need to understand.

Her hair swirled round her as she shook her head, her face growing animated. It blazed with an anger that made her eyes shimmer jewel-bright. 'I'm not some charity case, Damon. I realise your intentions are good but I don't need pity from any man.'

'Pity? It's not pity I feel for you.' It was on the tip of his tongue to blurt out exactly how he felt. But the look on her face stopped him.

She wasn't ready to hear. Not yet. She still didn't trust him, so why would she believe him?

Callie stared up at his wrinkled brow and the grim lines around his mouth. No. He really didn't understand. He'd only tried to help her. It wasn't his fault he didn't love her.

Suddenly her anger seeped away. She was tired. So very weary.

'I know how you interfered in my affairs.'

That stopped him in his tracks. His head reared back.

'I owe my inheritance to you.'

'You were entitled to it. And I could easily cover the sum.' He spread his hands in a gesture of openness.

He'd looked just the same all those weeks ago talking to Paulo about endowing a charity. He'd seen the need and he had the cash. Of course he'd step in to fix the problem. That was the sort of man he was. Generous and with an overactive instinct to protect. To set things right.

Except she wasn't a charity. She was a woman in love with a man who saw her as a problem to be fixed. The knowledge seared a hole in her chest, making it hard to breathe.

She didn't want Damon as a benefactor.

She wanted him as her equal.

'And the cheap rent in your new building?'

His gaze flickered. Obviously he hadn't expected her to find out about that. 'The place is perfect for you. It seemed a crime not to help you start up there.'

'But I have to do it *myself*. Don't you see that?'

If just once he'd say he'd acted out of love for her, because she was special, the woman for him...but that was wishful thinking. He'd acted to give her a new start after discovering the hurdles she had to overcome.

'You won't accept my help?' He drew himself up straighter, the distance suddenly yawning between them.

She shook her head. 'It's not about help.'

'So perhaps it's about control,' he murmured. 'You said your husband was a control freak. What exactly did he do?'

Callie frowned, not following his train of thought. 'I don't understand. That's not relevant.'

'Won't you tell me?' The sincerity in his voice, the tenderness in his eyes undid her resolve. Even now he cared. He wanted to remedy the past.

Whereas she wanted to forget the past and build a future.

Pity the only future she could visualise was a fantasy, with Damon by her side.

She sighed and Damon tensed at the pain on her face.

'Alkis always set limits. People I couldn't see, places I couldn't go. I lost count of the design classes and small business groups I joined only to find I had to withdraw. It was no longer convenient or we were taking an extended trip, or he was unwell and needed me. Always some excuse.'

'You could have gone anyway.'

She shook her head. 'He'd have found out and life would have been unbearable. He always knew where I was. Over dinner he'd quiz me about people I'd met that day, people who'd spoken to me.' She looked up and saw Damon's frown. 'He had me watched all the time, reports made on my movements. There wasn't a thing he didn't know about.'

Damon wished her husband wasn't dead so he could take him apart piece by piece. The damage Alkis had caused with his twisted desire for control was appalling. No wonder Callie was desperate to assert her independence.

What damage had Damon done?

Unwittingly he'd tapped into a vein of ingrained vulnerability. Nothing he did now could convince her he wasn't like her bastard husband. He'd tried to help but she thought he'd taken control of her life.

Damon swore under his breath, cursing his drive to act decisively. Should he have held back and consulted her?

He winced, knowing the answer.

'You think I'm like him.' He turned and paced the room.

He'd taken for granted Callie trusted him. More, that she reciprocated his feelings.

Had he pushed her so far he'd lost her for good?

'No! Of course you're not.'

But the misery was clear on her face, in the way she wrung her hands. Her pain belied her words.

He wanted to sweep her up and cosset her and caress her and make love to her till she forgot her pain. And he could. He knew even now that he could overcome her scruples and seduce her with his loving.

But the pleasure would only be temporary. Sooner or later she'd turn those sad eyes on him again.

'How can I prove you wrong?'

She frowned as if he spoke a foreign language.

'What can I do to make you trust me?'

'I trust you, Damon, I just…'

Don't love you?

Don't want you controlling my life?

Can't live with you?

Damon had never felt so helpless. So desperate.

'Then tell me what I can do. What will make a difference?'

He'd do anything. If there were dragons to slay he'd conquer them. He'd fight battles for her, overcome any obstacles. His only hope lay in proving to her he was the one man she could trust with her life.

Her mouth twisted and she shook her head.

'You can let me go.'

CHAPTER FIFTEEN

'The new stock I mentioned has come in. Over on that wall.' Callie smiled at one of her best customers then moved away, letting the woman and her companion browse in peace.

It was almost the end of another long day and she was exhausted. Not from physical tiredness. She still got a thrill of pleasure from her work.

It was emotional strain that made her feel like a wrung-out rag.

Five months, three weeks and six days since she'd seen Damon.

With each day she grew more needy, hungrier for a glimpse of the man who'd dragged all her skeletons from where they hid in her cupboard, who'd made her face her greatest fears. The man who'd infuriated her and challenged her and disrupted her life.

Who'd supported her and listened to her and given her peace as well as pleasure.

The man she'd rejected because she was too proud to settle for anything less than his love. Because with him she'd finally convinced herself dreams might come true. And her dream was Damon—loving her.

Her heart plummeted. Now she had the independence and the opportunity she'd fought for so long. It was wonderful, satisfying and challenging. Proof that she *was* capable. That she was worth more than Alkis or anyone else, herself included, had thought possible.

But independence wasn't enough. Not now she'd had a taste of life with Damon.

She was greedy enough still to dream of what might have been. If only he'd loved her.

He must have cared for her a little, to go to so much trouble on her behalf. But being pitied and propped up was no life for her. To be cared for because he felt sorry for her—that would have destroyed her. Especially when he moved on to his next charity project.

Or worse, fell in love with another woman.

Callie tucked her hair behind her ears, blinking rapidly as she finished unpacking a consignment of lamps.

No, Damon didn't love her. He found her sexually compatible. She stirred his protective instincts. But in the end he hadn't tried to stop her leaving. That had hurt the most, the knowledge she'd been right, that what he felt for her was simply pity.

By now he'd have moved on. Found another lover. A man like Damon would never be short of female companionship.

Her teeth sank into her bottom lip in an attempt to stop a betraying wobble.

Callie avoided the news as much as possible, not wanting to see him with another woman on his arm. She wanted him to be happy but she couldn't bear the thought of him bestowing that special, bone-melting smile on someone else.

Her vision blurred.

'They're beautiful.' A warm voice behind Callie made her swing round, blinking hard.

A woman in her late fifties or early sixties beamed at Callie. Her dark eyes gleamed as she gestured to Callie's silk hangings on the back wall.

There were only two left of her series of seascapes. One day, when she had more leisure, she'd make some more. Her embroidery work had always been therapeutic, especially in the dark years of marriage when she'd had few outlets for her creativity and energy.

'I'm pleased you like them,' she murmured.

Truthfully Callie would be glad to see them go. Those seascapes held too many memories.

She'd begun them in the early days of widowhood: stormy scenes of lashing waves or foggy, deserted coastlines. She'd finished them in a burst of energy and happiness when she lived with Damon. In those the sea was clear and calm, the mood exultant.

Looking at them now, so vibrant and serene, Callie felt more than ever she lived in the shadows. Despite the thrill of her initial tentative business success, the joy was missing.

'My daughter tells me they're your work.'

'Your daughter?' Callie struggled to focus on the conversation.

'Yes.' The woman gestured to her elegant companion bending to examine a small bronze sculpture Callie had just put on display. 'She bought one a few weeks ago and I had to come and see the rest for myself.' Her smile widened. 'And the remarkable woman who made them.'

Callie remembered that hanging so well. Once upon a time she couldn't have imagined selling it. That scene reminded her of all she'd let slip through her fingers. Of the happiness that had shone so briefly. But in the end keeping it had been too painful.

'Thank you.' Callie wished she felt more enthusiasm for her work. She should be thrilled, but it was a struggle to summon the energy.

Yet the older woman's interest was genuine and Callie forced herself to focus.

'Would you like a closer look at them?' Together they walked towards the hangings.

'I sew myself, but nothing as beautiful as this,' her companion said. 'I can't believe what you've achieved with fabric and thread.'

'Why, thank you. What sort of sewing do you do, Kyria…?'

'Savakis.' Her dark, intelligent eyes took in Callie's instant reaction, watching calmly as she jolted to a stop, eyes widening. 'But please, call me Irini.'

* * *

Damon shot to his feet.

'She's where?' he barked into the intercom.

'In the foyer, Kyrie Savakis. Shall I tell Reception to send her up?'

'Yes. Straight away.'

Damon put the phone down, registering the bolt of electricity hot-wiring his body. His pulse leaped at the thought of Callie here. In his office.

His brain buzzed with possibilities. Why here? Why now? Thoughts crammed and jostled for consideration till he slammed a lid on them.

He sat back in his chair and propped his fingers under his chin.

Six months since Callie had run from him. Six torturous months in which he'd plumbed the depths of doubt, fear and despair. Letting her go had tested his resolve beyond bearing. Allowing her distance till she was ready to trust had almost killed him when his instinct had been to hold her close and prevent her leaving.

She'd left him no option but to stand helplessly and watch the woman he loved walk out of his life. That had gutted him, knowing he'd hurt her and there was nothing he could do to rectify the situation but wait and pray.

Today he'd reached the end of his endurance. He'd promised himself, after half a year of waiting, he'd visit her apartment this very evening. He'd given her enough time, surely, to deserve a second chance.

Why was she here?

His lips thinned. Whatever her intentions, what mattered was the outcome of their meeting.

There could only be one possible result.

The alternative, to continue life without her, was unthinkable.

He'd driven his staff, his friends and his family to their wits' end, pushing himself harder than ever, yet unable to stick to anything. He'd lost his enthusiasm for work, for socialising. Even for sailing.

He had to resolve this. Now.

* * *

'Enter.'

Callie stepped over the threshold of the massive doorway and halted, her heart leaping against her ribs.

Just as dark as she remembered. Just as virile and stunningly good-looking. If anything, Damon looked even better than before. Hungrily she devoured the sight of him.

With his sleeves rolled up, his top button undone and his tie missing, he looked as though he'd been working hard. His hair was slightly rumpled as if he'd dragged those long fingers back through it, as he'd once caressed her own locks.

Her thoughts juddered to a halt. Intimate images swirled before her and she had to shove them aside.

'Hello, Callie.' She couldn't read his voice, or his face, it was poker-blank. Unlike her own. She was sure her roiling emotions were visible for him to see.

'Hello, Damon.'

The door snicked shut behind her and she jumped, feeling the weight of tension bearing down on her.

'Won't you take a seat?'

'Thank you.' She stumbled forward, aware of him assessing every aspect of her appearance. She'd hurried here from the shop. Hadn't taken time to go home and change. Her clothes were neat but not glamorous. Suddenly she realised that after a long day her tailored jacket and skirt probably looked creased and tired.

Callie stiffened her spine and met his stare. Closer to him now, she noticed what she hadn't from the door—the lines of fatigue bracketing his mouth, the way his eyes seemed to have sunk a little as if from too little sleep. The grim cast of his solid jaw.

Her stupid heart pounded. He'd been working too hard.

But she wasn't in a position to remonstrate. She wasn't supposed to care.

Yet she did, so much it hurt.

'It was good of you to see me.' She hated her stilted voice, the need to hide behind social niceties and pretend she was calm when her stomach churned with nerves.

Damon inclined his head.

Did he deliberately try to make her uncomfortable, sitting on the other side of that vast desk, saying nothing?

It didn't matter. Her pride was sawdust and she didn't care. All that mattered was connecting with him again.

If he'd let her.

She'd thought today, when she met his mother, that there was a chance. Just a slim hope he felt something more for her than pity. The fact that he'd talked to his mother about her must mean something, surely? But, looking into his set face, she realised she'd come on a fool's errand.

Damon didn't love her.

Nerves stuck her tongue to the roof of her mouth for so long the silence thickened between them.

'Would you like some refreshments?'

'No. No, thank you.' She swiped her tongue over her dry lips as she tried to pull herself together.

'I came to apologise,' she said, meeting his direct gaze. 'I should have done it before but it took a long time for me to…sort things out.' She halted but he said nothing.

'I should at least have thanked you for your generosity in refunding what my uncle stole.'

He made a sudden, slashing gesture. 'Forget it. It was nothing.'

She leaned forward. 'No. You're wrong. It's meant everything. It's allowed me to make a new start. To prove to myself I'm capable of achieving something worthwhile.'

'And that's important to you?'

'Of course.'

He nodded, his mouth twisting in a lop-sided smile.

'And I wanted to tell you I'll arrange to start paying you back when—'

He shot to his feet. 'You'll do no such thing!' His voice reverberated through the still room.

For the first time Callie saw his eyes spark. She preferred him this way. Even furious was better than the distant aloofness she'd seen since she arrived. Her pulse quickened at the memory of Damon when roused.

'Is that why you came? To settle a debt?' Despite the glint in his eyes, his voice was cool.

Callie's insides nosedived. That was it, then. It had been a ridiculous, forlorn hope that absence would make the heart grow fonder. That Damon would realise it was love he felt for her, not sympathy.

Her throat closed on bitter salty tears she refused to shed. She groped for the bag at her shoulder.

It was over. Time to move on.

Perhaps one day years from now she'd remember what they'd once almost had without the terrible wrenching sense of loss. Fatigue dragged at her limbs and the familiar leaden weight settled on her shoulders.

'Is that all?'

Callie nodded, avoiding his eyes. 'Yes, that's all. Thank you for seeing me. I hope…I hope things work out well for you.' Hurriedly she stood and spun round towards the door, her eyes misting.

'Wait!'

Damon's voice pulled her up short. But it was the artwork on the wall before her that rooted her to the floor. Her eyes bulged as she took it in.

'Come and sit down again, Callie.'

Numbly she shook her head. She blinked but it was still there, a massive appliquéd scene directly opposite Damon's desk. Where he'd see it whenever he looked up.

Her knees began to tremble. Out of the corner of her eye she saw movement. Damon approaching. Yet she couldn't drag her eyes from the piece before her.

'You've got my picture.' Her voice was a reedy thread of sound.

'I have.' His voice was grave. She tore her gaze from the wall and tried to read the gleam in his midnight eyes.

Not just any picture. Her favourite. The one that meant so much to her she'd once planned never to part with it. The secluded, pine-fringed beach where they'd met.

'Having a glimpse of paradise between business meetings

keeps me sane.' His mouth tugged up on one side, creating a deep, sexy groove in his cheek.

'It's not paradise.' Her voice was hoarse. 'It's—'

'I know exactly where it is.' He stepped close till he took up her whole vision. There was nothing but him. Callie breathed in the spice and man scent she'd missed for so long. Her eyelids flickered.

'That's why I asked my sister to get it for me.'

His gaze challenged. But it was all Callie could do to tamp down the rising bubble of excitement and disbelief inside her.

'That doesn't bother you?' he challenged. 'That you didn't know she was buying it for me?'

Callie shook her head, feeling a fizz of energy at the sudden glitter in his eyes.

'There's more,' he said. 'Not just that my sister told me about your work and I asked her to buy this piece.' His jaw firmed. 'You might as well know I asked her to visit your store in the first place. To see how you were.'

Warmth rose at the idea of Damon wanting to check on her. It took a moment to realise some of that warmth flowed from his grasp of her hands.

'Did you ask her to buy other things?' She tilted her head to one side, trying to read his expression even as her heart pounded a distracting rhythm.

'No. That was her idea. She was so enthusiastic she began telling her friends.'

'I've had a lot of word-of-mouth referrals.' But they were genuine, not orchestrated by Damon.

'You're not upset?'

'How could I be upset that you cared enough to look out for me?'

His whole body stilled, eyes narrowing.

'That's not all.' He looked so sombre her heart stuttered. 'I wanted to talk with you about it but you'd made it clear you didn't want anything to do with me.'

'What did you do?' She couldn't believe it was anything terrible but the look on his face worried her. She saw the white lines rim his firm lips, heard his clipped, distant tone and guilt speared her. She'd hurt him.

'I had words with your uncle.' A flash of satisfaction lit his expression. 'I persuaded him his interests would be best served by expanding his horizons. He's taken up an offer to manage one of my enterprises in the Caribbean. His wife isn't well enough to travel. She'll stay in Greece, preparing for your cousin's wedding.'

'That was your doing?' Astonishment filled her. Callie had spoken to her aunt just days ago. She sounded like a new woman, freed of Uncle Aristides' bullying influence. 'You've made a terrible mistake,' she blurted out. 'He'll ruin your business!'

The sudden rich rumble of Damon's laugh was like a blanket wrapping around her. 'Don't worry. His responsibilities aren't quite as broad as he first thought and he'll be strictly monitored. He might even have to work for a change.'

But behind the laughter Damon's expression was serious.

'You did that for me?' Callie could barely take it in. This was like a fantasy come true.

'And for Angela and your aunt.' He stood straighter. 'You'll say I was managing your lives.'

She shook her head. 'I think it's wonderful.'

'Truly?' His eyebrows arched. 'Even though you left me because I was like your husband, taking charge of your life?'

'No!' Callie reached out and put her hand on his arm. A surge of energy shot through her as she felt his living warmth. Her heart raced.

'You're nothing like Alkis!' The thought horrified her—that he'd believe such a thing. 'You're warm and generous and caring.' Her fingers clenched round his forearm, willing him to believe. 'You're...special.'

His penetrating gaze seared her.

'Then tell me, Callie, why did you walk out when I was about to ask you to marry me?'

* * *

Damon felt the spasm of shock rip through her taut body. Saw her eyes widen. In pleasure or pain?

His gut churned. Anxiety pulled every muscle and sinew tight. He'd given her six months to realise what they had together was special. Had he any hope at all?

'Don't, please.' Her jade eyes shone with distress and Damon felt a blow hammer his heart, robbing him of breath.

'You don't need to…' She looked away, the picture of misery.

Not as miserable as he'd be if he let her go again. It had nearly killed him the first time, even knowing he had to let her have her freedom if she was ever to return willingly.

'Don't need to what, Callie?'

She blinked and he touched a finger to her cheek, feeling the tears slide down her soft skin. His lungs contracted at the sight of her pain.

'Don't cry, *Callie mou*. Please.' It tore him apart to see her in pain.

'I know you feel sorry for me. But please—you can't marry me out of pity!' She hiccoughed and he wrapped his other hand around her, tugging her close.

It had been so long since he'd held her. Too long. His heart seized at the feel of her here, where she belonged.

'What are you talking about, *glikia mou*?'

'I…I…' Huge, tear-drenched eyes met his and, despite his confusion, he felt the inevitable spark of desire igniting.

'I've fallen in love with you,' she said in a rush. 'You must have realised that. But I can't bear to think of you staying with me out of pity.'

'You think I'd do that?'

She nodded, eyes overbright. 'Everything you did for me— I understand it wasn't personal. That it was altruistic, your need to right wrongs, but—'

'Altruistic be damned!' He hauled her even closer, wrapping his arms round her as if he'd never let her go. Impressing her body against his.

'That's why you left? You thought I felt *sorry* for you?'

She nodded against his chest and elation buoyed him as never before.

'The proposal still stands, Callie. I want you to marry me. I even have a ring to prove it.'

'Please, no. It wouldn't work. It—'

'Stop objecting for a moment, woman, and listen.'

She looked up then and he smiled. Damon's face felt as if it was cracking, so wide was his grin, so profound the relief that he sagged back against the desk, pulling her with him, off balance in his arms. Her warm, soft weight, all feminine curves and scented secrets, was like heaven after the purgatory of the last six months.

'I want to marry a woman who's deliciously sensuous, beautiful, talented, opinionated, determined. Someone I love.' It felt so good finally to say the words.

'Love!'

'Yes, love.' The weight of the past six months lifted off his shoulders in that moment.

'You love me?' Astonishment coloured her voice.

Damon spanned her waist with his hands and lifted her high, stepping away from the desk and swinging her round. She was light in his arms. As light as his heart. Her husky, surprised laughter floated all around him.

Who'd have thought happiness could be encompassed in one remarkable woman? He lowered her to the floor.

'I love you, Callie. I would be your husband, if you trust me not to run your life.'

'Really?'

'Really.'

'Damon.' She sounded choked up as tears flowed again. But he focused on her brilliant smile, knowing she cried from a joy that matched his. 'I trust you. I love you so much. I never want to be away from you again.'

The world stopped as he drank in her words.

Then Damon's primitive, possessive side urged him to seal the bond with more than a kiss. To take advantage of the long sofa against one wall and possess his woman instantly. It had been too long and he was so needy.

His arms tightened and he swung her off her feet.

'What are you doing?'

The feel of her in his arms was heady temptation.

'Taking you out before we get sidetracked,' said the civilised Damon who knew women enjoyed the trappings of romance. 'We'll celebrate with an intimate dinner for two after we collect your ring. And we'll call my family. It's time you met them.'

He strode for the door.

'I've met your family.' Her eyes glowed up at him in a way that made his heart hammer.

He jolted to a stop as her slender hand pressed against his chest. Her cheeks were flushed and her eyes slumberous.

'What I want now is you.'

Damon's heart filled as he looked down at her.

'I always knew you were my sort of woman, *glikia mou*. What a life we'll have together.'

RUTHLESS TYCOON, INEXPERIENCED MISTRESS

BY
CATHY WILLIAMS

Cathy Williams is originally from Trinidad, but has lived in England for a number of years. She currently has a house in Warwickshire, which she shares with her husband Richard, her three daughters, Charlotte, Olivia and Emma, and their pet cat, Salem. She adores writing romantic fiction and would love one of her girls to become a writer—although at the moment she is happy enough if they do their homework and agree not to bicker with one another!

CHAPTER ONE

CESAR was not in the best of moods as he swung his Bentley down the small street into which his sat nav had guided him. It was a little after nine in the evening and the weather, which had looked promising in London for taking his car out for a run, had become increasingly poor the farther east he had travelled. Flurries of snow had kept his wipers busy for the past forty-five minutes.

When he had arranged a meeting with his brother, this venue was not what he had had in mind. In fact, his club in London had been his preferred choice, but Fernando had insisted on meeting in his God-forsaken stamping ground of Kent, a place which held no interest for Cesar and therefore one which he had never seen the need to visit.

He now cursed under his breath as he pulled up in front of a building that had all the charm of a disused warehouse. For a few seconds after he had killed the engine, he stared at what looked suspiciously like graffiti on the walls and wondered whether his faith in computer technology had been misplaced. Had that disembodied female voice which had guided him away from the city centre got the directions all wrong?

With a sharp, impatient click of his tongue, Cesar swung himself out of his car in search of a door of sorts.

He would personally donate his car to the nearest vagrant if his brother lived in this dump. Fernando was not the sort of guy who *did dumps*. In fact, Fernando was the sort of guy who specialised in avoiding them at all costs.

Cesar did his best to swallow his anger at having to deal with this massive personal inconvenience. He was here for a specific purpose and, to that end, there was no point in dwelling on the fact that his Friday night had been ruined. Nor was there any point in getting annoyed with his brother. By the end of the night Fernando would have enough to deal with, never mind his lack of foresight in arranging this meeting, in the dead of winter, miles away from civilisation.

The door was cunningly concealed amidst the graffiti and, for a few seconds after he had pushed it open, Cesar took time to adjust to his surroundings.

This wasn't what he had expected. Disused from the out-side the place might well appear to be, but once inside, the picture was vastly different. A few dozen people were milling about what seemed to be a club of sorts. To one side of the semi-darkened room, a cluster of leather chairs and sofas were scattered around low tables. Elsewhere people stood drinking by a long, sleek bar which curved in a U shape to encompass most of the back of the room. To the left there appeared to be a raised podium and yet more chairs.

It didn't take long to spot his brother, talking in a small group, animated as he usually was and the centre of attention.

Having specifically told Fernando that he wanted to have a one-on-one meeting to discuss the small matter of his trust fund, Cesar was enraged to now discover that he had been conned into attending what looked like a private party. The subdued lighting didn't give him much of a clue as to the nature of the guests involved, but he didn't have to exert his brain too much to work out that they would all be his brother's usual cronies. Blonde bimbos, gambling partners and general wastrels who shared the same ambitions as Fernando to spend the family money as flamboyantly as possible whilst simultaneously dodging anything that smelled remotely like hard work.

Cesar grimly thought that his brother was on the wrong track if he thought he could avoid discussing his financial future by conniving to have a bunch of chaperons around him.

By the time he descended on Freddy, all of the group bar one had departed and Cesar treated his brother to a smile of pure displeasure. He didn't bother to look at the crop-haired youth standing next to him.

'Fernando,' he said through gritted teeth. He held out one hand, his cursory nod to courtesy. 'This is not what I expected.' It had been several months since he had laid eyes on his brother. In fact, the last time had been at a family gathering in Madrid, where yet again Cesar's attempts to interest his brother in the fortunes of the company had met with a resounding lack of interest. It was then that he had told Fernando in no uncertain terms that he would be putting his trust fund under the microscope. It was within his power to defer it until such time as he considered it wise to release it and he wouldn't hesitate to use his power of attorney. 'Get your act together,' he had warned, 'or kiss sweet goodbye to that lifestyle of yours.'

Of course, Fernando had responded by staying as far away from the company head office as he physically could.

'I thought…Friday night…' Freddy's smile was pure charm. 'Live a little, big brother! We can talk tomorrow. Actually, I wanted to show you…' He spread his hands in a gesture to encompass the room and Cesar looked at him in cool silence. 'But I am being rude.' He turned to the woman he'd been talking to who had been displaced by Cesar striding in front of her. 'This is Judith—Jude—meet my brother, Cesar... What can I get you, Cesar?' He edged away. 'Whisky? As usual?'

'And I'll have another glass of wine, Freddy.' Jude had to take a few sideways steps until she was standing directly in front of the most intimidating man she had ever set eyes on in her life.

So this was the famous Cesar. No wonder Freddy had been quaking in his proverbial boots at the prospect of having a meeting with him. He was a good four inches taller than his brother and where Freddy was good-looking in an approachable, flirtatious kind of way, this man was stunning. His face was dark and lean and, with its perfect bone structure, somehow forbidding. This was a face that could chill to the bone.

She did her best to smile. This elaborate set-up had been meticulous in the planning. Freddy had been so desperate to introduce his brother to the place he had bought. It was a converted warehouse which was halfway to becoming the sexy jazz club of his dreams, waiting only for the injection of cash from the trust fund which, he had told her worriedly, was in danger of being wrenched away before he could get his hands on a single penny of it. He had invested heavily in the place but it would get no further without Cesar's approval.

How better to get his brother's backing than to entice him into it, show him *what it could be*, prove to him that he was no longer the layabout playboy kid brother he had always been. He had invited all the right people to help him create the perfect setting, including her. Bankers were there, lawyers, a couple of accountants, everybody who had had any input in his burgeoning venture.

'Freddy's told me a lot about you.' She was wearing her flats and had to crane her neck to look up at him.

'Well, I have no idea who you are, nor do I know why Fernando has arranged to meet me here.' He frowned at the girl standing in front of him. He had barely noticed her and he knew why. With her short dark hair, she hardly oozed femininity.

Inherently Spanish, Cesar had a very clear image of what a woman should look like and this wasn't it.

'Do you?' he asked coolly.

'I think he wanted you to meet…some of his friends…'

'I've met Freddy's friends in the past. Believe me when I tell you that I have no desire to meet any more.' That said, he hadn't met *this particular one* before and she certainly wasn't the sort his brother usually went for. In fact, just the opposite. So what was she doing here? He looked at her narrowly, his shrewd brain coming up with possibilities and playing with them. 'Who are you, anyway? And how do you know Fernando? He's never mentioned your name to me in the past.' His brother had a lavish lifestyle and was cavalier with his money. Cesar knew because he had access to all Fernando's bills. He also knew that his brother was fond of spending money on his women. From the age of eighteen, the boy had been a magnet for gold-diggers. This one didn't have the outward appearance of a gold-digger, but Cesar was suddenly keenly interested in finding out what her connection was to his brother. He looked across the room to where the clutch of sofas was being studiously ignored by people who seemed to prefer standing. In a minute Fernando would return with drinks and Cesar was pretty sure a round of boring and pointless introductions would then commence. With his suspicions suddenly roused, he nodded curtly to the sofas.

'I've had a hell of a long trip here. Let's sit and you can tell me…all about your relationship with my brother.'

Jude wondered how an invitation to converse could sound like a threat. Having disappeared in the direction of the bar, Freddy had obviously been waylaid. This was one of Freddy's bad habits. He was capable of striking up a conversation and getting lost in it until he was forcibly dragged away.

'I don't have a relationship with your brother,' she said as soon as she was sitting on one of the mega-expensive sofas artfully arranged at an angle to the wall. The mood lighting here was even more subdued and Cesar's face was all shadows and angles. She laughed nervously and drained the remainder of her glass. 'I feel as though I'm being interviewed.'

'Do you? I have no idea why. I'm just interested in finding out how you know Fernando. Where did you meet?'

'I'm helping him work…on a project…' Jude's brief had been simply to promote Freddy's new-found gravitas and work with him in convincing his brother that he could make a success of his venture.

'What project?' Cesar frowned. As far as he knew, his brother hadn't been near any projects, at least not since his school days, when they had involved felt-tip pens and maps.

'He might want to tell you that himself,' Jude said vaguely, and he sat forward, leaning towards her with his elbows resting lightly on his thighs. Six foot two inches of pure threat.

'Look, I came here to have a serious talk with Fernando about his future. Instead, I find myself in a bar, surrounded by people I have no desire to meet and now treated to some mysterious nonsense about a project Fernando hasn't mentioned to me. What work, exactly, are you doing on this so-called *project*?'

'I'm not sure I like your tone of voice!'

'And I'm not sure I like whatever game it is you're playing. How long have you known Fernando?'

'Nearly a year.'

'Nearly a year. And how close have you become in that time?'

'Where are you going with this?'

'Let's just say that I may not see a great deal of my brother, but I know the way he operates and long-standing platonic friendships with the opposite sex have never been high on his agenda. He's always liked his women willing, able and bedded. He's also always been predictable in his preferences. Blonde, busty, leggy and lightweight in the brains department. So where do *you* fit in?'

Jude felt outraged colour seep into her cheeks and she took a few deep breaths to gather herself. In the silence, Cesar continued remorselessly, 'If he's spoken to you about me, then you are clearly more than just a *business acquaintance...*' He invested that with thinly veiled scepticism. 'So what exactly, are you, then?'

Saved by the bell. Or rather, saved by Freddy, who appeared with drinks on a tray. Cesar watched her expression of relief. He was taking in everything, from that quick look that passed between them to the way his brother leaned towards her and whispered something in her ear, something to which she shook her head and removed herself just as soon as she feasibly could. He lazily watched her departing back, allowing his eyes to rest briefly on the movement of her rear. She might look like a boy but there was something unconsciously sexy and graceful about the way she walked. He'd get back to her later. Something was going on. He could *feel* it, and he wasn't going to let up until he got to the bottom of it. But, for the moment, he would bide his time.

Watch and wait. A very good motto, he had always maintained and he stuck to it as the predictable round of introductions began and he was treated to a suspiciously *normal* group

of people. Where were the bimbos? The pampered young
men with their idle, vapid conversation and roving eyes? Disconcertingly, everyone here this evening seemed intent on
discussing investments with him.

By the end of the evening he found that he was almost
enjoying the mystery.

Outside, the snow was now falling much harder. Amidst the
throng of people dashing out to their cars, which were parked
in a designated area at the back of the building, unlike his
which was skewed at an angle at the front, Cesar spotted Jude
wrapping a long scarf around her neck and stuffing her hands
into her pockets. The lights had been turned on in the foyer
and he could see her properly now. Her short hair was streaked
with auburn and her face was not at all boyish. The opposite.
Long, dark lashes fringed widely spaced brown eyes and her
mouth was full and lush, at odds with the gamine appearance.

Fernando may have always had a soft spot for the obvious
but who was to say how a gold-digger could be packaged? The
more subtle, in a way, could be all the more deadly.

And there she was again, talking in a fast, low undertone
to his brother. Talking about *what*?

'I hadn't planned on staying the night,' Cesar said to his
brother, barging in on their conversation, which came to an
abrupt halt. He wasn't looking at her but he could feel her eyes
on him and mentally he flexed his muscles, intrigued at
whatever was stirring beneath the surface.

'Ah.' Freddy smiled apologetically. 'There's an excellent
hotel in the city…'

Cesar frowned. 'Don't you have a house locally?'

'Well. Apartment, in actual fact. Pretty small…'

Cesar glanced across at Jude, whose eyes were studiously
averted, and his mouth tightened a fraction.

'It's snowing pretty heavily,' Cesar said bluntly, 'and I have no intention of driving around in circles looking for somewhere to stay. What's the name of the hotel?'

'Name of the hotel…' Freddy glanced quickly at Jude, who sighed in resignation.

'I have a phone book at my place,' she said grudgingly. 'If you drop me home, I can reserve a room for you.'

'Drop you home? How did you get here?'

'I came with Freddy.'

'Did you now…' Cesar murmured. He smiled and inclined his head to one side. 'Well, that sounds like an offer I'm in no position to refuse… And tomorrow, Fernando…we need to have a little chat…'

'Of course, big brother!' He slapped him warmly on the back and gave him a semblance of a hug, which came naturally to neither of them.

Cesar, accustomed as he was to a stilted relationship with his brother, nevertheless felt a twinge of genuine regret at the lack of real warmth between them. The loss of their parents when he had only just been out of his teens should have brought them closer together. Instead, it had done the opposite. With the mantle of the family's empire resting heavily on his shoulders, Cesar wondered if he had failed in his main duty as a brother—to love him. He had had to don his responsibilities quickly and he had been impatient with Freddy's lack of ambition which he had seen as weakness. He shoved aside the irksome thoughts—he'd worked hard to provide a stable and secure life for his brother. He'd done his best.

'My car's out at the front.'

'Why didn't you use the car park at the rear?'

'Because, believe it or not, I was inclined to think I had arrived at the wrong address when I got here. I never suspected that the place was functional or that there was a parking area at the back.'

Freddy beamed. 'Clever, isn't it? We can discuss all of that tomorrow.' He was already backing away and Jude eyed Cesar warily. The last thing she wanted was to be cooped up in a car with him, go back to her house with him, but she had no choice. Freddy couldn't possibly take him back to the apartment—not with Imogen there.

Just thinking of that little secret by omission made her flush guiltily. Imogen should have been at the little party tonight. She was, after all, the key player in the game, but Freddy had insisted that she be kept out of sight. At least for the moment. Having met Cesar, Jude could understand why, because Cesar was a man in whom suspicion was deeply embedded. She could sense it in his conversation, which had been a thin cover-up for a cross examination. One look at Imogen, her long blonde hair, her big blue eyes and her legs that went on for ever, and Freddy's trust fund would have been written off for good. The fact that she was nearly seven months pregnant with Freddy's baby would have brought on cardiac arrest.

'We could just drive into the city,' Jude said once inside the car, which was as comfortable as any of those wildly overpriced sofas Freddy had insisted on buying for the club. She glanced worriedly at the snow, which was falling thickly white. 'I don't live a million miles from here but my place is down some narrow country lanes and this car might not make it.'

'This car,' Cesar informed her, reversing and swinging the car in the right direction, 'is equipped to cope with anything.'

'Anything except snow in Kent in the middle of January. For that, you really need something a bit more robust. These sorts of fashion cars might be all right for London but they're rubbish out in the country.'

Cesar gave her a look of pure incredulity but she was frowning out of the window, busily trying to work out how fast he could reasonably travel without ending up in a ditch.

She directed him out to the main street which, at a little past one in the morning with the snow pelting down, was deserted. It took a ridiculously long time to clear the city, then came a series of winding country lanes, each one more treacherous than the last.

'How the hell do you make out in these sorts of conditions?' Cesar muttered under his breath, every ounce of concentration focused on getting them to her house in one piece.

'I have a four-wheel drive,' Jude admitted. 'It's old but it's pretty reliable and it can get through just about anything.'

'As opposed to this fashion statement I drive.' He glanced over at her, then back at the road.

'I could never afford a car like this in a million years. Not that I'd ever want one. I don't see the point of them.'

'It's called comfort.' Cesar realised that he didn't know the first thing about her. What job did she have? Aside from helping his brother on some so-called *project*, which could be anything from doing his accounts to colour coordinating his wardrobe. He would need to find out more about her to ascertain what her motives were. For the moment, however, he was too preoccupied with controlling his car in these conditions for too much detailed questioning and, as he rounded a corner at a snail's pace, he began to wonder how he was going to find his way back into the civilised roads of the city and the comfort of a hotel room.

'I would choose practicality over comfort any day of the week.'

'I gathered as much from your choice of clothing tonight.'

'Meaning what?'

'Meaning—is your house going to be coming into view any time soon because, if I go any slower, we might just as well get out of the car and walk the remainder of the way.'

'It's just up ahead.' She pointed to a dim light, barely visible through the downfall, but she was mentally chewing over what he had said about her clothing. Yes, she had worn her jeans because they were comfortable and it hadn't been a fussy affair. She hadn't been the only one there wearing jeans. So maybe most of the women had worn something slightly more formal, but she had looked presentable enough!

She glanced down at her thick black duffel coat and her black boots, which were perfect winter garb although they did seem a little incongruous against the cream luxury leather of his car. Then she slid her eyes across to where he was frowning in concentration at what was trying to pass for a road.

He might be the rudest man she had ever met, but there was no denying that he was frighteningly good-looking. In a scary way, she amended. Not her type at all. He made the hairs on the back of her neck stand on end.

As the car tackled the last lap of the trip, she heard the squeal of tyres and then…nothing.

Cesar swore under his breath and glared at her.

'It's not *my* fault!' she protested immediately.

'How the hell would you have made your way back here? On foot?'

'I would have…' she stopped in the nick of time from telling him that she would have stayed at Freddy's apartment, which would have involved no narrow snow-ridden country lanes, as it was in the city centre—if he couldn't accommodate his own brother, then how could he have possibly accommodated *her*? '…stayed at Sophie's place,' she said quickly, thinking on her feet.

'Damn car!' He scowled and flung open his car door to a sheet of white. 'We'll have to walk the rest of the way.'

'You can't just leave your car here!'

'And you suggest…?'

'I suppose we could try pushing it.'

'Are you completely mad?' He began walking in the direction of the light and Jude half ran to keep up with him. 'I'll have to return for it as soon as the weather shows some sign of clearing.'

'But that might not be for hours yet!' It was occurring to her what that meant and she didn't like it. 'You've got to get to a hotel!'

'Well, why don't you wave a magic wand and maybe the weather will oblige us both by stopping…*this*!' In retrospect, he should have insisted on Fernando travelling to London to see him. In retrospect, he should have stopped at the first sign of snow because he could not afford the luxury of being snowbound *anywhere*. Even on a Saturday, he had vital conference calls to make and meetings to arrange via e-mail with people on the other side of the world. Fernando might be able to lie in when the weather looked a little challenging, but not so for Cesar! He ground his teeth in frustration and raked his fingers through his hair which, in the brief amount of time it had taken them to reach her front door, was already dripping from the snow.

At least the house was warm. Or rather cottage because, from what he could discern in the inky blackness, it was small, white and with a picture-postcard picket fence. Inside was as quaintly pretty, with old wooden floors and a feeling of age and comfort. In short, it was a million miles away from his marvel of pale marble, pale leather and abstract paintings—investments which had cost an arm and a leg.

'Phone book…phone book…' Jude was muttering to

herself as she looked under tables and behind chairs. 'Ah. Here we go. Right. Hotel. Any in particular?'

'Forget it.'

'What do you mean, *forget it*?'

'Look outside.' He nodded in the direction of the window and Jude followed his gaze with a sinking heart. This was turning into a blizzard. He would need a snowplough to clear the roads for his car and a tractor to transport him to the city centre. Other than that, it was madness to even think about leaving the house.

'But you can't stay here!'

'Why not?' Cesar looked at her narrowly, weighing up whether to pursue his line of thought or leave it until the following morning considering the lateness of the hour. 'Would Fernando object?'

'Freddy? Object? Why on earth would he object?' They were both in the small hallway and she felt as though her breath was being sucked out of her. He was so *tall*! He was also removing his coat and she gave a little squeal of horror. Chatting pleasantly to the man for half an hour and singing Freddy's praises was all well and good but enforced overnight companionship was a completely different matter. 'You can borrow my car to get into town!' Pure genius. 'The comfort level's a bit low but you'll make it there in one piece, at any rate, and a hotel would be a lot more comfortable than the floor here…'

'Floor?'

'I know. Appalling.' He was now hanging his coat on the banister and she wanted to fling it back at him, demand that he put it on and send him firmly on his way. 'Small house.' She pointedly kept her duffel coat on so that he would get the message.

'Forget about trying to shove me outside, Jude. I'll leave in the morning and if I have to sleep on the floor, then so be it. I'm certainly not going to risk my life in your clapped-out car in this weather.'

'Oh, very well,' she snapped, edging back a few inches as he stepped towards her.

'So why don't you take your coat off and show me which particular part of the floor you want to designate to me?'

'There's a guest bedroom,' Jude admitted grudgingly, 'but it's very small and very cluttered. You'd find it a very challenging space to sleep in.'

Cesar strolled past her towards the general area of the kitchen, inspecting the surroundings as he went. No signs of his brother in the house, at any rate. At least no photos, no bits of male paraphernalia which, in his brother's case, would probably have been hugely expensive, garishly coloured jumpers or any one of those ridiculous hats which he collected. In fact, no signs of any male occupancy at all.

'Would you like a guided tour?' Jude asked acidly, arms folded. 'Or are you happy just nosing around on your own?'

Cesar turned to her and gave her a long, leisurely appraisal. Not only was she *not* his brother's usual trademark busty blonde, she was also *not* the usual trademark giggly airhead. He really would have to work on finding out just what her job was and how it involved his brother. Maybe the weather could work to his advantage, he thought. Trapped in the confines of her own house, she could hardly disappear if the questions got tough. He smiled slowly, relishing the prospect of asserting his authority and letting her know, in no uncertain terms, that he was not a man to be messed with.

'No,' he said lazily, eyes back on her mutinous, flushed

face. 'The guided tour won't be necessary. At least not at this hour of the morning.'

'Fine. Then, if you follow me, I'll show you where you can spend the night.' Up the stairs, which creaked protestingly under his weight, and to the left, pausing only so that Jude could yank a sheet and a blanket from the airing cupboard. 'I'm sure you know how to make a bed,' she told him, handing over the linen. She was pretty sure he didn't. Like Fernando, he would have been spared the necessity of doing any menial tasks thanks to a background that had seen him raised with all the help that money could buy. It was only after he had met Imogen that he had discovered that *fast food* wasn't just a pre-theatre dinner. She was reliably informed by her friend that he could complete most household tasks now but with record slowness and only dubious success.

She would have liked to have witnessed his botched attempts at bed-making, but she let him get on with it while she swept aside all her stuff and, by the time she looked around, the bed was perfectly made and he was looking at her with an amused smile.

'Up to your standards?' he asked, raising his eyebrows, and she had the grace to blush.

'The bathroom's next door and we share it, so if I'm in it then you'll just have to wait your turn.' She was suddenly flustered as he reached for the top button of his shirt. 'I'll make sure that there's a towel for you.' She backed towards the door as a sliver of hard, muscled, bronzed torso was revealed.

'What's with all the drawings?'

Her mouth went dry as he reached the final button and began to undo his cuffs.

'Are you an artist?' He walked across to the pile of sketches which she had dumped on the ancient pine table, which had begun life as a dressing table but was now used as a surface on which any and everything found its way.

Jude snatched her drawing from his hand and returned it to its place. 'I'm a designer, *actually*.' Thank God she kept all her work in her architect's chest downstairs or he would be rifling through those as well. 'I just do a bit of sketching now and again as a hobby.'

'Well, well, well. *A designer.* Interesting.'

'Yes, it is,' she responded tightly.

'Actually, I meant that it's interesting to discover that you have a proper job. Most of the women who have cluttered up my brother's life have only paid lip service to the work ethic. In fact, the last one to grace my presence was a flightly little thing with a sideline in glamour modelling.'

Jude tried hard not to think of Imogen. What, she wondered with an inward shudder, would he have thought of a *stripper*? She and Imogen went back all the way to pigtails and hop-scotch. A couple of poor choices on the boyfriend front had found her working in a nightclub, saving hard so that she could continue her studies and get the qualifications she needed to become a primary school teacher, but Jude doubted whether the man looking at her now would find an ounce of compassion for that sob story.

He appeared to have read her mind because he continued, musingly, 'Naturally I had to ensure that that particular relationship was stillborn.'

'Why?' Jude asked uncomfortably. Images of her pregnant friend rose in her head. 'There's nothing wrong with glamour modelling...'

'A glamour model and my brother equate to a gold-digger out to fleece a golden goose.'

'That's a very cynical way of thinking...'

'It's called the realities of life. Another reality of life is that I would do anything within my power to ensure that my brother is not taken advantage of. Flings with women are all well and good, just so long as they leave the picture. Any unsuitable ones who try to stick around…would have *me* to contend with…' Always a good idea to lay down one or two ground rules, Cesar thought. She might blush like a teenager and appear to have a face as transparent as glass, but he was savvy enough to know that neither of those two things necessarily added up to a personality as pure as the driven snow.

'Well, thank you for that,' Jude told him coolly. 'It's always illuminating to hear what other people think, even if you don't agree with what they say. Although I'd guess that you don't really give a damn whether people agree with what you have to say or not.'

'Bull's eye!' With a quick, easy movement he stripped off his shirt and tossed it on the ground. 'I'll have to dry these in the morning.' Intriguingly, she looked as though she had never seen a man half naked before.

'You're going to sleep…in the… *What are you going to wear to bed?*'

'What I usually wear.' He looked at her in genuine surprise. 'My birthday suit. It's very comfortable. You should approve.'

Jude thought of him sleeping naked, with only a small bathroom separating their rooms, and felt faint. Of course, this was because she had taken an instant dislike to him and, in fact, disapproved of pretty much everything he had had to say, but the image of that muscular, lithe body flung over her sheets and blankets lodged in her head like a burr.

'I'll get you something!'

'You have men's clothes stashed away in your house?' Cesar's ears pricked up but she didn't say anything. She had backed right out of the door and he waited, thinking, until she reappeared two minutes later and tossed him a T-shirt. It was big all right. It was also bright pink.

He could hear the laughter in her voice as she said, 'That should fit. Have a good night's sleep!'

CHAPTER TWO

AT SIX-THIRTY the following morning, the snow had stopped
but outside was a landscape of pure wintry white. Very attractive for a postcard, Jude thought sourly, but not so handy
when it came with her house guest, the thought of whom had
kept her tossing and turning throughout the night. He should
never have mentioned that he slept naked. The minute he had
told her that, the image of him without his clothes had lodged
in her head and all her mechanisms for a peaceful night—
counting sheep, planning her day, thinking about the projects
she had on the go—had been ruined.

Her highly efficient heating system had kicked in over an
hour previously and the house was already beautifully warm.
It was also beautifully silent.

She crept stealthily out of her bedroom, wondering whether
to use the bathroom and then deciding against it just in case
her visitor woke up. She had decided overnight that the less
contact she had with him, the better. He was disturbing and,
much as she loved Freddy and Imogen both, she didn't see
why she should have her life disturbed by a virtual stranger.
Of course he would surface at some point but before then she
could at least snatch a cup of coffee in relative peace.

She crept down the stairs, which didn't creak because she weighed so much less than he did, and expelled one long relieved breath when she was in the safety of her kitchen.

Like everything else in the cottage, it was small but beautifully proportioned, with two beams across the ceiling, an old but serviceable Aga and a much worn kitchen table, which she had bought second hand from a shop which purported to sell antique pine. Freddy's apartment in the city centre was shiny and new and kitted out in a style that could only have been achieved by an interior designer with a limitless budget. She caught herself wondering what his brother's place looked like and immediately stamped on her curiosity.

She was happily pouring hot water into her mug, back to the kitchen door, when an all too familiar voice said from behind, 'Great. I'll have one, too.'

Jude started violently, with the kettle in her hand, and she gave a cry of shock and pain as hot water splashed over her wrist.

Cesar was next to her before she could turn around and give him the full benefit of her annoyance at finding her privacy invaded.

'What have you done?'

'What are you doing down here?' The man looked bright-eyed and bushy-tailed, as though he had been up for hours, and he was back in his trousers and shirt, although he had appropriated one of the baggy old zip-up sweats which she kept on a hook by the front door for those rare moments when her conscience got the better of her and she decided to go to the gym. It drowned her but on him was pulled tight, leaving her in no doubt as to the build of his olive-skinned muscular body.

'Give me your hand.'

'I know what to do.' She turned away, her heart racing at the sight of him, and switched on the cold water, but he was there before her, holding her hand under the tap and then gently patting it dry with one of the tea towels on the Aga.

Jude watched, mesmerised, those long brown fingers against her pale skin, barely able to breathe properly. His clean masculine scent filled her nostrils and made her feel giddy.

'Clumsy, clumsy,' he tutted under his breath and she glared at him.

'You gave me the fright of my life,' she accused. 'I didn't expect you to be sneaking around at this hour in the morning! You're a guest! Guests stay in bed until they think it's appropriate to emerge!'

'I'm a morning person. Up with the lark, so to speak.' He guided her towards a chair and sat her down. 'Do you have any antiseptic cream? Bandage?'

'I'll be fine as soon as you give me back my hand.'

'Nonsense. As you said, this is my fault.'

Jude couldn't disagree with that. She told him where to find her first aid kit and watched in silence as he efficiently bandaged her hand, treating her with a great deal more concern than the scalding warranted. Much to her discomfort because halfway through the procedure, and having recovered from the shock at having him sneak up on her from behind, she became acutely aware of what she was wearing. A baggy T-shirt, along the lines of the one she had tossed at him earlier on. It reached mid-thigh but thereafter she was fully exposed and all too aware of the unprepossessing image she presented to a man who obviously didn't do casual, judging from his remark about her jeans outfit the night before.

She hunched forward in an attempt to conceal the jutting peaks of her breasts and then realised that she was thereby exposing them to an overhead view so she sat up and glared at his dark head as he put the finishing touch to the bandage.

'Now stay right there and I'll finish what you started.'

'What have you been getting up to down here? How long have you been up?'

'Oh, I only managed to grab a couple of hours' sleep,' Cesar said, his back to her as he made them both a mug of coffee. 'Perhaps it was the novel experience of sleeping in a pink T-shirt.'

Jude took some comfort in imagining him looking ridiculous. Had he been wearing it right now, she figured she might have coped with him being in her space without her body feeling as though it were on fire.

'Then—' he placed her mug of coffee next to her on the table and sat down '—I tried to get the Internet working but it refused to oblige.'

'Phone lines might be down,' Jude said glumly. 'A heavy fall of snow can sometimes do that. It can also be a bit quirky at times.'

A bit like its owner, Cesar thought. He had had time to think things over and had come to the conclusion that nothing would be gained from browbeating her. She was clearly as stubborn as a mule and, from what he could see, given to baring her claws. Far better to put away his armoury and use weapons of a different nature to find out what exactly her role was in his brother's life.

'I then decided to use my time profitably so I went to check on the car.'

'And you got it started?'

'Started but nowhere to go with it. Snow's pretty deep.'

'Couldn't you have scraped the snow away? You're a strong man,' she added boldly. 'Men do stuff like that.'

'Sure, if I'd wanted to spend the next eight hours outside in the freezing cold—and here's some more bad news. The sky looks grim and the weather reports are talking about more snow in the next twenty-four hours.'

'They can't be!' Jude all but wailed.

'Hazard of living in this part of the world. I can count on the fingers of one hand the number of times I've seen snow in London.'

'How can you be so…so *calm* about all of this?'

'Why get hot and bothered about something over which I have no control?' Sure, he had uttered a few ungentlemanly curses when he had discovered the lack of Internet connection but he had now resigned himself to the fact that the business world would have to spend at least part of the weekend without him. For Cesar, this was no small thing. Work was his driving force. It took precedence over everything and everyone.

'Because you live for your work! You practically have a bed in your office!'

'And how do you know that?'

'Freddy told me.' It had slipped out before she had time to catch it and Jude shot him a sheepish look. He might rub her up the wrong way but she knew that she would have hated the thought of being discussed behind her back. 'He just mentioned it in passing,' she amended.

'You two seem to share quite a close relationship…considering it's purely professional…'

'I never said that it was *purely professional*…'

'But you told me that you were working on a project with him.'

'I am. Was. Am.'

'Past tense? Present tense? Which is it to be? And you never said precisely what this so-called project is.'

'I told you, that's something I know Freddy would want to

tell you about himself.' She belatedly remembered that she was supposed to support him whenever and wherever possible. 'And it's very exciting.'

'Well, I can't wait to find out what it's all about. I'm literally on the edge of my seat. If my little brother is involved, then it's sure to be a non-starter. His business sense has always been fairly non-existent.' He finished his coffee and pulled out a stool so that he could prop both feet up—something, she noted, he seemed quite at ease doing considering he was in someone else's house. 'So he told you that I'm his workaholic brother, did he? In between discussing his mystery project?'

'You make it sound as though it's a crime to be friends with Freddy.'

Cesar decided not to inform her that it would only be a crime should she want to adjust her position from *friend* to *spouse*.

'I'm just curious. Project to friend? Friend to project? What was the order of events? How did you meet?'

Jude looked at him warily. That earnest expression on his face didn't fool her a bit. He was taking small steps around her, looking for clues.

'I'm a designer,' she mumbled, trying to sort out how she could avoid divulging details about their meeting, which had happened courtesy of Imogen. 'And he needed some stuff doing...'

'Oh, yes. The stuff he wants to talk to me about. And, at that point, did you know how much Fernando was worth?'

'I knew that's where all your questions were leading!'

'I'm that obvious?' Cesar asked indifferently.

'Yes, you're *that* obvious, not that you care! I have to go and get changed.' She stood up and gave him a withering look, which had zero effect. He still carried on calmly looking at her, as though he had all the time in the world to wait until she decided to deliver the answer he wanted to hear.

'Please don't bother on my account,' Cesar drawled, taking in the shapely legs which had been disguised the night before in their jeans. For someone with dark hair and dark eyes, she was delicately pale and her skin was like satin. He had become used to a diet of women who slapped on make-up. Jude, he absent-mindedly noticed, was wearing none and her face was fresh and smooth. She had a sprinkling of freckles across her nose and he imagined that she might have been a tomboy, climbing trees and doing everything the boys did.

Jade ignored him. 'I haven't been eyeing up your brother as marriage material so that I can get my hands on his fortune,' she said tightly. 'And it's totally out of order for you to repay my hospitality by insulting me!'

'Come again?'

'I could have…left you to find your way round Canterbury in the snow so that you could source a hotel!' Theoretically. He wasn't to know that the pleading look Freddy had given her had warned her that he needed help just in case Cesar found himself programming his sat nav for his brother's apartment—a very strong possibility considering his lack of familiarity with the city and the deteriorating weather. Okay, so maybe *hospitality* implied more than had actually been delivered, because *hospitality* implied a smiling welcome, but she was sticking to her guns. 'You could have ended up lost and trapped in that silly car of yours.'

'*Silly car?*'

Jude made an inarticulate, defiant sound under her breath and glared at him. 'I'm not a gold-digger. I'm not even materialistic! I don't believe that money can buy happiness. The opposite, in fact! I've worked with loads of really rich people who have been miserable as anything. *In fact,*' she tacked on meaningfully, 'are *you* happy because you work all the hours God made so that you can accumulate more money than anyone could possibly spend in a lifetime? Freddy says that you bury yourself in your work because you've never really recovered from…' She went bright red and covered her treacherous mouth with her hand.

'From *what*…?' Cesar asked softly.

'Nothing.'

'What did my brother say?'

'I really need to go and change now!' She fled. She didn't understand how she could have been so thoughtless, just lashing out at him because he had accused her of being a gold-digger. What he'd said meant nothing to her. She should have been able to hear him out and shrug it all off because whatever he thought was never going to be her problem. Instead…

She locked the bathroom door and leaned against it for a few seconds with her eyes closed, before turning on the shower and taking her time under the cascading water.

She felt better once she had showered and even better when she had jettisoned her silly nightie in favour of her favorite fitted jeans and a tight long-sleeved T-shirt. For some indefinable reason she defiantly wanted to show Cesar that she at least had a figure of sorts!

The smell of bacon sizzling greeted her halfway down the stairs and her stomach churned in immediate response. If this was Cesar at the stove, then he was clearly more domesticated than she'd thought he'd be, imagining this brooding billionaire to be the type who had never knowingly sought out any culinary device. She walked into the kitchen and watched for a few silent seconds as Cesar popped some bread in the toaster and then began to beat eggs in a bowl.

'You ran away before you could tell me what other little gems Fernando has shared with you,' Cesar said without turning around.

'I'm sorry.' Jude took a deep breath and went to sit at the table. She stared at the bandage, then looked at Cesar's aristocratic profile. His face was a lesson in beauty, his features sharply, powerfully defined. A portrait artist would have given their right arm to paint him. He had rolled his shirtsleeves to the elbows. His hands were sinewy and strong and she looked away quickly. 'I told you that you were out of order to insult me in my own home and I was out of order to bring up something which is none of my business. Can we call it quits? Maybe start arguing about something else?'

'I take it he told you about Marisol,' Cesar said flatly. He had never found himself in the position of talking about his private life before, even though his late wife was not exactly a subject that was out of bounds. Hell, check his profile on the Internet and up the information would come.

'I'm very sorry.'

'For what? For not, as he insinuated, recovering from her death?' He leaned against the counter and met her gaze coolly, steadily.

'Like I said, it's none of my business.'

'You're right. It's not, but if you want to make it your business, then feel free to look it up when your Internet connection's been restored.' Had he never recovered? Was that the general consensus whispered behind his back? No one had ever dared say anything like that to his face, not even his uncle in Madrid, to whom he was close. The thought of other people having opinions on his state of mind made his mouth tighten in anger but there was no point in venting any of that anger on the woman sitting opposite him. He never allowed other people's opinions to have an effect on him and he wasn't going to start now.

Briefly, though, he thought about his late wife, Marisol. She had been dainty and, peculiarly for a Spanish girl, fair. Cesar, just eighteen at the time, had taken one look at her and had known, in that instant, that he had to have her. It had been a union blessed by both sets of parents and Marisol, for that brief window when she had been alive, had lived up to every expectation. She had been the sweetest woman he'd ever met. She had cooked amazing meals, had not once complained at the hours he kept. She had been a woman born to be protected, looked after, sheltered and he had been more than happy to oblige. What man wouldn't, for a soothing domestic life?

And since Marisol, although he had never contemplated a replacement, he had always been attracted to the same kind of woman. Unbearably pretty and willing to be at his beck and call. As luck would have it, things usually deteriorated with them when his boredom levels were breached, but that never bothered him. He wasn't in it for the long haul. Did that mean that he *had never recovered*? That he couldn't live life fully after a tragedy that had happened more than ten years ago?

He frowned at the wide brown eyes staring back at him and thought, irritably, that he would have been hard pressed to find a less soothing woman than her. Didn't she know that men weren't attracted to women who approached life like a bull in a china shop? He was fast coming to the conclusion that if his brother *was* involved in any way with the woman, aside from platonically, he was a candidate for the loony-bin.

'And you can stop oozing sympathy,' he grated.

'I'm not *oozing sympathy*. I was just wondering how come you never settled down with someone else.'

'Why haven't *you*?' He returned to his task of making

them something to eat. It was unusual to find him behind a stove and his repertoire of dishes was limited, but he had never taken advantage of the family fortune in the same way that his brother had and consequently was more than capable of fending for himself.

'I believe in kissing a few frogs so that I can recognise the prince when he comes along.'

'And how many frogs have you kissed?'

'I lose count.'

Several kissed frogs but only one who had become close enough for her to be seduced into thinking that he might be *the one*. It had been three years ago and it had ended amicably enough when he had sat her down and gently broken it to her that she wasn't the woman for him, that he hoped they could remain *friends*. Remaining *friends*, she had later concluded, was just the coward's way of exiting a relationship with the minimum amount of fuss. If a guy didn't want some woman crying all over him then he did that gentle smiley thing and carried on about remaining *friends*, but a let-down was still a let-down and in retrospect Jude could have kicked herself for not at least asking him *why*. Instead, she had stuck out her chin and saved her tears for after he'd gone.

She had no intention of telling any of that to Cesar, however, and she was thankful that he wasn't looking at her because, when he did, he always gave her the impression that he had some kind of weird insight into what was going on in her head.

'That many…'

'Yes, *that many.*'

'And why did none of these frogs turn out to be the prince in disguise?' He put a plate in front of her, brimming with bacon and eggs, far more than she could have eaten in a month of Sundays.

'How is it that you can cook a meal and make a bed and your brother is so hopeless?'

'Is that your not so subtle way of changing the subject?' Cesar sat down, fork in hand, and began tucking into his breakfast, which was roughly double the amount he had set in front of her. 'I find that it pays to be able to do everything for myself, even if I might choose not to, and that includes cooking and cleaning.'

'Fine. In that case you can make yourself useful around here if you can't drive back for a couple of hours...' Jude glanced outside at the unpromising sight of snow flurries, which seemed to be reminding her that the weather forecasters might have had their fingers on the button when they'd predicted more snowfall. 'I'm pretty useless at both.' Their eyes met for an instant and Jude flushed. 'Or at least uninterested.'

Cesar grunted. It was a grunt, Jude decided, that was laced with criticism. She could just *feel* it. The man didn't have to actually *say anything* to make his opinions clear. Poor Freddy, written off by his big brother because he didn't like wearing a suit and going into an office every day to stare at charts and profit and loss columns, having his ideas greeted with those grunts of disapproval.

'I guess you're one of those ultra-traditional men who think that all women should either be chained to a stove or else whistling a merry tune as they push a vacuum cleaner up and down the stairs,' she said tetchily.

'I admit that when it comes to the opposite sex I have pretty traditional views—am I letting myself in for a feminist lecture now? Because you seem to be very sensitive on the subject.'

'Of course I'm not sensitive on the subject,' Jude scoffed, stabbing a piece of bacon with her fork. She thought of James, the disappearing ex-boyfriend who had left smiling and apologising and wittering on about remaining friends. Eight months ago she had heard through a mutual acquaintance that he had since married a sweet blonde thing who had instantly become pregnant and they were both busily doing up a house somewhere in Wiltshire in preparation for the new arrival.

'Most men are…' he said provocatively. 'Fernando included.'

'Is that your way of warning me off him, should I have ideas above my station lurking at the back of my mind?' She stood up, plate in hand, and went across to the sink, from which she had a spectacular view of increasing snow.

When she looked around, it was to find him clearing the rest of the table. In an ideal world he would have remained sitting, she supposed, having enjoyed a lavish breakfast prepared by his woman, who would tidy the kitchen without asking for help and then make him comfortable in the sitting room with a newspaper and a roaring fire. Curiosity reared its unwelcome head again and she caught herself wondering what these women of his looked like. Freddy had told her that he apparently had killer appeal when it came to the opposite sex.

'Maybe—' she smirked '—Freddy isn't quite as traditional as you think.'

Cesar looked at her sharply and Jude shot him a mysterious smile. In actual fact, traditional-hearted Freddy had found his perfect match in Imogen because, never mind her past occupation, she was as conventional and feminine as they came and always had been. Barbie dolls had been her favourite toys at the age of seven, pink her favourite colour at the age of fourteen and she was a dream in the kitchen. While Jude had been playing football with the boys, her best friend had been experimenting with make-up and, for every botched meal Jude had scraped into the rubbish bin in Home Economics class, Imogen had produced its faultless equivalent. And enjoyed it!

'Meaning what?'

'Meaning you don't give your brother enough credit.'
Well, that was certainly true enough. She had worked with
Freddy from every angle when it came to the jazz club, had
heard him explain his ideas lucidly and persuasively to accountants, had seen his fledgling plans slowly come to
fruition without hitches…

'I know Fernando better than you think.' Did he, though?
Would Fernando be attracted to a fiery, opinionated, mutinous,
downright exasperating woman like this one? A woman who
said whatever was on her mind and hang the consequences?
Fernando, Cesar thought, would never be able to handle a
woman like her! She had said that there was no romantic involvement between them. Was there? It annoyed him that his
usual unerring accuracy at reading women seemed to be
letting him down now.

'Even though you never see him?' Jude asked sweetly. She
began washing the dishes.

'I don't see my brother because I literally don't get the
time.' Cesar walked towards the kitchen door, thought better
of leaving and turned back to look at her with a disgruntled,
exasperated expression. 'Yes, I work damn long hours. When
I took over the company, it was in the throes of internal war-
fare. I stabilised it and hauled it into the twenty-first century,
selling off what I had to and sinking money into speculative
investments that paid off. None of that gets done sipping
cocktails on a beach in the Caribbean or hitting the slopes in
Aspen!' He raked his fingers through his hair and glowered
at her as she continued to pile the dishes haphazardly on the
dish rack. 'I've never known my brother to rise to the challenge of anything,' Cesar heard himself saying. 'And that
includes his choice of women.'

'And you do?' Jude turned to look at him. He was leaning against the door frame and the strength of his personality seemed to fill the kitchen, unseen but powerful and suffocating.

His lack of an immediate answer supplied the information she wanted.

'My choice of women is not the issue here.'

'You should give Freddy a chance. He feels…'

'Feels what…? I'm all ears.'

'*Inadequate* compared to you. He feels that you'll shoot him down in flames because he hasn't followed in your footsteps. At the snap of your fingers, his trust fund will go up in smoke and I don't suppose that's the nicest feeling in the world.'

'He's told you all this, has he? Or are these loose interpretations based on a one-year relationship?'

'He's told me.'

'Have you had sex with him?'

'*What?*'

'You heard me. You are clearly sleeping with Fernando, because your conversations seem pretty meaningful.'

'Our conversations are *normal*.' Jude was bright red, her hands clenched at her sides. '*Normal* people discuss how they feel about things, what their hopes and dreams are…' And these had been with Imogen present, just random, casual conversations over spaghetti bolognese at his flat, with some music playing in the background and the three of them all having one too many glasses of wine and putting the world to rights. Cesar might invest something meaningful into her last statement but Jude wasn't going to supply him with a blow-by-blow description of who said what and where and how and when.

'You've vaguely answered part two of my question but what about part one?'

'No, I haven't slept with your brother, not that it's any of your business.'

Cesar looked at her carefully. 'Tell me something… If you're so close to Fernando and you spend hours spilling your hearts out to each other and bonding, why is he so desperate to get his hands on his trust fund at this precise moment in time? He's been more happy to lead a carefree lifestyle on the allowance he gets for doing no work whatsoever, yet the last time I spoke to him he sounded desperate… Bit of a puzzle, that…'

'His project,' Jude stammered uneasily. And the fact that, while he did indeed get an allowance, he had always funded his lifestyle by sending his bills to Cesar to be paid. Cesar had, through devious means, known pretty much where his money went and could practically track the progress of his relationships by the gifts he had bought for whatever girlfriend he'd happened to be seeing at the time. In short, he had always been accountable. Silk dresses and diamonds, weekend breaks in exotic countries, hotel bills for two—his personal life vetted to a large extent by Cesar, who would step in if he deemed it necessary. Cesar, he had confided in Jude, was very hot on protecting the family fortune from unsuitable women but that had never bothered Freddy because he had never had any intention of getting too wrapped up with anyone. If bills for nursery equipment and baby gear began appearing on the statements, then Cesar would descend with frightening speed and it didn't take a genius to figure out what his reaction would be when he saw Imogen. The trust fund would give him independence.

'If I approve whatever scheme he has in mind, then I would be more than happy to invest in it and set aside the headache of putting Fernando in charge of staggering wealth when he has yet to prove that he would know what to do with it. So did he mention *why* the hurry?'

Jude tried to look as though she might be searching her memory bank for any helpful information on that front, then she shook her head and shrugged. 'I guess he just wants to take control of his life. I mean, he *is* nearly twenty-five…'

'Ancient.'

'*You* were younger than that when you took charge of your empire, or whatever you want to call it.'

'I was responsible.'

'Of course. Silly me. Crazy to think that you might have had a trace of recklessness in your body.'

'If by *reckless* you mean a healthy, active sex life with an interesting variety of women, then, I assure you, you couldn't be further from the truth. If, on the other hand, you mean an ability to squander money on passing pleasures without any thought to the future, then you're spot on. I'll willingly confess to being ridiculously cautious…'

Jude blinked as her active mind hived off on the same unwelcome tangent that had kept her tossing and turning the night before.

Her breasts felt heavy and tender and the brush of her lacy bra over her nipples was almost painful.

'I think…we should think about what we're going to do with the day,' she said hastily, folding her arms squarely in front of her. 'I agree it would be silly for you to try and dig that car of yours out of the snow when there's more falling, but there's no point getting under each other's feet.'

'You should give lessons on how to be the perfect hostess.'

'I've got some work I can be getting on with. In my office. Well, I have a little room off the sitting room that I use as an office, anyway. You can…'

'Make myself scarce?' He pushed himself away from the door frame, his sharp mind tallying their conversation and replaying it. She had been sincere in her denial that there was anything sexual between herself and Fernando but, that being the case, why her unease the minute his questions became too probing? Why did she behave like a cat on a hot tin roof in his presence?

He looked narrowly at her and the heightened colour in her cheeks, then his eyes drifted to those arms tightly folded over her chest. A very protective gesture, he thought. He knew that he could be intimidating. He liked that. It often helped to keep people at a distance, especially for a man like him, someone at the very pinnacle of his field, which was a situation that encouraged on the one hand sycophants, on the other predatory sharks who wouldn't hesitate to cosy up to him while clutching knives behind their backs. It also helped as a silent reminder to any woman that, however physically close they got, he was not up for grabs.

Maybe that was it. Maybe she got jittery in his presence and, face it, he was an intruder in her house, snowbound and with zero means of transport out. Or maybe those whispered conversations he had noticed between his brother and her pointed to something going on under the surface, something that made her nervous around him.

Or maybe—and he mulled this last option over with a little kick of satisfaction—just maybe he made her nervous for a perfectly understandable reason. He was a red-blooded man and she, if he wasn't mistaken, was a woman who was all fire where it mattered if only she knew it. Couldn't pretty much everything in life go right back to the elemental?

CHAPTER THREE

IT WAS lunch time before Jude emerged from her office, where she had spent her time redoing her sketches for a loft conversion which, according to the couple who had employed her, had to make them feel as though they were somewhere by the sea. It was a tall order for a Victorian house on the outskirts of a city.

The first thing that greeted her was the sight of Cesar, bare-backed, with a stack of freshly cut logs next to the open fire, which was in full swing.

'Just in case the power goes,' he explained. 'If it can snow like this out here, then anything's possible.'

Jude nodded. The sight of his bare skin flickering in the glow from the open fire seemed flagrantly intimate, although he looked at her innocently enough before walking across to the bay window and nodding at the leaden yellow-grey skies outside, barely visible through the now heavy snowfall. 'The Internet connection's still AWOL so I figured I might as well make myself useful. Manage to get much work done?'

'Work?'

'You've been cooped up in there for four hours!'

She thought of the discarded drawings tossed into the waste-paper bin because her thoughts wouldn't leave her alone. 'Yes. It was very useful.' She made a big effort to stop gaping and actually walked into the sitting room, which was wonderfully warm.

'I've switched off the central heating in the room,' he told her. 'Hope you don't mind.' Cesar had been stared at before. Many times. But never like this, never by a woman who so obviously didn't want to look at him and yet couldn't help herself. It was fiercely erotic. He had, and he hadn't mentioned this, also hand-washed his socks, his boxers and his shirt. At the moment his nakedness against the zipper of his trousers was threatening to need adjustment.

'How did you know where to find the wood?'

'Little shed at the back of the house. Not that tricky, really.' He prodded the fire with the poker, making sure that his back was towards her so that he could give his body time to cool down. Eventually, when he had himself under control, he strolled towards the chair and wiped his face on one of her T-shirts—the very one she had thrown at him the night before.

'Well, thank you. There was no need. The central heating's very efficient in this house. I make sure of that. Shall I get you something to put on? One of my T-shirts?'

'I'm not sure they would fit,' Cesar drawled, 'unless it's one of those baggy ones you seem to like sleeping in.'

Jude refused to be goaded by his remark. Instead, she hurried upstairs and snatched the biggest of her T-shirts out of the chest of drawers because the sooner he covered himself up the better. He obviously hadn't stripped on purpose. He had stripped because chopping logs and starting a fire was a sweat-inducing job, especially once the fire really got going. He wasn't to know that his semi-nudity was just fuelling all sorts of unwanted thoughts in her head. She could swear that her eyesight had gone bionic because she had even been able to make out a trickle of perspiration along his ribcage.

'Well, at least it's not pink,' he said, reaching out and casually brushing her outstretched hand in the process. 'I don't think my male pride could have stood it.'

'Stood what?'

Keep your eyes focused on his face, my girl, and you'll be all right. Definitely don't give in to the temptation to stare at the way his muscles ripple whenever he moves his arms. Or the fact that he has flat brown nipples and a tangle of dark underarm hair.

'Being on public display wearing a girlie colour.'

This was a different Cesar to the grim-faced one who laid down laws and issued threats. This one was smiling at her. A crooked, amused smile that made her toes curl.

'Real men aren't afraid to wear pink,' she said automatically, and Cesar kept her eyes locked to his.

'Trust me. I'm all man.'

'I should go and get us both something to eat. You must be famished after a morning chopping wood. I have some… er…pasta…' she gabbled, taking a step back towards the kitchen. 'I can rustle something up. I'm not great, I have to warn you…but I do a good carbonara…spaghetti…nothing fancy…' The pale blue T-shirt sported a cartoon character but somehow he didn't look silly in it. If anything, it made him more frighteningly masculine, accentuating his biceps and the lean hardness of his stomach.

'Carbonara…spaghetti…nothing fancy…will do just fine, and yes, I'm famished, but I didn't want to start rummaging in your kitchen for food. I know how territorial women can be about men rummaging through their cupboards…I'm surprised you managed to work with your hand bandaged…'

'It doesn't hurt.' She stumbled over her words, instinctively flexing her fingers to prove her point. 'You made a big deal over nothing.'

'Maybe I enjoyed it,' he came back, quick as a flash. 'Don't you know that there's nothing a man finds more appealing than a damsel in distress…?'

'I'm not the damsel in distress type. If you wait *right here* I'll go and fix us lunch.'

She might have guessed, five minutes later, that giving him an order to do something would have the opposite effect because, in his new, confusing good mood, he appeared in the kitchen just as she was fumbling with an onion and debating whether to get rid of the wretched bandage so that she could actually move slightly quicker than a snail.

'Allow me.'

Jude stiffened but didn't look at him as he relieved her of the knife and began expertly peeling and chopping the onion, giving her the far less onerous task of pouring them both a glass of wine because, he told her, it was as dark as night outside and, besides, when did he ever get the chance to consume alcohol at lunch time?

It was a passing remark but it struck him that he very rarely gave himself any chance to really enjoy his leisure time. He had wined and dined many women over the years but courtship was a game he played and the final outcome was already written on the cards before the first meal was even halfway through.

This was different. He might not have been here of his own volition but now that he was, and without the benefit of work as a distraction, he found that he was actually enjoying chopping an onion, frying bacon, playing the domestic man that he never was because his interaction with women never evolved into doing tasks together. He took them to expensive restaurants and sat next to them in theatres and made love to them in his vast bed, but never this.

He saluted her with a raised glass once their concoction was made and nodded to the kitchen table.

'Aren't you a little bored being cooped up here?' she asked tentatively. 'I don't suppose this is what you usually get up to on a weekend.'

'No, it's not.'

'What *do* you get up to?' Curiosity got the better of her and she looked at him over the rim of her glass.

'I work by day and play by night. Occasionally, I skip the play bit if I'm busy.'

'Who do you play with?' Jude blushed, confused to have asked the question but the wine had loosened her tongue, as had his change of attitude. She was no longer on the defensive, wondering where the next barb was coming from, and, released from that constraint, she went beyond her surreptitious appreciation of his masculinity to an even deadlier appreciation of the complex, intelligent, witty *person* behind that formidable, unbearably handsome mask. She began to really see why he was such a killer with the opposite sex. He wasn't being remotely flirtatious and yet there was something indefinably magnetic about him.

She barely noticed how much she was drinking. She was too busy listening to his casual admission that he hadn't, actually, *played* with anybody for the better part of six months. Had she? With the tables neatly turned on her, Jude heard herself ruefully admitting that her playtime stretched a whole lot longer than his. Then, even more surprising because she had never really talked about her ex-boyfriend to anyone, not even to Imogen, who had obviously known the bones of what had happened, she heard herself baring her soul to Cesar.

'So there you are. You were right on one count—men are pretty predictable in the kind of women they go for and it's not the kind of woman *I* am.'

For some reason Cesar felt a spurt of anger towards the unknown stranger who had brought home to her that life was a pretty disillusioning business.

'And stop me now before I get even more maudlin.' Jude laughed and stood up so that she could begin setting the table. 'Too much wine, I'm afraid. One more glass and you'd better watch out. I'll start feeling weepy and sorry for myself.'

'I have very broad shoulders.'

'I know. I'd noticed.'

There was an electric silence. She may have only consumed one glass of wine but not even that slight tipsy, reckless feeling could blind her to the fact that she had just blurted out something horribly private that should have been kept to herself.

And he was looking at her in a very peculiar way.

'When you were…stoking the fire…' she continued lamely, dropping her eyes. At times like these, wouldn't a curtain of long hair have been convenient! She could have hidden behind it. 'I don't often get semi-clad men in my cottage…'

'No, not for a few years, at any rate…'

'I knew I shouldn't have told you that,' Jude said with a hint of bitterness in her voice. She brought the pan over to the table and curtly told him that he could help himself. Guests first and he *had*, after all, cooked it all himself.

'Why do you say that?'

'Say what?'

'That you shouldn't have told me about your ex.'

'Because I don't need you, *or anyone*, being in a position to use information against me at some later date. I don't need anyone to feel sorry for me. I *made a choice* to give myself a break from guys after James and I'm not ashamed of that.' She attacked her food fiercely and glared down at the coil of spaghetti around her fork.

'You really loved this guy, didn't you.'

'I cared about him,' Jude said stiffly. 'I wouldn't have stayed with him for over two years if I hadn't.'

'Stayed with him in the expectation that the relationship would eventually lead to marriage?'

'I suppose.'

'And you never spotted the cracks?'

'I honestly don't want to talk about this.'

'Fair enough. Although…'

It was just one word but it drew her in and she said sullenly, 'Although *what*? I know you're just dying to tell me what's on your mind.'

'We're stuck here.' Cesar shrugged. 'A little conversation passes the time of day and it's not as though I can get through to any of my colleagues. Have you tried the phone? Lines are down. I could always use my mobile…' though the temptation wasn't there, for some reason '…but no charger, so I'm conserving the battery.'

'They're not!' She went over to the phone and then looked at him. 'They are.'

'Yep. Only outside contact I've had is with Fernando to let him know I'm safe and sound and not buried under ten foot of snow somewhere on the outskirts of the city. And you'll be relieved to know that I didn't mention that I had spent the night here. So…no landline, no computer access, limited mobile access—what choice do we have but to make do with each other's company?'

'Is that why you've started to be a bit more pleasant?' It was almost a relief to snipe at him. Just back then—talking to him with the wine flowing through her veins and his smile making her feel all hot and bothered and self-conscious—she had felt like someone walking on the edge of a precipice, with a sharp drop on one side and the comfort of safety on the other.

'I'm intrigued by the irony of someone who is at liberty to psychoanalyse my relationships with women as a response to the death of my wife twelve years ago and yet seems unable to see that her self-imposed exile from emotional involvement with men is her response to a failed relationship.' Cesar forked some food into his mouth and carried on looking at her. 'You're not eating.'

'My appetite seems to have disappeared.'

'Because you're uncomfortable being asked about some guy who led you down the garden path and then dumped you. I'm not the monster you seem to think I am and I'm not laughing at you because you've been celibate for a while.' What he could have added but didn't was that, with no access to the outside world, he now found himself doing something he had never done before. Cesar was taking an interest in a woman beyond the physical. Mostly, his conversations with the opposite sex, unless conducted in the working arena, were laughably superficial. He didn't encourage emotional outpourings.

'Okay, maybe I'm a bit over-cautious when it comes to men, maybe I just don't like getting too close. In fact, your brother is the first guy I've really felt comfortable with for ages,' she admitted and she knew why. Freddy was no threat. He wasn't going to try and pounce on her. He was wrapped up with Imogen and was therefore a safe bet for friendship and it had to be said that having a man as a friend was a huge plus because men brought a different take on all sorts of things. She had forgotten how invaluable they were when it came to putting things into perspective.

'Is that a fact?' Cesar murmured softly, watching the smile on her face.

'I know.' She looked at him, still smiling to herself. 'I know you've had your problems with Freddy, but you'd be surprised at how practical he can be when it counts.'

'Practical…' Well, that, Cesar thought, was a first when it came to recommendations. He stood up and, when she followed suit, told her to go and make herself comfortable in the sitting room. Why waste the fire?

'I should help tidy these things away.'

'You're an invalid.'

'Hardly. Oh, yes, forgot. Damsel in distress.' She glanced down at the bandaged hand with sudden amusement. 'I'm beginning to see that I've played things all wrong. Maybe, instead of trying to be independent, I should have been dropping hankies on the ground and batting my eyelashes so that dashing men would fall at my feet in their eagerness to help me out.'

Cesar was tempted to tell her that he couldn't picture her batting her eyelashes although, when he looked at her, he could see that she had very long eyelashes indeed, eminently suited to playing coy. Where other women enhanced theirs with mascara and eye make-up, for her there was no need.

'Maybe you should,' he said non-committally, but as she disappeared towards the sitting room, leaving him with a sink-load of dirty dishes and the novel experience of washing them, he had plenty more to think about. That faraway, dreamy look in her eyes when she had sung his brother's praises. What did that mean? The random thoughts that had been playing around in his head since the night before now coalesced into something a lot more concrete and a lot more disturbing.

So she hadn't yet slept with Fernando. He was convinced

of that. The woman didn't seem to have the ability to dissemble. He also believed that she had been hiding out from involvement with any man because she had been burnt before.

Where Fernando figured in this jigsaw puzzle was now becoming a little more obvious. He had no one in tow at the moment. Cesar knew that because there had been no charges recently for classy weekend breaks or expensive items of jewellery. For Fernando, whose lifestyle was nothing if not predictable, that could only indicate one thing. He was currently without a woman and, from the looks of it, had been for a while.

Cesar rested both hands flat on the edge of the kitchen sink and gazed thoughtfully at the steadily falling snow.

He had dropped his accusations, had adopted a different approach and, sure enough, he had got what he wanted or at least he had got the pieces he had needed to turn the puzzle into a mathematical equation he could solve.

Jude, reading between the lines, had been in a deep freeze and he didn't know whether her thaw when she met Fernando had been deliberate or whether it had been accidental, but thaw she had. He had seen that in the expression on her face when she had talked about him and heard it in the tone of her voice.

She had given him a load of spiel about not being materialistic but that, he now cynically considered, was something that had to be taken with a huge pinch of salt. People were fond of throwing their hands up in the air and spouting forth about the best things in life being free, but show them a shedload of cash and the free goodies suddenly didn't seem quite so tempting.

Had she decided somewhere along the way that a friendship, played right, could lead to financial security for the rest of her life?

He thought of her and irritably shrugged off the nagging

unease that her sharp, straightforward, argumentative personality was at odds with the picture he was piecing together. She
seemed as keen, in her own way, as Fernando was in getting
hold of the precious trust fund. How many times had she
mentioned all his brother's marvellous and hitherto unseen
virtues of common sense and responsibility? Sure, she might
be innocently complimenting him because she was his friend
and nothing more. On the other hand, she could be fuelled by
motives that were a hell of a lot more suspect.

He ignored the little voice in his head that was telling him
that Fernando was a big boy now, well capable of taking care
of himself, that he could make his own choices as far as
women were concerned and that really, maybe the two of
them genuinely had a good thing going and that hell, she was
a damn sight better than some of his other catches.

Instead, he focused on the fact that their interaction at that
club had not been the interaction of a man and a woman in the
throes of a passionate affair after months of mutual teasing.
There had been a few whispered conversations, a few furtive
looks when they had thought themselves unobserved, but no accidental brushing of bodies and no mysterious disappearances.

So where did that leave him? Was she an out-and-out gold-
digger? And, even if she was, was it really any of his business?
Hand over the trust fund and walk away. He could do that.
Leave Fernando to make a mess of his life in the full understanding that rescue down the line would not be part of the deal.
Or withhold the trust fund and protect his brother's financial
interests, except at what point would the protection end?

He frowned darkly, waiting for an answer to come to him
the way it always did. There was no situation over which he
couldn't have complete control and this, surely, was another
but no answer materialised in his head. Instead, he just found

himself thinking that *he wanted her*. It was something elemental. It defied logic and had caught him on the hop but it was still there, that powerful surge of his body when he looked at her and when he caught her looking at him.

He pushed himself away from the counter top and headed for the sitting room, where she was sitting on one of the sofas with a magazine in her hand and her feet tucked under her.

Although it was not yet completely dark, she had switched on the lights. Outside, with the falling snow, there was a twilight hue that made it feel much later than it was and the scene of roaring log fire and woman curled up on sofa just needed the addition of faithful Labrador to turn it into a picture from a magazine.

She looked up from whatever she was reading and Cesar strolled into the room and sat at the opposite end of the sofa.

'Does it bug you that you can't get in touch with anyone?' she asked, just to break the silence. The way he was looking at her made her stomach flip into knots.

'I'm getting used to it. I might have to start having the occasional retreat without my computer or mobile.'

'But with a change of clothes.'

'That would work,' Cesar drawled. 'I've washed my boxers and I'm more than happy to put them on and stick these things in the wash, but if you find that offensive…' He grimaced at the trousers, which had now seen a night at a club and a stint in the driving snow gathering logs, not to mention the grubby business of chopping them and getting the fire going.

'I'm not sure that that's a very good idea.' Suddenly the room seemed a lot smaller, the fire a lot hotter and her skin as tingly as if electric currents were pulsing underneath it. 'And I haven't got any tracksuit pants that would fit. I…er…'

'So you *would* find it offensive…'

'Not at all. I'm not a prude.' She laughed lightly and reminded herself that he was just a guy and a guy who had been pretty insulting towards her. More to the point, *she* might be able to recognise that obvious sexual appeal of his but her effect on him was rather different. Not only, by his own admission, was she not the sort of woman he found attractive, she was the sort of woman he found the least appealing. He liked them subservient and background. She was independent and outspoken. He had made the most of being cooped up in her house and had seemed to enjoy the unexpected break of having to indulge in doing things which he never did because he could pay someone else to do them for him but that didn't mean that he was no longer the cold-eyed, suspicious man who had quizzed her on her motives. It *would* make him suspicious if she became jittery at the thought of seeing him in a pair of boxer shorts. Which were, in effect, no more revealing than swimming trunks.

'I could always remain safely tucked away in my bedroom until I was fit to come back downstairs,' he murmured, lowering those magnificent eyes of his so that she couldn't tell whether he was joking or not.

Jude made a decision. 'If you give them to me, I'll put a wash on.'

'Only if you're sure…'

'Why shouldn't I be?' She gave another tinkling laugh to indicate surprise that he might think otherwise and stood up, stretching, because her legs were now stiff from her awkward sitting position.

'No reason. I just wouldn't want to embarrass you…' Cesar looked at her with a little half smile and his eyebrows raised, the picture of pious solicitude. 'I won't take them off here. Nothing underneath. Boxers still drying on the radiator upstairs.' His voice was apologetic and polite. 'You may not embarrass easily, but far be it for me to put that to the test. I'll leave them outside the bedroom door. Just give me a couple of minutes...'

He was in high spirits by the time he hit the sitting room, this time wearing the ubiquitous T-shirt and his silk boxers, now dry if a little crisp.

He would never have guessed in a million years that having to play truant from work would have such unexpected benefits. He'd certainly meant it when he'd told her that he would have to start arranging some more down time for himself because he hadn't thought once about any e-mails he might have received, to which he needed to respond, nor had he been particularly bothered by the fact that his cellphone was switched off. He could have contacted his secretary, informed her that she had to get to the office and fill him in on whatever numbers he needed for client contact over the weekend, but he had rejected that idea even before it had fully taken shape. Incommunicado was working just fine for him, as it happened.

He went across to the fire. On the mantelpiece was a selection of books, most of them semi-architectural, a few dedicated to iconic designers and a couple of fictional works. He slotted out one of the architectural ones and was leafing through it when he sensed her by the door.

'You don't mind, do you?' he asked, casually lounging and seemingly engrossed in the print in front of him.

Jude opened her mouth but nothing emerged. Seeing him standing there, with the light from the fire flickering over his hard, bronzed body, made her throat run dry. The tingly feeling was back, this time accompanied by a desperate need to sit down because her legs felt like jelly. She knew that it was absolutely imperative that she stop gaping like a teenager.

It would be mortifying and disastrous if he suddenly looked up and spotted her doing her goldfish impression, right down to the bulging eyes, but she couldn't wrest her eyes away from the fabulous perfection of his body. His stomach was flat and hard, his muscled legs long and lean with perfectly shaped calves and thighs. He stood there, indolently leaning against the wall, and he resembled a classical Greek statue. Living and breathing, she reminded herself shakily.

'No, of course not.' She remained hovering by the door, rooting through her brain for some excuse to vacate the room in favour of some other part of the house, where she could get her breathing stabilized.

'You never told me what sort of design work you do,' Cesar mused, slowly turning to face her. The curtains had been drawn and the overhead lights switched off in favour of the two lamps on the tables either side of the sofa and the standard lamp in the corner of the room.

'You never asked,' Jude stammered.

'Why are you dithering by the door?' He snapped shut the book, tucked it under his arm and strolled to the sofa, where he proceeded to sit down and extend his long legs on the low table in front of him. Then he patted the space next to him, which Jude chose to ignore in favour of the less challenging one on the chair by the fire. Arguing with him, bristling and fending off accusations seemed like a walk in the park compared to the weird, gut-wrenching sensation of having an amicable conversation while looking at his semi-clothed figure.

'There's an architectural theme to your books.'

'I began studying architecture,' Jude said, eyes above waist level, 'but I had to quit because it was too long and I needed to go out to work.' He tilted his head to one side with a show of immense interest. 'My mother had just died and my sister's husband was laid off at just the wrong time because they had a newborn. The proceeds from the house…well, it wasn't much and she needed it a lot more than I did…'

'Tough call,' Cesar said sympathetically.

'These things happen. I really enjoyed interior design so I decided that that was the next best thing and, as it turns out, I'm pretty good at it because I can offer more than just a load of advice about colour and soft furnishings. I can help with all the fundamental stuff to do with restructuring houses so they get my knowledge without the big bill at the end. If a qualified architect gets involved, he usually just has to sign off on drawings that have already been done.' She couldn't resist a smile of pride.

'Talented lady.'

Jude flushed with pleasure at the compliment. 'I get by,' she told him with a little shrug. 'I may not be rolling in money but I've been able to buy this cottage and most of the mortgage has been paid off because my sister's husband went back out to work a year and a half ago and she's managed to repay me the money I gave her. Not that I asked for it.'

'And she lives around here?'

'On the other side of the world, actually. Australia.'

'So you're here on your own…' Was that how she and Fernando had become so close? Two lonely souls gravitating towards one another? He reopened the book, which had been resting on the sofa next to him. 'This place…' he said slowly. 'Where is it? I like it. Like the dimensions of the rooms…' He gave her a lazy look from under his lashes and saw her fractional hesitation before she came across to where he was sitting. Deliberately, he kept the book on his lap, frowning down at the series of black and white photos spread across two pages, so that she either had to circle the sofa and lean over him or else…yes, as she was doing now…sit next to him.

'That's one of my favourite apartment renovations,' she said, keeping her distance, which was awkward because it involved angling her body to see the pictures without toppling onto him. 'Ferrea has managed to combine comfort with modern, clean lines. Some apartments can lack soul if they're too avant-garde but look there…' she pointed to details '…he uses a lot of wood in crucial places and the addition of those beams…brilliant…' She leaned closer to him in her enthusiasm and stiffened as she brushed against his arm. It was just a feathery touch but it resonated through her in deep, disturbing waves which made her pull back sharply.

When she sneaked a look at him, it was to find him staring right back at her with his bitter chocolate eyes. His expression was shuttered and yet, strangely, she seemed able to read intent there and that made her draw in her breath as the colour rose into her face and her eyes widened in acknowledgement of everything that was not being said. Or maybe she was misreading the situation. She had been on her own for a long time. Maybe her imagination had become over-developed in direct proportion to her isolation.

She became aware that she was holding her breath and also that he was still looking at her.

'I guess,' she said, clearing her throat and blinking, 'that's just about one of the few modern places I could actually see…see…er…myself living in…' She gave a nervous laugh and gestured around her. 'I mean…you can tell that I'm the kind of person who goes for the weathered…look…' Her voice faded because he raised his hand and curved it at the nape of her neck. Then he began stroking her, just his thumb against her skin, moving in tiny circles that sent fireworks through her body.

Jude had no idea what was going on but she wasn't fighting

him, and somewhere deep inside she realised that she had been imagining just this moment, when he would reach out and touch her.

She closed her eyes on a sigh as he pulled her gently towards him...

CHAPTER FOUR

For Cesar, this felt *right*. He curled her into him and the kiss, which started softly explorative, became deeper and more urgent. She gasped when they finally broke apart and sucked in a lungful of air.

'What's going on?'

'A kiss. What would you *like* to be going on now?' Cesar questioned softly. It was odd but this was the first time he had ever held a woman with short hair. Had he always been so predictable in his tastes? He glibly criticized his brother for always being attracted to the same type of woman, but he was no different. Neither of them had ever looked outside the box for anything different and he realised that he had never sought anyone who could challenge him. He had never wanted anyone to break through the layer of steel he had concocted around himself. Intimate conversations had been discouraged, as had any games of domestic bliss. Relationships without depth had been safe because they could never threaten the predictable course of his life.

Now this woman.

Cesar frowned, thrown by a surge of complex, conflicting thoughts, but then he relaxed. This felt right because it made sense. He was attracted to her, even though she ticked none of the usual boxes and, more than that, by taking her, wouldn't he be safeguarding his brother from a potential gold-digger? She made all the right noises about not wanting money and said all the right things about just wanting Fernando as a friend, but money was a powerful magnet and, just in case she had the slightest thought of worming her way into Fernando's affections, what better way to prevent that than by making her his own first?

It made no difference to Cesar whether she was after money or not because he, unlike his brother, was well equipped to handle any sort of woman. He, unlike his brother, could handle *anything*.

'We were…talking about designers…' she stammered, reaching out for the first thing she could think of that might restore normality, but she couldn't drag her eyes away from his beautiful face. She felt as though she were drowning.

'So we were…' Cesar agreed. He angled his long body into a more comfortable position on the sofa, never releasing her, just shifting her into position.

With no messy, tumbling hair everywhere, he could really appreciate the grace of her neck, the slimness of her shoulders, the exquisite daintiness of her heart-shaped face.

He slid his hands to span her waist and slowly caressed the satiny smooth skin with his fingers. 'You were telling me about that apartment…how much you admired the guy who designed it…' He gently parted her legs with his thigh, a small but significant movement because now she was straddling him and he could move his leg against her while he continued to look earnestly into her eyes.

Cesar didn't know quite how he was managing to maintain this level of self-control when what he wanted to do was rip off her clothes and indulge in the glory of making love to her.

Nor did he know just how long he had been nurturing those thoughts. When had his suspicions morphed into lust?

The material of her trousers felt abrasive against his naked thigh.

Jude sighed and her eyelids fluttered as the heat and moisture built up inside her until she felt incapable of doing anything but riding the growing tide of desire.

He was moving his leg against her crotch and she liked it. God, how she liked it! She pressed herself against his muscled thigh and a wave of sensuous pleasure drained her of all coherent thought. Her sigh turned into a moan when he placed his hands on her bottom and pushed her down hard against him so that now her swollen, sensitised nub was being massaged even through her clothes.

'Shh…' Jude silenced him, and Cesar looked at her with a mixture of lazy triumph and a powerful, uncontrollable, surging *craving*. Her eyes were closed and she was arched back, the flats of her hands on either side of him so that their bodies only met at that point where his leg was rubbing against her.

Cesar was desperate to touch her but mingled with the conviction that she wanted him was the nagging thought that she really didn't *want* to want him. It was just that her body had managed to ambush her logic. If he began touching her intimately, if he made a move to strip her of that tight little T-shirt that was the ultimate in tease because he could see so much and then the rest was left to the imagination…would she back off? Would her eyes fly open and logic reassert its rightful place?

Never hesitant in bed in his life before, he was taking on board the unaccustomed realisation that he would have to let her come to him. He would have to let her initiate that first move. Whether she knew it or not, she was in the driving seat and he had no choice but to relinquish the steering wheel to her.

The frustration was agonizing, so when she did lower herself, blindly seeking out his mouth, he couldn't resist pulling her against him. His kiss was an assault on her senses as his tongue delved into the softness of her mouth.

Jude groaned. She could feel his hardness pushing against her as she lay down against him and instinctively she reached down with one hand and felt it, then she slipped her hand beneath his boxers and wrapped her fingers around the massive, throbbing shaft of steel.

Her body seemed to be operating on autodrive. Sex with James had been a pleasant business. Nothing like this.

'Don't begin what you can't finish…' Cesar said hoarsely, and Jude opened her eyes and gazed into his.

'What would you do if I decided to walk away?' she teased unsteadily. She had wondered what it would be like to see this big, powerful man in the grip of something beyond his control. She was seeing it now, as she continued to massage him until he was forced to put his hand over hers and squeeze tightly.

'Continue our in-depth…our…'

She scrambled to pull the T-shirt over his head and, for a few seconds, revelled in the sight of him. She ran her hands over his broad chest, loving the hard definition of muscle against bone.

'My turn now, wouldn't you agree?'

Jude smiled and reached to yank off her top, but he was there first, ridding her of it in one fluid movement and stopping her before she could unclasp her bra at the back. Instead, he cupped her breasts and began playing with them, teasing her nipples through the lacy covering.

'Neither of us is going anywhere,' Cesar told her thickly, 'so what's the rush? I want to enjoy every inch of your beautiful body and I want to take my time.' He scooped one small, ripe breast from the bra and almost lost control of himself.

Outside, night was rushing in. In the flickering light, he could see the fine film of perspiration making her face shine like smooth satin. He lowered her breast towards his mouth and felt her tremble under his hands. She was as supple as a cat, her slight, slim body yielding to him as he began suckling on her pink, hardened nipple.

She was hardly aware of him easing her jeans off, although she helped by wriggling free of them and she tried very hard not to be frantic when she tugged down his boxers.

'Maybe we should go upstairs…' she murmured.

'The sofa's more than big enough for the two of us. Besides, why waste a good fire?' He rolled her onto her back and they swapped positions.

Jude looked up with a slow, curling smile as he pinned both her hands above her head and then lowered himself on her so that he could continue to lavish his attention on her breasts.

She kept her hands raised behind her, half hanging off the back of the sofa, even when he had moved his. Arched like this, his mouth on her nipples as he nuzzled and sucked, sent fire shooting through her body.

She couldn't keep still. Little moans escaped as she twisted in a fever of longing and, as he eased himself lower, she curled her fingers into his hair, pushing him down and parting her legs, inviting him to taste her in a way no man had done before.

She shuddered as he trailed his tongue against the flat planes of her stomach, circling it around her belly button. She knew she said something at that point, something that made him give a low, sexy laugh, then his exploring mouth was moving lower until she could stand it no longer and he slipped his tongue into her.

In the same way as she had massaged him with her hand, so he teased her with his tongue, sliding it up and down over the swollen bud until she was bucking against him and gasping with the effort of not reaching her climax against his mouth.

Dimly, she was aware of the fact that there was no contraception to hand. This was a situation for which she had never catered and she wasn't one of those thoroughly modern young women who kept a stash of protective measures *just in case*. There had been no *just in case* episodes in her life before.

She tried to work out whether she was in a safe period and decided that she was, although she realised that her mental arithmetic was a little sketchy just at the moment.

So when he finally levered himself onto her and asked her, unsteadily, whether she was protected, she had no hesitation in nodding.

He thrust into her and began moving deeply and firmly, and then faster as they both surrendered to their bodies. She cried out and jerked up just as he gave one final powerful thrust that sent him over the edge.

He was still breathing unevenly when his shuddering orgasm eventually eased him from its grip, as if he had run a marathon and was struggling to catch his breath.

He turned onto his side and pulled her against him, tucking her leg between his. Her hair was damp against her cheek and she looked drowsy. Drowsy and satisfied, he thought. Ever confident about his abilities in the bedroom, he found himself resisting the temptation to ask her whether it had been good for her, whether it was the best sex she had ever had. Since when had he ever been concerned by crazy notions like that?

'I don't know what happened just then.' Jude could feel her heart beating like a drum inside her chest.

'We made love.'

'I know *that*, but I...I don't *do things like that*. I mean, hop into bed with a man I barely know.' Dawning reality was making her think that she should probably get up and get dressed but he had his arms around her and her body was suddenly lazy and weak.

'Believe it or not, neither do I.'

'You're right. I don't believe it.'

Cesar laughed softly and stroked her hair back. 'Okay, I admit I haven't led a celibate life since Marisol died, but this level of spontaneity...'

'You mean you court your women before you hop in the sack with them.' It was so silent in the cottage that she could almost hear the beating of their hearts. 'Don't you ever get lonely?' she asked, and Cesar stiffened as he felt the push against his self-imposed barriers. This was one of the most intimate questions he had ever been asked.

'You don't have to answer that one,' Jude said quickly. 'Not if you're scared to.'

'Scared?'

'Maybe not *scared*, as such.'

'Of course I don't get lonely! I have a very active life, as it happens.'

'Right.'

'Your tone smacks of disbelief.' But he laughed. He felt too damn relaxed to let her get under his skin. Must be something in the good old-fashioned clean country air that had gone to his head. He stroked her thigh and then pushed her legs apart so that he could cup her between them, just gently resting his hand there. He could already feel himself ready to make love to her all over again, like a sex-starved teenager bedding a woman for the first time.

'Course I believe you. I bet you play lots of sport, go out a lot and have women flocking around at your beck and call.'

'Yes to all three.'

Of course he was just being honest. For a man like Cesar, women were just a pleasant distraction in his life. This sort of situation would be unusual for him and not just because it would have veered wildly away from his normal routine of pursuit and capture, not just because they had fallen together against all odds—it would have been unusual because she wasn't his type.

'Where do you go?' she asked, stifling the discomfort she felt at knowing that she had slept with a man who would walk out of her life the minute the snow stopped falling and he could climb back into that expensive car of his and drive away. 'You said that you go out a lot. Where to? Theatres? The cinema?'

'Theatres, yes. Cinema—can't tell you the last time I went to see a movie. There's not enough time in the day for such mindless luxury.'

In her head she was getting a picture of a man who seldom relaxed and the more glimpses she got of the man, the more she wanted to know more.

'Theatre is a luxury,' she pointed out.

'Theatre is either entertaining clients,' Cesar told her drily, 'or else being entertained by them. Life in the concrete jungle is one great big exercise in back-scratching.'

'Sounds fun.'

'I can think of better things to do.' He grinned and let her know just what he had in mind by reaching out to touch her breast. 'Are you ready for me again?'

'We *could* talk…a bit…'

'Why?'

In that split second, Jude knew that her curiosity had been a mistake. They had made love, done the most intimate things imaginable with one another, but in all other respects they were still worlds apart. Discovering one another was not on Cesar's agenda, at least not beyond the extent of getting to know her in relation to his brother.

'You're right. Why talk when there are so many better things to do? I mean, I've been on my own for a while…'

She stroked his back and felt him stiffen.

'What are you trying to say? Are you telling me that you're using me as a refresher course?'

'What on earth are you talking about?'

Cesar shifted so that he could pull back from her, look her squarely in the eyes. 'You know what I'm saying, Jude. You haven't been with a man for a while and here I am.'

'Ah.' Dawning comprehension. Cesar might find talking a bore, he might use women for recreational purposes only, but he didn't like the idea that for once the shoe might be on the other foot. She knew that it was wrong to encourage him to misinterpret her behaviour but weren't some lessons in life salutary?

'You *are* quite a hunky specimen…'

'Hunky? Specimen?…Specimen?'

'Don't tell me that I'm the first woman to tell you that…' Jude found that she was enjoying the wicked one-off opportunity to have Cesar on the back foot. 'I mean, what girl in her right mind *wouldn't* enjoy a string-free romp in the hay with you? Especially if she happens to find herself marooned with you, so to speak?' To prove her point, she leaned forward and kissed him slowly, lingeringly and provocatively on his mouth.

This was a Jude she didn't recognise. She had taken her relationship with James seriously and one step at a time. She had made sure that she got to know him over a period of time before they progressed onto a physical level. She certainly would never have encouraged him to think that she was using him for sex! Nor would she have hopped into bed with him after a few hours because they happened to be in the same place, at the same time and with the same thing on their minds.

'I don't believe I'm hearing this,' Cesar said repressively but she could feel him responding to that kiss and it gave her a heady feeling of power.

'Why not? *You* enjoy sex with women without any desire or intention of having a *relationship* with them…'

'You're playing with vocabulary.'

'Am I?' Jude gave a perplexed frown. 'Sorry, I thought I was just being honest and straightforward. I always speak my mind. You know that. You said that yourself.'

'I have relationships with women.' Cesar wasn't sure why he was launching into a debate on a non-subject, but he felt self-righteously aggrieved at her spurious accusations. 'Just not relationships that will end up leading down the aisle. You ask any of the women I've dated in the past. They'll all tell you that they had a damn good time with me.' He shot her a wolfish grin that made her blood run hot with desire, but she kept her expression serious. *This* was talking and she knew it was dangerous but she felt driven to get beneath that iron exterior to the real man, even though her head was telling her that it was a pointless exercise.

'If you say so.' She shrugged. 'Talking's overrated anyway,' she told him truthfully. 'You can talk until the cows come home and think that you really understand someone, only to discover that you didn't know them at all.'

'And, on the flip side of the coin, you can spend two minutes in someone's company and realise that you know them completely.' He cupped one of her breasts and teased her pouting nipple with his thumb. The rough abrasiveness of his finger sent feathery sensations all through her body until she could almost feel herself melting.

'Hmm,' she sighed, curling her body against him and moving sinuously against his erection. 'My parents did, you know. One look across that crowded village hall and their future was sealed.'

'Which, theoretically, makes me as good a candidate for everlasting love as your ex. You'd better make sure you don't fall for me.' Cesar realised that he was guilty of making the most provocative statement he could think of but he was still a little irritated when she laughed as if he had cracked the joke of the century.

'Oh, *please*,' Jude said, sobering up but still smiling. 'I would need sectioning under the Mental Health Act if I was ever fool enough to do that.' *Fall for him?* It was a crazy, disturbing thought that made her denial all the more vigorous. 'You're probably the last man on the face of the earth I could ever fall in love with.' Just to silence that little voice in her head that was reminding her that she had managed to climb into bed with him, which would have been unthinkable two days ago.

'I'm crushed,' Cesar murmured, his hand moving down to idly play between her legs. 'You're very bad for the ego. Most men would be insulted to think that they were being used as a stud.'

'But you're not…' And she almost wished he was, but sex for the sake of sex, unsullied by any annoying emotional complications, was the kind of language he understood.

'I'll come back to you on that one…'

This time round their love-making was fierce and urgent. When he had touched and caressed every inch of her body, he rolled her so that she was on top of him, driving down on him while she continued to kiss his face, his neck, the broad span of his shoulders.

He didn't know what time it was when he eventually surfaced. His legs felt stiff and he had to angle himself off the sofa because she had fallen asleep on his shoulder. As he moved, she stretched and made a soft sound, then squirmed back into sleep mode.

For a few seconds Cesar stood, naked, looking down at her, trying to get her measure.

She bristled and hissed like a wildcat, but then there had been moments when she had been shy and cautious and tentative. One minute she acted the stammering girl, the next she was telling him that he was nothing more than a pick-me-up for someone who needed a little sex. Who the hell was she?

One thing for sure—if she had decided to seduce Fernando, for whatever reasons, the poor boy wouldn't have stood a chance. As he watched her, she stirred and opened her eyes. There was no post-coital smile on her face, nor was she making the slightest effort to entice him back between the sheets.

This in itself was a little annoying. Cesar was accustomed to women using all manner of guile to keep him in bed once they had managed to get him there in the first place.

'Have you checked the weather?' They had been lying on the throw which she used as an attractive cover for the squashy sofa and she half wrapped it round herself now and wriggled into a sitting position.

She could, shamefully, have stayed lying there on the sofa with him for the rest of the day but she had felt when he had eased himself off and had kept her eyes closed, feigning sleep. She wasn't sure how she had managed so spectacularly to jump into a pot of boiling water, but jump she had. They had made love and as they had dozed, entwined like the perfect happy couple, she had had time to think and they *weren't* the perfect happy couple. In fact, they were neither perfect nor were they a couple in any way imaginable. Even the happiness part was debatable because, while she had been on cloud nine when they had been making love, reality had had time to do its job and yank her very firmly back down to earth.

Cesar was a highly sexed man and, caught up in an unusual situation, he had taken what he had sensed had been on offer. Somehow he had managed to twig that she was attracted to him and he had acted on that nebulous feeling with the unerring instinct of a man accustomed to women falling over themselves to get near him. No phone, no computer—what better way to pass the time than making love? He was a man who would be able to distance the act from emotion, but what about *her*?

She had wanted him and had made love to him because he fascinated her. There were feelings wrapped up in the melting pot and she knew that she had to stand back and take stock before those inconvenient feelings dragged her down deeper.

'About to.' He walked across to the window and squinted at a black and white landscape. 'Snow's stopped.' He dropped the curtain and turned to look at her, pink and rumpled and cool as a cucumber.

'That's good. Look…' Jude licked her lips nervously '…about what happened…'

'You mean the business of your using me to satisfy your sexual needs…?'

'It wasn't quite like that,' Jude admitted grudgingly.

Cesar strolled to where their heap of frantically discarded clothes were piled together on the floor and extracted his boxers, which he slipped on. 'Well, that's some much needed balm for my battered ego,' he said, fishing through the bundle and separating them.

'We both got carried away. Cooped up here, with the snow outside…a bit like people who do crazy things when they're on holiday. It was just something that we'll have to pretend never happened.' She took a deep breath.

'And what if I don't feel like going along with the pretence?'

'Why wouldn't you?' She had fed her curiosity and was beginning to see how women could be brainwashed by men who just weren't good for them. She intended to get her speech in before he could deliver his.

'What if I think that what happened between us was pretty good? What if I think that there's no conceivable reason why we have to *pretend* it away?' He shrugged. 'So the snow stops and life gets back into gear…' He strolled towards her. 'Are you telling me that that would make a scrap of difference to the chemistry between us? In fact,' he continued smoothly, 'are you telling me that if I decide to kiss you right now, you're going to turn away because you've been able to tell yourself that you are no longer attracted to me?'

Jude hadn't bargained for anything but ready agreement from him and she looked at him in some confusion.

'That's not the point.'

'Then what is…?'

'The point *is*…' Now he was perched on the sofa next to her, his weight depressing it so that her body inevitably slid against his. 'The point *is*,' she repeated patiently, 'we both acted out of character. I don't…I'm not the kind of girl who just hops into bed with someone on the spur of the moment and yes, I know I might have given you the impression that I was just using you, but I don't do stuff like that. The fact is that if I choose to get involved with a man, then I want more out of it than just a romp in the hay.'

'Clarify.'

'We're different people, Cesar. We don't think along the same lines and what you look for in women is not what I look for in men.'

'Oh, well, everything's as clear as mud now.'

'Don't pretend you don't know what I'm saying. You distract yourself with women…'

'Because I'm really deeply unhappy and lonely…haven't we been here before?'

Jude could feel all her well thought out arguments begin to unravel at his mildly amused, mildly indulgent tone of voice. This was not the aggressive reaction she had expected and now she felt as if she were on thin ice. Wasn't that huge ego of his supposed to respond with predictable fury?

'You're right on one count,' Cesar said thoughtfully. 'Leaving aside the loneliness, deep unhappiness issue, I don't get involved with women because I don't want anything long-term out of the relationship, but do you…?'

'Do I what?'

'Want something long-term out of this?'

'I'm not going to waste my time with someone who's a commitment-phobe and, like I said, you're not the sort of man I'd envisage being a life partner,' Jude told him bluntly. 'I don't mind admitting that I've made a mistake and move on from there.'

'Move on to…what?'

'To someone I think I can build a relationship with, and if it doesn't come to anything, then that's fair enough, just so long as we both start with the same intentions. No one knows what the future holds but we can all start out with high hopes that it's going to be leading somewhere. You don't, Cesar. You start out with the assumption that all your relationships are destined for the bin and they do. You've been married and it was wonderful and since nothing will ever compare to that, then as far as you're concerned, there's no point in trying. You take what you want and then you walk away, and please don't tell me about all the lucky women who have thoroughly enjoyed being with you and would never have dreamt of asking for more.'

A dull flush had spread across Cesar's high cheekbones. 'Finished?' he asked coldly.

'You probably think I'm being stupid…'

'Your choice what decisions you make with your life but while you're in the mood for sermon preaching you might want to think that, while you're waiting for your dream to come true, life's passing you by.'

'You're right. My decision.'

'I was about to go and have a shower. After that, I'm going to go and see how deep my car's buried under the snow.' He had never begged for any woman in his life before and Cesar wasn't about to start now. She had made her point perfectly clear. 'Just out of interest, what *is* your ideal guy?'

'Someone kind and thoughtful,' Jude said defensively. She wasn't sure how he had managed it, but it no longer felt noble to be holding out for the perfect man. Was she wasting her life waiting for a dream? And if Cesar was that far off the scale in terms of suitability, then how was it that he had the ability to make her heart beat faster and her pulses quicken? How could he make her feel so *alive* when all her common sense pointed to the fact that he was all *wrong*?

She was beginning to feel faint as she took stock. She might say one thing and tell herself that she believed it, but somehow the man had crawled under her skin. What had started out as dislike had turned into something else and now she was very much afraid that she had committed the fatal sin of beginning to fall for him.

'Someone who doesn't think that he's God's gift to womankind,' she carried on fiercely. 'A gentle kind of guy…' Except James was like that and where had *that* ended? Cesar was nothing like that and yet…

'Why did you sleep with me?'

'You should go have your shower.'

'I will just as soon as you say it.'

'Okay! I slept with you because you're…you happen to turn me on! Satisfied?'

'Perfectly. You forget, I only know how to use women. I just wanted you to say it aloud, though, so you can remind yourself that sometimes having fun is its own reward. An empty bed is never grateful for the moral high ground.'

He headed for his shower. He damn well needed something to cool him down! He had managed to get the last word, but it had been an empty victory.

Of course, he told himself, rubbing himself dry with the towel and then glaring at his reflection in the mirror, women like that were bad news for a man like him and he should have been thanking her for being honest and upfront. And, hell, who was he to complain about jettisoning someone because they didn't fit the bill? He had jettisoned countless numbers of women in the past, maybe not with quite such unadorned frankness, but it all counted for the same thing.

Stuck inside this cottage had made him stir crazy! The minute he got back to civilisation, he would forget the woman, climb back onto the dating bandwagon, from which he had been away for a disturbingly long time, rediscover the guy who worked hard and played hard and didn't get involved with long, futile discussions about emotions, which frankly were best left alone.

Hell, he hadn't even been able to shave for nearly two days! His facial growth was now more than just designer stubble. He was beginning to look and act like a caveman.

With any luck, the snow would disappear as quickly as it had come and he would be able to leave this God-forsaken part of the world and resume his life.

At least, he thought, bringing all his will power to bear to eradicate her annoying, lingering image from his head, one thing was sure. She wasn't after his brother in search of elevating her lifestyle. Whatever nuances he had sensed between them had been in his imagination. The only thing the woman was after was a knight in shining armour. She wasn't into the finer art of subtlety. Oh, no. If she had been in any way, shape or form interested in his brother, then Fernando would have been married and en route to papahood by now!

He decided that he would let this whole business be a salutary lesson to him—keep close to the devil you knew…the ones you didn't were too much of an infernal headache!

CHAPTER FIVE

JUDE later wondered how she'd managed to get through the remainder of their snowbound isolation, but two weeks later, chewing it over in her head as she had been doing ever since she'd watched him close that front door quietly behind him, she knew that he had been the one to pull it off.

He had disappeared for his shower and, when he had returned, he had followed her heated plea to the very last letter. She had asked him to pretend that nothing had happened and he had. He had checked on his car, which had taken a long time because of the banked-up snow. In his absence, she had tidied the little sitting room and each cushion she had plumped had been one more gesture towards putting away for good the wild moments they had shared together. In under an hour, the room had been restored to its original impersonal cosiness, with the absence of the wretched throw, which she had put in the wash.

She had even lit two scented candles because she could detect the aroma of their love-making, and she wanted no reminders.

They had eaten in the kitchen, discussed the weather in civilised voices and retired to their separate bedrooms at the earliest possible hour.

And every ultra-polite question he had asked, his fabulous

eyes shuttered and expressionless, had been like a knife twisting inside her. At the time she had wondered how on earth he could have been so utterly detached, but now, thinking about it, she knew why. Cesar wasn't the sort of man who was swept away on great tides of emotion. Nor had he invested any feelings in her. He had slept with her and had enjoyed it, and he probably would have carried on an affair of sorts for a while after, but that hadn't been enough for her and he had accepted that with a casual shrug of his shoulders because he could take her or leave her. He was a man for whom emotional involvement was an unnecessary complication. He had been down that road and, whether he would ever admit it or not, had buried his ability to *feel* with his wife.

Overnight the snow had begun to melt and in the morning she had awoken to find him fully dressed and ready to leave. He had already been out to try the car and had managed to get it pointing in the right direction. He had left the engine running, he said. Her interpretation of that was that the faster he could get away, the better. A running engine was the equivalent of a taxi outside blowing its horn.

Since then she had heard nothing from him, although she had been to visit Freddy and Imogen and it seemed that the fate of the precious trust fund was assured. Cesar hadn't fallen over himself in admiration of the bar, but nor had he demolished the idea after five seconds, which had been Freddy's fear.

She was busying herself with her latest project, half thinking about her drawings and half thinking about Cesar, when the phone rang. As usual, there was a heart-stopping second when she thought that it might be *him*, even though she had told herself that he couldn't possibly call her because he didn't know her number, so common sense told her that of course it wouldn't be him.

But nor had she expected a distraught Freddy stumbling over his words until she asked him to slow down because she couldn't understand a word he was saying.

'I am at the hospital,' he said shakily.

'Hospital? Why? What's wrong? Are you hurt?' Jude felt a rush of panic as in the space of seconds she contemplated the worst. She swivelled her chair around and leaned forward, clutching the receiver to her ear.

'It's Imogen. She's been rushed in.'

'But the baby's not due for another couple of months.' She felt a fine film of perspiration gathering on her forehead.

'You have to come, Jude,' Freddy told her with rising panic in his voice. 'She's in theatre right now and I'm going out of my mind with worry!'

'On my way.'

'And you have to…to tell Cesar…'

'Tell him *what*?' Just the mention of his name made her nerves flutter. When she had last seen Freddy, he had told her that while Cesar had reluctantly given his blessing to the bar, he hadn't wanted to press his luck by telling him about Imogen because who knew what eruptions might follow. Cesar, in over-protective mode with the family fortune, was an unpredictable animal. It was, he had told her, a tactical omission and not an outright lie. So now, with dismay, she had some inkling of the favour that was about to be asked.

'I'm in no frame of mind to explain about Imogen,' he said and Jude could hear the worry in his voice. Placid, good-natured, girlie Imogen was the quiet but steady rock in their relationship. Freddy, with his effervescence, had never been a candidate for winning any awards when it came to holding out in a crisis. Her heart went out to him as she imagined his panic.

'I know I probably should have confessed everything the

last time I saw Cesar. He was being particularly receptive but…but…'

'Okay. And I'll get to the hospital as soon as I can. You'll have to give me your brother's number, Freddy…'

Fifteen minutes later and Jude was on her way to the hospital. She hadn't bothered to change out of her dungarees, just slinging on a wooly jumper over them and wrapping a long trailing scarf around her neck. The snow had completely disappeared and after the cold snap had come a spell of un-seasonably warm weather. Everywhere people were tut-tutting about global warming and complaining that they never knew what to wear when they went out.

She had yet to phone Cesar. That was something she had decided to defer until she got to the hospital and at least made sure that Freddy and Imogen were going to be all right. Both her cellphone and the scrap of paper on which she had written Cesar's various numbers were burning a hole in her pocket, hovering on the edge of her anxiety, just enough to make her feel queasy.

She made it to the hospital in record time but naturally took ages to park. By the time she ran through the doors of the maternity ward, she was totally stressed out and a pressure headache was beginning to build in her temples.

Freddy found her before she found him and he looked as frightful as she'd figured he would. The baby was fine, he told her, but had been rushed off to intensive care. It was a girl.

His eyes filled up and he looked away quickly. 'I've been told to have her christened immediately…just in case…'

'Don't do the *just in case* scenario, Freddy,' she said quietly, giving him a hug and then standing back with her hands on his arms. 'You'll just make yourself even more worried. How's Imogen doing?'

'She's lost a lot of blood…'

'But she's…going to be okay, right?'

'They won't say. The next few hours are important. Jude, I have to get back to her… Have you…?'

'I'll phone him in a minute. I wanted to get here first and make sure that both of you were all right. All *three* of you,' she amended with a reassuring smile. 'Is Imogen awake? Will you give her my love? I'm going to stay here for a while, Freddy…' She hoped that didn't sound grim but he seemed relieved by that and left her a few minutes later with the un-enviable task of calling his brother.

Jude made her way to the café, her nerves stretched to breaking-point. The smell of the hospital made her feel faint. In a room upstairs her closest friend was hanging on and in another room the baby she and Freddy had looked forward to having was struggling with the complications of being born prematurely. Nowhere in a hospital was it possible to feel calm. Even in the cafeteria there was the ominous feeling of people waiting for news, good or bad.

She bought herself some coffee and retreated to the farthest corner table, out of earshot, not that anyone would be likely to pay her conversation the slightest bit of attention.

Freddy had given her a handful of numbers, but in fact the first number she dialled—his mobile number—was answered within a couple of rings.

Down the line, the reception so clear that he could have been sitting next to her, came that rich, low, velvety voice that had reduced her to jelly. She hadn't thought, especially with everything going on and her head in a whirl, that it would have the same effect now, but it did.

'Cesar, it's me. Jude,' she clarified, just in case he had for-gotten her existence.

Miles away, in his London office and with his secretary sitting opposite him, Cesar felt himself freeze. He gestured to his secretary to vacate the room and she did, closing the door behind her.

To his intense frustration, the past two weeks had been hellish. His formidably controlled mind had refused to obey orders and the memory of her had seeped in through all sorts of cracks and crevices which he hadn't known existed. He had found himself losing concentration during meetings, an un-heard of occurrence, and at the least convenient moments his imagination would steal in like a silent thief to capture his thoughts and he would have to physically rouse himself away from the temptation to gaze out of his window and just think. Of her. The smell of her and the feel of her, which lingered in his head like a fever he couldn't shake.

Now, hearing her voice on the line, brought all his rage at his weakness rushing to the surface.

'And to what do I owe the honour?' he asked coldly.

'Look, I know you're probably surprised to hear from me…'

'How did you get my number?'

'That's not important. Cesar, something's happened…'

He detected the urgency in her voice and he restlessly sprang to his feet and walked across to the impressive floor-to-ceiling windows of his plush office, which overlooked the hustle and bustle of the financial district. Somewhere inside him a knife twisted.

'What are you talking about?' he demanded, his breathing uneven. 'Where the hell are you?'

'I'm…I'm at the hospital…' There was no point explain-ing anything down a telephone. The minute Freddy had asked her to call his brother, Jude had realised that she would have no option but to see him again, even if seeing him was the last thing she wanted to do. 'Would you…would you be able to get here? I'll explain everything when I see you. I'm sorry if I caught you on the hop…'

'Name.'

'Sorry?'

'The name of the hospital. What is it?'

He scribbled it down on a piece of paper and shoved the paper into his pocket. He had several meetings lined up for later in the afternoon and was scheduled to leave the country later that evening. None of it mattered.

'Tell me what this is about,' he said in an attempt to regain his self-control. 'I am a busy man.'

'I know and I'm sorry but I'd rather not say on the telephone, Cesar. But it's important.'

'I'll be there in half an hour.'

That brought a reluctant smile to Jude's lips. 'How are you intending to do that? Fly?' She had an image of him swooping through the clouds like Superman. He might be able to do most things but that one was definitely out of his reach.

'Correct.' Cesar was already calculating how long it would take to get there on his private helicopter. Not long. 'Where will I meet you?'

Jude was about to ask him what he meant when it clicked that he would probably own a fleet of helicopters and private jets. He was, as he had said, a busy man and busy men didn't waste time dealing with the vagaries of public transport if they could possibly avoid it. 'I'll be in the cafeteria,' was all she said and, with all the necessary information imparted, she was treated to the abrupt silence of disconnection. He had asked relatively few questions and had given no indication of curiosity, for which she was thankful. Of course, he must suspect that Freddy was involved and, whilst she felt for him having to make a journey with maybe some pretty dark thoughts in his mind, she also knew that what she had to say would, at least, be more bearable than what he possibly suspected.

Only when she was on her second cup of coffee, which was surprisingly good and surprisingly cheap, and after she had once more visited the ward for an update, of which there was none, did she begin to feel the pounding of nerves.

She aimed for distraction by reading one of the tabloids provided on a table by the cash tills, but she couldn't resist the temptation to glance up every five seconds, it seemed, and search the doors to the cafeteria for him.

She told herself that this was a meeting of necessity and that if Cesar threw a fit because his brother had chosen to keep Imogen's existence quiet, then she would be the one in the firing line. Didn't they say that the messenger was always the one to be shot?

As luck would have it, she had finally been distracted by the gossip page when she became aware of Cesar's presence by the shadow thrown over the table. She looked up slowly, giving herself time to fix her expression and harness her composure, but it didn't work because the very minute their eyes met, she felt all her self-control give way to a sickening attack of nerves.

She had hoped that in the interim her lively imagination had exaggerated his powerful, brooding beauty and the ferocious impact it had on her nervous system. It hadn't. If anything, in his dark tailored trousers and crisp white shirt, with his jacket hooked carelessly over one shoulder, he looked even more dangerous and magnificent. And utterly cold.

She half rose and then sat back down with a tight smile. Hell, he had been so *civilised* the last time they had been in the same space together that the very least she could do would be to return the favour with a little sangfroid of her own.

'Would you like some coffee?' she blurted out, only belatedly realising that it was a pathetic attempt at a greeting since she was neither a waitress nor a hostess.

'What I *want*,' Cesar grated, 'is to be told why I am here.'

He pulled out the uncomfortable plastic chair and sat down. He had spent the entire trip in a state of heightened anxiety and was ridiculously relieved to see her looking fit and well, if haggard. There were shadows under her eyes and her short hair was tousled, as though she had been running her fingers through it. His eyes skimmed over her outfit, which appeared to be some kind of workman's overalls.

'It's a long story, Cesar…'

'Is my brother all right? Just answer me that.'

'Freddy's…fine.'

'And…you…?' He felt himself struggle with the question.

'I'm fine, thanks for asking.'

'Then what the hell is going on?'

Jude tried hard not to react to the imperious tone of his voice. Of course he was going to demand an explanation! Cesar being Cesar, he wouldn't ask polite questions or tiptoe around with pleasantries!

'I'm going to tell you! If you'd just stop *snarling*.'

'I don't have the time or the inclination to sit here while you try and get your thoughts in order.'

'It's…it's about your brother, Cesar.'

'You said that he was fine.' For some reason, he had assumed that there was nothing wrong with his brother, had assumed that, because she had made the call, then whatever the situation, it concerned *her*. Now, with the muted sounds of people shuffling in the cafeteria and the depressing smell of antiseptic cleaners mixed in with unappetising food, Cesar contemplated the possibility that his ferocious anxiety had been misplaced.

In a split second it dawned on him that there had been many opportunities in the past to try and heal the distance between Fernando and himself but that maybe his time had run out for second chances. He clung to the fact that she had told him that his brother was fine, even though they were sitting in a hospital so clearly he wasn't quite as *fine* as she said.

'He is. Sort of.'

'Fine. Sort of. *Get to the point, Jude!*'

'It's not that easy!' And particularly so when he was glaring at her as if she had mutated into something unsavoury that had crawled out from beneath a rock. She guessed that he had had no choice but to be polite to her when he had been holed up under her roof, but now he had options and he had chosen the option of showing his full-blown aggression. She had dragged him away from his precious work, was blathering and dithering instead of telling him why she had done so and he wasn't about to exert any patience with her because time was money and she had cut into his time.

But how on earth was she supposed to explain about Imogen in a few brief sentences? She had vaguely thought about what she was going to say. Now she wished that she had jotted it all down on some paper so that she could just hand it to him to have a read and then ask questions. A bit like a comprehension exam.

'Do you remember asking me…why Freddy seemed so keen on sorting out the matter of his trust fund as quickly as possible? When he had always been happy to go with the flow and let you settle all his bills?'

'Go on.' This wasn't what he had been expecting by way of an explanation, but then he might have guessed that anything to do with her would defy all his laws of predictability.

'Well, there was a reason.' She looked at him warily. It was hard to believe that for a window in time she had felt relaxed enough to share anything with him. Right now she was looking at a stranger, a cold, distant, watchful stranger. 'And I can understand why Freddy did…well, what he did…'

Cesar, reading between the lines, seeing the uncomfortable expression on her face and the anxious fidgeting of her hands, adding it to the fact that he was currently sitting on an orange plastic chair in a hospital, came to the only conclusion his logical mind could find.

'Are you trying to tell me that my brother has had some sort of money problem that he's kept to himself? I knew he gambled, but has it got out of hand?' Cesar cursed softly to himself. He had controlled his brother's lifestyle for his own good, making sure that he kept an eagle eye on his outgoings so that he could forestall any potential problems. But what if his brother had *had* financial problems? What if there had been a shortfall somewhere and he had been too scared to come running to him, knowing what his reaction would be? That would make sense. In a moment of rare self-examination, Cesar acknowledged that he could be unsympathetic and dismissive.

'Has he got into some kind of trouble and ended up in hospital because of it?'

'Freddy hasn't gambled for months, Cesar. No…'

'Drugs, then. Is that it? Is that why I'm sitting here?' He raked his fingers through his hair and for a moment she felt a powerful tug on her heartstrings as she looked at this big, controlled man torn by incomprehension and deserted by his usual self-assurance.

She reached out and touched his hand. For a second there was a bond between them, as if a bridge had sprung up between the massive chasm that was dividing them, then he shook off her hand.

'Stop, Cesar,' Jude said firmly. She sat on her hands just in case they decided to do something crazy again without her permission. 'You're jumping to all sorts of conclusions. Freddy hasn't got a gambling problem and he isn't a drug addict either. The opposite, in fact. He's as focused as he's probably ever been in his whole life and that's the thing... there's a reason why he's changed...'

'Just spit it out, Jude, because I'm getting tired of the endless riddles.'

'He's in love.'

'*He's in love?* And he's in hospital because of a...what... *broken heart?* Tell me, who exactly is the object of my brother's affections?' His eyes narrowed suspiciously on her face and Jude looked back at him, outraged at the implied insult in that questioning gaze.

'Not me, if that's what you're thinking, Cesar! Do you imagine that I would have...could have....if...' She took a few deep breaths and told herself that she shouldn't be offended because Cesar was just being Cesar. Suspicious to the point of absurdity.

'He's in love and has been for a long time with a girl called Imogen.'

'That's impossible,' Cesar dismissed, pushing back his chair so that he could extend his long legs at an angle. 'The name means nothing to me.'

'Don't be so superior, Cesar!' Jude snapped. 'You live in a bubble, do you know that? A magical world where you think you know everything there is to know about everybody!'

Far from having any impact on him, Cesar lounged back in the chair and shot her a look that questioned whether she had taken leave of her senses. On several counts, he felt considerably relieved. Firstly, his brother was fine. Secondly,

Jude was fine. Thirdly, for a second there that whole *Fernando in love* thing had done something crazy to his composure, for a second there he had thought that Jude was the woman involved. She wasn't.

'I'm really struggling to see where all this is going. So my brother fancies himself in love. He's been there before and he'll go there again.'

'He hasn't and he won't and you still haven't asked why you're sitting here if the only reason I wanted to see you was to tell you that Freddy's found the girl of his dreams.'

Cesar had the grace to flush. Relief seemed to have distracted him from the main issue. In fact, relief on several fronts had weirdly distracted him from what should really be annoying him, namely the fact that, at great personal inconvenience, he had sequestered the company helicopter on a mission that could probably have waited.

'You said. Her name's Imogen.'

'And she was rushed to hospital today to deliver their baby, which was born prematurely.'

The silence that greeted this slice of information was deafening. For once, Cesar was utterly and completely dumbstruck and Jude didn't know whether to laugh at his expression or duck for cover.

'You're kidding.'

'Do I look as if I'm kidding? Freddy called me up this morning in a complete state of meltdown. He's been here for the past few hours, out of his mind with worry. Hence he volunteered me to tell you…to tell you the truth about Imogen…'

'Why was I kept in the dark about this?'

'Could you *keep it down*, Cesar?' she hissed. 'Have you forgotten where we are?'

'Is there somewhere else we could go?' he asked abruptly.

'No, there isn't. At least not within walking distance and I want to stay here. Imogen is my closest friend. You once asked me how I met your brother. Well, it was through Imogen and the reason this was kept from you was because Freddy was afraid that…'

'You both lied to me.'

'We didn't *lie*…' Jude didn't want to get into this offshoot of what she had to say. She had known, almost within minutes of meeting Cesar, that any form of deception would not have sat easily with him and, whilst she had chosen to label it, as Freddy had, *a slight evasion*—a slight *temporary* evasion— she was uneasily aware that she had been an accomplice to something Cesar might well consider insupportable.

'I think I need to go and see my brother.'

'It's not a good time to start an argument about this. In fact, I won't allow it.'

'You won't allow it?'

She recognised this as a tone of voice that could have halted an army in its tracks. However, Jude wasn't about to let Cesar loose on Freddy. Even if he gave her his word that nothing would be said about the revelations, she knew that, inevitably, he would be physically incapable of *not* expressing an opinion. Cesar lived in, and was accustomed to living in, a world in which he had absolute freedom to say what he wanted. Today, she determined, wasn't going to be one of those days.

'That's right. I'm not going to let you confront Freddy…'

'You misunderstand me. I never said anything about confronting my brother…'

'You don't have to,' she said bluntly. 'Freddy's not in a very good place right now and he doesn't need you making things worse.'

Cesar was lost for words. Never in all his adult life had anyone forbidden him from doing anything. The words *allow* and *Cesar* had never actually occurred in the same sentence and here she was now, glaring at him like a headteacher dealing with a recalcitrant pupil.

'I think we should talk,' Jude continued, ignoring his outraged expression. 'I can explain why Freddy chose not to disclose any of this to you...'

'As did you. Even when we were in your house, making love.'

Jude went red. She didn't need any reminder of that. Her mind did a very good job on its own of not letting her forget.

'Maybe it *would* be a good idea to find somewhere else to talk,' she conceded, half to herself. 'We're occupying seats other people might need more than us.' And, besides, she wanted privacy to speak with him, even though she knew that no one was listening or would care what they were talking about, even if they were sitting right next to them at the same table.

'Scared I might blow a fuse?'

'I know you wouldn't do that.' At least, not at that very moment in time. She stood up. 'I'll just go and see Freddy, let him know that I won't be around for an hour or so and I'll meet you back here.'

Cesar knew that there was nothing to prevent him from going with her but he contented himself with a curt nod. He needed time to himself to think, at any rate. On the surface was the business of being deceived, but scratching the surface was the far more overwhelming reality that Fernando had a baby, that he had managed to keep secret an entire chunk of his life because...

He watched her get eaten up by all the people coming and going and rubbed his eyes wearily with his fingers.

It was turning out to be one hell of a day. Rather than churn over in his head all the thoughts which seemed too big for him to absorb, he flipped open his cellphone and put a call through to his secretary, whom he had left wearing a baffled expression and holding a dossier of paperwork which, she had stammered, was urgent. Efficient as she was in every way possible, the one thing she apparently couldn't deal with was a boss acting out of character.

Her bewilderment was almost audible down the line when he told her that all his appointments were to be cancelled until he informed her otherwise. Anything important should be e-mailed to him. She couldn't have sounded more shocked if he had told her that he was about to take a trip to the moon.

He snapped shut the phone just as Jude was weaving her way back towards him.

For the briefest of moments, just the span of the blink of an eye, he forgot everything. He only saw *her*, her slight figure which, as he knew from first-hand experience, was as sexy as hell, the stubborn, elfin attractiveness of her face, at present lost in distraction, the short hair that could have looked disastrous and instead was inexplicably appealing.

What the hell was she wearing? He'd never seen such a shapeless garment in his life before, not helped by the over-sized jumper she had thrown on over it. A jumper which he recognised as one of those hanging on a hook by her front door.

She focused on him at the same time as he reined in his mutinous train of thought. How the hell could he be distracted at a time like this, when there were a thousand and one questions bouncing around in his head?

'I've spoken to Freddy,' Jude said, not sitting down. She grinned. 'Things are looking good for both mother and daughter. Their baby's going to be kept in hospital for at least a couple of weeks, maybe longer, but the doctors say she's doing incredibly well and Imogen's smiling, which is always a good sign. I've told Freddy that we're just going to grab a coffee somewhere in town but that we shouldn't be long.'

She didn't add that Freddy had wanted to talk to his brother himself because she wanted to make absolutely sure that she had had a chance to put Cesar in the picture and hopefully deflate any tendency to erupt. If Cesar knew that Freddy was no longer in quite the same state of shock, she was pretty sure that he wouldn't now be getting to his feet and putting on his jacket.

'My car's in the car park.' She turned away and killed the treacherous thought that maybe, just maybe, there was a little part of her that *wanted* to carry on talking to Cesar, even though she had no idea how relaxing the conversation was going to be. To be brutally honest, even though she knew that the conversation was probably going to be hellish. Just being in his presence, like an addict driven to feed an unhealthy habit, was irresistible.

'I never asked,' she said as they headed towards her car, 'how did you manage to get here so quickly?'

'Helicopter.'

'I'm sorry to have dragged you away from your...meetings...'

'I know. You already apologised. Is *that* your car?'

Ah, something on which to focus that was neither the delicate situation at hand, which she would leave until they were sitting in front of their energy-boosting coffees, nor her rapidly beating heart which was signalling to her, with every sickening thud, that she was still as knocked out by the man as she ever had been.

She could lose herself in a pointless but much needed quibble about the incredulous scorn in his voice.

'Have you got a problem with that?' She faced him squarely, hands on her hips, before unlocking the door the old-fashioned way, as central locking was still a dream when her Land Rover had hit the roads. As were most other automobile gadgets the rest of the Western world took for granted.

'Lots of problems,' he said, defusing the situation, much to her annoyance, 'but that definitely isn't one of them.'

CHAPTER SIX

WITHIN half an hour they had parked and were making their way to a coffee shop. The short drive had been conducted largely in silence. Cesar seemed heavily preoccupied with his thoughts, staring through the window, and Jude was content to skip the stilted conversation about nothing in particular.

'They haven't decided on a name for the baby,' she said eventually, to break the silence. 'Freddy thinks maybe Maria after your mother and Florence after Imogen's mum.'

'What is she like, this woman…?'

'We can talk about that…once we're sitting down, having a coffee.'

'I need something stronger than a coffee!'

Jude nodded. Well, it *was* nearly five-thirty. She veered away from the coffee shop and towards a restaurant/bar which opened all day for food and drink. It was spacious, very modern, comfortable and, at this hour, virtually empty. By seven-thirty it would be packed solid with an after-work crew.

'Right,' Cesar said as soon as the waiter had scuttled off to get their drinks—mineral water for her and a whisky for him. 'You were going to tell me what this woman is like. I presume not the sort you would bring home to meet the parents if

Fernando has kept her a secret.' He shot her a twisted, cynical smile. 'No one keeps a woman locked away unless they're ashamed of her.'

'It's nothing like that. Of course Freddy's not ashamed of Imogen! Why would he be? She's a wonderful girl and I should know that better than most. I grew up with her.' The bottle of mineral water looked dangerously insufficient to cope with Cesar on full throttle.

'How ironic to be singing the praises of someone who, until today, didn't exist as far as I was aware. Suddenly she's out of the cupboard and you're telling me that she's the next best thing since sliced bread. Now, why would that be?'

'Because of the trust fund.'

'Ah. So you and my brother connived to keep this all under wraps until the trust fund business was settled, is that it?'

'We didn't *connive*, Cesar.'

'No? Well, I'm racking my brains to think of a more appropriate word.'

'You're not going to make this any easier for me, are you?'

'Did you expect me to?'

'No,' Jude admitted. She picked up her glass and swirled it around for a while, watching the bubbles scatter on the surface, then she took a sip of the water. 'And that's why Freddy felt that he couldn't confide in you.'

'I have never tried to run my brother's love life.' Cesar shrugged magnanimously. 'He has always been free to do whatever he wants to do with any woman he wants to.'

'Just so long as whatever relationship he had remained transitory. He told me that his role was to marry a woman of independent means.'

Cesar's mouth thinned. Yet more confidences, more whispered secrets. 'I never laid down any rules about that.'

'But it was understood. Cesar, there's no use pretending that you're not really protective about all that money in your bank account! You practically accused *me* of being a gold-digger the first time we met!' She told herself to calm down and not get off the topic because she could hardly hold the torch for being transparent when she had kept Imogen's importance to Freddy to herself. 'Imogen doesn't come from the sort of privileged background that you would have found acceptable. At least, that's what Freddy thought.'

'He should have told me so himself, man to man. He wanted the trust fund—no, wrong use of word here—*needed* the trust fund, presumably because the woman in question was up the spout, but instead of laying his cards on the table, he chose to approach it through a side door. In cahoots with you.'

Jude reddened uncomfortably. 'It wasn't like that. He knew that you wouldn't approve. In fact, he knew that you'd probably try to intervene and of course you had the trump card because you pulled all the financial strings.'

'Forget about whether the woman came from a privileged background or not. There must be some other reason why he never breathed a word of her existence to me.' They could keep going round and round in circles about the upside and downside of enormous wealth, about the measures taken to protect it, but they would get nowhere because, in the end, they would have to differ. Reality meant no time for useless discussions. Cesar needed to flush out the whole story and then decide how he played it from here.

He was, he acknowledged, shaken to the core and, much as he felt concern, as any human being would, for a woman who had been through what must have been a nightmarish ordeal, he still had to think with his head.

Naturally, the woman sitting opposite him wouldn't understand that. Anyone who'd spent her life looking for a knight in shining armour clearly had no use for her head.

'He thought that you would write her off as being after his money because of…of the way she looks…'

Cesar sat back and finished his whisky in one long swallow. Now they were getting somewhere. 'And how would that be?' he drawled. 'No, let me guess. Blonde hair? Big blue eyes? Lush, sexy body?'

'Something like that,' Jude mumbled. She took a deep breath and said in a rush, 'And she worked in a nightclub. Actually, that was where they met.' What was the point of a partial truth?

'In a nightclub. Doing what? With her blonde hair and blue eyes and sexy body? Hmm. The books, maybe? Or a receptionist?'

'Not quite.' She looked at him, at his shrewd, cold, calculating, fabulous eyes and mentally winced. 'She…um…waited on tables, so to speak.'

'So to speak…?'

'Well, if you must know, she was a stripper. Of sorts. Nothing crude, of course.'

'No. Far be it from me to think anything of the sort.' A picture was beginning to form in his head and he didn't like it. He had no problem with Fernando dating a stripper—hell, he was a red-blooded male and had always had a taste for blondes—but what had been the stripper's motives? How long before she *forgot* to take her contraceptive pill and *accidentally* fell pregnant?

'I can see what you're thinking, Cesar, and you're wrong. They're head over heels in love and Imogen is one of the nicest people you're ever likely to meet. I grew up with her and there isn't a mean, avaricious bone in her body!'

'Except that now she's had a baby and presumably was behind Fernando's sudden urge to get his hands on his trust fund?'

'That was *his* idea. He'd been thinking about doing something for himself…'

'And naturally coming to work for the family business was never one of the plans mooted…'

'You know how Freddy feels about office work. The thought of sitting behind a desk like you do, staring at a computer screen and going to meetings…well, it was never going to be his cup of tea.'

Cesar had to stop himself from giving her a description of exactly what he did. Instead, he focused on the problem at hand.

'Anyway, he was going to tell you everything…'

'I'm sure. Just as soon as I gave him the green light to get his hands on his money. Have you any idea how much he will be worth?'

'Lots?'

'And, of course, by the process of association, how much this friend of yours will be worth.'

'Her name is Imogen.'

Cesar shrugged. 'Does he intend to put a ring on her finger?'

'Of course he does!'

'Dammit! The boy should have come to me before he got himself embroiled in this situation!'

'He's not *embroiled* in anything!' Jude snapped indignantly. 'He's walked into this relationship with his eyes wide open and he's *happy*. Doesn't that mean anything to you? No, it probably doesn't,' she said acidly. 'I guess you've forgotten what it was like to be head over heels in love and looking forward to starting a life together.'

'Marisol was embraced by the family,' Cesar said. 'There

was no question mark over her head as to whether she had inveigled her way in because she could smell the whiff of bank notes.' He thought, with some surprise and discomfort, that whereas she had always been at the back of his mind, the rosy picture against which every woman he had ever dated was measured, this had not recently been the case. Recently, his head had been filled with the image of another woman, one who didn't fit the mould and, he told himself with remorseless iciness, fitted it even less now. A woman capable of sleeping with him and holding her secrets to herself. Her extremely *costly* secrets.

'And you're very fortunate that you found the perfect love match. Did you think that you'd be able to dictate to Freddy whom he should marry? What background she should have? What the colour of her hair should be?'

'Don't be ridiculous.'

'I'm not being ridiculous! This is exactly what he was afraid of.'

'That I would have his welfare at heart?'

'That you wouldn't give him a chance! He's not a kid any more, Cesar! And you liked his jazz club idea. Freddy told me that you did. It's well thought through and he's put a lot of effort into costing it. Do you think a *kid* would have been able to do that? He's even gone into detail about what sort of acts he would have and he'll make a success of it because his heart's there, and he has so many of the right connections.'

'Where are you going with this?'

'Give him the benefit of the doubt.' Jude knew why she was fighting their corner. They weren't there to do it themselves. Imogen was closer than family to her, and while it might well have been better for Freddy to have spoken to his brother *man to man*, as Cesar had put it, his priority at the moment had to be the woman he loved and their tiny baby daughter. But she still had her own problems to deal with, her own tortured thoughts to put to rest, her own screwed-up heart to try and piece together. Just sitting opposite him was sending her nervous system into frantic overdrive.

'Have you *ever* treated him like an *adult*, Cesar? Capable of making the right decisions for himself?'

Cesar flushed darkly and scowled at her. 'I'm beginning to see why he sent you to do his dirty work. You're like a pit bull.'

'That's a horrible thing to say!' Jude looked away quickly, her eyes filling up. Where was a handkerchief when you needed one? Or even a bit of wretched self-control?

She wiped her eyes harshly with the sleeve of her jumper and then stared down into her half-empty glass of water. She only saw the pristine white handkerchief when it was thrust in front of her and, when she stubbornly refused to take it, she only realised why he had withdrawn it when she felt his fingers on her chin, tilting her face up so that he could carefully dry her eyes.

The breath caught in the back of her throat. His eyes were the colour of dark, bitter chocolate and she felt as though she might drown in them given half a chance.

'I apologise for that last remark,' he said gruffly. 'It was uncalled for.' She wasn't a crier. Cesar didn't know how he knew that but he *just did*. She might have crazy girlish notions of love and romance but that didn't make her soppy, which was why the tears still glistening in her eyes had had such an effect on him.

And God, now that he was touching her, he wanted to touch more. He wanted to dip his head and capture her mouth with his, feel the coolness of her lips and the sweetness of her tongue against his. He wanted to slip his hand behind those hideous overall things until he felt the warmth of her breast and then he wanted to touch that ripe pink nipple, stroke it with his fingers until it hardened and made itself ready for his mouth.

He had to make a Herculean effort to drag himself back down to earth.

'You can keep the handkerchief.'

Jude gathered her scattered wits and tried to think straight even though she could still feel where his fingers had been in contact with her skin, leaving their mark as boldly as if she had been branded.

'Okay.' Cesar sat back and looked at her carefully. For a second there, he had been caught up in some rip tide of sensation but he had to remember that he wasn't born yesterday, whatever sob story he got fed. 'I admit the jazz club idea might work out if Fernando is prepared to go the distance and do the work and I'm willing to give him credit for trying to get some sort of focus in his life, but I still have serious misgivings about this woman...'

'You won't when you meet her,' Jude told him quickly, sensing the smallest of chinks in his armour and determined to exploit it before it disappeared. 'Which, hopefully, will be soon.' Her worry over Imogen and the baby was playing havoc with her emotions and she felt another weeping jag approaching. She diverted it by blowing her nose and standing up. 'In fact, we should get back to the hospital, see what's going on. Freddy hasn't called so I'm hoping that everything is going to be all right.'

In fact, it was another hour before they did, finally, get to see Freddy. The traffic back to the hospital was a nightmare and the car park was an endless line of cars trawling in search of an elusive space.

Jude looked at Freddy's face and knew immediately that

Imogen was through the worst. She also knew, without having to be told, that he wasn't looking forward to having the inevitable chat with Cesar, but she had done enough to smooth the path and after popping in to give an exhausted Imogen an enormous hug and then stopping in to see the very, very tiny baby with masses of dark hair, which made her want to cry all over again, she headed back to her cottage.

She didn't know what was being said between the two brothers. Cesar was as hard as granite and with little time for the grey areas that made up most people's lives. His own life was so ordered and so controlled that he expected everyone else's to be the same and was intolerant of any deviation.

So why did she…feel so acutely tuned in every time she was around him? Because he was intransigent and autocratic? Because there was a lump of ice where his heart should have been? Because she was in love with him?

The realisation was not accompanied by the clap of thunder or an explosion of fireworks. It just sneaked into her head quietly and unobtrusively, confirming what she had known in her heart for a while. He filled up every part of her and she couldn't talk herself out of it or reason it away.

He represented just the sort of person who, on paper, was the last man on the face of the earth she should have been attracted to, but whoever said that love was contained and logical like a game of chess?

Seeing him that afternoon, she had felt as though her world had been tilted on its axis. Now, back in her house, she wondered miserably if it could ever be levered back into position. Even when she had been gritting her teeth and trying not to explode at his all-knowing, all-consuming *pigheadedness*, she had still felt something inside her melting and taking flight.

And when he had touched her…

She sternly reminded himself that the reason he had touched her in the first place, accidental contact though it had been, was because he *had made her cry*. She had been emotional, anyway, having to deal with everything that had taken place, and being *insulted* had just been the final straw. He had called her a *pit bull*! She masochistically replayed the insult over and over in her head in the hope that she might shore up her weakened defences but she was having little success as she made herself something to eat, when she heard the rap of her front door knocker.

Her immediate thought was that it would have to be Freddy.

Sandwich forgotten, she wiped her hands on the dungarees, which she had yet to get out of, and flew to the door.

She blinked in confusion at the sight of Cesar standing on her doorstep. For a few brief seconds she almost wondered whether her mind was playing tricks on her, but that didn't last long.

'I thought you'd want to know what's been happening at the hospital.'

'Sure.'

'Then why don't you invite me in?'

'How did you get here?'

'I borrowed Fernando's car. He's going to be spending the night there.'

She felt her heart begin to pound and contemplated telling him that he had caught her at a bad moment, that she was on her way out, but *where*? And still dressed in her *dungarees*? And wouldn't the lie be more of an indication of how much he affected her than if she treated him in much the same manner as she would treat anyone?

'How is Imogen? The baby? Has there been any improvement? Would you like something to drink? Tea? Coffee?' She could *feel* him behind her as she walked back to the kitchen, avoiding the sitting room, which would be too much of a reality check for her.

'Imogen is steadily improving. The baby is doing as well as can be expected. Better. Apparently, she is a healthy birth weight for…a baby of that prematurity. I'll have a coffee.'

With her back to him, aware of him pulling out one of the chairs and sitting down, Jude said tentatively, 'And how was Freddy?'

'How was he about…what? His girlfriend? His *child*? Or his cover-up?'

Jude stiffened, but she didn't swing round to face him. Instead, she continued making them some coffee, only slowly turning around when she could hand him his mug.

'I thought that maybe you had come here to tell me that you had had a change of heart, had listened to some of what I had to say. If I'd known that you were just going to repeat the same things you said to me earlier on…'

'I listened to what you said,' Cesar told her flatly.

'And?'

'I naturally expressed my disappointment that he hadn't seen fit to tell me about…this bit of his personal life…' He held up one hand to stop her before she could speak. 'Don't worry. I'm not the monster you think I am. I appreciate that my brother is going through a difficult time at the moment. I was…very controlled…'

He looked exhausted.

'Naturally I mentioned that I would have to think carefully about releasing the entire trust fund at his disposal…'

'Oh, great. In other words, you got your message across loud and clear that you don't trust the woman he loves and wants to marry.'

'In other words, I let it be known that I'm willing to sink

money into this venture of his—certainly he will get a proportion of his trust fund…'

'And Imogen? Did you get to meet her at all?'

'I thought it better to leave her to recover first.'

'And you're going to head back to London now? Or are you
going to stick around for a few days, moral support for Freddy?'

Cesar hesitated. His sparse retelling of the facts had not
allowed for the unexpected empathy he had felt towards his
brother nor for the truth, which was that he had paid her words
a great deal more attention than she probably assumed. A
month ago, he would have dealt with his brother according to
the facts as written on a sheet of paper. Namely a blonde
stripper, an unknown quantity, had got herself pregnant and,
to that effect, his brother wanted to get hold of a vast sum of
money in the naive belief that he could throw it at some ill-
conceived venture, half of which could feasibly end up in the
hands of a woman who had taken advantage of his gullible
nature. Ergo, no trust fund.

But something in him seemed to have shifted.

When, for instance, had his brother started fearing him?
How had they reached the point where a fundamental life
change could be kept hidden?

Cesar had heard the condemnation in Jude's voice and it
had got his back up. It had also given him pause for thought.

Yes, he had been incredibly lenient with Fernando. Indeed,
for the first time in many years, they had embraced on parting.
And, before he'd left the hospital, he had actually gone to see
the baby at the centre of all the fuss and had stood watching
it for an inordinately long time in the incubator, amazed that
something so small could be so perfectly formed.

Of course, he would reserve judgement until he had met
the mother of the child, but he now found himself in the

position of being prepared to give the woman both his brother and Jude held in such high regard the benefit of the doubt.

All in all, and hot on the heels of cancelling all his appointments until further notice, his secretary would have been reaching to call the medics were she to see him now.

But underneath it all, and against his better judgement, he could still feel a thread of anger running through him like poison that Jude had deceived him.

He conveniently sidelined the thought that he had justified sleeping with her—*seducing her*—because he had believed that he might extract whatever she was hiding. The only thing that occupied his mind now was the fact that she had lain in his arms, had made love to him and still managed to conceal something potentially highly damaging to the Caretti empire. She would doubtless call it loyalty to his brother. His experience with the money-grabbing women that circled him like hawks had taught Cesar to call Jude's secret-keeping a deliberate act of treachery.

And rumbling beneath this was his anger that she had turned him down, had swept aside their love-making as if it had been an unfortunate disease, something passing that needed to be eradicated by pretending it had never taken place.

'I might just stick around...' he drawled, looking at her coldly. 'After all, I'm going to have to make my own value judgements on this person.'

'I told you...'

'I know what you *told* me but surprisingly I'm finding it hard to believe a word you have to say.'

'That's not fair!'

'No? You haven't got an honest bone in your body, have you, Jude?'

'I explained to you why I did...what I did.'

Cesar knew that this was a conversation destined to go nowhere. He also knew that he *was* being unfair, at least to her. And he didn't quite understand why he couldn't leave it alone. He shouldn't have made the trip out here. There was nothing to gain from a pointless confrontation—but he had got into his brother's car and it had been as though his rational thought processes had closed down.

'Look at the big picture from *my* point of view,' he suggested in a voice that would freeze the fires of hell. 'You and this woman have been friends since childhood.' He drained his coffee and stood up, aware that he was on a roll and that he should make an effort to stop. But, looking at her… It enraged him that he could still *want* her, after all of this. He had never felt so out of control in his life and it wasn't a good feeling. He didn't understand it and he didn't need it. The woman had cast some sort of spell over him and he wanted her conclusively out of his life.

He began walking towards the front door. He knew that she would follow him and she did.

'You tell me that I should take your word for it that the woman is as pure as the driven snow, innocent of any ulterior motives.' He turned to look at her and leaned indolently against the door frame. She had that ferocious look on her face—an expression that suggested that, given half a chance, she would have grabbed the largest, heaviest object to hand and slugged him with it. 'The fact that she met my brother in a nightclub where she works for a living taking her clothes off…'

'She doesn't *take her clothes off*! At least, not *all* of them…'

'Immaterial. You get the gist.'

'I think you should leave.'

'And I will. When I'm finished saying what I have to say.'

'I might have guessed that you didn't come here just to

bring me glad tidings,' Jude said bitterly. 'I might have guessed that it would have just been too much to have sympathised with Freddy and just be happy for him.' Had she actually been fool enough to have imagined that he had wiped her eyes *with tenderness*?

'Don't get me wrong. I would be overjoyed if I thought that Fernando was about to embark on a life of undiluted joy and fulfilment with a woman who loved him for the person he was and not the significant amount of money he brings to the equation. And believe me when I tell you that I'm really going to be totally impartial when it comes to sizing up the situation...'

'As impartial as any dictator is ever likely to be...' Jude muttered under her breath, forcing Cesar to lean towards her words. Which he didn't but somehow he could guess its tone.

'But I can't help wondering whether a conspiracy of sorts was involved...'

'*A conspiracy of sorts?* What on *earth* are you talking about?'

'How am I to know that you two didn't contrive a convenient meeting with Fernando? You would have known his name and, even if you didn't know his pedigree, it wouldn't have been hard to guess that he had money. My brother in a nightclub is an open book. I should know. I've had the unhappy pleasure of being with him in one once. A few minutes on the Internet and you could have sourced his background in under ten seconds.'

'I can't believe you're telling me this, Cesar!' But she could. At least, she could believe it of the man standing in front of her like an implacable rock, his face harshly condemnatory.

'Why?' he demanded in a silky voice. 'Why can't you believe it?'

'Because you should *know* that I'm not that type of person! We've been through this.'

'So we have, but think about it—how much do I *really* know about you? How much do I really *know you*?'

Jude felt cut to the quick by that remark. Did he mean it? Surely, after all they had shared, he knew that she would be incapable of such a horror? Her back stiffened as she adopted a defensive pose. No, she was *not*, absolutely not, going to justify herself to him! But the thought of seeing him walk away with the worst things in his mind made her want to weep.

'If you really think that about me, Cesar, then what can I say?'

It wasn't what he wanted to hear. The truth was, he didn't know *what* he wanted to hear.

'So true. What *can* you say?'

'You put so much importance on money, Cesar. You can't understand that, at the end of the day, it doesn't really mean very much. Yes, it can get you the company helicopter and the designer car, but those aren't things of any value.'

'Still going for the altruistic line, Jude? I might have believed you once, but in the light of what's unfolded, you'll have to excuse a certain amount of cynicism on my part.'

'Why? Why do I have to excuse it? You think the worst of me. You think that I would do anything for a bit of money.'

'Everyone has their price.'

'That's a horrible thing to say.'

'Is it? And here I was thinking that I was being utterly realistic.' He looked down at the glowering face and smiled grimly. 'What a shame.'

'What is?'

'Shame that you don't agree with me, because if everybody has a price then you would discover that I could be a very generous lover…and we made such good lovers, didn't we, Jude?'

He reached out and touched her face.

Jude froze. For a while, all she felt was the perfection of his skin against hers, reminding her that she had given her soul to the devil. She wanted to curve into his touch, hold his hand and lead him to her bed.

She pulled away sharply, her breathing uneven and painful, and placed her hand firmly on the door knob. She couldn't actually open the door as he was still leaning against it, but he stepped aside and she pulled it open quickly, shaking.

'How long do you plan on staying?' she asked tightly.

'Why? Would you want to take evasive measures?'

'Can you blame me?'

'Maybe not.' Cesar shrugged. He had said what he wanted to say. More. Too much. And some of it had left a sour taste in his mouth.

'Just…' she looked up at him, her eyes clear and steady despite the fact that her thoughts were all over the place '…don't let whatever you think about me affect your decision about Freddy's trust fund. Or your opinion of Imogen.'

'Still fighting the fight?'

'Still hoping that there's a place inside you that I can appeal to, some bit of you that isn't totally jaded.'

Cesar flushed darkly. He didn't like the picture she had conjured up but, in all fairness, he could hardly blame her. However, that was not something he intended to impart, so he gave her a curt nod and left through the open door, straight to his brother's car.

From the doorway, she watched as the car revved and then swung neatly round, doing the fastest three-point manoeuvre she had ever seen in her life. When she closed the door, she felt drained. The day had started badly with Freddy's call and it had gone downhill since, picking up speed with Cesar's appearance on the scene.

Now, she was shattered. The nagging headache which she had managed to keep at bay was returning with a vengeance. She needed and wanted nothing so much as to have a hot bath and climb into her bed, but then what would she do once there? Stare up at the ceiling in the darkness and think about him? Think about what he had said? He surely couldn't have meant it…could he? Could he really think that she had plotted and connived with Imogen to cheat someone out of his money?

He would meet Imogen and realise that he had been wrong, and in fact some small part of her sensed that everything he had said had been an overreaction to the bombshell that had been laid at his door.

He had lashed out but he had lashed out at *her* and that really hurt because, even if she never saw him again, and it was unlikely that would happen, he had been left with the wrong impression.

Which made her think of all those long days lying ahead, days in which he would play no part, a life in which he would have no say.

He had been cruel and blinkered and cold and she tried very hard to resurrect some good, healthy dislike but she couldn't. She couldn't resurrect anything but the way he had made her feel when his fingers had touched her skin.

CHAPTER SEVEN

WITHIN a fortnight, both Imogen and the baby were out of the hospital. Little Maria was already beginning to gain weight and Freddy, the proud father, was fast-tracking his jazz club venture, which had now received Cesar's financial backing thanks to the release of a fair amount of the trust fund.

'I'm on probation,' Freddy had told Jude sheepishly, 'and I can't say I blame him. After all, I *have* spent a goodish amount of my adult life squandering my money, so he's going to be careful, really.'

Whatever Jude's personal feelings about Cesar, she was very happy for Freddy. Maybe Cesar had found himself cornered but, whatever the reason, he had cut his brother some slack and, better than that, had been thrown into the novel situation of having to defer to Freddy on his expertise when it came to the practicalities of opening a club. It was doing Freddy's sense of self-worth a power of good.

And today was the Big Day. A little sooner than expected, and a lot smaller than Freddy's extended family might have wanted, but still happening. A register office affair in Marylebone, followed by a lavish lunch at one of the top restaurants, which had closed its doors to the public for the day.

The honeymoon, Imogen had told her, was to be put on hold for a few months but, radiant with her newborn, she didn't seem to mind in the slightest. Nor did she seem in the least bit critical of her brother-in-law-to-be. He was, she had told Jude, very charming and she couldn't understand why there had been all this fuss about him in the first place.

Jude had refrained from pointing out that, yes, sharks might not bare their teeth *all the time* but that didn't mean that they weren't capable of inflicting grievous bodily harm. She should know.

It was all now one Big Happy Family. Winners all round. Except, of course, for *her*.

She gazed at her reflection in the mirror. She looked like someone recovering from a bad bout of flu. Hollow eyes, face a little too thin, anxious expression.

In a little under two hours she would be standing in that register office, and it would be the first time in nearly three weeks since she had seen Cesar, although the passing of time had done little to soften the blow of his final departure from her life. Every cruel word he had said had been imprinted on her mind with such force that she relived the moment even in her sleep.

She had chosen her outfit carefully. It was a loose jade-green woollen dress, just reaching her knees, and with an attractive empire line that gave it a youthful appearance. A sensible buy, all things considered. She had even bought herself a fancy coat, something in which she would never have thought to invest, but she felt that she might need courage when it came to meeting Cesar and what better to give courage than an image-boosting outfit?

Now all she had to do was apply sufficient make-up to deal with the worried face.

By the time her taxi arrived she looked a great deal better than she felt. The dress lived up to the expectations she had had when she had bought it two days previously, as did the high black shoes and the fancy coat. Her black bag was a little too oversized to be labelled anything other than useful, but what was she to do? She still had her hundred and one things to stuff in.

The worst of it all, she thought, was that she *had* to meet Cesar. She couldn't go along and hope to get lost in the crowd. She *had* to meet him and, for the sake of her sanity, she *had* to talk to him.

She looked at that little, perfectly innocuous piece of plastic on her dressing table and felt the same shiver of fear as she had when she had bought it two days ago.

It had not occurred to her at any point that she might be pregnant. She still wasn't too sure when the notion had begun to form in her head that her period was overdue. Even then, she had uneasily put that down to stress. Wasn't that supposed to affect the body in mysterious ways?

In fact, she was still telling herself that she had absolutely nothing to worry about when those dark blue lines informed her that, yes, she had something to worry about. A great deal to worry about.

Since then she had done nothing but oblige. She had worried.

She had also replayed Cesar's last conversation with her, in which he had accused her of conspiring with Imogen to con Freddy out of his money, some hideous joint venture, which she was certain Cesar couldn't possibly believe.

She told herself repeatedly that he had overreacted because he had been enraged by what he had seen as a case of deliberate deception, that people often said things in the heat of the moment which they didn't mean. Not really.

But it was down to *capability*, wasn't it? He might not really believe that she had conspired to do anything with anyone. In fact, he might have zoomed off in his car, come to his senses and realised that the idea was ridiculous, but at the back of her mind she wondered feverishly whether he thought that she was *capable* of manipulating someone else for her own personal gain.

If he thought that, then how was he going to react when she broke the news to him that she was pregnant?

She had told him, when they had made love, that she was protected. She hadn't exactly explained that she had believed herself protected thanks to the ancient and apparently wholly unreliable method known as *the rhythm method*. He had probably assumed that she was on the contraceptive pill, although why he would assume that she didn't have a clue, considering she had told him just how long it had been since she had slept with anyone. But assume it he must have or else he would have taken charge of contraception himself.

Cesar wasn't looking for commitment, let alone an unwanted pregnancy. In fact, when it came to women, Cesar wasn't looking for anything beyond sex.

The ride to the register office was a nightmare. There was an awful lot of traffic, giving her ample time to stare vacantly out of the window and turn over in her mind the various hideous scenarios that could be awaiting her.

She almost wished that she had made an appointment to see him in his office although, at the time, she had wondered whether he would have even taken her call.

She had opted for today because she had known that he would be there and would have to see her, have to talk to her. Somewhere quiet after the reception was over. At any rate, it didn't make a difference *where* the conversation happened, she told herself now as her stomach churned away. There was no suitable place.

The guest list had been narrowed down to twenty-five people. Some relatives from Spain, close family, and then friends. A trip was planned for later in the year to visit the rest of the family, when Maria was a little older and more able to handle the change of environment.

When the taxi eventually pulled up outside the building, Jude could already see the guests congregated on the steps. At the top of the steps was Cesar, talking to Imogen, one hand in his pocket, his coat lifted by the breeze.

Jude got out of the taxi and took a deep breath before walking the gauntlet from the pavement to the entrance, noticing that, while Cesar briefly broke off his conversation to glance in her direction, he very quickly returned to what he was saying to Imogen, making it clear that while he had noted her presence, he was indifferent to it.

So time, she thought wretchedly, hadn't diminished his bitterness towards her.

He had made his peace with his brother, accepted Imogen as his soon-to-be sister-in-law, and yet the olive branch was visibly not being waved in *her* direction.

She was the last to arrive and offered her apologies to Imogen, while smiling down at a bundled-up little Maria, who was beginning to fret, waving her fists around, her tiny face puckered into a cross frown.

'I've only just fed her,' Imogen confided, 'but she's already hungry again. She eats like...well, like Freddy...' Imogen laughed. 'Are you okay? You look a little drawn, Jude.' This in hushed whispers as they headed indoors, out of the bright but cold sun.

'Just working really hard,' Jude said in a strained voice.

Her eyes darted towards Cesar's back. 'You know how it is…' She hadn't breathed a word of what had happened between herself and Cesar, and Imogen, thankfully, had been too busy to ask questions.

'We'll have to go out soon,' Imogen promised. 'When my life gets a bit less frantic. I feel pretty strong now, but it's amazing how a little thing of just six and a half pounds can turn an adult into a zombie.'

'Well, you look very glamorous for a zombie,' Jude said truthfully, smiling. Radiant, in fact.

And for the next forty-five minutes or so she was spared the agony of dwelling on her situation. The service was short but heartfelt and the couple looked deliriously happy. In fact, even an ingrained cynic like Cesar would have been hard-pressed to think that they were anything but truly in love.

Jude wasn't going to put that to the test, though, by meeting his eyes. Indeed, she kept hers well averted from his dark, striking face, although, as she signed the registry book, she was all too aware of him standing next to her like a block of implacable, unforgiving granite.

She wasn't entirely sure when she would draw him to one side and, like a coward, she kept her distance for as long as she could and as much as was physically possible, given that they were both seated opposite one another at the same table.

She wittered away with seemingly endless enthusiasm to one of their cousins, a nineteen-year-old boy who was heavily into football, something about which she knew precious little but was learning fast by asking all the right questions and displaying all the right interest.

Every so often her eyes would slide of their own accord to Cesar's dark, unbearably handsome face as he engaged the people around him.

She could barely appreciate the wonderful meal, which seemed to stretch on for eternity, course after course after course, and then the toast, a short, witty few words given by Cesar in which no reference was made to Imogen's far from illustrious background or the suspicions that had driven him to assume the worst of their relationship. The man was a consummate actor, Jude thought acidly, charming the crowd in the same way that he had charmed her out from behind that wall which she had erected around her emotions and behind which she wished she was still firmly secure. His own wall was obviously made of far sterner stuff.

It was nearly five by the time the meal was cleared away, at which point her stomach was doing a very merry jig.

She had barely uttered a word to Cesar but, as he glanced at his watch, a sure prelude for him leaving, she followed him to the restaurant door and tentatively placed her hand on his arm.

In the process of slipping on his coat, he turned to her and looked from her face to her offending hand and then back to her face.

'Cesar...hi...' She licked her lips nervously, traipsing along behind him as he left the restaurant. 'How are you?'

'As you can see, never better. Is there something you wanted?'

'You're not still angry with me, are you?'

'Why would I still be angry with you?' Dark, hard eyes clashed with hers. 'You over-estimate your importance, Jude.' Naturally he had known that he would be seeing her but it was still a bad moment for Cesar. She looked more fragile than he remembered, which made him think of her vulnerability when she had lain in his arms. It was a thought he did not want to entertain and he slashed it before it could take root by recalling her deception. He had been taken in by that honest, transparent face and her blazing outspokenness. Never let it be said that he wasn't a man who didn't learn from his mistakes.

He felt duly fortified by that thought and stared down at her icily.

'I…Cesar…we need to…to talk…'

'Do we?' He looked at his watch, just as he had in the restaurant, reminding her that he was probably off to do something. It was Saturday evening and she didn't imagine that he would be spending it alone. In fact, that was something Jude had studiously avoided thinking about. Another woman in his arms was just too much to bear.

'I know you've probably got something to do…somewhere to go…' She invited disclosure.

'Nothing and nowhere that you need know about.' He signalled to his driver, who magically appeared as if out of thin air. In fact, Cesar was looking forward to a meal on his own at an Italian restaurant close to where he lived and an evening in front of his computer, downloading e-mails and reading three reports. This despite the fact that he had been invited to several company affairs which, he knew, might have improved his ongoing foul mood but which had seemed impossibly tedious. Too tedious to attend.

'Of course. I was just being polite.'

'Well, consider yourself relieved of that particular burden.' His driver hurried around to the passenger door and pulled it open for him but, instead of getting into the back seat, he found himself leaning against the car door and looking down at her. 'As far as I'm aware we've covered pretty much everything there is to say, wouldn't you agree?'

'Not *everything*, as a matter of fact.'

'No?' In a minute his car would be moved on. Traffic wardens were very hot in this part of London. Still, he found he continued to loiter, watching her derisively although he had told himself, at irritatingly frequent intervals over the past couple of weeks, that he was well rid of her.

'Maybe we could go and grab a…a coffee somewhere…' Jude offered, even though she had already had two cups after the meal and knew for the baby's sake she really couldn't have any more caffeine.

'I'm trying to think of a single reason why I would want to have a coffee with you.'

Jude rested her hand on the open door. 'Because I want to talk to you and it's the very least you owe me.'

Cesar gave an incredulous laugh. 'Run that by me again?'

'You might just want to shove me out of your mind, but we…we're going to keep meeting up every so often and we need to try and work out how we can do that without ignoring one another. If we ignore one another, Freddy and Imogen are going to start asking questions.' It was the only thing she could think of to say because she wasn't about to drop her bombshell on a busy road in central London with his driver waiting impatiently inside the car.

'You'd better get in,' Cesar said impatiently. 'In a minute we're going to cause a traffic jam.'

She ducked down past him into the back seat of the Bentley and shuffled over so that he could sit next to her. It was hard to tell whether he had decided to talk to her because what she had said made sense or whether he had just got fed up of standing outside his car, obliged to speak to her because clever positioning of her hand prevented him from getting into the car and slamming the door in her face.

'I…I gather you and Freddy have reconciled your differences…' Jude began hesitantly.

It seemed pitiful to be indulging in small talk when there

was something far more important to discuss, but she wasn't going to just blurt it out. If she could somehow get him to thaw just a little bit towards her, it would, she reckoned, make things a lot easier.

'I was given precious little choice.' Cesar leaned towards his chauffeur and instructed him to go to the restaurant, then he turned to look at her. 'Presented with a fait accompli, I could either have stuck to my guns and deprived Fernando of his chance to prove himself or else release his trust fund and give him the independence he wanted.' He shrugged elegantly. 'If he were man enough to get a woman pregnant, and I gather that it was not entirely an unplanned event, then he will have to be man enough to handle his finances and raise a family.'

Everything was very civilised, but Cesar's eyes remained cold and shuttered.

'And…what about Imogen? Have you softened your opinion towards her?'

'Is that why you wanted to talk to me? So that we could compare notes?'

Jude looked away, but it was difficult. His closeness, the intimacy of being in the back seat of the car with him, those deep, black, penetrating eyes—it affected her like a drug seeping into her veins and making her thoughts woolly.

'I thought you would have been a lot less forgiving than you were.'

Cesar was loath to admit it, even to himself, but so had he. In all events, he had seen his brother distraught with worry at the hospital and then afterwards had seen them together, the way they looked at one another, and had grudgingly admitted to himself that maybe some things weren't as black and white as he cared to think.

Furthermore, even in her weakened state, Imogen had

managed to get him on his own and had suggested—no, *insisted*—that she sign a pre-nuptial agreement. She had also, to his surprise, on some paper, worked out a pretty accurate formula for what she thought his brother should be given from the trust fund and it roughly coincided with his own estimate. He had had to do a quick rethink on his preconceived ideas.

'I will, naturally, be taking an active interest in my brother's venture,' was all he said, 'at least until it's up and running.'

'Freddy says that you don't know a huge amount about how clubs are run…' she said with a little smile.

Cesar felt himself grudgingly descend from his polar iciness and he admitted drily, 'It's true. Fernando has discovered the one area of expertise in which I am fairly ignorant and he's naturally revelling in the discovery. In fact, I think it's made his day.'

'Who can blame him? Living in your shadow must have been a tall order.'

'I'll take that as a compliment.' He knew that this was how she had managed to get under his skin. Cesar, in his daily life, was surrounded by people who bowed and scraped and put themselves out to be included in the magic circle that surrounded him. Jude, albeit unwittingly, seemed to carry a metaphorical pin around with her, specifically designed to burst his rarefied balloon.

'It is,' Jude agreed readily. 'I never thought I'd hear you say that you were ignorant about anything, so that means that there must be even more dimensions to you than I thought.'

'Even more?'

The car pulled smoothly up in front of a small bistro, sparing Jude the embarrassment of having to explain her back-handed compliment.

After that brief respite her nerves were beginning to kick

in again, but she forced herself to remain calm as they went in. Cesar was obviously a regular and they were treated to the best table in the restaurant, a small one tucked away at the back where the noise level was lower and two oversized potted plants gave the illusion of semi-privacy.

'I can't eat a thing,' she said.

'Can't you? I didn't notice you stuffing yourself at the reception.'

He'd noticed how much she had eaten?

'I'll just have some…some orange juice, I think.' She snapped shut the menu and then stared down at it, as if in search of inspiration.

'So…' Order for some calamari and drinks placed, Cesar sat back in his chair, one arm loosely draped over the back, and looked at her. 'Are we succeeding in this important mission of acting like civilised adults?'

'Did you really mean it when you said that you thought I'd been involved in some sort of plot with Imogen to fleece your brother of his trust fund?'

'Is that why you wanted to talk to me, Jude? Because you wanted to clear your name?'

'Amongst other things,' she mumbled.

'Amongst *what* other things?'

'Why don't you answer my question?'

Cesar looked at her carefully. Hell, it was no skin off his nose if he told her the truth. Anyway, like it or not, she had a point. She and his brother's wife were close friends and he envisaged that his relationship with his brother was set to improve. They were certainly going to be thrown into each other's company more than they ever had been before, with this whole jazz club situation. Chances were high that he and Jude would bump into one another now and again. The baby's christening, for a start, would be a big family occasion. It made sense to drop the hostilities.

And it had clearly been preying on her mind. That instantly made Cesar feel pretty good.

'I confess I may have said one or two things that possibly weren't entirely accurate, that being one of them.'

'What were the others?'

'Has this been worrying you?' he asked casually. The calamari arrived, just the right amount considering he had eaten a hefty lunch only a few hours previously.

He imagined her losing sleep over what he had said, tossing and turning at night, unable to function by day and desperate for him to release her from her misery. His mood went up a couple of notches. It made a pleasant change from that reception lunch when he hadn't been able to miss the way she had leaned into his cousin, Jorge, practically draping herself around the poor boy and hanging on to his every word as though he actually had something other to talk about than football.

'I just didn't think it was right for you to walk out with such an unfair impression of me.' Now that the moment had arrived, Jude discovered that she was dragging her feet, dreading when she had to tell him about her pregnancy.

'Okay. I've had a chance to get to know your friend and I would be lying if I said that I could imagine the pair of you plotting to do anything. Are you satisfied now? It's rare for me to be wrong about anything or anyone, but in this instance I may have reacted in fury. Don't forget you were the one who contrived to keep something very important a secret.'

'So did Freddy,' she pointed out, fiddling with her glass.

'Freddy had an ulterior motive.'

'So did I. I was being loyal.'

'You were my lover. Your loyalties should have been with me.'

'What else?'

Cesar looked up with a speared piece of calamari on the way to his mouth. 'What else…what?'

'You said that you said *one or two* things that weren't entirely accurate. Well, you've mentioned one thing. What's the other?'

He took his time with this mouthful of food, then washed it down with some of the white wine. He had drunk nothing at lunch and the cold wine tasted good, especially when combined with his improving spirits.

'I was enraged by what I considered your deception. I obviously still am, don't get me wrong. However, I don't consider you a gold-digger, not that I would sell my soul on that certainty. Face it, if you could lie once, you could lie a thousand times, but from what I've seen of you, I don't think you are capable of using Freddy for his money. There. Consider your character suitably exonorated, an excellent basis for civil conversation between us in the future.'

'Civil conversation…'

'Correct. Why?' He shoved aside the plate and leaned back in his chair so that he could look her squarely in the face. 'Were you expecting more?'

Something akin to pleasure raced through his veins, making this unexpected meeting well worth the temporary inconvenience. For starters, he was enjoying her company, much as he didn't care to admit it, even to himself. He wasn't too big to acknowledge that she had had more of an effect on him than he had anticipated when he had walked out of her house.

That said, of course he wasn't going to take her back. He

had offered her a chance for involvement and she had blown it. Furthermore, she had proved to be a traitor.

However, he wasn't going to deny that there was something satisfying about knowing that she was ready to come crawling back. Doubtless she had had time to really think about what he had said and ponder the truth, which was that isolating yourself from all contact with the opposite sex on the off chance that the right guy would come along with a ring in his hand and a marriage proposal on his lips was sheer lunacy. Dreams were all well and good but not when they interfered with day-to-day existence. Hell, *he'd* never had much time for idle dreaming, had he?

For a passing moment, the image of his brother flashed into his mind—his brother laughing with Imogen as they'd cut that little wedding cake at the reception. His eyes had been tender, loving, *besotted* and she had been smiling back at him with a similar expression.

'No, of course not,' she was saying awkwardly. 'Why would I expect more?'

'No idea, because there's nothing more on the table.' He signalled for the bill. Was it his imagination or did something resembling anxiety shadow her face?

'Look, this is difficult for me but there's something I need to tell you.'

Cesar stilled, sensing a level of urgency in her voice that went beyond some simple desire for them to try and *get along* for the sake of convenience. She was also fiddling like mad with the linen napkin on the table, although when she caught him noticing the nervous gesture she immediately stopped and placed her hands on her lap.

'Go on, although I haven't got all evening.'

'No.' She remembered that he probably had a date with a

leggy blonde or some other model-type creature. He had pointedly refrained from telling her exactly what he had to do later which, in her head, could only mean one thing.

'Do you remember…at the cottage? When we…made love…?'

The question came from nowhere and, taken aback, Cesar frowned. 'Of course I remember, although I thought that we were both going to pretend that that had never happened.'

'I *did* say that at the time, didn't I…'

'Have you since discovered that *selective amnesia* is a little harder to do?'

'Virtually impossible.'

'So you don't want anything more than for us to just sit here chewing the fat…but by your own admission, you can't get me out of your head…'

'It's not as clear-cut as that… I don't know quite how to say this and you're probably not going to like it but…Cesar, I'm pregnant.'

Cesar froze. The silence between them was so bottomless that, even with the dull clatter of noise around them, Jude felt that she would have been able to hear a pin drop.

'You're kidding, right,' he said finally, but his voice was raw and he had gone slightly ashen.

'I'd never kid about something like that.'

'How do you know?'

'Because I did a test two days ago. In fact, I did the test three times. Those tests are pretty much one hundred per cent accurate.'

'You can't be. You asked me if I remembered when we made love at your cottage. I do and I distinctly remember you telling me that you were protected.'

'Yes, I know and I thought I was. I really did. I mean, I

worked out when my period was due and I should have been perfectly safe but…'

Cesar was in a state of shock. When she had told him that they needed to talk, he hadn't known what to expect. It hadn't been this. Was that why she had been so desperate to know whether he had really believed her capable of using his brother? Because really she had needed to find out whether he thought her capable of using *him*?

'Was this deliberate?' he felt obliged to ask because nothing could be taken on trust, but he knew the answer already from the look on her face.

'Of course not!' Jude told him fiercely. 'Don't you think I was as shocked as you are now when I…when I did that test?' She felt her eyes threaten to fill up again but she blinked the tears away and clenched her fists.

'Okay. I believe you.'

She felt a wave of relief. From the various scenarios which had played in her head, most had featured an accusing and disbelieving Cesar, who saw her as someone who had intruded into his life and, having infiltrated, had used the situation to her own advantage.

At least that nasty possibility was out of the way, leaving her to face the stark reality, which was that she and Cesar no longer shared an intimate connection, that she had only ever been a sex object to him, easily and quickly disposable. Now that she was pregnant, nothing was destined to change but they would have to work out some sort of civil arrangement whereby they could deal with the situation.

In all her girlhood dreams, being pregnant by a man who didn't love her had never featured. Plan A had always been to have children in a loving relationship. She now had to face some pretty harsh facts. She was on Plan B and she would just have to deal with it.

'I haven't come here to ask anything of you,' she told him quietly. 'I'm pretty realistic.' She smiled sadly. 'We had a very brief fling but there's nothing between us now so we just need to sort out…well, what happens when the baby is born…'

'What do you mean, *what happens*?'

'About…visiting…I know it's early days but…it's probably better to deal with things now…or at least discuss them… I know this is a bombshell…'

'That has to be the understatement of the year.'

'Anyway, perhaps I could give you a few days to think about things, let it sink in…?'

'Let it sink in? It's already sunk in!' He raked restless fingers through his hair and looked at her, imagining *his* baby in her tummy. Fatherhood had never been something he had contemplated. In fact, the concept was completely alien to both his way of thinking and his lifestyle.

'Nothing has to change for you,' she said quickly. 'This is *my* situation.'

'*Your* situation? What planet are you on, Jude? Whether you like it or not, this is fifty per cent *my* doing.'

'But it's my fault that I'm pregnant. I wasn't careful enough. I should have thought.'

'It's pointless debating whose fault it is or isn't. Right now we need to get out of here, go somewhere where we can talk privately.' He stood up and beckoned for the bill at the same time. 'My apartment's just round the corner. We'll go there.'

CHAPTER EIGHT

CESAR'S apartment was literally a five-minute walk away. It made sense to be out of the restaurant, to go somewhere more private to talk, but Jude still felt nervous as they walked along in silence, she huddling into her coat while he seemed lost in his thoughts.

She reminded herself that he had now moved on from her, which made her think of his ruined date. The poor blonde was probably waiting at some table in some unknown restaurant, checking her watch and tapping her long scarlet fingernails impatiently as it dawned on her that she might have been stood up. Jude didn't feel at all sorry about that. In fact, the thought provided her with a few moments of well-deserved amusement.

'We're here.'

She snapped out of her pleasant daydream and looked up at the sharp, clear lines of a four-storey Georgian town house with its neat black railings fringed by two impeccably groomed shrubs. It reeked of money and the impression was cemented by the array of flashy cars parked on either side of the wide street. Even in the darkness, this was clearly a part of London reserved for the immensely wealthy, a far cry from the cheap and cheerful hotel room she had reserved for herself for the overnight stay.

Inside, the large flagstoned hall was dotted with yet more well-manicured plants and she followed him to the lift, which took them up two flights to his apartment, which occupied the upper floors of the building. Two complete floors!

Jude looked around her for a while, forgetting the seriousness of the situation that had brought her to this place.

The floors were pale blond wood and here, on the lower of the floors, was the sitting area, the kitchen and several other rooms which she could only glimpse. Up a curving iron staircase were the bedrooms and bathrooms, how many she had no idea. It was incredibly neat and clean and had the perfect appearance of a place that would not disgrace the cover of a house magazine.

'Nice place,' Jude said politely. She tentatively made her way to one of the sprawling cream leather sofas but was hesitant to sit on it.

'It won't bite,' Cesar said drily. 'It's only a piece of furniture.' The bracing night air had taken some of the edge from his initial shock. He wouldn't go down that road of thinking just how his life was going to change. There were so many areas to contemplate that it seemed better to scrap the thought altogether. The main thing was that he was going to be a father and pondering the consequences wasn't going to get him anywhere. 'I'm getting myself a cup of coffee. Do you want one?'

'Thank you. No. I think I've probably had more than my fair ration today.'

Her eyes strayed to the huge abstract paintings on the walls and the weird pieces of sculpture that had been artistically positioned on the mantelpiece of what was a very modern fireplace.

She looked back at him as he sat on one of the low matching leather chairs facing her.

'I'm sorry.' If she hadn't realised how much this was going

to upset his life, then being in his apartment was a lesson in finding out because it reflected *him*, the man. Here was a person with no use for clutter or lack of order, two things that followed in the wake of a child. 'I've given this some thought,' she said hesitantly, 'and I've worked out that you won't have your life disrupted. No, please, Cesar…' This when he was about to interrupt. 'I can take care of the baby on my own and, naturally, you can visit whenever you want to or whenever you have the time…'

'Visit whenever I want…? When I have time…? We're not talking about an art gallery here, Jude. We're talking about a child—*my* child.'

'Well, yes, I realise that…'

Cesar sipped his coffee and continued to look at her while she, in turn, stared miserably at the intricately weaved Persian rug under her feet.

'I'm not sure you do,' Cesar countered. 'No, my parental rights will go way beyond occasional visits when you give the go-ahead. For starters, there's the question of money. You might like to think yourself not materialistic but no child of mine is ever going to endure any kind of hardship. Both your future and the future of my child will be secure. Of that you have my word.'

He allowed several seconds of silence to elapse, giving her time to absorb what he was saying.

'Hardship? Cesar, I have a job! I know I may not earn what you consider sufficient to live on, but your idea of an adequate amount of money is…well, completely different to most people's…' She looked round the apartment. The paintings on his walls probably cost as much as most people's holidays abroad. More. 'This isn't real life!'

'Agreed, but this is *my* life and it's the life my child will enjoy.'

'What are you trying to say?' She unconsciously rested her hand on her stomach as the colour drained from her face. This was something she hadn't considered. What if he decided that he wanted the child? Wanted to fight for sole custody of her baby? Would he do that? 'You won't take my baby away from me!'

'Of course I am not going to take your baby away from you!' Cesar was genuinely appalled at the suggestion. 'What sort of man do you think I am? I realise the need for a child to have its mother, to have *both* its parents, which brings me to the point I'm trying to make.'

Jude nodded, half listening to him, sagging with relief that she had jumped the gun for no reason.

'…so you see, whilst I am prepared to put financial security on the table, a child needs more than just that. As you have said a dozen times, it's not all about money…'

'Right.'

'And having both parents around means more than me driving to Kent once a week for a three-hour visit. When I say that I intend to be there for my child, I mean it. I intend to be there on a permanent basis, as in living on the premises. With you. With our child. Together. A unit. Married.'

It took Jude a few seconds to process that information, then she replayed it in her head just to make sure that she wasn't imagining that word, *married*.

'Are you telling me that you want to *get married*? *To me?*' Jude laughed incredulously. 'That's the most ridiculous thing I've ever heard in my life.'

Cesar stiffened. 'No child of mine will be born out of wedlock.'

'*Born out of wedlock?* Cesar, this is the twenty-first century! In case you hadn't noticed, pregnancy and marriage no

longer necessarily go together! Besides, isn't it a bit hypocriti-
cal to say something like that when you were prepared to bend
the rules for your brother?'

'I was prepared *to protect my brother at all costs from
someone I thought might be using him for his money.* Different
thing. Anyway, we're getting off topic here.' He stood up and
began pacing the room until he finally stopped directly in front
of her, then he sat on the sofa next to her so that she had to
propel herself back a couple of inches to stop herself from
falling against him.

'Surely you have to concede that a two-parent family is
superior to a one-parent one.'

'Yes, *in an ideal world*, but we're not living in an *ideal
world*, Cesar.' In an ideal world, there was nothing Jude would
have wanted more than to have been asked to be Cesar's wife
and for a couple of wild seconds she was ashamed to find
herself buying into a beguiling fantasy picture in her head of
a family of three, blissfully happy, doing normal family
things. It didn't last long.

'Why would you ask me to marry you, Cesar?'

'Isn't it obvious?' He frowned. Okay, so all of this had
come as a complete shock to him but he was now doing the
honourable thing and, in his head, the *only* thing and, instead
of fairly leaping at all the benefits being thrown on the table,
she had firstly laughed at him and now seemed to be asking
him for accountability on his offer.

'Cesar—' she sighed '—you can't just marry someone
because she happens to be pregnant with your child and then
assume that it'll all work out fine. We weren't even going out
together! Would you be sitting here with me *at all* if this
hadn't happened?'

'That's not the point.'

'But it *is* the point.' She could see that, having made the ultimate sacrifice and proposed marriage, it hadn't occurred to him that his offer might be rejected. 'Did you ever think about getting married again? Starting a family? No, don't answer that because I already know the answer and it's no.'

'Things have changed...I've never been in this position before...'

'And there's no need to put a ring on my finger because you *are*...' Jude wondered whether she was being crazy. She loved him! She could think of nothing greater than going to bed with him at night and waking up to him in the morning, and if she were married to him, he might just come to love her after a while. Relationships were things that were built gradually over time, weren't they? Each brick going down making it stronger and more durable.

But what if it didn't work out that way?

The voice of realism stole into her head and swept aside all her romantic illusions. It wasn't an ideal world after all and a man trapped in a marriage soon became a resentful man, even if he had built the trap himself and willingly jumped in. Cesar had grown accustomed to a life of freedom. How long would it take before he wanted that freedom back?

'I know you think you're doing the right thing,' she said gently, 'but my answer has to be no.'

'It isn't just about the child,' he told her roughly. 'I...I still want you...'

'But I may not want *you*...'

'Shall we put that to the test?' He curled his fingers into her hair and pulled her towards him, unleashing all the cravings she had been storing up ever since he had walked out of her house.

Jude shuddered against him as his mouth crushed hers, hot and urgent and demanding.

She was trembling as he swept her off the sofa and carried her to his bedroom. When he laid her on his bed, she began sitting up, gathering the strength to walk away, but her mouth dried as she watched him pull off his clothes, revealing bit by bit that wonderful body that had haunted her dreams.

Yes, he wanted her. Still. The proof was there in front of her eyes and, while this had nothing to do with love, it was so powerful that she gave a little groan of despair. Her feet were dangling off the bed and she still had on the high-heeled pumps, which she now kicked off.

He disposed of her dress in one swift, easy movement and then her tights, which were tossed on the ground to join the chaos of discarded clothes.

When he nuzzled against her lacy bra, Jude whimpered and ran her fingers along his shoulders. She could trace every muscle and sinew. She arched her spine so that her rosebud nipples pushed against the constricting fabric and then closed her eyes as he pulled aside the bra, allowing her breasts to push free.

Already, her breasts were becoming more tender with the pregnancy. Now, the feel of his tongue delicately licking the tautened bud was achingly pleasurable and she wanted it never to stop.

She half opened her eyes, watching that dark arrogant head as he devoted all his attention to teasing her and it was a massive turn-on.

As he continued to lick first one sensitive nipple before moving on to the next, he ran his hand along her body, over her still flat stomach and then down to her matching lacy briefs, where he tantalised her by allowing his fingers to rest there just for a moment before slipping his hand under the cloth so that he could play with her.

Every inch of her body screamed with wanting him to take

her but he was being wonderfully, maddeningly gentle as he continued to suckle on her while teasing her moistness with his fingers.

In a gesture of thrilling intimacy, he slowly made his way downwards and kissed her stomach, fluttery little kisses that had her spellbound, then farther down, he carried on kissing her and finally parting that aching place so that he could drive her crazy with his tongue.

Jude arched up to meet that exploring mouth and writhed against him as the sensations he was unlocking started coming quicker and quicker.

By day she had replayed in her head the harshness of his parting words, using it as a tool for self-protection, but by night this was what she had dreamed of—the slide of his tongue in her, the feel of his hands roaming over her body, possessively claiming it as his own. She had the weird sensation that she was living a dream.

She heard her own disembodied voice crying out his name as he thrust into her, taking her with sure, slow strokes that sent her wild.

It was a while before those waves of pleasure finally peaked and subsided, leaving her spent.

'We're good together,' Cesar murmured. On his side now, he pulled her into him. 'You tell me that you don't want to marry me, but at the bottom of every successful marriage is a foundation of passion, and you can't deny that there's passion between us.'

'I'm not denying it, Cesar.' She placed her hands squarely on his chest and created some distance between them. She was feverishly trying to work out how she had succumbed to him, but she didn't have to look far for the answer. If she hadn't loved him she would have had the strength to be indifferent to his advances. She certainly would have had the strength to have realised that climbing into bed with him was one sure way of undermining her resolve.

They both had the baby to consider and sleeping with Cesar was sure to complicate matters.

'But it doesn't mean that I'm going to marry you for all the wrong reasons.' She spun onto her side and was getting out of the bed when he pulled her back to face him.

'We're not doing this again!' he grated. 'Pretending that nothing happened just then. You're just going to have to wake up to the fact that we enjoy making love.'

'I haven't said that we don't! I'm just saying that it was a mistake.'

'Really? That's not what your body was saying when I was touching it.'

'Cesar, it's not enough and I think I should be going now. I've said what I wanted to say. There's no reason why we have to meet again, at least not until it's closer to the date and then we can discuss everything in more detail.' She wriggled off the bed and began hunting down her clothes, feeling very exposed.

When she looked over her shoulder, it was to find him propped up on one elbow, watching her.

'You need someone to take care of you.'

'I'm pregnant! I'm not ill!'

'And living in the middle of nowhere isn't very convenient for me.'

'Guess what, Cesar. This isn't about what's convenient for you and what isn't.' Dress now on, she stood up and fished her shoes out from under his trousers.

'You can't get back on your own.' He sprang out of bed and hastily began putting on his clothes.

This had turned out to be one hell of a day. In fact, the past couple of months would go down on record as the most life-changing he had ever experienced. He was finding it more and more difficult to remember the tranquillity of his brief marriage to Marisol. That time almost seemed unreal. Sugary and unreal—nothing like the grittiness of what he had recently been put through.

'Of course I can!'

'I don't intend to disappear until you think it's time to summon me back on the scene!'

'I'm not asking you to disappear!' She turned around to find him standing right behind her. 'But everything's going to be just a matter of routine for the next few months!'

'I will have to break this news to the public at large, including my family in Spain. My *very orthodox* family. What am I supposed to tell them? That I'm going to have a baby but the mother doesn't want anything to do with me?'

'Is that what this is all about? Appealing to convention?'

'There's nothing wrong with convention.'

Cesar was baffled and enraged that, even after making love, even after confessing that she still wanted him as much as he wanted her, she continued to dig her heels in. She wanted a knight in shining armour? Was he not that knight in shining armour, promising her a ring on her finger and a lifetime of ease? She would never have to worry about money, would be able to devote herself solely and entirely to the raising of their child. How many men, confronted with an unplanned pregnancy, would have done as much? It all seemed to make sense to him but yet again he was discovering that nothing made sense where this woman was involved.

Presented with a problem, he'd come up with a solution and a pretty damned good one, but not good enough, apparently.

'Where are you staying?' He shoved on his shoes, minus the

socks because she was already flying to the door when she should have been lying in his arms, still languorous from making love and looking forward to making love all over again.

She gave him the name of her hotel, one which was unfamiliar to him but, judging from the sound of its location, not one in which the mother of his unborn child should be staying and he told her so.

Jude flashed him a look that gave him her answer. From being a block of ice at the wedding, he had now become rampantly over-protective and solicitous and it would have been amusing if it hadn't been so sad. He had probably thought that enticing her back between the sheets would have softened her up, that she would have reconsidered and decided that yes, she was willing to have a marriage of convenience because it was what tradition demanded. As far as he was concerned, they would get married so that the dishonour of having an illegitimate child was avoided and have a sexual relationship until such time as he got tired of her, because lust only had a short lifespan before it faded away into boredom. And then she would stay at home, enjoying all the things that his money could buy her, while he had his discreet affairs. He would respect her as the mother of his child but he would never love her as a woman and as his wife. That was not one of the things he was willing to put on the table.

'Okay, I'll drive you there myself but it's not suitable. I have connections at some of the best hotels in London. I could get you a room at any one of them.'

'I don't want a room at any one of them!'

'Why the hell do you have to be so stubborn?' She was at the door now and, more than anything else, he just wanted to scoop her up and carry her back to his king-sized bed, where he could keep an eye on her because it seemed that the minute she was out of his sight, he lost control of his life. Hadn't that been the case for the past three weeks? Even seeing her earlier at the wedding had unsettled him, had distracted him from the business of his brother getting married. How the hell was he going to face the prospect of her, pregnant with his child, *doing her own thing*?

'I'm stubborn? Honestly, Cesar, you should take a look in the mirror. You're the most stubborn man in the world! You just won't take *no* for an answer!'

'I'm trying to be practical…and you have to be willing to compromise…'

'I *am* compromising. I came and told you, didn't I? I could very well have decided to keep you out of the loop. I *could* have sloped off and had the baby and you would have been none the wiser.'

'That wouldn't be your style, Jude. You're far too honest for that. Besides, where would you have sloped off *to*? And don't you think that Fernando and Imogen would have been a little curious when you started putting on weight? Anyway…I accept that you might want to go away and think about what I have asked…'

'Remember what I said about your stubbornness and in-ability to take *no* for an answer?' But as they walked towards the car she had to smile to herself.

'Believe me, you're only now discovering just how stubborn I can be.' Already Cesar was thinking about the situation and coming up with a fresh strategy. She wasn't prepared to marry him…*yet*…but he would still need to be around. He wasn't going to settle for doing a vanishing act until he got a phone call at three in the morning telling him that he was a father.

Besides…and in the darkness of the car, his eyes slid over to her neat profile…it had been disconcertingly easy to take this bombshell in his stride. Of course, he was a man capable of dealing with pretty much anything that life had to throw at him because, with the exception of health problems, there was nothing that could not be sorted out with a cool head, but he found himself a lot less disturbed by the notion of parenthood than he might have expected.

'Okay—' Cesar raised his shoulders in a gesture that indicated magnanimity in defeat '—for the moment I will accept that you have reservations about my offer. Although,' he couldn't help adding, 'I don't understand why, but I don't want to argue with you. Now is not a time for arguing.'

'No, it's not.' After all the tension of the past couple of days and the past couple of hours, Jude gave in to a moment of wickedness. 'After all, I *am* pregnant, and pregnant women shouldn't argue. Something about stress being bad for the baby…'

Cesar swerved the car over to the pavement and stopped. 'Is that what the doctor told you?'

'Why have you stopped?'

'Because I won't be accused of doing anything that might jeopardise this pregnancy.'

'Cesar, I was joking!' She looked at him, surprised at his reaction. 'Are you trying to tell me that you're *glad* that I'm pregnant?'

'I'm trying to tell you that…you shouldn't stress…' Put on the spot, Cesar was not going to commit himself to saying anything that might be misconstrued. *Glad* was a pretty big word. 'I'm here and I can take anything in my stride.'

'Oh.' Jude couldn't hide her disappointment. He had taken all this a lot better than she had expected, but then he had been put in an unenviable position and maybe, having resigned himself to the inevitable, he *was* now getting used to the idea of having a child. Maybe, just maybe, even *liking* it. But that didn't mean that he was pleased that *she* happened to be the mother. Like he said, he was just taking it all in his stride.

'But if *I* can take this in my stride and accommodate it into my life, then I feel that *you* should be prepared to meet me halfway.' That little word *glad* was still niggling somewhere at the back of his brain, in the same place, in fact, where he had stored away the explosive notion that he had been *missing* something in his life. It was just an unsettling feeling he had had seeing his brother, Imogen and their baby and, unused to dealing with anything less than complete satisfaction with the path he had chosen for himself, he had opted to shelve the feeling rather than deal with it. 'And I mean *literally* halfway.'

'Is this suggestion going to stress me out?' Jude asked lightly.

'No. In fact…' Cesar looked at her with a certain amount of self-satisfaction '…the opposite. It's going to make your life a lot easier and it'll give me peace of mind.' He started the engine and pulled away from the kerb, back on course to her hotel. 'I want you closer to me,' he said. It felt strange to say something like that to a woman but he let it go. These were exceptional circumstances. 'I'm a traditionalist. You know that and you're just going to have to run with it.'

Jude sighed, indulging his arrogance, which was so much part and parcel of the person he was.

'The mother of my child can't be allowed to run wild in the back of beyond, refusing all offers of help from me through sheer pride.'

Given such an array of misconceptions, Jude struggled to find one in particular on which she could latch. *'Run wild?'*

'I can see you know where I'm coming from.' Up ahead was her hotel, which wasn't the run-down one-star Cesar had imagined. In fact, he had to admit that it looked perfectly all right, although nowhere near the standard he was used to. Next to him, Jude seemed to be struggling to say something.

'*Back of beyond?*'

'I give you *snowbound.*'

'*Sheer pride?*'

'You said it. I see we're on the same wavelength here, which is a good thing because…' *you're going to move.* Cesar nearly said it but remembered in time that that phraseology would be like waving a red rag to a bull and right now tact was called for. '…I think it would be an immensely good idea if you move a bit closer to me. I'm not saying central London. I realise you have your work out there, but correct me if I am wrong—you freelance, so you could work from anywhere, right?'

'Yes, but…'

'Thought so. You could easily rent your cottage. Holiday let of some sort. People are always wanting to have weekend breaks in the middle of nowhere, for reasons I, personally, have never understood. So you let your cottage and I buy you somewhere a bit closer, somewhere I can actually get to quickly without having to use the company helicopter. There are some extremely pleasant areas around London that boast accessible road and rail links.'

Jude opened her mouth to inform him of the ease of transport from her cottage in most weather conditions, that she had furnished that cottage from scratch and it was her pride and joy and that he could take a running jump if he thought that he could manoeuvre her into his point of view just because he happened to be something of a dinosaur when it came to this unique situation. Instead, she said faintly, 'You can't just *buy* me a house.'

'Why not?' They were at the hotel and he parked his Bentley and turned toward her.

'Because people don't *do* stuff like that.'

'I thought we'd already established that I'm not like other people. Anyway, you are entitled. What do you look for in a house?'

Jude, who had no intention of accepting any such thing, was nevertheless distracted by the thought of *his* house—all modern flooring, expensive rugs and uncomfortable leather furniture that was designed to be displayed rather than sat on.

'Certainly not anything like yours,' she said and he gave her a disarming grin that sent her pulses racing.

'What's wrong with my apartment?'

'I hate leather furniture. It's too cold in winter and sticks to your legs in summer. And wooden flooring should be authentic. And paintings of lines and circles don't make any sense.'

'Anything else?'

'And don't you miss having a garden? Some small square patch of lawn? Somewhere you can sit in summer with a glass of wine?'

'No. What else do you hate about my apartment?'

'Sorry.' Too late now for an apology, she supposed, but while he seemed so open to criticism, she couldn't help adding, 'It doesn't look *lived in*.' She wondered what his house with his wife had looked like. Had it had a woman's touch? Flowers in vases? Recipe books bought with optimism but destined to sit on shelves in the kitchen unopened? Pictures of family members in frames? 'What was your house like in Spain when you were married?'

Cesar frowned. He hadn't really thought of that before. He had thought about Marisol, had put her in a safe keeping place in his mind, but the house? When he thought of a house, he thought of Jude's house—its casual warmth, the cosy clutter, the log fire burning in the sitting room.

'Big, as a matter of fact.' He should really let her go now, into her hotel, but it was comfortable being in the dark car with her. He rationalised that this was all part of the process of establishing an easier relationship with her. She was no longer just a woman with whom he had had a brief fling and who had caused him to lose a bit of sleep by bruising his ego. She was much more important than that now. He had a *duty* to sit here with her, to talk, to watch those fascinating expressions flit across her face, ambushing all her hopes of ever being mysterious and unreadable.

'I can't remember how many bedrooms…or sitting rooms, for that matter. Lots of marble.'

'Wow. Very grand.' Of course that would be his preferred taste in houses.

'Very grand,' Cesar agreed. 'A present from her parents.'

'Useful parents.' Jude laughed ruefully. 'Although I think I rather like the thought of small and cosy.'

'I know.'

'Anyway,' she said briskly, before his fond trip down memory lane had her bursting into tears, 'I'll be gone now. I feel exhausted.' She yawned as tiredness threatened to overwhelm her. She remembered what he had said about wanting her closer to him but suddenly she felt too weary to reopen the debate. Also, it wouldn't hurt to have just one night to indulge her romantic notions and wallow in the warmth of him telling her that he wanted to marry her, wanted her *as his wife*, that, failing that, he wanted her close to him. She would leave reality out of it and just pick the bits and pieces of his conversation that she wanted to hear. What was the harm in that? She would call him in the morning and tell him that having a house bought for her was entirely out of the question and he would have to play by *her* rules.

* * *

Three days later and Jude was still trying to get through to Cesar, who was, according to his secretary, out of the office closing a deal. Nor was he attainable on his mobile, which really brought home to her once and for all that her fragile, spun glass, you're-the-mother-of-my-child status was a figment of her imagination. All that mattered to Cesar was his work. It took priority over everything. As she was sitting in front of her bowl of cereal, idly thinking about what she had to do but mostly rehearsing what she would say to Cesar when she finally managed to get hold of him, she was jolted out of her thoughts by the sharp sound of her doorbell.

She opened the door with her cup of tea in her hand and there he was, materialising yet again out of thin air and making her wonder whether it was physically possible to summon someone up just by thinking very hard about them.

Jude's treacherous heart skipped a beat. At seven-thirty in the morning he looked gut-wrenchingly handsome and she scowled, remembering her frustrated efforts to get through to him.

'What are you doing here?' she demanded. 'I've been trying to get hold of you!'

'Is that *all* you ever wear?' Cesar eyed the shapeless dungarees with gleaming eyes.

'Where *were* you?' Jude repeated in a shrill voice.

'Important stuff. You'll have to go and get changed into something more…less utilitarian.'

'Why? I'm not going anywhere with you!'

'And forget about being stubborn. There's something you need to see.'

CHAPTER NINE

'Is THIS the deal I was told you were working on?'

They had just finished walking around the house which Cesar had threatened to buy and which Jude had spent the past three days deciding against, with her refusal becoming more eloquent in her head the longer she had tried to reach him by phone and failed.

It had taken them less than an hour to make it to the small hamlet on the outskirts of London, during which time he had pointedly refused to tell her the reason for his sudden urgency to take her out, instead keeping the conversation light. Every time she had tried to bring the subject back to the speech she had rehearsed, he had danced round her remarks and told her that he would talk seriously once they were out of the car and he could concentrate fully on what she was saying. As if he ever had the slightest difficulty in multi-tasking.

And now here they were.

He had clearly paid a great deal of attention to every word she had said about his apartment because there was an ostensible absence of anything modern in the house, although Jude could tell at a glance that everything was of a superbly high standard. The country-style kitchen with its small green Aga and the four-poster bed with its patchwork quilt—exquisite and no expense spared.

'This is the deal I was working on,' Cesar agreed, his dark eyes raking intently over her face. He had had to move at the speed of light but, with a bottomless pit of money at his disposal, Cesar had had no trouble in locating the ideal house in the ideal village which was within ideal driving distance of both his work and his apartment.

'Just look around before you say anything,' he had told her the minute he had seen the protestations rising to her lips. 'If you don't like the idea then I'll respect your decision.' He had banked on the house doing his work for him by wooing her and, although he wasn't certain of success, he was sure he had a better chance of her agreeing to this concession than he had three days ago when she had turned down his marriage proposal flat.

She had made all the right noises at the small, attractive mature garden with its own little orchard with apple and plum trees, had paused to admire the rough old beams in the house, the open fireplace with the date engraved on the mantelpiece and its border of original Victorian tiles, had run her hands over the Aga, which kept the place beautifully warm, and had admitted to him in the bedroom that she had always wanted a four-poster bed.

Cesar could feel triumph vibrating in the air between them. 'Well,' he asked pleasantly, 'what do you think of it? Do you like it?'

'Who wouldn't?'

They had retired to the kitchen and were now facing one another across the pine table, in the centre of which was a vase of wild flowers.

'It's the right distance from central London,' Cesar said,

working his sales pitch carefully because experience had taught him that one errant word would have her scuttling into defence mode. He still couldn't quite grasp why and how she could have seen his marriage proposal as some sort of insult. He had offered her the highest prize and she had rejected it but there was nothing to be gained from dwelling on that. 'And it's a commutable distance from where you are now. You could easily make it back if you need to for work purposes, or to visit friends…'

Temptation dangled in front of her eyes. Cesar didn't love her but he was driven to take care of her because she was carrying his baby. Of course, she would never, ever marry him for all the reasons she had told herself over and over again, but it was kind of comforting to know that he could be *right there* should she ever have the need to call on him and *right there* when their child was born and he wanted to visit.

'I could buy the house today,' he said, his dark velvety voice seducing her. 'The owners have moved to the Far East and they're willing to sell the furniture or what bits of it you might want… You could move in by the end of next week…' He allowed that cosy image to form in her head.

'We haven't even *discussed* this!' Jude objected. 'It's crazy for you to think that you can just go and find me somewhere else to live because it suits you, without even bothering to consult me!'

'Would you have agreed to go on a house hunt with me?'

'Maybe not but that's not the point.'

'Of course it's the point. You would keep putting obstacles in the way and making life as difficult as you possibly could for me. I made a managerial decision and chose the option that would suit us both.'

'I'm not one of your employees, Cesar! Someone you can boss around and give orders to!'

'I wouldn't consider buying a house for any of my employees. Now you've seen this place, tell me what you don't like about it.'

'It's not about *the house*. Of course I like the house! I've already told you so. It's about the *presumption*.'

'You mean the presumption that I might want a situation that works in some small measure for me as well as for you. So you like the house, it's in a brilliant location. So your real objection is that you wanted to have the opportunity to dig your heels in and exercise your right of refusal. You are carrying my baby and now that you have that leverage to blackmail, you intend to use it to the fullest. Is that it?'

'Of course it isn't.' Jude gave him a sulky look because, put like that, he somehow made her sound petty.

'And I don't *dig my heels in*,' she continued and Cesar raised his eyebrows in blatant incredulity. 'There's a difference between *digging your heels in* and *having an opinion*,' she carried on, her mouth downturned.

'Give me a concrete objection, Jude, and spare me the postulating.'

'I have heaps of stuff in my cottage…'

'Transporting whatever you wanted to bring could be done in the snap of a finger…'

'But moving house is a really big deal. Anyway, I can't let you *buy* this for me…'

'Could you let me buy it for my child?' Cesar shrugged because the whole matter of finance was immaterial to him. The cost of the house was an infinitesimal drop in the ocean for him. 'If you like, the house can remain in my name, held in trust for our child. These small concerns barely matter.'

Jude heard the sound of arguments forming in her head and being washed away by the ebb and flow of Cesar's logic and determination.

And her own clawing love for him was undermining all her objections. She liked the sound of his familiar drawl, thrilled to the prospect of knowing that he was within easy reach, was guiltily aware that she really craved the thought of being the sole focus of his attentiveness at least for a few months, even though the short-term fix would probably do even more long-term damage to her mental state.

'Well…' She drew the syllable out and Cesar knew that he had won. She would move in. He was surprised at how relieved he felt at that thought.

'I still don't much like the idea of accepting this…' Jude felt obliged to point out because she wasn't about to be brow-beaten on all fronts '…but I guess I can compromise and then, when the baby's born, we can take it from there…'

'Whatever you say.'

In actual fact, it was a little over a fortnight later when Jude moved her final set of project designs into the house and during that time she had found it hard to cling onto her picture of Cesar as the arrogant man who only wanted her because of an accident of circumstance, a man who would just as soon set her up as his wife as he would leave her to her own devices the minute he got bored of her appeal.

She had to constantly remind herself that the voice which had guided her away from accepting something that should never be offered without love was the voice that should be heeded, because Cesar was on the charm offensive. He phoned her, helped her sort out the rental of her cottage, single-handedly made sure that every stick she wanted to take with her was duly transported. She had no idea what havoc this was wreaking with his precious work life but when she tried to ask he waved aside her questions as though they were an irrelevance. In the end, Jude gave up. She accepted his presence and kept to herself just how pleasurable she found it being in his company, especially like this, when they weren't arguing.

They also weren't in any way *touching*.

He greeted her with a careful peck on the cheek and said goodbye in the same way. It made Jude feel like an inanimate object, one which he was duty-bound to protect, though not so treasured that he was inclined to caress.

He had pressed the fast forward button on the physical attraction part of their relationship and arrived at that place which she had foreseen slightly further down the line. Instead of feeling more justified in knowing that she had done the right thing in turning him down, she just felt horribly hollow and empty.

A week after she'd moved in, she gave in to the perverse desire to put this to the test.

Cesar had phoned her earlier in the day and told her that he would be taking her out to dinner. Dinner with Cesar invariably involved a very expensive restaurant. Making do with what happened to be lying about in the kitchen was no more than a fond memory of two days snatched in her cottage when a lack of choice had seen him play at domesticity.

He showed up at the house promptly at seven. He must have quit work at a ridiculous hour, especially considering it was Friday, the day before the rest of the world rested, when he was inclined to work long into the night on anything that couldn't survive a weekend break. He was, tellingly, no longer in his work gear. The weather had improved steadily over the weeks and he was in a pair of jeans that lovingly moulded his muscular legs and a navy-blue jumper, the cost of which was only apparent in the very small logo on one side.

'I've decided to cook something,' Jude said, leading him through to the sitting room, into which she had brought all her mementoes from the cottage, but retained the furniture that had been left there.

'I can smell it. Why?'

'Don't you ever get tired of eating out?'

'It's a lifestyle that's grown on me over the years. Have you seen my brother recently? He is beginning to look like a married man.'

This was the Cesar he had become, someone who could charmingly talk about anything and everything, but without the passion that had driven him in their past fraught encounters. Over the meal she had prepared, he chatted amicably about Freddy and the jazz club, which was due for its big opening night in three months. Already the signs were that it wouldn't take long to break even and then would prove to have been a profitable investment.

Cesar, typically, was not averse to some self-promotion on this front but laughed when she gave him a knowing look from under her lashes.

'Okay!' He raised his hands in mock surrender. 'You can't shoot a guy for trying.'

Jude started to clear the table and said casually, 'Do you think that I'm beginning to look fat?' She offered her profile for his inspection, knowing that her bump was there but still small, although her breasts had grown.

After his sarcastic remark about her very practical dungarees, she had put them aside for a while and was in a pair of black fitted trousers and a black long-sleeved jersey top with tiny buttons halfway down the front.

She was also not wearing a bra, having grown out of her old ones but not wanting to commit to unnecessary expenditure when she might well get bigger.

Cesar drew in his breath sharply.

The past few weeks had seen him taking his time with her, behaving in a manner that was alien to him when it came to women, particularly considering he had slept with this woman and she still haunted his mind, tantalising him with the memory of her body, which was filling out now, her breasts enlarging, her once flat stomach showing signs of the baby she was carrying.

But she didn't want him, or at least not enough, and he wasn't going to rock the boat by throwing her back on the defensive. Knowing that she would probably involuntarily respond to him if he touched her was worthless knowledge. He wanted her mind to respond as well as her body because her mind would not want to sweep the physical attraction between them under the carpet where it could lie out of sight and out of mind.

'A pregnant woman cannot be classified as fat,' he said neutrally. Of course he knew that she wasn't wearing a bra. He had known it the minute he had stepped through the door. It was also pretty obvious that her breasts had expanded as well. They would now be a full handful. And her nipples, he guessed, would also have swelled with the pregnancy, swelled and darkened. He didn't want to look at that sideways view being innocently offered for his inspection, he didn't want to see the outline of those nipples with their little firm buds pressing against the fabric of her top.

'I feel fat,' Jude said lightly, running her hands over her stomach. 'I think it's because I've always been so skinny and everywhere's bigger now. Not just my stomach.'

Cesar, invited to see what those other bits were, reluctantly looked at her breasts. 'To be expected.' He was surprised to hear his voice sounding so normal. 'I guess you'll have to start investing in bigger clothes. It goes without saying that any purchases will be put on the credit card I gave you.'

Jude sighed with a mixture of frustration and resignation. Point proved. If she ripped off her clothes now he would probably warn her about the dangers of catching cold in her fragile state. Had he even noticed that she had dumped the bra?

'Have you used that card *at all*?' Cesar took refuge in the sheer boredom of talking about spending and credit cards. If she only knew the effect she had on him, she would run a mile.

'Of course I haven't!' Jude snapped. The house came with a dishwasher but she preferred the cathartic process of washing the dishes herself, which she now began to do with great vigour. 'I *am* still working, still earning my own money and, in fact, in a month's time I'll be getting a rental income from the cottage so my finances are looking healthy. No need to dip into the vast Caretti reserves just yet!'

'You throw that in my face as though it's an insult to have it at your disposal!'

Jude could think of something else that was a lot more insulting, namely the way he had politely looked at her body and told her that weight gain was *to be expected*. It was the sort of thing her doctor might tell her before giving her a lecture on making sure to eat well and avoid alcohol.

She did quite like the idea of arguing with him because an argument would mean *heat* and *passion* of a sort, but pregnancy had mellowed her, so instead she made her peace and carried on making her peace for the remainder of the evening, which was pleasantly spent until he was ready to leave at a little after eleven.

He was going to be away for a few days from next Monday, he told her as he lounged against the door frame on his way out. Would she be able to manage?

'Of course I'll be able to manage,' Jude told him irritably. 'I keep telling you that you don't have to watch over me like a mother hen.'

'Great comparison. Guaranteed to make a man feel so virile.'

'I don't have to tell you that you're virile,' she said even more irritably. 'You know you are.'

'Oh, yes. So I am.' He reached out and touched her stomach, keeping his hand flat on the small mound, then rubbing it gently, which sent shivers of inappropriate excitement racing up and down her spine. She wondered what he would do if she grabbed his hand and pushed it under her T-shirt.

'I've bought one of those pregnancy books,' he admitted, removing his hand and sticking it into the pocket of his trousers.

'You've *bought a pregnancy book*?' Jude laughed. 'You never said. Is it your bedtime reading? I thought you went to bed with important reports and your laptop computer!'

'I've only dipped into it,' Cesar told her gruffly. 'And I would seriously advise you against reading one of those things. They're full of horror stories.'

'That's probably because you're squeamish.' Jude was still laughing at the thought of this big, dominant male reading a pregnancy manual and feeling queasy.

'You're talking to one of the least squeamish men to walk the earth. I am also incredibly robust, never a day's illness.'

'That's because you're so bossy that germs can't be bothered to attack you.'

'Things are good between us, aren't they, Jude? Admit it. We can talk like this, laugh… Tell me why you find it so damned difficult to commit to me! *I* was supposed to be the commitment-phobe.'

'Don't spoil the night, Cesar.'

And, besides…what was he committing to? Fulfilling his obligations as a prospective parent? Being a superb financial provider? Having an amicable relationship with her, one in which they would be able to behave in a civilised fashion for the sake of the child?

He would see all that as the greatest sacrifice but he didn't love her and from all appearances was no longer even physically attracted to her, which meant that he could throw out that word *commitment* as much as he liked. In the end it all amounted to him wanting to put in place a marriage of convenience because it suited him. The most dangerous mistake she could ever make would be to think that there wasn't a fist of steel within the velvet glove.

Cesar reined in his patience with difficulty.

'No. No, I wouldn't want to do that,' he said curtly. He looked away, then back down at her. 'You have all my numbers. Call me, okay?'

Jude had no intention of calling Cesar. She could recognise that there was a thin line between what she saw as making the best of her situation and digging a hole for herself. It could become far too easy to develop a dependency on a Cesar who was pushing the boat out with his friendly charm.

In fact, she looked forward to having some time to herself. She would really focus on her work; there were a couple of projects which needed to be completed. She would also visit Freddy and Imogen and remind herself of what a union between two people should be like because she couldn't afford to be lulled into thinking that what she and Cesar shared was a viable basis for anything more than a couple who would be sharing the upbringing of a child.

What Jude hadn't expected was to return to the house the following Thursday afternoon and have to deal with the unthinkable, the one thing which neither she nor Cesar had factored into the equation.

It was only a couple of spots of blood but at that point in time the bottom seemed to drop out of her world.

Outside, it was a glorious day. She had enjoyed her meeting with the young couple who had been impressed with her designs and she had driven back to the house in an upbeat mood, already looking forward to the distraction of loads of work after the baby was born, which would keep her mind preoccupied. She had concluded that a preoccupied mind was a sure-fire remedy to the daunting prospect of dealing with Cesar.

She could feel the slow swell of panic rising inside her like a destructive tide.

Should she remain where she was? Sit very still and hope that the bleeding stopped? She tried to remember what she had read about unexpected bleeding during pregnancy but her thoughts were all over the place. She was scared to check and terrified by the sickening possibility that she might lose the baby.

And she didn't want to call Cesar.

Her words were stumbling over one another when she eventually mustered all her courage and phoned her doctor. It was probably nothing to worry about, he said…*nothing to worry about!*…but, to be on the safe side, she should go to the hospital…he would phone ahead so that they knew to expect her… *Safe side? Hospital?*

Every word sounded like a death knell to the child growing inside her.

Jude wasn't sure how she managed to have sufficient wits

about her to call a taxi to take her to the hospital, or how she managed to circumnavigate the endless signposted corridors leading to the hundreds of different specialised wards, arriving at the right one, and all this done without breaking down and sobbing.

At some point during the anxious, convoluted journey, she had phoned Imogen and told her what was happening but keeping it light and repeating the doctor's refrain, not a single word of which she actually believed.

'No need to worry Cesar,' she said. 'He's only just back in the country. Very busy. Silly to get him worried for nothing…'

She had given herself stern lectures, had done her damnedest to protect herself from the heartache of being with the man she loved who did not return her love, had laid down the ground rules for dealing with his presence in her life for years to come. She had envisaged a time when he might tell her that he was involved with someone else, had fallen in love against all odds, had finally put the ghost of his wife to rest because he had met someone to whom he was willing to give his heart. And that, unlike all those conveniences the vast reserves of Caretti money could buy, was priceless.

All told, she had recreated a thousand scenarios in her head and all of them had been based on the assumption that they would be sharing a child.

She hadn't imagined a future *without* Cesar's child. She was young, her pregnancy had been straightforward. Not once had she worried about the technicalities of her body doing what it was supposed to do and taking this pregnancy to full term.

Now she was having to contemplate another future and it was one in which Cesar would have nothing to do with her because there would be no need, no duty to fulfil. He wouldn't need to be friendly, witty, attentive. He wouldn't want to have her in a house that was conveniently located so that he could have quick access to her.

True to his word, her doctor had telephoned the hospital in advance of her arrival and she was shown immediately to a bed in the maternity unit to await a scan.

As before, the usual soothing platitudes were rolled out. Jude nodded and pretended to believe them.

She underwent an examination, ignored what her consultant said about not worrying and was taken to have an ultrasound scan.

She wished that Cesar was with her. Then she imagined his face if everything started going wrong and realised that it was a blessing that he wasn't. For the first time it was brought home to her with remorseless clarity just how fragile their relationship was and just how weak she had been in allowing him to take over her life.

Her heart was beating like a hammer as she lay on the narrow bed in the darkened scan room and watched the monitor as the sonographer studied her baby. She was mesmerised by the detail she could see moving. Everything, she was told soothingly, was fine.

Jude realised that nothing was fine. This scare had been gifted to her as a learning curve. She had become complacent. She had fallen victim to her own fanciful notions. What was the point in giving yourself stern lectures and then going out and doing just the opposite? She had allowed herself to set up home in a bubble, won over by a few smiles and kindly gestures.

Besides, the doctors said that everything looked fine. They had also told her that she needed complete bed rest and had been vague when quizzed about worst-case scenarios, telling her that she shouldn't fill her head with nonsense but that she should just take it easy.

With her imagination now doing a merry jig in her head, however, Jude was managing to convince herself that the baby she was so desperate to have, the baby she had foolishly taken for granted, was a vulnerable life held in the balance, its future out of her control.

Changes would have to be made. What she and Cesar shared was a business arrangement and she had stupidly allowed herself to forget that.

Put aside the rose-tinted specs for a minute, she thought relentlessly, and what did she see? Someone keeping her sweet for the time being because it suited him.

What had he been doing, for instance, while he had been away? Cesar Caretti wasn't the average male. He was the stupendously sexy, immensely rich and powerful head of an empire. A man who was well aware of his sex appeal and had never dated anyone who hadn't resembled a model from a glossy magazine. In fact, he had probably dated a fair few *models from glossy magazines*. So was it really likely that he had been to New York and contented himself with business dinners and work? With no play on the side? Especially when he was no longer interested in *her* from a sexual point of view?

Unanswered questions grew in her head, proliferating and twisting themselves around her mind like ivy.

Of course, she would have to see him some time, probably when she was released from the hospital, where she had been advised to stay overnight so that they could monitor her vitals. The bleeding had stopped and, while her level of panic was now receding, her head seemed to have cleared.

She was feeling quite pleased with herself when she finally drifted off to sleep to the sound of trolleys being wheeled outside the little room into which she had been put.

She woke up to the sound of someone in her room, the

quiet pad of footsteps and then the scraping of a chair as it was pulled close to the bed.

Jude knew who it was without opening her eyes. It seemed that something about Cesar could send her antennae onto full alert even when she wasn't actually looking at him.

'How did you know I was here?' She reluctantly opened her eyes and was startled to find him sitting closer to her than she had thought.

'Imogen told me. Why the hell didn't you call me yourself?'

'I didn't see the need.'

Cesar controlled the temptation to explode. He had already had a word with her consultant and been told that everything appeared to be fine but that she should take it easy, at least for the next few weeks. Shouting was just going to stress her out.

'You didn't see the need.'

'No. And Imogen shouldn't have called you. In fact, I asked her not to. You've been away and the last thing I wanted was for you to rush here when you probably had work commitments.' She kept her voice as businesslike as possible. 'It was just a scare, as a matter of fact.'

'I think I have a right to know when you have *a scare*.'

Before, she thought bitterly, she would have subconsciously construed that as a thoughtful gesture that included *her*. It would have given her a warm, tingly feeling and she might have smiled at him and confided how worried she had been. She might even, depending on how much that warm, tingly feeling was, have mentioned that she was glad to see him. He would have taken her back to the house and used that gentle, concerned, friendly voice on her and she would have deluded herself into thinking that she meant something more important than just an incubator for his child. Not now.

'Hopefully, there won't be another,' she said politely and Cesar frowned at her.

'What's the matter?'

'What do you mean?'

'When I left you, you were sunny and upbeat. Is this change of mood because you're worried? The consultant said that there's no need to worry. Actually, the last thing you want to do is get stressed out.'

Because stress might affect the baby. I couldn't give a damn about your welfare!

'Of course.'

'You have to rest. No more working round the clock on fool projects. From now on, you'll put your feet up and listen to what the consultant said. I'll get a housekeeper in. Someone to cook, clean and run whatever errands you want her to run. There'll be no need for you to lift a finger.'

'They're not fool projects.'

'You'll do as I say,' Cesar grated. There was no point pussy-footing round her sensibilities. 'Your good health is the baby's good health, it's as simple as that.' He didn't know what kind of mood she was in but he wasn't best pleased with it. He had rushed to the hospital, worried out of his mind, and that cool voice of hers was getting on his nerves.

Simple as that. It always had been.

'Don't even think about telling me that you can do without a housekeeper,' he said, forestalling any possible idiot objection to this particular ground rule.

'I wasn't. I'm not stupid, Cesar. I realise that I'll need help around the house and I won't be driving out for any more of my *fool projects*, as you call them. At least not for the moment.' She remembered when Imogen had been rushed into hospital. The stricken look on Freddy's face when she'd seen him. That look had been all about love. In that moment she had known that he would have given up everything for Imogen, would have done anything for her.

Cesar's worry was reserved solely for the child she was carrying.

'I'm tired now,' she told him abruptly. 'It's been a long day and I want to go back to sleep.'

'You'll need some clothes.'

Jude hadn't given that a moment's thought. She was still in the hospital gown they had provided. She shrugged and nodded.

'Tell me what you want and I'll bring them.'

'There's really no need to trouble yourself, Cesar. Your driver can fetch what I need.' She stifled a yawn.

'Don't be absurd.' Cesar thought of his driver rifling through her underwear and he scowled with distaste. It was worse than unacceptable. It was obscene. 'I'll get what you need and I'll make sure that a housekeeper is in place by the time you get back to the house. In fact, I'll get my secretary working on that immediately.' He flipped open his cellphone and Jude listened as he gave orders. Orders that would be obeyed without question and handled with a level of efficiency that a high salary guaranteed. His voice was crisp, the voice of a man who knew that when he gave orders, they were obeyed. His secretary was *paid* to obey them.

He had used different tactics on her, though, but the net result was the same. He had given his orders, orders cloaked with smiles and concern, and she had obeyed them. She had even been paid, in a manner of speaking, because where was she living? In a house he had chosen in an area he had picked for reasons that suited him. The only fly he had found in the ointment had been her refusal to marry him, which would have legitimised his baby, but in every other respect he had persuaded her into the corner he had wanted and she had put up very little resistance.

But that scare had reminded her that she was essentially disposable and it was time she sat up and took notice of the fact before she found herself carried too far downstream on the current to ever get back to safe shores.

CHAPTER TEN

I've been doing some thinking…

Jude was back at the house and Cesar was on his way. The housekeeper had been employed in record time, had already cleaned the house for Jude's return and had now been dispatched to the supermarket with a list of food items to buy. This so that the house could be empty when Cesar arrived.

She looked in the mirror and carried on with the speech she had rehearsed. She'd been doing some thinking and, first of all, wanted to make sure that the correct documents were signed so that the house which he had bought was in his name. That would establish the tenor of the conversation straight away.

Thereafter, it would be easier to maintain a grip on her emotions, especially when she moved onto the thornier subject of the personal boundaries which needed to exist between them. Of course he would tell her that no boundaries had been crossed, that they were conducting a civilised, adult and perfectly amicable relationship because it would make things easier when it came to jointly caring for their child. She had her answer to that one all worked out. Dinners out went beyond *being friendly* and she wouldn't be put in a position of being *under his thumb*, a single woman to all intents and purposes but one with her life controlled by him. She would raise the issue of what would happen when one of them found a partner, someone meaningful with whom to share their life. Basically, she would let him know, in not so many words, that he was a bystander in her life when it came to her emotions.

Looking at her reflection as she applied some mascara, she wondered what this fictional character, destined to appear at some point on the horizon, would be like. Would she even recognise him as a possibility when her head was so full of Cesar? Even if he was carrying a placard which said *Look No Further, I'm The Man Of Your Dreams*? No one seemed to match up to Cesar. He was so much larger than life that, alongside him, all other men faded into the background. He had burst into her life and had dominated it and she had swooned and fallen in love like a tragic heroine from a Victorian novel.

She made a little grimace at herself and then walked through to the sitting room. From the sofa, she could look out onto the back garden and right now it was bathed in sunshine.

She heard the front door open and knew it was Cesar before he stepped into the sitting room. Those wretched antennae again! Gorgeous, sexy, incredible Cesar in a pair of cream trousers and a rugby shirt which, he'd explained to her some time in a past that now seemed like another lifetime, was a leftover from his university days when he'd been captain of the rugby team.

Jude felt her heart give its usual little flip.

'Obeying doctor's orders,' he said approvingly. 'Good.' He sat down on the chair facing her and crossed his legs. She'd told him to come at four and he'd spent the last three hours edgily aware that he was looking at his watch way too often

and wondering why she had told him a specific time when
before she had been happy enough for him to pole over
whenever he felt like it.

'How are you feeling?'

'Fine. Thank you.'

Fine? Thank you? That same politeness fringed with just
a touch of frost. Or was that just his imagination playing
tricks on him?

'And the housekeeper? Working out all right? Where is
she, anyway?'

'Annie's working out fine and she's at the supermarket right
now. I asked her to go because…I really think we need to talk…'

Cesar had no trouble in recognising that tone of voice. He
had used it himself in the past, usually on women whose role
in his life had gone beyond their sell-by date. Then he would
take them out for an expensive meal and over liqueurs would
tell them that they *needed to talk*…

'Talk on.'

Jude noticed that the easy smile had left his face. In its
place was that shuttered expression which had once chilled
her to the bone. 'I…I did a lot of thinking yesterday, Cesar.
When I thought that…well, when I thought the worst…and I
realise that we really need to sort out one or two details…'
She cleared her throat and waited for him to say something.

'What details?' Cesar eventually asked.

'This house, for instance.'

'Is in my name. As you asked.'

'Good.' His dark, watchful eyes were unsettling, making
her stumble over the brisk, no nonsense tone she had planned
on using. 'And…and we need to discuss what happens if and
when either of us meets someone else.'

'Are you telling me that there's someone else?'

'Of course not! Look at me, Cesar. I'm pregnant!'

Of course there wasn't anyone else. It had been a ridiculous question but he had found himself asking it anyway.

'But there might be. One day. Just as there might be for you.' She half hoped that he would deny such a preposterous thing but naturally no such denial was forthcoming and why should it be? He had offered her marriage, had told her that she was eligible for money, as if she were an employee who was worthy of a pay rise after a satisfactory probationary period. He had never said anything about fidelity. She gave voice to something that was only now occurring to her.

'Why did you ask me to marry you, Cesar?'

'Not this again!'

'I know you're a traditionalist. I know you don't like the thought of having a baby born out of wedlock. But was it also because you didn't want any other man on the scene? Muddying the waters with the upbringing of your child?'

'That thought never crossed my mind!' But Cesar flushed. Had it crossed his mind? Even subconsciously? Was that why he felt more comfortable with her living closer to him? Because he could keep an eye on her? He didn't like the thought of being possessive. He had never been a possessive man. Indeed, had never felt the need to know the whereabouts of any of the women he had dated in the past, although he had always known that none of them would have thought about straying. Even with Marisol…yes, he had been protective. She had been very feminine and very helpless, had needed his protection…but possessive?

'Where is this going?' he asked harshly. 'Have I not complied with every request you've made?' She had been fine a few days previously. What had changed?

Jude saw that dark flush that had stained his high, aristocratic cheekbones when she had asked him about his reasons
for proposing to her and knew, with a sinking heart, that she
had hit a tender nerve. He would tether her to him, would
make it impossible for her to ever find anyone else because
he would have no other man interfere in his child's life. It was
a game played by his rules and only his rules.

'I'm laying down a few ground rules,' she told him steadily.
'I thought that I was going to lose the baby. In fact, right now
I'm taking nothing for granted.'

'Has the consultant said anything to you that he kept
from me?' Cesar demanded, frowning. 'If he has, there will
be hell to pay!'

'This doesn't have anything to do with the baby.' Jude
looked away. She didn't want to see his expression close over.
'This has to do with me. Actually, with *us*.'

'If we're talking about *us*, I thought we were getting along
just fine until I came back to England to discover a black cloud
hanging over you.'

'We *are* getting along just fine,' Jude told him. 'But I think
it's important to remember that we're not *friends*. We're two
people who made a mistake by sleeping together and getting
more than either of us bargained for. Let's not forget that we
wouldn't, actually, be here having any sort of conversation if
I hadn't discovered that I was pregnant. I appreciate all that
you've done…'

'Will you stop talking to me as though I'm a stranger!'

'And stop shouting at me in my own house!'

'But it's *not* your own house, is it?'

There was a tense, electric silence and then Jude said
slowly, the colour draining from her face, 'Is that it, Cesar?
Your house and therefore I have to abide by your rules? Toe

the line because you've paid for the roof over my head? The roof, incidentally, that I don't remember *asking* for?'

'This is ridiculous!' Cesar said fiercely.

'No, it's not!' She thought of his trip to swinging New York. 'Okay, here's a question. How would you feel if I *did* meet someone down the line—someone I wanted to play a big part in my life? Someone who would inevitably come into contact with our child? Have an influence over him or her? Would that be all right with you? Or would I have to abide by *your* rules so long as I'm living in a house *you* paid for?'

Cesar dearly wanted to inform her that *she* could do as she damn well wanted to do, just so long as *his* child was kept out of it, but images of her with another man made him clench his jaw in fury.

'Don't worry about answering that, Cesar. I know the answer from your silence. You…you think you can do whatever you want while I stay in the house you paid for doing motherly things!'

'Do whatever I want?'

Jude realised that somewhere along the line her cool, calm, mature speech had gone down the pan. Now, she felt like bursting into tears.

'I mean, what did you get up to in New York?' she was appalled to hear herself ask, especially when he was looking at her as though she had taken leave of her senses. 'Not that I care. I'm just saying that to *prove a point*. You are free to do whatever you want, and I expect to be free to do whatever *I* want as well.'

'So let me get this straight,' Cesar said tightly. 'If I told you that I went to New York, met up with an old flame and spent three very sexy nights with her, you wouldn't be bothered.'

'Did you?'

'At the risk of flying in the face of all your preconceptions, no, I didn't.'

'That's not to say that you won't some time in the future,' Jude goaded him, relieved to death by what he had said but already bleakly contemplating a time when his answer would be different and hating herself for knowing that she would always care enough to ask and to be hurt.

'And, of course, if I did, you wouldn't try to stop me.'

'What would be the point? You're a free man, Cesar. Even if we got married, you would still be a free man and there'd be nothing I could ever do to hold you back.'

Cesar thought that once he had been a free man and any hint of a woman trying to tame him would have signalled the immediate end to a relationship. But did a free man lose track of work because his mind was too taken up with one very stubborn, very frustrating woman with short dark hair and a line of conversation that had absolutely no respect for his barriers? And did a free man count the hours until he could see the one woman who consumed his every waking moment? He found it hard to remember when he had last been a free man.

Now she was talking about Marisol, telling him what might have been true once upon a time. He held up one hand, cutting her off in mid-rant and waited until she had subsided into silence.

'Everything you're telling me is true,' he admitted roughly, leaning forward, elbows on his knees. He ran his fingers through his hair, a gesture with which Jude had become so familiar that it brought a lump to her throat.

'I loved Marisol. Hell, we were so young and had so little time together. Too little time to really find out each other's faults and yes, I put her on a pedestal.' His coal-black eyes tangled with hers.

Jude wanted to put her hand over his beautiful mouth

because she didn't want him confirming everything she had just said. She realised that in all her mentally rehearsed speeches, he had largely been a silent listener.

'She was…compliant, soft, subservient…'

'I know. I think you've told me this before. She was everything I'm not.'

Cesar nodded in confirmation. 'Which makes me wonder whether we were ever really suited.'

'What?' She raised her head and focused her wide brown eyes on his face.

He felt a giddy, strange sensation, as though he were standing on the edge of an abyss, looking down.

'I always thought that sweet and subservient was what I wanted until I met a headstrong, mouthy, argumentative woman who had the nerve to question everything I did and said and thought.'

Jude found that she was holding her breath, wondering whether she was hearing properly, but the expression on his face told her that she was. He looked oddly vulnerable. It wasn't an expression she had ever seen before. She wanted to reach out and go across to him, sit on his lap, stroke his face, but she also didn't want the spell to end.

'When I left your cottage, I really thought that I could return to London, that my life would pick up where it had left off. I was accustomed to women being transient. Sure, my ego was hurting because you'd sent me on my bike when I wanted to prolong what we had, but I told myself that it was for the best. Thing is, I couldn't get you out of my mind.'

'You couldn't?'

Cesar shook his head wryly.

'That's probably because…you know…the sex thing… wanting the one thing you thought you couldn't have…'

'Are you fishing, by any chance?'

Jude grinned reluctantly at him. 'Sort of.'

'Fishing for what?'

She shrugged and watched as he covered the distance separating them, until he was sitting on the sofa by her so that she was squashed to one side to accommodate his big body. Very happily squashed because she had missed him being close to her, feeling the warmth of his body. He was so vibrant, so *aggressively alive* and he made her feel the same. Without him, she was a shadow, lacking definition.

'It's not the sex thing. In fact, it's nothing to do with sex. Sure, when I think about you, I feel horny, but I also feel…incomplete. I guess what I'm trying to say is that I love you. I can't think of you with any other man and it's got nothing to do with wanting to protect my kid from someone else's influence. It's got to do with something a hell of a lot more primitive than that. I think it's called jealousy.'

'You're *jealous*!' She smiled a wide sunny smile and took one of his hands in hers, liking the way he played with her fingers.

'I think it's a side effect of being in love.'

'And I love you, too.'

'If you love me, why won't you make an honest man of me and marry me?'

'I was waiting, Cesar, for you to say the right words and now you have. I'll marry you whenever you want me to.'

They were married six weeks later in a very small, very intimate ceremony with just family and close friends. By this time Jude was back on her feet, although all work commitments that involved her driving were put on hold.

Like Imogen, there was no honeymoon and, like Imogen, Jude didn't mind in the slightest. She was so happy that she wouldn't have minded if she never left the country. She was content to be wherever Cesar was, even if that meant staying put in her little house with him, eating meals in and looking after the garden, for he had moved out of his apartment. She no longer recognised him for the workaholic she had first met and he had even been making noises about moving farther away from London when the time was right. For a man who had once considered Kent the back of beyond, this was a big step.

After what turned out to be an uneventful pregnancy, Olivia Caretti was born on a bright, sunny afternoon and seemed determined to compensate for all the stress that had surrounded her conception by coming into the world with very little fuss.

She had a head of very dark hair and was a very sweet-tempered baby, calmly accepting the doting attention that was lavished on her with happy gurgles. She was christened several weeks after her birth. Imogen was her godmother and Freddy her godfather, with strict instructions never to allow her near any clubs, including his, which was fast developing a reputation as the best jazz club in the county.

Life could not have been happier.

And now, with winter fast approaching and Christmas just around the corner, the air was fragrant with the anticipation of buying their first Christmas tree together.

'The first of many,' Cesar had told her the night before, after they had made passionate love and had lain in bed, just talking while their baby slept in the room next door. 'And, pretty soon, I'm hoping you give me a reason for us to move a little farther out into something a little bigger...'

'What kind of reason?' Jude had known exactly what he was talking about and for the past five hours she had been waiting for just the right, special moment to tell him what she had to tell him.

'What kind do you think, Mrs Caretti?'

'Well, now, funny you should say that because we might have a very good reason in…oh…eight and a half months time. I did a test this morning, Mr Caretti, and it seems that you're as virile as you keep telling me, after all…'

* * * * *

& *A sneaky peek at next month...*

By Request

RELIVE THE ROMANCE WITH THE BEST OF THE BEST

My wish list for next month's titles...

3 stories in each book - only £5.99!

In stores from 16th November 2012:

☐ *His Chosen Wife – Anne McAllister,*
Christina Hollis & Susanne James

☐ *Christmas with Him – Jackie Braun,*
Christine Rimmer & Shirley Jump

In stores from 7th December 2012:

☐ *Billionaires & Babies – Maureen Child,*
Katherine Garbera & Emily McKay

Available at WHSmith, Tesco, Asda, Eason, Amazon and Apple

Just can't wait?

Visit us Online

You can buy our books online a month before
they hit the shops! **www.millsandboon.co.uk**

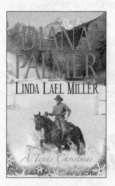

The World of Mills & Boon®

There's a Mills & Boon® series that's perfect for you. We publish ten series and, with new titles every month, you never have to wait long for your favourite to come along.

Blaze®
Scorching hot, sexy reads
4 new stories every month

By Request
Relive the romance with the best of the best
9 new stories every month

Cherish™
Romance to melt the heart every time
12 new stories every month

Desire™
Passionate and dramatic love stories
8 new stories every month

Have Your Say

You've just finished your book.
So what did you think?

We'd love to hear your thoughts on our
'Have your say' online panel
www.millsandboon.co.uk/haveyoursay

- 🌹 Easy to use
- 🌹 Short questionnaire
- 🌹 Chance to win Mills & Boon® goodies

Visit us Online

Tell us what you thought of this book now at
www.millsandboon.co.uk/haveyoursay